# Praise for *Dating Dr. Dil*

"Nisha Sharma's *Dating Dr. Dil* is what would happen if you put all my favorite romantic comedy tropes into a blender: a frothy, snarky, hilarious treat with a gooey, heartwarming center. The perfect addition to any rom-com lover's shelf."

— Emily Henry, #1 *New York Times* bestselling author of *People We Meet on Vacation*

"What a joy! *Dating Dr. Dil* is further proof that Nisha Sharma is a mega-talent who can do it all. Anything Nisha Sharma writes is an auto-buy for me."

— Meg Cabot, #1 *New York Times* bestselling author

"Bursting with character, spicy tension, and laughs, *Dating Dr. Dil* is the enemies-to-lovers dream book!"

— Tessa Bailey, *New York Times* bestselling author of *It Happened One Summer*

"Hilarious, swoony, and oh so sexy. . . . *Dating Dr. Dil* will steal your heart. Take it from me, seeing a man utterly ruined by love has never been more satisfying!"

— Adriana Herrera, *USA Today* bestselling author

"*Dating Dr. Dil* is my rom-com wishlist come to life: a determined heroine, a stubborn (but secretly squishy) hero, and banter for *days*! Prem and Kareena have a sizzling chemistry that weds the sheer delight of an enemies-to-lovers tale with the swoons of an unforgettable romance. *Dating Dr. Dil* needs to go to the top of every romcom fan's TBR pronto."

— Sierra Simone, *USA Today* bestselling author

"Replete with endearing references to Indian, specifically Punjabi, culture. Kareena and Prem are engaging protagonists, and the relationships they each share with their closest friends are fresh and fun."

—*Kirkus Reviews*

"*Dating Dr. Dil* has all the feels of a 'woe is me' tale, but then it shifts to 'I can do anything I set my mind on'. . . If you love a romance filled with chaotic dating and families pressuring our couple to find their soulmates, then you won't want to miss *Dating Dr. Dil*."

—Romance Reviews Today

"Nisha Sharma's new rom-com, inspired by *The Taming of the Shrew*, promises to be charming and hilarious."

—Book Riot

## Also by Nisha Sharma

If Shakespeare Was an Auntie Series
*Dating Dr. Dil*

The Singh Family Trilogy
*The Takeover Effect*
*The Legal Affair*

Young Adult Novels
*My So-Called Bollywood Life*
*Radha and Jai's Recipe for Romance*
*The Karma Map*

# TASTES LIKE SHAKKAR

A NOVEL

## NISHA SHARMA

**AVON**

*An Imprint of HarperCollinsPublishers*

HarperCollins books may be purchased for educational, business, or sales promotional use. For information, please email the Special Markets Department at SPsales@harpercollins.com.

FIRST EDITION

*Chai illustration by Shwetofficial/AdobeStock*
*Jewelry illustration by Shorena Tedliashvili/AdobeStock*

Library of Congress Cataloging-in-Publication
Data has been applied for.

ISBN 978-0-06-300114-5

23 24 25 26 27 LBC 5 4 3 2 1

*This one is for the people in my past who've judged me by my weight and underestimated my worth. Your poor math skills have only added to my value.*

## Trigger Warnings

Fatphobia (in discussion)
Deceased parent (in discussion)
Racial bias

## IMPORTANT CAST MEMBERS

**Bhua:** Bobbi's aunt

**Bindu:** Sister of the bride. YouTube influencer and expectant mom

**Chottu:** Benjamin's younger brother. Future CEO of Naan King Emporium

**Dadi:** Kareena's grandmother

**Deepak:** Benjamin's best friend. Equally important in Benjamin's life as Prem

**Gabbar Singh:** Benjamin's father. The Naan King

**Gudi:** Benjamin's younger sister. Living her best life in Hawai'i

**Gwen:** Messina Vineyard's event coordinator

**Kareena:** Bride, and Bobbi's best friend. Equally important in Bobbi's life as Veera

**Loken:** Bindu's husband, and Kareena's brother-in-law

**Mamu:** Bobbi's uncle

**Neha:** Wedding decorator

**Prem:** The groom, and Benjamin's best friend. Equally as important in Benjamin's life as Deepak

**Sukhi:** Bobbi's younger cousin

**Sana:** Veera's twin sister

**Veera:** Bobbi's best friend. Equally as important in Bobbi's life as Kareena

## THE AUNTIES: A COMMUNITY OF WOMEN WITH AN AGENDA

**Falguni** Auntie: Wears orthotics and crocs. Former political correspondent

**Farah** Auntie: Former engineer. Extremely tech savvy

**Mona** Auntie: Fashionable with the excellent blowout and Chanel sunglasses

**Namrata** Auntie: Veera's mother. Connected in the wealthy NYC Indian community

**Sonali** Auntie: Extremely religious auntie

Let me be that I am and seek not to alter me.
　　　　　—*Much Ado About Nothing*, William Shakespeare


*Indians Abroad News* Relationship column:
Everyone has room for improvement.
　　　　　—Mrs. W. S. Gupta, Avon, New Jersey

# PROLOGUE

*Ten Months Ago*

## Benjamin

Benjamin would do anything for his family. Not the family members he was related to, even though he'd sacrificed quite a bit for them over the years, but his two best friends, Prem Verma and Deepak Datta. When they asked him for something, he always said yes because they showed up for him when he needed them, too. Like when he cut his hand with a paring knife and Prem came in the middle of the night to stitch him back up. Or when Deepak helped him develop a business plan for his first restaurant. He texted them daily, confided all his ambitions, and knew all their secrets.

But right at this moment, he was rethinking that policy and his relationships. Specifically with Prem. Had the man really convinced him to use his day off to attend a Bollywood-themed house party in suburban New Jersey?

When Prem asked Benjamin to act as a decoy so he could spend time with a woman named Kareena Mann, Benjamin figured he would merely eat free food, drink the booze, and answer a few questions from aunties.

He did not expect to meet Bobbi Kaur.

For months he'd used careful maneuvering tactics to avoid the notorious wedding planner. She, like many before her, had been trying to convince him to turn one of his restaurants into a catering venue. He'd finally been caught in her line of sight at this New Jersey Desi house party. Because apparently, Bobbi Kaur was Kareena's best friend.

Benjamin stood, arms crossed, listening to her ramble on about the cost-benefit of working together. Prem was going to seriously owe him after this.

"I'm not interested," he said, cutting her off. "I'm a chef, a restaurateur. Not a caterer for thousand-person Indian weddings in New Jersey. I don't do buffet lines offering butter chicken and naan."

Her jaw dropped, but she recovered quickly. Straightening her shoulders, she said, "I understand your hesitation, but I really think—"

"No, thanks."

Her professional façade began to chip away. "Chef, you said I get five minutes, and it hasn't even been two yet. If you weren't going to listen to me, we should've just stayed downstairs." She motioned to the guest bedroom in Kareena Mann's house. It was small, with six-inch-tall statues of gods and goddesses sitting on a tiny platform in the corner. On the other side of the room, opposite the home mandir setup, was a narrow daybed with a printed bedsheet that reminded Benjamin of his grandmother's house in Amritsar. The mustard-yellow paisley design mocked him now.

"There is nothing you can say that's going to change my mind," he said. "I only agreed to come up here because it looked like Prem and your friend Kareena needed a minute. I'm sure you can find someone else easily enough."

"Not someone with your traditional aesthetic," she said. "That's why I've been trying to get in contact with you for weeks. You're truly talented, and so many of my clients dream of having your food to celebrate their important day. This particular client wants to organize their entire wedding around *your* availability."

She looked so earnest, so determined, with her thick black lashes framing deep brown eyes. Her plump red lips set in a line.

He hated the hard sell. That was part of the reason why he didn't want to work for his father's company. People were so damn pushy when food should be about pleasure and enjoyment. But Bobbi didn't seem to get that.

There was no question that this woman was an irritation. From her words, to the traditional Patiala salwar she wore. She had big eyes, big lips, big hair, and a big, beautiful shape. The shrewd look made her even more stunning.

And more irritating.

"Still a no," he added.

This time professionalism faded like mist melting in sunlight. "Do you have a problem with me?" Bobbi snapped. She planted her hands on her hips.

"I have a problem with someone thinking they know what's best for my business."

"Oh, so it's an ego thing."

"What? No, I'm saying you're pushy," he said.

She fisted her hands now. "God, this is the reason I can't stand working with Punjabi—"

"—with Punjabi men like me?"

His irritation began to boil. How could she be mad at him when she was the one who approached him? And for her to be prejudiced against all Punjabi men? Well . . . fair. But that just made him even angrier that she was probably right. He may not be her ideal person, but she definitely wasn't his, either. He had no intention of pairing up with someone, especially not a career-obsessed woman like Bobbi.

She rushed on, her indignation climbing with each octave. "I hate when people like you are so dismissive, disrespectful, and arrogant."

He shifted toward the exit. "Find a different chef, Kaur."

"Don't patronize me." She threw herself in front of the door, arms spread wide. There was a look of panic in her eyes. "These clients only want *your* food at their events. I told them that I would do my best to secure a meeting. I didn't expect you to be at my friend's party today, and I would prefer if we had a conversation in different circumstances about their wish list, but it's important. If you could just listen to what they're offering for their three-day, midsize affair—"

"I'm going to get myself a drink," he said.

Her eyes narrowed. "I still have two minutes left of my time."

"Move. Otherwise, I will move you."

"Yeah, I doubt that . . . oh my god!"

He gripped her hips and lifted her clean off the ground so he could set her aside. She let out a breathy squeak that had him smirking. So, Bobbi liked to be tossed around.

Benjamin grabbed the handle, but she'd squeezed between him and the door again. Their chests brushed and he froze. She looked up at him, lips parted. Her deep brown eyes darkened.

Well, wasn't this an interesting development?

He placed his hands on either side of her head and shifted his feet to bracket hers until she was surrounded.

"I don't think this is a good idea," he said softly.

"Wh-what do you mean?" Her lashes fluttered again, and she looked down at his mouth then met his eyes. He was close enough to see the soft wetness on her plump bottom lip.

She smelled of gardenias. The sweet scent was intoxicating, and he wanted a taste so badly. "I mean that if this doesn't stop, we both might do something that we'll regret," he said.

Her hands rested on his pecs, and the touch sizzled his skin. He let out a ragged breath. What the hell?

He expected her to shove him, but her fingers brushed the gold chain at his neck and curled in the fabric of his kurtha top. Her manicured nails tangled in his chest hair.

His blood began to hum as she slowly consumed his senses. The sound of that slight hitch in her breathing had him shifting closer. All he wanted was a taste now. He leaned forward to smell more of the perfume she must've dabbed at her throat. His lips coursed over the shell of her ear.

"Your heart is pounding," she whispered against his shoulder.

He rested his large palm at the center of her chest, feeling the soft curve of her breasts against his fingers. The steady rhythm was as fast as his own. "So is yours," he said.

He leaned closer, and Bobbi's head fell back against the door. The sound that came out of her mouth had his toes curling. They were now chest to chest, noses brushing against each other, lips centimeters apart.

Then when their eyes met, her bold stare seared him like a hot iron. Benjamin knew that this was all a mistake. Good god, he was in the temple room in a house full of strangers! If anyone caught them together like that . . .

Jumping back, he blurted out, "I'm sorry. I'm so sorry. That was uncalled for. That was, uh. My bad."

She looked confused and straightened her salwar. "I—I don't get it. We were both . . . What happened?"

*Tell her.*

*Tell her you think she's sharp, and you appreciate her determination even though you don't think working together would help your business.*

*Tell her that you googled her, and you respect her as a business-woman, but that she looks like the marrying type, the kind that would make your parents happy and make you undoubtedly unhappy.*

*Tell her that you intend to die a bachelor.*

*Tell her if anything happened between you two, then things would get very, very complicated.*

"You're not my type," he blurted out.

Bobbi froze, then she recoiled, pressing back against the door.

He watched realization dawn on her face as she looked down at her clothes, and back up at him. Her hands smoothed over her wide hips, and her shock morphed into hurt.

Why would she . . . Oh.

*Oh shit. I fucked that up.*

"No," he said, stuttering over the word. "No, no, that's not what I meant."

All the warmth in her face frosted over. "I think I know exactly what you meant," Bobbi said. "But this account is important enough to work with someone like you."

"I'm not like that!" he said, hands up in surrender. "I'm not like the—"

"Like what?" she said, feigning innocence. "Like every other Punjabi man who has come into my life looking for someone skinny and sweet, with fair skin and pedigree?"

"What? God no, that's not what I'm saying at all."

*Tell her. Tell her that the exact opposite is true.*

"This has nothing to do with you, Bobbi. I don't want to mass-produce food to a group of people who probably have no taste."

"What, now I'm tasteless?" she balked.

"No, I never said *you* were tasteless. But your job isn't exactly the best—"

"I fucking love my job," she snapped. "I *live* for my job."

"Yeah, that's exactly the problem!"

He winced again. It was as if he couldn't stop saying the wrong thing to her.

This time her hands balled into fists. "You know what? I can ignore your prejudices and how you don't find someone like me attractive. There are plenty of men who do, and who respect, admire, and adore me."

"Holy shit, Bobbi, I never *said* that I don't find you attractive!"

"But I would *never* stoop so low that I would ever consider someone insulting my job, too. Get fucked, Chef. Thankfully it won't be with me."

She turned, twisted the handle, and stormed out of the room. He heard the bedroom door down the hall slam shut.

"I am such an idiot," he said.

The sound of a soft metal chime clattered behind him, and he swung around to face the temple platform. The bell that was used as part of ceremony chanting had fallen over on its own. The murtis, statues lined up in a row, all stared at him as if condemning him for his idiocy.

"Yeah, I'm done here." He bolted out of the room, down the stairs, and through the front door. He just needed a minute. A second to figure out his thoughts.

And to beat himself up over hurting someone who he knew didn't deserve it.

Damn, he was so embarrassed about how badly he handled that; he didn't even think he'd have the guts to talk to his best friends about it. Some secrets family didn't need to know about.

### *Indians Abroad News*
Relationship column

It's best to pretend that you do not know your children have been alone with their potential partner. We must be honest with ourselves: we snuck around behind our parents' backs, too.

Mrs. W. S. Gupta
Avon, New Jersey

# CHAPTER 1

*Present Day*

# Bobbi

*Note left on Bobbi Kaur's kathi roll:*

*Paranthas are universal, but also uniquely Punjabi.*
*Sweet paranthas? Salty? Deconstructed?*

Bobbi Kaur was convinced that men—heterosexual *Punjabi* men—ruined everything.

They were chaos creatures who turned leisurely Sunday brunches into wedding work. Okay, if she was being honest with herself, she didn't mind the wedding work too much. Ever since her best friend got engaged, she'd been dying to start planning Kareena's special day. It was just that in her expert opinion, weddings were a lot more fun without men.

"I'm really happy renovations for your mom's house are coming along," Bobbi said. "But we've always had Sunday Bellinis at my apartment. Besides, I have the whiteboard for brainstorming." Not to mention, a fully functional kitchen. She clutched her tablet to her chest before lifting one foot then the other. Her sandals were probably not the best footwear for exposed plywood flooring.

Kareena Mann removed a coffee cup from a carrier that she'd

set on a folding table and handed it to Bobbi. "Prem and I thought it might be more convenient for everyone if you and Veera came to the house to talk about the wedding. Then we can start ripping up the carpet. We're going to do hardwood throughout the first floor, and we need to finish before the cabinets come in."

Bobbi took the coffee and inhaled deeply.

After one tentative sip, then another, she looked over at the living room that was now visible from the kitchen space. The wall that had separated the two rooms came down the week before. Sad beige carpet remained with divots where furniture used to be.

Change was good, Bobbie thought. Seeing her friend take her childhood home in Edison, New Jersey, and move into the next phase of her life felt special. Bobbi was still adjusting to Dr. Prem Verma, though. The former TV doctor from the South Asian *Dr. Dil Show* had been the best thing to happen to Kareena. Which meant that despite being a cis-het Punjabi man, Bobbi would love him, too.

"Why don't we get started while we wait for Prem?" Bobbi asked. "We can pretend this is a formal client meeting and I can talk about how my uncle opened an elite Indian wedding planning business twenty years ago, then met my aunt, who is a retired florist, and how they raised me within the business and blah-blah-blah, I'm here today."

Kareena held up her palm to stop her speech. "A business that hopefully you'll be running one day."

"I doubt that," Bobbi said. Even though she'd desperately wished for creative control. But ever since she lost the big wedding account almost a year ago thanks to one unruly chef who refused the biggest paycheck she'd ever negotiated, Bobbi's uncle had seemingly lost faith in her ability to host spectacular weddings. Now that her younger cousin was also in the business, it was hard to ignore the fact that they were most likely training her to take over.

Bobbi held up her tablet like she was modeling it. "I've made a ton of mood boards for a small, intimate wedding that you and Prem can afford. Just like you always talked about when you were drunk at those slam poetry nights you dragged me to in college. Don't you want to see?"

"As tempting as that sounds, both you and Veera need to be here before we get started so we can fill you in on a few updates," Kareena said. "And I want to remind you that you were just as drunk during slam poetry."

"I had to be whenever Denise Franco got up there to sob for five minutes about her high school boyfriend."

"Denise Franco," Kareena said dreamily. "I wonder what she's up to now. Did she ever get over her high school break up? She never accepted my LinkedIn request, you know."

"Probably for the best." Bobbi looked at her smartwatch. "I guess we can wait, but I'm surprised Veera isn't here yet. Our best friend is usually fifteen minutes early. Should we text to see where she's at?"

"I got a message that she's on her way." Kareena began tapping her toe and looked at her phone. She set it down, then seconds later, picked it up again.

Alarm bells began to ring in Bobbi's head. "Oh god, what is it?"

"What? Oh, it's nothing."

"Kareena!"

"I'm serious," Kareena said. She twisted her fingers together. Her classic solitaire diamond ring glinted in the overhead light. "After my sister and Loken settled in Princeton, we received a bit of news. We want to tell you all together. It's going to affect the wedding planning."

"Wait, this has to do with *Bindu*?"

If there was one person who could get Bobbi's blood boiling, it was Kareena's spoiled younger sister. Bindu always seemed to get everything she wanted while older sis Kareena was stuck with scraps. Kareena was so forgiving because she viewed her sister like her child. But Bobbi knew that Bindu was just a user. No matter what happened, Bobbi would not let that snotty brat ruin the wedding. Kareena gave so much of herself to everyone that she deserved a special day that was all about her.

"I'll take care of your sister for you."

"It's not like that," Kareena said with a shake of her head.

"Then is it your grandmother?"

"No," Kareena said. "It's not my grandmother. She's relatively content now that she's spending half her time in India and half of it in Florida with Dad where it's warmer. She hasn't said much yet, but I'm sure that will change once we get into the planning details."

"Not if I can help it," Bobbi murmured. That was someone else who Bobbi had beef with. There was an underlying level of toxicity that existed in so many South Asian family relationships, but Kareena's grandmother was next level. And Kareena, forged in the fires of grief and love, gave that woman too much of herself.

"When everyone shows up, I promise it'll make sense," Kareena continued. "I wanted to tell you and Veera about it a week ago, but it's been hard to coordinate schedules."

"Time is moving so much faster than it used to," Bobbi said quietly.

Kareena hummed in agreement. "Did you ever think that we'd be here planning weddings and coordinating calendar invites when we were first in that dorm room all those years ago?"

"No," Bobbi said, smiling at the memory of a less complicated, less lonely time. "Everything changed. And it's going to continue to change." Because one of them had a man.

The sound of the garage door rumbling open had Bobbi standing to attention. It had to be Prem. Finally.

Kareena's face brightened. She ran a hand over her button-down shirt and dark wash jeans.

She looked happy. Relaxed.

The mudroom door opened from the hallway off the kitchen, and Prem walked in with a bottle of champagne in one hand and what looked like a brand-new tool bag in the other.

Okay, she understood why her friend was smitten. Prem was gorgeous, with wide shoulders, a sharp jawline covered in light scruff, and black hair styled back in a neat cut. He also looked like the sun and the moon set with Kareena.

"Hey, sorry I'm late," he said. He went to his fiancée first and dropped a kiss on her upturned mouth. "I wanted to check the renovation site for the community center before I left, and the contractor stopped me for some questions. Hey, Bobbi."

"Hey, Prem," she said, smiling. "How does it feel to renovate your health center and your home at the same time? That's a lot of construction."

He grinned. "It feels fucking fantastic." He dropped the tool bag at his feet and put the bottle of champagne down on the folding table. "For Bellinis," he added. "As you requested."

"Any problems at the site?" Kareena asked.

He began listing all the concerns and his plans to address them. His vision for creating a holistic health clinic for members of the South Asian community had been the reason why he started as a host on a medical talk show, apparently. And now that he'd secured enough investors, he was a year away from his dream becoming a reality.

"As much as I hate to interrupt your work," Bobbi said, "I really think we should get started. We've got a lot of decisions to make, starting with date and location." She was buzzing with ideas now that she could see both of them together, imagining their lehenga and sherwani.

A knock echoed through the empty house from the front door. "Oh, that should be Veera and the guys now," Prem said. "I'll get it."

Bobbi felt her heart seize in her chest. Nope. No way. She whirled toward Kareena. "*The guys?*" she hissed. All happy thoughts shriveled up in a nanosecond.

"Now, Bobbi—"

"Don't you 'Now, Bobbi' me," she said, leaning closer. "You knew that douche nozzle was going to be here? Why didn't you tell me?"

She had the decency to look sheepish. "Because I wanted you to come, and you wouldn't have if you knew Benjamin was coming."

There was laughter and conversation coming from the front foyer, trickling down the hallway now.

"I can handle a lot of things, ranging from beach weddings during a hurricane siren to a five-year-old who gets his tongue stuck to the butt crack of a swan ice statue. But Benjamin Padda is the *worst*. I do not want to be in the same room as him."

"He's one of Prem's best friends," Kareena replied patiently. "Like you and Veera are to me. Come on, can you please play nice? I don't know what he did to you—"

"It doesn't matter," Bobbi said. She was so embarrassed about the whole scene that she'd never told her friends what happened in that pooja room upstairs all those months ago.

"It matters to Prem. He's a good friend, Bobbi."

"Remember after you and Prem announced your engagement," Bobbi whispered as she leaned farther across the makeshift table, "we went out to dinner as one big group? Bunty and I fought all night, then he got pissy and walked out and everyone blamed me."

Kareena raised a brow. "That's because you told everyone at the bar that Benjamin was the son of the Naan King, heir to a frozen naan empire, and he was buying everyone shots called Naan-er Naan-er. You know he's sensitive about his family's frozen food company."

The conversation was now distinguishable from down the hallway.

Then Bobbi's breath caught in her throat, threatening to choke her. Benjamin "Bunty" Padda came into view in all his glory. Like so many Sikh Punjabi men she knew, he towered over everyone. He had a thick beard, his jet-black hair styled, and his T-shirt fit across a wide, rippling chest. A silver kada bracelet glinted on one wrist with a twenty-five-thousand-dollar Rolex on the other. A gold chain with a pendant rested at the base of his throat, matching the gold ring he wore on his right hand. He carried a large paper bag in his arms.

She had a flash of memory, of those arms picking her up and putting her aside. She looked away, hating that her cheeks warmed.

She focused on Deepak, who stood next to him. Why couldn't she think of Deepak in the same way? Prem's other bestie looked classically handsome in contrast. He was a poster child for a finance exec who preferred wearing polos in his downtime.

Behind him, Veera's expression brightened, and she waved in greeting. Veera, their sweet, nerdy bestie, was the most relaxed out of the trio, with her braid already coming undone.

"—I mean, the chilis were picked yesterday," Benjamin said to Prem. "The chutney that I made is world-class. I just wish you had appliances so I could've made this fresh for you."

He stopped in the middle of the kitchen and the corner of his mouth curved. His eyes locked squarely on Bobbi. "It's the most gorgeous woman in the room." He tilted to the side and winked at Kareena. "No wonder Prem couldn't stop staring when he saw you for the first time."

"You're going to get murdered, brother," Deepak mumbled in the back.

"*Bunty*," Bobbi said, her chin angling upward. She felt a spark of evil joy when Benjamin's eye twitched at the sound of his nickname. "I don't know why you're still talking when literally no one cares about . . . what was it? Chilis? A little cliché, don't you think?"

"Bobbi." His voice turned saccharine sweet. "Your high-strung attitude hasn't killed you yet?"

"Why do you ask?" she replied. "If you want me dead, all I have to do is try your food."

"You'd at least die happy then. Unless of course you prefer that soupy butter chicken garbage you serve at your weddings."

"I've heard that frozen naan has gotten increasingly more popular, Naan Prince," Bobbi said cheerfully. "Maybe I should call your dad to see if *he's* interested in working with me."

There was that glorious eye twitch again.

"Hey, that sounds like a great idea," he said, snapping his fingers. "I bet you can't tell the difference between fresh and frozen, anyway. Can you even appreciate traditional cuisine?"

"I prefer originality. Not . . . what was it that you do? *Elevated* Indian street food? It's so cliché it makes me gag."

His smile spread slowly. "If you're into gagging, I can help you make that happen. Hey, question for you. Has a man ever fallen in love with that prickly attitude of yours?"

She rolled her eyes. "I'd rather hear dogs howling outside my window in Jersey City all night than hear a man tell me he loves me."

His smile slipped. "Probably a good thing. They'd die of cat scratch disease."

The comment hurt like a quick jab to the chest. "Aren't you howling at someone new these days, Bunty?"

"Why? Jealous, Bobbi?"

"Why don't you suck my—"

A loud piercing whistle cut through the kitchen. Bobbi glanced over at Veera, who'd stuck two fingers in her mouth to make the sound.

Deepak held up a fist, and Veera tapped hers against it.

"Come on, guys," Prem said. He looped an arm around Bobbi's shoulders and squeezed. "We have a lot to talk about. Can you put down your swords for a few minutes? Benjamin?"

"Yeah, Bobbi, why don't you—"

"Bunty!" Prem and Deepak said together.

Benjamin held up a hand in surrender. "Fine, fine. Truce. I'm done."

"I somehow doubt that," Bobbi mumbled.

Kareena gave her a pleading look. Damn it, this was not how the meeting was supposed to go. Now Bobbi would have to brace herself for this man making fun of her samples, her color choices, her invitation recommendations, her floral design selections. Not because he preferred a specific aesthetic, but because Benjamin had an opinion about everything. Especially if it related to her.

"Come on," Benjamin said to the group. He put the bag on the folding table and began pulling out containers. "Let's eat."

The smell hit her first, then the sight of fresh hot paranthas stuffed with deliciousness wrapped around veggies with spicy mint chili chutney. He'd made kathi rolls. She loved kathi rolls. That jerk.

Bobbi watched as her cozy trio was now a group of six. Everyone grabbed foil-wrapped rolls while talking over each other, smiling and laughing. The champagne bottle popped, and Deepak generously poured it into red Solo cups with mango juice.

Benjamin held out a kathi roll to Bobbi. "It's not catering, but I made one for you."

"I'm fine. I ate before I came."

His eyebrows furrowed, as if he knew that she was lying. But since their fight almost a year ago, when he'd told her that she wasn't his type, when he'd judged her so openly, she refused to eat at his restaurants, or eat anything he made.

"Suit yourself," he said, and put the roll back on the table.

The conversations and laughter continued until Bobbi decided enough was enough.

She clapped her hands to get everyone's attention. "I thought we were supposed to plan a wedding?"

"Why don't we have breakfast first?" Kareena asked, kathi roll in hand.

"Now you're stalling." She'd known Kareena for way too long to *not* pick up on the signs.

"Stalling?" Veera asked, looking back and forth between Kareena and Bobbi. Her loose braid began to come undone around her face. "What do you mean?"

"She's been keeping a secret. Both Kareena and Prem."

Everyone turned to look at the couple. They glanced at each other, and Bobbi's shoulders relaxed when they nodded.

"We have some news," Prem started. "But first, I think it goes without saying that all of you are the Mann-Verma wedding party. Or #VermannGetMarried."

They all groaned.

"As in 'vermin'? Yeah, we're going to have to work on that," Bobbi said dryly.

"There's something else," Prem said. "We have a venue."

"*What?*" Bobbi asked. She had sent over a list of properties months ago. She was ready to clear her schedule to do site visits and interviews. She never expected them to handle things on their own. "When did this happen?"

As if reading her mind, Kareena looked apologetically at Bobbi. "Bindu is pregnant," she said. "It moves our timeline up a bit because once the baby is born, it'll be harder for my family to, ah . . . make time to celebrate Prem and me. That's why we had to start making decisions as soon as possible."

"Congratulations to Bindu!" Veera said with a salute of her glass. When no one joined her in cheers, she shrugged and drank the rest of the contents in her cup.

"I honestly don't give a shit about Bindu's timetable," Prem added, "but we went to Messina Vineyards in South Jersey for a colleague's wedding a few weeks ago."

Bobbi gaped. "*Messina?* I know I added that to the list I sent you, but they book two years out because they're in such demand. If you want something within eight months, Messina will be tough." Truthfully, she'd been dying to host a wedding at Messina Vineyards, but it was nearly impossible convincing her clients to wait so long for their big day. The other problem was the venue didn't have an Indian chef, and they didn't have a policy to allow outside caterers. That was a big no-no for most of her weddings.

"We got really lucky," Kareena said, her eyes sparkling. "There was a cancellation while we were there, and after paying a large deposit, we got it."

"The date is in four months," Prem added.

"*Four months?*" Bobbi shrieked.

"Goddamn," Benjamin murmured, pressing a finger to his ear. "Say it louder for the next town over, why don't you?"

Four months to pull off a South Asian wedding? Appalling. The only upside was that would put them in early October, and the weather would be perfection. The views in South Jersey were stunning that time of year.

"Bobbi," Kareena said softly. She reached out across the folding table and touched Bobbi's hand. "It goes without saying that we want you to plan the wedding. Everything else is in your hands. We'll pay you, your staff, whatever your fee."

"My services are a gift," Bobbi said, waving a hand, even though that meant she'd be planning another wedding during the busiest time of year. Her uncle would not approve. "We can work out the fee for my staff. And Veera is going to help."

Veera's head snapped up from her kathi roll. "What?" she said with her mouth full.

"We'll also set up a system for you to pay vendors directly," Bobbi continued.

"Great," Kareena replied. "Thanks, Bobbi."

Bobbi opened her tablet and began making notes. "There is a lot to do, but the venue is always the biggest hurdle, so I'm glad that's confirmed. The most important question is what will the budget be?" She knew that Kareena's father had set aside money for each of his daughters to pay for a wedding or a down payment on a house. Since they were currently standing in Kareena's gutted kitchen, Bobbi knew that's where the money had gone. "Prem, are your parents going to contribute, or are you two still planning on paying for this on your own?"

Prem and Kareena looked at each other, holding a silent conversation in public, before Prem said, "My mother and father have apparently been hoarding money for years. They want to pay for our wedding." He named a figure that had everyone in the kitchen swearing.

Bobbi nodded. Since two-thirds of Indian families spent an average of half of their net annual income on weddings, it wasn't surprising to her. God bless parents who would rather spend money on parties than on things like retirement. It definitely kept her in business. "I have more questions. How long is the wedding? One day, two, three, or five? How many people are coming from India? Prem, will your family in California fly out early? We'll have to secure the hotel block. You'll forgo save-the-dates and go straight to invitations. The clothes! We need time for alterations. I have a form that I need both of you to fill out by tonight so I can get started."

Benjamin cleared his throat and raised a hand. "What's the plan for the food? I don't want my best friend eating subpar garbage. Does this place do Indian food?"

Bobbi's shoulders straightened. She opened her mouth to let Benjamin know exactly what she thought was subpar garbage when she caught Veera's eye. Her best friend shook her head as if to say *let it go.*

Damn it.

"Benjamin, we know you don't do catering," Kareena said hesitantly. She leaned against Prem's side, and their fingers linked together as a unit. "But the venue agreed to work with us if you, with your reputation and expertise, would be willing to create the menu and guide the chef. Bobbi can help coordinate—"

Bobbi clutched her tablet to her chest, holding her breath. No, she could not work with Benjamin. Absolutely no way, considering how she had begged him for help in the past.

As if he was reading her mind, he looked at her, then ran a hand over his beard. "For Prem's wedding, I'd be happy to help."

"Wait a minute," Bobbi said, holding her arms up like a T. "Are you two really asking for Bunty and me to work together?"

Kareena and Prem looked at each other, then smiled. "Yes," they said in unison.

Benjamin looked like he was truly taking this heinous idea seriously. Then to her horror, he flashed her a smile. "Hey, this is my best friend's wedding. Bobbi, looks like you have yourself a wedding planner partner."

"This cannot be happening."

# CHAPTER 2

## Benjamin

Benjamin put the empty chutney containers into Deepak's double wide stainless-steel sink. He reached for the faucet, then paused. Bracing against the sink ledge, he dropped his head.

Damn. Why was it always like that when he was with Bobbi? Ever since they met in person almost a year ago at Kareena's family party, he just couldn't seem to get it right. He had no idea what he could do to make things better with her.

Okay, maybe he could start with being nice. But when he antagonized her, she was at least looking at him. Talking to him. After Prem and Kareena had finally become official and they'd all gone out together to celebrate, he'd tried being cordial, tried making up for the way he dismissed her so harshly on their first meeting.

She'd ignored him and the silence was so much worse than her sharp, pointed words.

Now . . . well, now they hated each other.

No, technically, she hated him.

*You're not my type.*

He'd said the worst thing he possibly could. What he meant to say was:

*You and I would never work out.*

*I want someone who doesn't work as much as I do.*

*I'm never home. Hell, I don't even have my own place as a thirty-five-year-old man, and I have no intention of getting married.*

Benjamin twisted the faucet and began rinsing out the containers. Hot soapy water always reminded him of his days as a kid in the back of a restaurant trying to prove that the son of a frozen food company CEO belonged in a real kitchen. His thoughts were his own in those long hours, just as they were now.

In Deepak's professionally designed home that resembled a farmhouse in the French countryside with its high ceilings and open shelves, Benjamin dried the containers with a dishcloth and set them aside. Just as he finished, the sound of the front door echoed from the bottom level of the four-story brownstone.

"Yo!" Deepak called out.

"Kitchen," Benjamin called back.

Deepak pounded up the stairs and appeared a moment later in the doorway. He still wore the same clothes that he'd put on that morning for Prem's wedding planning brunch, except he now carried a canvas backpack with him.

"Did you just get back?"

Benjamin nodded. "I checked on Phataka Grill, and then a few new restaurant sites. What about you?"

"I stopped by the office to handle some stuff for my dad." He dropped his backpack on a barstool. "Did you like any of the locations?"

"A few," Benjamin replied. "Some right here in Brooklyn. I appreciate the leads."

Deepak walked around the giant square butcher block island to retrieve glasses from the corner cabinet. He popped open a bottle from the bar cart next to the cabinet and poured two fingers in each glass. He slid one of the glasses into Benjamin's waiting hand.

They tapped rims and took their first tentative sips. The smooth aged whiskey slid down Benjamin's throat, warming his chest.

"Hey, is there a kathi roll left from this morning?" Deepak asked. "The one that Bobbi didn't eat? I'm starving."

Benjamin straightened. "Uh, no, it's gone," he said. He was not going to tell Deepak that he'd slipped the kathi roll into Bobbi's bag when she wasn't looking so she could have something to eat for later. *It was a peace offering*, he'd told himself. "Let me make you something. What's your poison? Sandwiches? Pasta? Daal roti? You're pretty stocked up."

Deepak waved a hand in dismissal. "I can order takeout. You don't have to constantly cook for me."

"It wouldn't be any different than when we were in college." Benjamin unhooked a cast-iron skillet and placed it on top of the metal grates of the Maison La Cornue Le Château range. He poured in a healthy amount of oil to coat the bottom before setting it to preheat. "Besides, it's the least I can do. I'm in your space all the time."

"I have a four-story brownstone with two living rooms, a rooftop deck, and a dedicated parking spot out back with a patio. It's just me. I have no idea why I bought this ridiculous showroom. You'd be doing me a favor by keeping me entertained."

Benjamin had to hide a smile behind his glass. Not unlike himself, Deepak did what his parents expected, including investing in real estate that was ridiculous for one person but perfect for a future family. However, that's where the similarities stopped. It was only a matter of time before Deepak's parents presented rishtas, and Deepak found a match he was willing to settle down with. Then he would turn his showroom house into a home.

Which meant that Benjamin would have even more family to claim as his own.

"If I end up opening my next restaurant here, then I'm going to have to get a place just so I can start storing my things," Benjamin said. "I still haven't decided on New York yet, though."

"Come on, Bunty." Deepak rolled his eyes before sipping more whiskey. "There is so much opportunity out here. This should be a no-brainer."

"There is so much opportunity in California, too," he replied. His first restaurant, Namak, was a small hole-in-the-wall that had reservations for weeks in advance. The menu was fresh, approachable lunch-brunch fare. Benjamin had sold some of his Naan King Emporium company shares to his brother, taken the profit, and made even more money with it from Namak. Then, after accumulating enough from his first restaurant, he started his second. Phataka Grill in Jersey City focused on trendy evening-hours grilled food. Business was booming. But now he wanted to go after big game. The Kohinoor diamond of his restaurant empire. The Michelin Star. The question was, did he open the restaurant on the East Coast, when his immediate family was all located on the West Coast?

He was already heavily involved as a member of the board of his father's company. It made sense for him to stay in California. But if he did, would he lose the last pieces of joy he'd created for himself outside of the Naan King empire?

More importantly, if he stayed on the West Coast, would he lose the close connection he had with his two friends?

Benjamin put his glass down, then walked over to the fridge and started taking out tomatoes, onions, lemons, and limes. A block of cheddar cheese joined the list of ingredients along with a bag of lime tortilla chips and some fresh garlic. There was a marinated flank steak he'd intended to use earlier that day, which he could repurpose. He began prepping the ingredients while his best friend added more whiskey to the glasses and pulled out a stool from under the counter to sit.

"Sheet pan nachos?" Deepak asked.

"Yeah." As if he would default to anything else this late at night. It was one of the first few regular meals he'd made for his friends when they were in college.

"You should put that on the menu at your new place," Deepak mused. "It's always a crowd pleaser."

"Not exactly elevated Indian street food," he said, thinking of the dig Bobbi made earlier that morning. He slid the Japanese blade against the honing rod, then flipped it in his hand, testing the weight. With one swipe against his dish towel, he positioned the white onion and then diced it with easy, quick movements.

A cell phone buzzed, and Benjamin watched out of the corner of his eye as Deepak retrieved his phone from his back pocket and looked at the screen.

"What is it?"

"An obligation," Deepak mumbled. "Hey, can I ask you a favor?"

"What's up?"

"Veera," he said with a sigh.

"Our best friend's best friend? What about her?"

"It's not about Veera per se," Deepak continued. "It's about her family's company. They're doing work for mine, and they invited us to a corporate fundraiser event for South Asians in the tristate area. My mother is going to try to set me up if I don't come with someone. You interested in being my plus-one? If you're still in town."

It looked like Deepak was already getting rishta offers. How many more nights would Benjamin have like this before he was by himself?

Now he was feeling sorry for himself when he really should be thrilled that his friends were finding happiness. They were moving on with their lives in the best way and he was watching them become better versions of themselves.

He sniffled.

It was the onions though, not his feelings. The onions always made him a little misty-eyed even after all this time in the kitchen.

"Do I need to wear Indian clothes or a suit?" he asked, as he diced the tomato next.

"A suit," Deepak said. "And a mask. It's some masquerade theme."

"I don't know about the mask but the suit I can do," Benjamin said. Then, because he couldn't help himself, he added, "Now that Prem is settling down, are you ready, too?"

Deepak ran a hand over his face. "To be honest, I think I became ready to settle down months ago. But wrong time, wrong woman. Now I'm afraid that I'll be stuck with second best for the rest of my life."

Benjamin laid the steak in the hot, seasoned cast-iron pan and heard the musical sizzle. "Wrong woman? Who were you dating back then?"

Deepak shook his head. "It doesn't matter. She'll be at this fundraiser though. Bobbi will be there, too."

"Bobbi?" Benjamin turned around to face him, tongs in hand.

"Bobbi's uncle's company is the one planning the event."

Benjamin nodded, then went back to the pico de gallo. He crushed garlic, squeezed lemon and lime juice, and poured it over the tomato and onions to sit for a few minutes before returning to the meat. "Are you sure you want me there? I mean, Bobbi and I might start a riot."

"Bunty," Deepak said in that all-knowing tone. "I've asked you this a few times already, but I'm going to do it again. What happened between the two of you?"

Benjamin had kept his mouth shut, and since Prem didn't know any of the details from Kareena, Bobbi must not have said anything, either. It was a secret between the two of them. A secret that he revisited at night when he was alone, remembering the feel of her hips in his hands.

He began assembling the nachos. "It's complicated. Complicated and best left in the past."

Deepak's brow arched. "It's definitely not in the past if every time you see each other you want to slit each other's throats."

Benjamin slid the tray into the oven, grabbed a towel, and flipped it over his shoulder before wiping his hands on the end. "I could ask you the same about Veera."

Deepak's mouth flattened into a straight line. "We're friends. But you and Bobbi? You're mortal enemies."

"'Mortal enemies' is a strong word for two people who just don't want to spend time together."

"Remember the celebration dinner where she got you to buy the bar shots called Naan-er Naan-er? You had the kitchen burn or under season everything she ordered out of spite. This may not be the Hunger Games, but in New Jersey? That's as close to mortal enemy as you get."

Benjamin let out a sigh. "Just tell me where I need to buy a mask, man."

# CHAPTER 3

## Bobbi

*Note left in Bobbi Kaur's purse:*

*Heart meat. Not too gamy to eat. Especially if it's spicy. Adding to a menu.*

Bobbi loved planning events at Cipriani's on Wall Street. The venue and the staff were always prepped and professional, the pre-approved vendors were excellent, and the large two-story space with wide marble pillars and state-of-the-art acoustics was a delight to decorate. She'd ordered two-story-tall sheer curtains to stretch between the pillars to give the space an ethereal look. A large metal tree sculpture was positioned in the center with masks hanging from the lower branches for those who forgot their own. Round tables circled the sculpture and spread across the second level.

Everything looked perfect, just the way she planned.

When security opened the entrance doors and the check-in table began to direct guests, Bobbi cued the twelve-piece band to start their soft instrumental set. Once the staff looked like they were directing foot traffic without any hiccups, she pressed a hand to her earpiece.

"App rotations can start now," she said.

"Copy," a member of her team said from the kitchen.

The youngest employee on their planning team, Bobbi's cousin Sukhi, slid up next to her, tablet in hand. She wore a soft peach lehenga that came with a matching mask hanging from her wrist. "This was such a cool idea, Bobbi," she said.

Bobbi slung an arm around Sukhi's waist. "Masquerades only work if the attendees are invested in the theme. Nice job on ordering all the extra masks in different shapes and sizes."

"It was a lot of fun," she said, her ponytail bobbing. "I'm so glad I got to work with you on this event. I feel like I've learned so much. I hope Mom and Papa give me the opportunity to lead my own events after grad school because I know with your help, I'll be ready by then."

"Patience, grasshopper," Bobbi said. "They're still heavily involved in my events, and I'm the oldest wedding planner they have. It'll be some time before you get to operate solo, too. Now you're on check-in duty. There is a line forming so you may want to pitch in to keep things moving."

"On it," Sukhi said, and bounced off.

"She's as eager as you were when you started," a voice said from behind her. Bobbi turned to face her uncle. He'd pulled out his classic tux for the event since he had been invited as a family friend. It had been so long since he'd attended a party as a guest, Bobbi mused.

"I'm surprised that she changed her mind about joining the business," Bobbi said as she reached up to automatically straighten the bow tie at the older man's throat. She used to fuss with it just like this when she was a child watching him launch his planning business from home.

Mamu patted Bobbi's hand. "Not everyone takes to it as quickly as you did, beta."

"There," she said, admiring her handiwork. She patted the silk lapel of his jacket. "I remember when the business really started to take off. I was what, fourteen? Fifteen? Sukhi was just a toddler back then. She used to pitch a fit when I was helping with centerpieces at our dining table and wouldn't play with her. She's grown up so fast."

Mamu's eyes turned misty. He cleared his throat. "Both my girls are adults now. I'm so grateful for you, beta."

"Same, Mamu."

A line formed between his brows as they furrowed. "But there is one thing . . ."

"Oh, here we go."

He motioned to the drapes. "The sheer pinks and golds were a risk. If they didn't work, we would've had to pay out of pocket. And the table settings are a bit modern, no?"

She thought about her plan, her hopes for taking more of a leadership role in the business as Mamu and Bhua took a back seat. Damn Benjamin Padda for being the reason she lost a big account.

To be fair, she'd been way too enthusiastic and promised at least a meeting with the chef, and when she wasn't able to deliver, it was understandable they dropped her. But since then, her uncle had questioned her about every decision she'd made just like he used to when she'd first started managing events on her own. Mamu was a sweet man with so much talent, but he was also a traditionalist.

Bobbi, on the other hand, was praised for her revolutionary ideas in Indian weddings. Or she used to be, before Mamu tightened the leash.

"Don't worry. I know what I'm doing," Bobbi said smoothly, even as she motioned to the staff manager to start the second round of appetizers.

"Still, I think you're doing too much—"

"There you are!" Veera's voice was a delightful interruption. She looked stunning in a lehenga that shimmered in the dark lighting. The turquoise faded into a black hem at the skirt, and the blouse had elegant detail along the cap sleeves and the sweetheart neckline. She carried a mask with peacock feathers sprouting from the side.

Bobbi opened her arms for a quick hug. "Hey there, gorgeous."

"You have to say that because you're my bestie. Hi, Uncle."

"Hi, beta," Mamu replied and patted her gently on the cheek. "You do look so pretty."

She tucked her hands into her lehenga pockets as if to show them that she had them, then did a quick twirl. "It's the outfit that makes the impression. Since this is the first major fundraiser we're hosting, I wanted to make sure I look the part," she said. She brushed a curl off her face. "And since my sister is in India for the next six months setting up our global office in Goregaon, my mother's attention is all on me."

"It's less about clothes and more about you that makes you beautiful," Mamu replied.

Someone called his name from the wings, and he waved. "Duty calls. Bobbi, page me if you need anything. If anyone has comments about the—"

"It's *fine*. Go have fun."

He waved and ambled off into the wings.

Veera motioned to Bobbi's retreating uncle. "Still on your case?"

Bobbi nodded. She let out a frustrated sigh. "I have a perfect track record, but I make one mistake and he won't let me forget it."

"Well, I think you're amazing," Veera said. She turned so she could stand next to Bobbi and look at the inflow of guests, masks in hand, heading to one of the six bar stations positioned throughout the expansive space. "Thank you so much for handling this for us."

"Thank you so much for the giant paycheck from your company," Bobbi replied. "This is going toward the down payment on my new place. And toward Kareena's bachelorette party."

Veera's eyes lit up. "We have to get on that. Four months until the wedding doesn't give us a lot of time. Hey, how goes the planning?"

"Great," she said.

"Great?" Veera prodded. "Seriously?"

"Yeah," Bobbi said. She waved to a familiar face, a former client who pointed to the curtains and gave Bobbi two thumbs-up.

"I just have to get Kareena to try on some wedding clothes and we'll be right on track." Well, almost on track, she thought. There was the food situation, which she hadn't addressed yet. Because that meant she'd have to have a conversation with Benjamin.

He'd slipped a kathi roll in her bag at their last meeting. What did that even mean? Was it because he was judging her, assuming that she was hungry? And why did she eat it instead of throwing it away when she'd sworn off his cooking?

Just as the thought of food crossed her mind, wait staff carrying spring rolls and sweet-and-sour chutney paused in front of them. Veera's eyes lit up.

"Oh, I'm starving!" She reached for a spring roll when a voice cut through the noise.

"Veera, don't you dare!" The sound was high-pitched and reedy, with a faint accent from New Delhi by way of boarding school. Bobbi turned to face Veera's mother, who shimmied over in her white sequined sari.

"Damn it," Veera muttered, and smiled sheepishly at the wait staff person before they walked away. "Hi, Mom."

"'Hi, *Mom*', ka bacha," she said, and ran a hand down Veera's arm affectionately. "You can't get your hands greasy before you say hellos. This is an important event for your father's business. You are supposed to be welcoming our clients and employees. Hello, Bobbi. Wonderful work, darling."

Bobbi leaned forward for an air-kiss. "Thank you, Namrata Auntie. We aim to please. You look stunning."

"Thank you, thank you." She eyed Bobbi's black suit. "Is that what you're wearing?"

Bobbi grinned at the tastefully veiled judgment. "I'm going to change in the back room once I'm sure the tech team has a handle on the auction software on the tablets."

Auntie waved a hand. "With the number of engineers in this room, someone can help figure it out." A person caught her attention out of the corner of her eye, and her hand shot up and waved. "Oh, look. It's Kumar Uncle. Veera, you remember Kumar Uncle? His son is in town. You should talk to him for your sister."

Bobbi looked at Veera, who was equally perplexed.

"Why would I talk to his son for Sana?" Veera asked. "She's a lesbian."

Veera's mother rolled her eyes. "Yes, I know, but he's gay, too."

Bobbi realized what she was saying at the same time Veera's expression morphed into a mix of horror and exasperation.

"Mom, that's not how it works. Sana only dates women. Kumar Uncle's son only dates men. Just because they're both in the queer community doesn't mean that they're interested in dating each other."

Veera's mother's eyebrows furrowed. "So, if Sana is only dating women, and Kumar Uncle's son is only dating other men, then who am I supposed to find for you? What do you date?"

"Trash mostly," Veera said. "Sana's been out for years. You should know better. Now you *promised* you'd behave tonight. Can you drop it?"

Namrata Auntie gently cupped Veera's cheeks. "Wanting my children to find companionship and happiness *is* behaving," she said simply. "Now stop hiding in a corner. I thought you were done with this habit. You can't always sit with your book at a party in the corner. I expect you to be on your *best* behavior. Start at the bar, please."

Veera glared at her mother, then turned to Bobbi. "Excuse me. I'm going to pretend that I don't know that people are insulting me when they insinuate that as a woman I know nothing about the stock market."

"Veera," her mother chided.

Veera put her mask over her face and practically moped her way through round tables and gold high-back chairs. The room was now filled with gorgeous lehengas, saris, and salwar suits. With men dressed in sherwanis and tuxedos. A sea of jewel tones and sparkle moved together, alive with elegant energy.

"Now, Bobbi," Namrata Auntie said. "Are you going to change into something traditional?"

"Yes," Bobbi replied. She motioned to one of her team members standing closest so she could hand her devices over. She quickly dispatched her head piece, the tablet, and the unit clipped to her waist. "I just hope that no one is going to be rude about my lehenga blouse. It's backless."

"So? Half the women here are wearing blouses that are backless," Auntie said.

Because she knew Namrata Auntie didn't share many of the same sentiments as other people in their community, Bobbi answered the question honestly. "You know how people treat fatness in our society, Auntie. God forbid a *healthy* Desi woman—because we still can't use the word 'fat' apparently—wear anything backless. I love the outfit and I just want to wear it, but I hate having to defend my choices when I don't owe anyone an explanation. It's exhausting just existing in a room full of these people sometimes."

Auntie's glare sharpened. "If anyone ever questions who you are or what you look like, if they say or do something, you come to me." She switched to rapid Hindi. "I'll have Uncle sink their portfolio so fast that they'll be crying for the rest of their sad, miserable lives." She reached out and cupped Bobbi's cheek. "Acha?"

God, this woman was scary, Bobbi thought. "Yes, Auntie."

"Nam!"

Bobbi and Namrata Auntie turned to the woman who stepped up in front of them.

"Deena," Namrata Auntie said. Bobbi watched in fascination as they air-kissed each other, then separated.

"Don't you look . . . young," the woman named Deena commented as she sized up Namrata Auntie's sari.

Bobbi's jaw dropped at the dig.

Auntie didn't look fazed in the least. "Deena, I didn't know you would be here. But then again, I was only familiar with the A-list important invitees. So glad we opened the event to others. My husband is a generous man."

Deena's expression turned sour. "Yes, I've heard about his generosity. Are you one of the women who gets the appreciation?"

"Myself and my daughters," she said smoothly. "Oh, I heard you have a daughter yourself now who has married into your family? Congratulations on your son's nuptials. So *rushed* though."

"Apologies we couldn't send you an invite, of course," Deena said coolly. "Just those who are close friends were included in our joyous occasion."

"Then it must've been a very small invite list," Namrata Auntie said. "It's a pleasure to see you, Deena, why don't you go have a drink? I heard you're a fan of an open bar these days."

Bobbi could see the thunderous expression on the woman's face as she was quickly shooed away. Bobbi grinned. "You're my favorite Auntie."

Namrata Auntie winked. "Just because I don't know my daughters' dating preferences doesn't mean I'm completely clueless all the time. When you finish changing, I'll introduce you to Koma Auntie. I hate her prickly attitude, but she has deep pockets, that witch. We'll try to guilt her into a bigger donation."

"Deal," Bobbi said, and then left Veera's mother to wreak havoc so she could change and enjoy the party herself. She waved to Veera from across the room, feeling sorry for her poor friend who looked bored senseless. When Veera caught her eye, Bobbi motioned to the dressing room in the back corner.

Then she slipped through the growing crowd until she reached the hidden corridor. It was a closed-off section next to the lounge people used for quiet phone calls. The party had just started, but the room was already occupied by a few individuals in tuxes with cell phones glued to their faces. Typical.

She unlocked the dressing room with the event code, and once she was inside, she removed her large tote bag from under the vanity bench. It took her moments to slip out of her suit and slip on a pair of biker shorts. Then she pulled the lehenga up over them, tying the thread at the waist. The blouse was a whole different matter. After removing her bra, she slipped her arms through the holes and then fit her breasts into the cups.

That's when Bobbi realized she'd made a grave error. The back was a series of crisscrossed strings that tied between her shoulder blades. There was absolutely no way that she was going to be able to tie it herself.

She reached for her phone and sent a quick message to Veera.

> **BOBBI:** Can you come to the dressing room? I need a quick favor.

She texted the door code as well, then tossed her phone aside.

Typical, she thought. Typical that she was always prepared for a fashion emergency, but when it was her turn to have one, she had no idea what she was supposed to do. What was she thinking, wearing a backless outfit? She should've known it wouldn't be easy to get in and out of something like this. Especially since she might have to move quickly if there was a party emergency.

While she waited, she pulled on a mask that covered half her face and pinned it to a jeweled band that fit around her head.

She'd just finished tying it when the door lock beeped. Bobbi pressed the cups over her chest as it opened. "Hey, I just need help tying the back and— What are you doing here?"

She met Benjamin's eyes in the vanity mirror, her cheeks heating at the thought of him seeing her in any state of undress. He wore a Phantom of the Opera mask in bone white and a fitted tux that stretched across his chest and tapered at the waist.

"Veera is stuck talking to some old dudes on her company's board," he said. "She asked if I could help you."

"I don't need your—"

"Okay," he said, and began backing out of the doorway.

"Wait!" she called out. She literally had no other options in this situation. She needed someone to tie the back so she could return to the floor. "Shit."

"Yeah, that's what I thought." He closed the door at his back. The room felt instantly smaller. Her breath caught as he moved closer. She was naked from nape to waist, her hair up in a careless twist, her hands over her breasts to stop from baring even more of herself.

"Just make it quick, Mr. Phantom of the Desi Opera," she said in a soft rush.

With his eyes on her in the vanity mirror, their masks adding another layer between them, he skimmed an index finger down the center of her spine, and she shivered hard. *Oh god.*

Her breath was ragged. "If you don't know how to tie it—"

"Relax. I know my way around strings and ropes better than most people."

The comment had her jaw dropping. What in the world? Was he insinuating that . . . no. No, he couldn't be. A cascade of images filtered through her mind, most of them with her tied to his bed. *Oh god.*

Benjamin gripped the ends of the string, then began lacing them through the loops on the left and right sides of the blouse. His movements were firm, and efficient, even as his knuckles continued to run along the sensitive curve of her hips.

She shivered again and arched her back. "B-Bunty—"

"You look good laced up in my knots," Benjamin said, his voice deepening as his fingers lingered. Then he tugged hard on the strings. She gasped as she bumped against his chest.

"Benjamin *Bunty* Padda!"

"You got the wrong guy," Benjamin replied, and tugged again. "Who is this person?"

Two could play at this game, she thought. "He is my best friend's fiancé's best friend," she said, gasping when his fingertips brushed the side of one breast. She felt a rush of heat straight to her lower belly. "He is insufferable, arrogant, and not my type."

The ties crisscrossed and Benjamin tugged hard. Her shoulders pulled back as the corset blouse fit into place. Bobbie's head fell back against his shoulder. She smelled his rich, musky cologne, and the spicy-sweet scent she instinctively knew was hot and hard skin.

"Why isn't he your type?" Benjamin whispered. She felt his breath against the shell of her ear, and her curls fluttered along the soft skin at her nape. "Is it because he was an idiot for saying something he didn't mean? Or because you feel absolutely nothing when he's close to you?"

She had to fight the urge to turn in his arms, to have him untie her as efficiently as he'd dressed her. "Is that an apology?" she whispered.

She felt the tight bow he'd fastened resting against her lower back now. He pulled the strings one last time until she was practically trussed up. There was no way that thing would move for the rest of the night.

"Bobbi, I've been apologizing since the moment I said those words," Benjamin replied in gruff Punjabi. He held her gaze in the mirror as his hands slid down her hips and pulled her back so that her ass rested against the top of his thighs. If she bent forward, and he bent at the knees just a little, they'd fit perfectly.

Bobbi grew damp, her pulse skipping at the thought. Then Benjamin's hand fell away and the moment was gone.

She turned to face him, but there was only cold air where he'd been standing. She watched his retreating back as he slipped through the dressing room door. She ran a hand over the front of her fitted blouse. What the hell was that? What had just happened?

### *Indians Abroad News*
### Relationship column

There is nothing like food to unite potential matches.

Mrs. W. S. Gupta
Avon, New Jersey

# CHAPTER 4

## Benjamin

**BOBBI:** Hey it's Bobbi. I got your number from Deepak after the masquerade fundraiser a few nights ago. We have to confirm the menu.

**BENJAMIN:** Okay. I'm on the west coast for the week, but I'll be back next weekend.

**BOBBI:** I have two events next weekend but I can do Sunday night.

**BENJAMIN:** Fine. Come to Phataka Grill.

**BOBBI:** I'll be there at 7:00 p.m.

Benjamin glanced at his watch and then attempted to discreetly call for a car service on his cell. If he didn't leave in the next ten minutes, he'd be at risk of missing his flight, and he absolutely hated to be late.

That, and he had a meeting with Bobbi.

A conversation with his father was the only thing standing in his way.

Gabbar Singh, the Naan King of California, sat in the high-back leather armchair across from him, nursing his morning chai. He was as tall as Benjamin, but lean. He wore an off-white beige suit because it was Sunday, and he always wore beige suits on Sunday workdays. His pagadi matched in color and was expertly tied around his head like the crown it was meant to be. His beard was combed and conditioned. A bright white color. The only sign that he was at home was his large bare feet, one of which was visible thanks to the fact that the ankle attached to it was resting on his opposite knee.

They had been sitting in silence for the past fifteen minutes.

"Dad, I better get going," Benjamin said. He wasn't sure why his father wanted to meet him in private so close to his flight to the East Coast.

"Your restaurant can do without you for a few more days. You should stay."

He waved a hand in an easy move of dismissal, which contradicted the hard, rapid-fire Punjabi. His words always sounded like bullets ricocheting in the air without the whirring thud of impact.

"You know I can't do that," Benjamin said gently, in an accent tinged with his American upbringing. "I have people counting on me to be there. Is there something you wanted to talk about?"

There was a loud, heavy sigh, then a beat of silence. "It's my health," he said gravely.

Benjamin's heart pounded. "Wh-what's wrong?"

"Nothing," Benjamin's father said. "Well, nothing yet. I have a feeling your mother is going to eat my head and then my health will suffer. Just like she would want it to."

"Fuck, Dad. You scared me." Benjamin pressed a hand to his chest and took a deep breath.

"That is because you are my scare-dy son," he said in English.

He chuckled. Then his expression grew serious. "Bunty, how many times have I told you the story of the Naan King Emporium? I grew my small business from two stores believing in my product to every major grocery retailer selling our goods. I don't want that to go to waste. But this October, when I share with the board my intentions, I'm afraid that will happen."

"Your intentions?"

"I'm retiring. My legacy will have to live on without me as I sail into the sunset."

"Sail into the sunset? What are you talking about?"

"Your mother has booked an around-the-world cruise for us as soon as I'm done. Twenty-eight days. Very good price."

Benjamin thought he'd be happy when his father finally announced his retirement. He wanted to believe that he'd clap the old man on his shoulder and pour a whiskey to celebrate. But Benjamin did neither of those things. Instead, he had a very clear understanding of where this conversation was headed. "Papa, I already spend a significant amount of my time helping the business. If you think I should come in as CEO to replace you, then you know that's not happening. I have restaurants . . ."

"Chudde paran apne restaurants," he grumbled. His white beard lifted up and down as his mouth twisted with displeasure. "I don't think your brother is ready. The board may not approve his nomination to be CEO."

"That's between you and Chottu," Benjamin said. He'd played mediator for most of his life between his father and his brother and it was always the same story. His father had never stopped questioning whether his younger brother had the skill and the courage to lead a frozen food empire because of one mistake Chottu had made in his early twenties. Meanwhile, his brother was the reason why the company had expanded as much as it had in recent years.

Hell, he was the reason why their Diwali Naan campaign was so successful.

"If Chottu leads," his father continued, unaware of Benjamin's spiraling thoughts, "he'll be making big mistakes. Did you know he wants to do a big media campaign for this ridiculous gluten-free line?"

Not the gluten-free conversation again, Benjamin thought. "Gluten-free is inclusive. There are people who can't eat gluten. It's a move we should've made years ago." A notification pinged on his phone. Two minutes until his car would arrive.

His father grunted. "Did you taste it?"

"Yeah," Benjamin lied as he set his empty chai cup down on the tray. "It's fine."

The idea of having to try gluten-free naan had Benjamin's stomach turning. Not that he had anything against going gluten-free. The truth he'd been hiding from this man sitting in front of him was that he, Benjamin Padda, *hated* naan. He'd been forced to eat it with every meal most of his childhood and had developed a bad taste for the thick, soft bread. But he'd never tell Gabbar Singh that. He rebelled quietly in his own way. In the restaurants he owned, he offered paranthas, rumali roti, bhature. But naan? No, it was tucked away in the corner under accompaniments.

"I can tell when you're lying, Bunty." His father sipped his chai again and grunted. "At least it freezes well."

"You have to trust Chottu to know what he's talking about. You've been grooming him for this role for years. And he's done a good job. He's wanted to do right by this company since he was a kid." Most of the time. Chottu was a walking *Indian Matchmaking* profile for the second-generation uber-rich Punjabi son with privilege in SoCal.

"And then there is your sister—"

Benjamin held up a finger. "Nope, no, you don't get to talk about her." He'd be here for an hour explaining to his father that both he and Mom were the reason why his sister had moved away for good. Now she was living her best life, traveling the world and writing her books in coffee shops or on a beach somewhere dreamy.

His father flicked his hands at him as if shooing away a fly. There was sadness etched in the creases around his eyes. He missed Gudi. They all missed Gudi. But Gudi was suffocated in Cali. And like Bunty and Chottu, the Naan King had shaped her destiny.

"Bunty," his father said, his voice gentling. "I'm getting older. Your mother is getting older. We're going to be traveling more. Your brother won't have my regular guidance once he's at the helm by himself. He'll be alone. But if you officially join as an advisor instead of this temporary consulting nonsense, the board will have more confidence in him as the next CEO. And so will I."

"I don't understand," Benjamin said. "I won't be doing anything more than what I already do, right?"

"No, it wouldn't be the same," his father continued. He let out a harrumph that had his entire body shifting in his seat. "You'd be in the office for any board meetings, and any senior leadership meetings. Chottu would bring you in for the bigger decisions. Which leads me to my last request. I know you're looking to open your next restaurant, and I want to support you. But more importantly, I want you to remember you're part of something bigger. Family first. You have responsibilities. That's why your mother and I think you should open your next restaurant on the West Coast. So you can be close by to support Chottu, your sister when she is home, and to see us as we get older and need you."

He'd already been considering the West Coast, but now the

decision felt so much more imbalanced. His family needed him. And he always wanted to be there if they needed him. They, and the profession he'd chosen as a chef and entrepreneur, were the reasons why he already felt like his family life was so full. So many people had told Benjamin that he didn't have an obligation, but in reality his success and every opportunity he had been afforded were because of the sacrifices that his parents had made . . . right?

"Papa, this is a big decision. I already support the business, I fly back and forth regularly, and when I'm here, I live with you in this house. I don't know what more I can do by joining as—"

His father held up a hand. "You don't have to decide now, but in October, I'll be announcing my retirement formally. If you want your brother to take over, then you're going to need to be there. Your presence will inspire support for Chottu. If you're not there, then well, I don't know what will happen. I don't think Chottu has my vision for success in mind, and the board knows that."

Ah, and there was that guilt trip, Benjamin thought. Another notification pinged his phone. He stood and straightened his suit-coat.

"If you keep nagging me with your speeches," Benjamin said lightly, clapping his hand on his father's shoulder, "I'm going to tell Mom that you don't want to go on her cruise."

The stern businessman his father had become shifted to terrified husband. "Don't you dare, Bunty. She'll make me suffer from her incessant lectures."

Benjamin called out over his shoulder, "Then you'll know how it feels having to sit through yours, old man!"

Benjamin went straight to his restaurant from Newark airport, his head buzzing with the conversation he'd had with his father. Was he really considering the West Coast for his next location because of his father's retirement? He loved his family, and he wanted to be there for them as much as he could, but he wasn't ready to sacrifice what was best for his dream.

He continued to mull it over through a conversation with his kitchen staff, his manager, and his wine distributor. When his laptop pinged with a reminder that Bobbi would be there within the next ten minutes, his focus shifted to seeing her again. If anyone could distract him, it was Bobbi.

In an effort to keep from fidgeting, he began opening the mail on his desk. He knew it was better to look like he was busy when she showed up. He didn't want her to think that he was eager to see her.

After a series of mailers and junk letters, he came across a nondescript envelope at the bottom of a stack of messages.

On the front was a note printed in bold letters.

Benjamin,

Here are the selections I made for Kareena and Prem's wedding reception. Please send this to the wedding venue once you've reviewed. We do not need to meet about this as it's already been decided. This is for your information only.

Best regards,
Bobbi Kaur

Bobbi was supposed to be at the restaurant any minute to pick out the menu items with him. Why would she go ahead without his input? He quickly tore open the envelope. His eyes practically fell out of their sockets at the menu.

Yellow daal? Boiled white rice? *Pizza?*

"What the fuck?" he said, his voice booming in the quiet office.

He picked up his phone to call Bobbi. He was going to tell her exactly what he thought of her little underhanded attempt at selecting the worst wedding menu options to make him look bad—

A knock on the door had him looking up. His hostess peeked her head inside. "A Bobbi Kaur is here for you. I brought her back like you asked."

*I'll just have to yell at her to her face.*

He nodded at his staff. "Thanks."

Bobbi came into view seconds later, her hair upswept, wearing a pair of high-waisted pants with a white sleeveless button-down tucked in the waistband. Her summer sandals were white and strappy, while her toes were painted a coral pink to match her nails.

She looked from his leather sofa and large glass-topped coffee table against one wall to the bar cart under two large flat-screen TVs with the news running on one side and security footage on the other, before she gave him a rueful smile.

"Nice."

He thought of that gorgeous naked back. The wide curves of her hips. The softness of her skin. And then he cursed.

"You've got to be kidding me, Bobbi."

Her eyes went wide. "I told you I'd be here by seven. What's your problem now?"

"My problem is this," he said, waving the paper she'd mailed him like a coward. "You're bold to even show your face after this attempt at undermining my authority."

"I don't know what *this* is." Bobbi dropped her large tote bag on the couch and sighed, as if she were about to deal with a child.

And if that didn't piss him off even more. He waved the paper like a battle flag.

"Do you really think Prem and Kareena are going to want kadai daal as their main course entrée? And what's this garbage about Costco brand ice cream for dessert? I thought you had better taste than to choose this garbage for the wedding!"

"Whoa, whoa, whoa," Bobbi said, holding her hands up like a T. "I haven't made *any* recommendations or decisions about the wedding food. That's why I set this meeting."

Benjamin stepped from around the desk and shoved the sheets of paper at her. "Then why would you have a messenger drop this off at the restaurant? I just opened the envelope, otherwise I would've called an emergency intervention earlier."

He watched as Bobbi focused on the typed note at the top of the page. "What the hell? I don't talk like that . . . oh my god." She flipped the page and began reading the menu selections. "Bindi and toast as an appetizer? Bunty, I definitely did not send this, and I absolutely would *never* pick bindi for a wedding. That's disgusting. This isn't from me. It has to be a joke."

Now he was offended all over again. Bindi was his favorite. "Why do you have a problem with bindi? You know, okra is the most misunderstood vegetable—"

"Bunty!"

"What? Okay, I'm sorry." He took a few deep breaths, even though he still had no idea what was going on. "I didn't mean to lose my shit. But you have to admit, it's convincing that a letter with the menu stuff arrives before our meeting today. And how am I supposed to know you don't have an assistant who wrote the note?"

Bobbi rubbed the tension crease between her brows before she collapsed in the chair opposite his desk. "I wouldn't put it past Kareena's sister to mess around with us just because she's a self-centered asshole. It's probably a prank from Bindu. Toss the letter."

The thought of his siblings doing something like that was incomprehensible to him. Kareena must've had a rough time as a child, he thought. He balled up the pages and dunked them in the wastebasket next to his desk. "Done." He swallowed his pride that sat in his throat like a lump, and added, "I'm sorry that I jumped to conclusions."

She nodded. "Thank you. In the interest of time, let me show you some sample menus that work really well for weddings the same size and scale as Kareena and Prem's event. This is just to get us started. If you prefer, I can send them to you by email as well." She removed the tablet from her bag, turned it on, and then handed it over to Benjamin.

Instead of sitting behind his desk, he came around to sprawl in the guest chair next to hers. His legs spread out, and his loafers almost bumped her sandaled feet. When she scrambled back, he had to hide a smile. Skittish.

He began to look over the documents in front of him, and his concern eased even further. Okay, he could work with this. Some tweaks, a few custom requests, and he'd be able to help put together something fantastic.

He was about to comment on the live grill stations when he heard a very audible grumble.

His head shot up even as Bobbi pressed a hand to her stomach.

"Are you hungry?" He felt awash in shame and horror that he hadn't even thought about feeding her before they got to work. Good god, what kind of idiot was he? His mother would've killed him for neglecting not only to offer her something to drink, but to have food prepped for their meeting.

"Don't worry about it," she murmured. "I'm heading home after this, and—"

"For once can you not be so damn stubborn?" he said. He got up from his chair and then left the office, slamming the door in his wake. Taking a left into the hallway, he glanced in the mirror hanging at the corner, then pushed through the right side of the double doors. The kitchen stopped, and every head jerked up to look at his entrance.

He went to the overhead warmers and glanced at the tickets. Table twenty-three, order for two, a plate of chole, and another piled high with soft yeasty bathure, a plate of vegetable biryani, some of their spiked chai in clay kullar cups. His wait staff came over. Jake was one of Benjamin's oldest employees.

"Chef, is everything okay?"

"Table twenty-three is yours tonight, right?"

"Yeah, young couple. Looks like they've been together forever. Out for a Sunday night meal. Familiar with the menu, too."

"You think they'd mind a delay?"

Jake shook his head. "Comp part of their meal and offer free dessert?"

"Yup, do it. Just let them know if they'd like to speak with me, I'm happy to come out and talk to them and apologize personally. Hey, Rez, I need you to redo the ticket for table twenty-three, please. Extra care with the plating."

Rez held up a thumb. "Yes, Chef."

He grabbed a tray and loaded it with the order along with two cutlery sets he pulled from the clean rack. "Thanks, Jake."

"You got it, Chef."

He called out before pushing through the double doors one more time, tray in hand, and then entered his office. He watched Bobbi's stunned expression from where she stood.

"Give me a minute," he said, and cleared some room on his desk with one hand before setting the tray down.

"There is no way you made this in three minutes," Bobbi said, eyeing the tray.

"It's someone else's order," Benjamin replied.

"Bunty, you can't just take someone else's order for yourself," she said, even as she leaned forward to inspect the food. "What kind of restaurant are you running that—"

He spooned rice on top of a fork and shoved it in her mouth midsentence. Her expression morphed into one of pleasure, and she closed her eyes. She chewed, and a soft moan escaped her throat.

*Damn.*

"I sent the wait staff to apologize for the delay, rushed their replacement order, and comped their dinner," he said gruffly. "Happy?"

Bobbi chewed, swallowed, then opened her mouth to respond, but he fed her more rice before she could stop him.

She slapped a hand over her mouth.

Her cheeks tinted with pleasure.

He hadn't felt so smug in a long time.

"Good, isn't it?" Benjamin scooped up biryani for himself and took a taste. He was so damn proud of his kitchen. When he saw Bobbi watching him, he pulled the tines of the fork out of his mouth slowly.

"Okay!" she blurted out, pushing her chair back to increase the space between them. "Just stop. What do you think you're doing?"

"Feeding someone who is hungry. Obviously."

Bobbi stood. She paced across the office and held up her hands. "I don't get you. Why would you do something nice for me?"

The words on the tip of his tongue were cutting, just as they had been since the moment they met. They'd been at odds with each other over something he said that he didn't mean, and her reaction and assessment of him as a person in response. But if they had to work together, wouldn't it be better if they just paused their ongoing battle?

The memory of her naked back, of her smooth, soft skin, flitted at the corner of his mind.

"Let's call a truce," he said. "A formal truce. No bullshit. I screwed up the way we met, and I apologize for that."

"Why call a truce now?"

"Because our friends are getting married. Because we have to work together, and because it really pisses me off that you won't eat at my restaurant." He didn't mean to add the last bit, but it was the truth. He wanted her to enjoy his food, to tell him what she thought of it, and to share it with him. He respected her as a professional, and a part of him was intrigued by the way she worked. He wanted to get to know all her.

They watched each other for a moment before she crossed her arms over her chest.

"Just for the wedding," she blurted out. "I'll play nice just for the wedding."

"For fuck's sake, fine," he said, and ran a hand over his beard. "Just for the wedding then. So we can get through the next three and a half months together."

He waited until she sat back down before pushing the tray toward her. "You know," she said as she inspected the chole, "it was probably a good thing nothing happened that day."

*Like hell.* "Yeah, I guess."

"I mean, you've made it clear in the few times our group has spent time together that you never plan on getting into a relationship."

He wanted to argue with her, to tell her that just because he wasn't interested in a serious relationship didn't mean that he wasn't interested in her. Instead, he opted for the safe response, even as he reached out to tuck a curl behind her ear. "I have . . . family to manage," he said. "And my career and bicoastal business isn't something that inspires women into believing I'm a good investment." Especially not someone who was dedicated to their job like Bobbi.

She nodded, and as if she'd read his mind, added, "And if I get into a relationship, I am looking for someone who can work around my schedule, too."

"Exactly. You get it."

"So, we should be grateful."

He rubbed the back of his neck so he wouldn't reach out to touch her again. "Yeah. So grateful."

Bobbi looked pleased with herself as she reached for the cup of chai and curled back in the chair to take a sip. There was pleasure in her expression now, and he had to hide a smile. He could make even better chai at home, but now was probably not the best time to mention that.

She saluted him with the kullar. "My Phataka Grill boycott has come to an end. Temporarily."

"I appreciate the pain you endured to have dinner at my restaurant." Benjamin took two plates and began divvying up the rest of the food between them. He handed her one, and then settled back with the other.

She tore a corner off the bhature to scoop the chole. "Do you usually feed women biryani and chole or is it just me?" she said.

"Just you. I didn't realize how much of a turn-on it is, too."

She put the plate down on his desk with a clatter.

He couldn't hide his grin now. He wondered if she flushed all over.

"If we're calling a truce, you have to behave."

*Like hell.* "Fine."

"Fine."

He waited until she picked up her plate again. "When you're done with that, I'll order rasgulla cheesecake. You have to taste my sweet, creamy dessert."

"Bunty!" Her cheeks were tinged with pink, and he could tell that her nipples beaded through her thin shirt before she crossed her arms over her chest.

"Bobbi," he said, laughing. "Okay, the truce can officially start now."

*Probably.*

# CHAPTER 5

## Bobbi

Bobbi stared at the blank expression on Gertrude's face. "What do you mean someone canceled it?"

Gertrude shrugged, her crisp white chef coat moving up and down like a starched boxy suit. "The day you made the cake reservation, someone called and canceled," she said, in her slightly accented English. "So I never pushed your deposit through."

That's exactly why Bobbi had come all the way out to Brooklyn. To find out why her deposit for Prem and Kareena's wedding cake never processed. If there was a problem with the wedding cake, she always wanted to deal with it in person. "Who called you about the cake, Gertrude?"

Gertrude shrugged again, even as she motioned for one of her team members to adjust the pastries in the case next to the old-fashioned register.

Bobbi tried to control her temper. She needed this woman way more than Gertrude needed her. "What name did they give you?"

"Your wedding planning company name. Then the name of the

bride and groom. And then your phone number. I thought it was a legitimate call."

"Why didn't you just check with me to confirm?" Bobbi said. Gertrude shrugged again. Bobbi pinched the bridge of her nose and began pacing the black-and-white tile floor of the German artisanal bakery. "I do almost all of my business with you! I wouldn't have some random person call on my behalf to cancel. I would've texted or called you directly."

The older woman continued to look bored. "I'm sorry, Bobbi."

She folded her hands and pleaded. "Can you put the cake back on the books?"

Gertrude shook her head. "You know I squeezed you in last minute as a favor to you. It's too late now."

"You are the only person I know who I can trust to make this cake, Gertrude. I order over fifty cakes a year from you. Please just this once bend the rules. This is for my *best friend*."

Frustratingly, the woman shook her head again. "I'm so sorry, Bobbi. You know I can't. I'm already at capacity. I can maybe try for December?"

What good would that do when the wedding was in October? Damn it, where was she supposed to find an artisanal baker for a cake this close to Kareena and Prem's event? She could go through all her backup bakers, but it was most likely a fruitless exercise. They'd all be booked too. Maybe her uncle knew someone? But he, and their two senior wedding planners on staff, usually took recommendations from her. And if her uncle even smelled something was wrong, he'd yank her off another wedding so fast.

"Gertrude, do you know anyone else who bakes delicious cakes almost as good as you?"

The woman shook her head. "No one is even close to me, darling."

"I know, that's the problem."

Gertrude was human enough to look sorry for Bobbi's state. "Next time," she said. "Next time someone calls, I only talk to you. Okay?"

"Yes, please. I appreciate that."

Gertrude pulled out a fruit tart from the case, placed it on a doily, then slipped it into a custom-cut box with her logo on top. "For the road. You look a bit stressed."

*Stressed* was a mild word compared to what she was feeling. Someone had first tried to sabotage the meal planning, and now the cake.

Gertrude had outdone herself with the design for it, too. Four tiers, for the four months Kareena and Prem circled each other, falling deeper in love. Buttercream frosting instead of fondant. A light yellow sponge with a Nutella ganache filling for the base, and interesting combinations for each tier. The whole masterpiece was topped with French macarons cascading down the side in an ombré of yellow. Mehndi designs in piped sugar icing were decorated with an edible glitter.

No one would ever be able to create anything as luscious as Gertrude with such an eye for detail.

Bobbi looked down at the pastry in her hand, then relented. She reached into her tote for her wallet and Gertrude shook her head. "It's the least I can do. I'll let you know if someone cancels and I can put you back in for that date."

"Thanks. I'll touch base next week about the Patels' cake, okay?"

"The thousand-person wedding?"

"That's the one."

Gertrude shook her head. "You live a very exciting life, Bobbi."

"I wish that were true," she said, waving before she stepped out the double doors and onto the sidewalk. The sun was brutal today, and the heat radiated off the cement. She tucked the pastry away and put her sunglasses on.

Her gut was telling her that someone had a vendetta, so she stepped out of the pedestrian traffic flow, scrolled through her phone, and made a call to find out if her hunch was right.

"Hello?" The soft, sugar-sweet voice of Kareena's younger sister answered on the second ring. "Bobbi?"

"Hi, Bindu, how are you?" she said with as much politeness as she could muster. She felt her thighs sticking together already in the humidity.

"Wonderful! I don't know if Kareena told you or if you saw my YouTube channel recently, but Loken and I are expecting a baby."

"Oh, that's right! Your sister is *so* happy for you. She can't stop talking about her future niece or nephew. Congratulations!"

"Really? Didi is excited?"

"Very. That's why she moved up the wedding! That way nothing will interfere with the attention that your child deserves."

"That's so sweet," Bindu said. She began to sniff. "I don't appreciate Didi enough. She's always been there for me. Even though she ruined my engagement party. But that turned out to be a blessing in disguise, too. Is that why you're calling? To ask me to help with the wedding?"

Bobbi heard the excitement in her tone and could tell that this woman had absolutely nothing to do with canceling the cake. She would've sounded smug at this point. No, Bindu was too busy focusing on herself. "I just wanted to ask if you had any recommendations for a cake vendor."

"Not off the top of my head, but I'll do some research," she said cheerfully. "I'll put the word out on my YouTube account, too. This might be a good thing for my mother-in-law to help with as well."

"Your mother-in-law?"

"Yup!" Bindu lowered her voice to a whisper. "I hate to be mean, but she is a terrible woman, and she is still so upset that Loken and I didn't have a wedding. Finding a cake vendor may be the distraction she needs."

"Great. Thanks, Bindu. Talk to you soon." Bobbi hung up the phone and groaned.

That was a complete waste of time, she thought as she canvassed the Brooklyn sidewalk. Bobbi would go home and regroup before figuring out her next steps. Once she had a solution, she could connect with Kareena and Prem to tell them what happened.

Never deliver a problem to a client without at least two options to fix it.

She tucked her phone away, and when she realized that there was barely any through traffic on the side street, she decided to walk to one of the cross streets to grab her ride share service, even if that meant baking in the sun. "Today keeps getting better and better," she murmured.

"Bobbi?"

She spun around on her platform heels and immediately recognized the familiar face. "Bunty?"

He was framed in sunlight, wearing a white button-down shirt, rolled up at the sleeves and open at his neck. His khaki shorts and sandals were casual. He had a swagger as he walked toward her.

Damn, his thighs were like tree trunks.

She jerked her head up so she wouldn't be caught staring below the waist. "What are you doing in Brooklyn?" she asked when he was inches in front of her.

"I stay with Deepak when I'm in town."

"Isn't he in Park Slope?"

"Yeah," Benjamin said. He adjusted his aviators. Damn, he

looked good in aviators. The thought had her shaking her head. What the hell was wrong with her?

"Then why are you in Carroll Gardens?" she asked, trying to distract herself.

"I had a meeting with a developer with leads on a new restaurant location a few doors down. We just finished when I saw you. What are you doing out here?"

She motioned to Gertrude's Bakery behind her with the classic white-and-mint-green-striped canopy over the doorway. "My secret weapon. Except Gertrude can't make Kareena and Prem's cake."

"Too short notice?"

"Yes, and also, I think someone is trying to sabotage Kareena's wedding."

Benjamin's jaw dropped. "You're joking."

"No, I'm serious," Bobbi said. "Before I can figure out who, I have to find a new bakery. Someone who can do a wedding cake that's out of this world. I don't think any of my backup options are going to work. Unless you have a pastry chef contact up your sleeve?"

He stroked his beard, the kada on his wrist glinting. "You know what? I might know someone. Do you have some time? And are you up for walking in this weather?"

She pulled at her blouse, hoping for the light breeze in the air to cool her just a bit. "Yes, to both, if it means we can get Kareena a cake."

"Come on, then," he said and motioned for her to follow him down the sidewalk.


During the five-minute stroll, they talked about Bobbi's theory that someone was out to ruin the wedding. Benjamin still looked skeptical, but he didn't interrupt before he stopped in front of an ice cream parlor with a paisley decal on the window. The word KULFI was etched in the center of the glass pane. The reference to milky, slow-churned South Asian ice cream was intriguing, but that did not solve Bobbi's problem.

She was about to tell Benjamin to stop wasting her time when he opened the door and called out a hello before stepping inside.

Bobbi followed. "I don't understand why we're here," she said.

"You will in a minute."

A woman with dark brown skin, a septum piercing, and a riot of silky black curls pinned on top of her head came out from the back room. She wore a white apron smeared with what looked like chocolate sauce. She was younger than Benjamin and Bobbi, but wore old, traditional jhumkas in her earlobes.

She was gorgeous.

"Benjamin!" she said, coming through the small gap behind the ice cream freezers so she could hold Benjamin's outstretched hands and present her cheek for a kiss. "What are you doing in my shop today?"

He motioned to Bobbi. "Bobbi Kaur. Wedding planner. Bobbi is planning my best friend's wedding to her best friend, and she needs a wedding cake. Bobbi, this is Sachita. We met through a mutual friend."

Bobbi's professionalism automatically kicked in. She held out a hand to shake. "Hi, it's a pleasure to meet you. I'm berating myself for not knowing about your store before." She looked around now, at the delicate details, the brightly painted walls, the rows of meticulously arranged ice cream coolers, and the framed neon menu board. "This looks like such a great place."

"I opened about a year ago, so we're still new. Benjamin, did you say wedding cake? I'll be honest, the last time I made a wedding cake was when I was apprenticing. I don't know if I can help you there."

That's exactly what Bobbi feared, but Benjamin held up a hand. "I know it's not something that's normally on the menu, but I have an idea. Do you think we could try a slice of your celebration ice cream cake? Bobbi really needs to try it."

Sachita looked as skeptical as Bobbi felt. "Sure," she said slowly. "Give me a sec."

She went into the back, and Bobbi nudged Benjamin's shoulder. "Please tell me you aren't wasting my time," she whispered.

"Trust me," he whispered back, setting the aviators on the top of his head. "Sachita knows her flavors."

"But it sounds like she doesn't know wedding cakes."

A moment later, Sachita returned, a thick slice of tri-layered ice cream cake on a large plate and two metal spoons. She handed them to Benjamin. "The celebration cake is usually for small birthday parties or anniversaries, but it's popular. I have a garden set up out back. No one is out there now. You're free to sit and enjoy."

Bobbi thanked her, then followed Benjamin through the narrow hallway to the courtyard.

It was small, like so many Brooklyn spaces. The trash was hidden behind a privacy screen, with greenery added as an additional barrier. The concrete slab was completely shaded and significantly cooler than the sidewalk, albeit still warm. The sound of cars warred with birds chirping overhead.

Benjamin pulled out one of the iron patio chairs for Bobbi, then twisted the other one around so that he straddled it and leaned against the back. When he held up his spoon, Bobbi looked at him, then the utensil, before realizing what he was doing. Whenever Prem and Kareena had dragged both groups of friends out together, Prem, Deepak, and Benjamin had the same ritual. Bobbi picked up the second spoon then tapped it against his, smiling when she saw the satisfaction on his face. They both dug into the cake.

"I think the bottom is a brownie crust, then with chocolate cake and vanilla cake breaking up the ice cream layers," he said. "There is Turkish coffee ice cream, orange and fennel ice cream, and the top is her signature malai."

Bobbi inspected the colors and the different textures. Those flavors should not go together, she thought. But Benjamin knew what tasted good. His restaurant was by far her favorite, because he did such interesting things with food.

When she slipped the spoon into her mouth, she knew in that instant she'd found another diamond. Well, Benjamin had found it, but she was now savoring it, and it was out of this world.

Her eyes closed and she experienced every flavor and texture. From the coffee to the orange fennel to the smooth sweet cream and chocolate cake. It was thick, rich, and creamy, all melting together with icy coolness on her tongue. A perfect antidote to the heat. The taste had her moaning deep as pleasure consumed her. She slowly slipped the spoon out of her mouth. Orgasmic.

After she swallowed, she opened her eyes again. Benjamin was staring at her.

"What?" she asked.

He jerked and banged his knee against the table. He winced and rubbed his injury. "Damn it. Uh, it's good, right? I mean, yes. It's good."

She had no idea what had gotten into him. She scooped up more ice cream while he grimaced. "You think Sachita can turn this into a wedding cake?"

"Without a doubt. Four tiers, different combinations like this. Simple cake décor. Because it's ice cream, have her assemble on-site, and then make it a showpiece by incorporating dry ice around the base to keep it cool. When it's wheeled out, the vapors from the dry ice will add to the display."

Bobbi nodded. The one thing she always prized herself on was working with suppliers who provided unique experiences. This would definitely be a unique experience for Kareena and Prem. And knowing her best friend like she did, ice cream was a win-win.

She leaned forward on the warm patio table, scooping more of the orange fennel, Benjamin waiting for his turn before he did the same. Bobbi thought about the beautiful woman inside. Benjamin had said that he knew Sachita through a mutual friend. That shouldn't irk her the way it did. They were nemeses calling a temporary truce, right? She thought about keeping her mouth shut but decided that was not her style.

"Question, before I go in there and try to convince Sachita to make a four-tier ice cream cake. Are you two dating?"

His eyes widened at the question. "What? No. We just met a few months ago. She was the one who suggested I look in this part of Brooklyn for my new location."

"Are you thinking about dating her?"

Benjamin shook his head. His response was quick and confident. "I'm . . . preoccupied at the moment."

Bobbi couldn't dwell on what that meant. Preoccupied as in dating someone else? Or preoccupied because he was looking for his restaurant location? "Do you have any plans to ask Sachita out before the wedding?"

"For fuck's sake, Bobbi," Benjamin said. Irritation marred his face.

She held up a hand. "I have to ask. If you complicate this business relationship, then it could get ugly for Kareena and Prem's wedding."

"There is nothing there. We're new friends. *Colleagues*."

"Fine," she said. "I mean, she seems sweet. And she's gorgeous."

There was that irritated look again. "So are you, but *we* aren't dating. No, wait . . . scratch the sweet part. Because let's be honest, you are a total pain in my—"

"Bunty, I swear to god, shut up." Leave it to him to give her a backhanded compliment. But the thought that Benjamin preferred Sachita to her still circled her mind. Bobbi was aware of the world and how it perceived the way she looked, and she couldn't help but wonder if Benjamin had the same perceptions.

He crossed his arms over the top of the chair and rested his chin on them. "Are you really asking me about Sachita in particular or the way that Sachita looks in general?"

She jerked back, her spoon still empty. It took a lot to surprise her, but Benjamin seemed to do so consistently. She sure as hell didn't expect him to call her out. Bobbi was fortunate that she had always been loved and taught to love the way she looked and how she felt about herself. But that didn't mean she was comfortable sparring with other people and their prejudice every day. She knew after years that some people would never change, and it made her wary about whether Benjamin was one of them.

"A lot of Punjabi men have a history of fatphobia," she finally said.

Benjamin bit into more cake, nodding. "I'm not going to argue with you, and I'm not going to tell you that you're wrong because I've seen it in our community. I respect you for wanting to protect yourself from it. But, Bobbi, I don't have a problem with your body. From the first moment I saw you, I *never* had a problem with your body."

"Okay," she said. She heard a ring of truth in his tone, and that was enough for her to trust that maybe, just maybe, he hadn't been talking about the way she looked when he said that she wasn't his type.

"No, wait. That's not true."

Bobbi froze. "*Excuse* me?"

"If we're calling a truce, that means we have to be honest with each other." He tilted to the side and slowly looked her up and down in one sweeping movement. "Your body *does* matter to me. It was one of the first things I noticed about you in that room at Kareena's house. But in the months that I've known you, and that you've irritated me, I also noticed your stubbornness. Your intelligence. Your loyalty to your friends. That's just as important if not more. It hits my list of things that I find attractive."

Her face felt hot, and she remembered the vivid fantasy that she had of Benjamin tying her down. "Let me guess, your *list* also includes having to be a virgin, rich, a great musician, and have rich dark ebony hair."

Benjamin tilted his head back and laughed. The sound was deep and rich, sending a thrill up her arms. "No," he said. "Her hair can be whatever god intended it to be."

"I don't even know why I bother." She got to her feet. "I'm going to talk to Sachita about this cake."

He slowly slid the spoon out of his mouth, and Bobbi knew that she was blushing again. "You do that. I'm glad I could help."

The only reason why she needed his assistance in the first place was because of the cake cancellation. She still had to deal with whoever was trying to ruin Kareena and Prem's wedding. Unfortunately, she didn't have a lot of time. "Bunty, I'm going to have to call in reinforcements to find the shaadi saboteur. We need to stop whoever is doing this from creating even more problems."

"Reinforcements?" He looked momentarily confused before his eyes bulged and his mouth fell open. "No. No way, Bobbi.

Getting them involved is a bad idea. They are chaos, and they'll only make this whole situation worse."

"They love Kareena," Bobbi said. "They'll do whatever it takes to make sure this wedding goes off without a hitch. And honestly, I have too much on my plate to take this on myself. The summer is my busiest season and I'm at capacity."

He followed close on her heels as they crossed the courtyard. "But, Bobbi," he whined. "Does it have to be the aunties?"

# CHAPTER 6

## Benjamin

**BOBBI:** Are you purposefully leaving recipes in my to-go containers, or is it by accident?

**BENJAMIN:** On purpose

**BOBBI:** Why?

**BENJAMIN:** To always remind you of my creative ingenuity

**BOBBI:** That would take a lot more than nonsensical notes. I don't understand half of what these mean.

**BENJAMIN:** They're part of my creative process. It's how I come up with new and interesting dishes. All you have to know is that you inspired them.

**BOBBI:** Okay, that's kind of . . . sweet?

**BOBBI:** By the way, since you're witness to two different sabotage attempts, I need you to come to lunch with me and the aunties next weekend. Are you in town?

**BENJAMIN:** Yes, but why can't you just talk to them?

**BOBBI:** No.

**BENJAMIN:** No . . . ?? That's it?

**BOBBI:** Yup. See you next weekend.

*One Week Later*

**BOBBI:** Confirming lunch. Are you ready to meet the aunties?

**BENJAMIN:** No.

**BOBBI:** Too bad. Here is the rundown: these four women are Kareena's mother's best friends. They helped raise Kareena after her mother died. You have Farah Auntie, who is a former software engineer. Then there is Mona Auntie, who always has the perfect hair and designer sunglasses. Falguni Auntie wears crocs but don't let that fool you. She's the most progressive. She used to be a political correspondent in India. Then there is Sonali Auntie. Sonali Auntie is . . . well, she's very religious.

**BENJAMIN:** Do I really have to be here for this lunch?

**BOBBI:** Yes. See you tomorrow.

Benjamin propped his hands on his hips and stared at the empty table in the corner of his restaurant next to the large windows. The

Jersey City sidewalk was packed with afternoon foot traffic, and his lunch hour was brisk. He had reservations through 2:00 P.M., and a packed house that night. He'd launched his summer season menu to rave reviews, and people were coming out in droves to try it.

In fact, he was pretty sure that the table he was looking at now would've come in handy for his restaurant patrons, but no. He'd promised Bobbi that he'd save it for an auntie lunch.

Why did it have to be at his restaurant? And more importantly, why did he have to be there? Bobbi was more than capable of handling everything all by herself. Hell, even the president could trust the fate of the country in her hands because she simply oozed that much confidence.

Jake came over to the table and stood next to him. "Chef, everything okay?"

"Yes, it's fine. Can you take care of table fifty-six for me?" He motioned to it. "We have a party coming in at one. I know it's outside of your section, but switch a table with Kavita. Please have their water ready to go as they sit."

"Sparkling or filtered?"

"Filtered, no ice. And there might be a few jalapeno, lychee, or mango margarita orders. Let Rahul know to go heavy on the alcohol otherwise they're going to ask them to remake it. I already told the kitchen to make everything that comes from fifty-six extra spicy, but if any of them say no spice whatsoever, then gives you their health history, it needs to be American Wonder Bread–bland. I don't think that will be the case."

Jake chuckled. "Do you know these people?"

"I know *of* them," Benjamin said. Every child of South Asian immigrants knew *of* the aunties. He clapped Jake on the shoulder. "As well as I know my own mother. I'll most likely get roped into sitting down, so I'll help out when needed."

"You got it."

A figure caught his eye through the restaurant window and his jaw went slack.

She was wearing a dress today in a brilliant cobalt blue. It hugged her hips and ended in a flirty hem right below her knee. The halter neck left her arms bare, and her wrists had stacks of gold bangles. Then there was that thick black hair in a high pony-tail.

He tracked her every step as she walked toward the front door. "Ahem."

Benjamin turned to look at Jake, who had a toothy grin on his face.

"Chef, you need a napkin? You have a little drool right here." He pointed to the corner of his mouth.

"I'm going to stick you with the aunties more often," Benjamin said.

"Just calling it like I see it. You two a thing?"

His head volleyed back and forth between Jake and the win-dow. "What, Bobbi and I? No, absolutely not. I mean, she's gor-geous. Just look at her. Of course, she's beautiful. But no. Can you imagine how disastrous that would be if things didn't work out? We spent the last year at each other's throats. And I'm opening a new restaurant that may be on the . . . whatever. This is just a temporary truce. And even if anything were to happen, Bobbi is as dedicated to her job as I am. It would be a mistake."

"You sound like you're trying to convince yourself there."

Benjamin shook his head. "I love women. I'm grateful to them. To my mother. To my sister. And the fact that they are my friends and colleagues. But just because I love women doesn't mean I have to be *in love* with a woman. You know the restaurant lifestyle is shitty. I'm living that bachelor life."

"If you say so," Jake said, and then crossed the room to the bar to load up on the water pitchers.

"I do say so," Benjamin mumbled. He walked over to meet Bobbi at the front entrance, weaving through tables until he reached the desk where she was speaking to his hostess. Her eyes brightened when they met his. Her thick black lashes fluttered once, then twice as she scanned him head to toe.

He flexed his pecs to make sure that if she was looking, she got a good view.

"Hi," he said.

"Hi," she replied. "The aunties are parking in the garage next to the train station. They should be here any minute. It depends on Falguni Auntie. If she didn't wear her orthotics, then it'll take them longer."

"Orthotics. Got it." He did not need to know that information, but he had a feeling that was how most of this lunch was going to go. "I set a table aside for you. Now, I have a lot of work to do—"

"Oh no you don't," she said, and grabbed his arm. "You're the only other person who knows someone is trying to ruin Kareena and Prem's wedding, which means that you're stuck in the vault with me until we figure this out."

He was about to rebut her ridiculous argument when he felt her fingers flex on his bicep.

Did she just . . . did she just squeeze his muscle? His heart pounded as he looked down at her glowing, upturned face.

The very thought of her finding him irresistible enough to cop a feel had him grinning like a fool.

"What?" she said warily.

At that moment, the glass door swooshed open and four women strode into Phataka Grill. They looked exactly like Bobbi had described in her text message.

First there was Farah Auntie, who carried a backpack with a tech company logo on it. Then came Sonali Auntie with her salwar kameez and streak of red powder in her hairline, most likely from temple that morning. The third was Falguni Auntie. She was indeed wearing her orthotics. And last was Mona Auntie with her perfect blowout and Marilyn Monroe sunglasses.

None of them said a word as they looked at Benjamin first, then Bobbi, and then to Bobbi's grip on his arm.

Benjamin and Bobbi sprung apart.

"Aunties!" Bobbi said cheerfully as she opened her arms for a hug.

There was a lot of squealing that happened after that, as the four women took turns first enveloping Bobbi in a big embrace, then doing the same to Benjamin.

He leaned down, bending at the knees to get to their height as he accepted each of the hugs. He didn't know these women personally. Just that they were Kareena's mom's best friends who helped raise Kareena once her mother passed away. But Benjamin had aunties too. Women from the community who befriended his immigrant parents. They would scold him if he did something wrong, feed him even if he didn't ask for a meal, and praise his success. Luckily for Benjamin, and for Kareena, the aunties had the capacity to be fierce supporters.

The last person who embraced him, Falguni Auntie, whispered in his ear, "Don't think we didn't see that move with Bobbi, puttar. We're watching you."

Yes, he thought. Definitely fierce supporters.

Of Bobbi.

And if that wasn't terrifyingly auntie-like, he didn't know what was.

"I can take you all to your table," he said, stepping away from

Falguni Auntie, who still had eyes on him. "What would you like to drink?"

"Tap water is fine," Mona Auntie said. "But no ice."

"No ice for me."

"No ice here, either."

"Definitely no ice."

At the reserved table, Jake was already pouring ice-less water into the glasses to the surprise and joy of all the women.

"Mona, you sit here," Sonali Auntie said, motioning to a chair.

"No, no, I want to sit on the end," Falguni Auntie said. "Farah, you okay to sit here?"

"Yes, I'm fine."

After a few minutes of musical chairs, they all managed to take their seats with Bobbi at the head. Benjamin turned to go, but she glared at him so hard that he shriveled into the empty chair at the other end of the table.

Farah Auntie reached out and patted his arm. "Such a beautiful restaurant, Benjamin. And the service is already impeccable. Your parents must be so proud."

"Thank you, Auntie. Yes, they are. What can I get you all to drink from the bar?"

Sonali Auntie patted her chest. "Oh no, I don't drink alcohol."

"Oh, don't listen to her," Farah Auntie said, clicking her tongue in dismissal. "At the Venkatraman party, she finished an entire bottle of rosé on her own."

"I thought it was fruit juice," Sonali Auntie replied.

Benjamin grinned. "Well, we have rosé here too, but we also have a wonderful jalapeno-mango margarita that tastes like spicy fruit juice."

The way they all agreed so fast, with hands in the air waving, he thought he was at bingo night and they'd all just won the jackpot. He couldn't help but grin at their enthusiasm and went to put the order in himself. When he returned with the drinks and placed them in front of everyone's plate, he was met with a round of "shaahbaash, beta."

Because the margs were extra spicy and extra liquored up, not a single woman had a peep of complaint. When he finally sat back down, Bobbi called for everyone's attention.

"I wanted to talk to you about something that's happening with Kareena's wedding planning."

"Is it the Dholki?" Falguni Auntie asked. "Because we definitely want to throw a Dholki party for Kareena."

"What's a Dholki again?" Benjamin asked, curiosity getting the better of him. "Is that a bridal shower?"

"Sort of," Bobbi replied. "The Dholki is when the women get together and sing folk songs. The word Dholki refers to this hand drum that is used to set the beat."

"I have a microphone and portable speaker," Sonali Auntie said. "And a digital song book. My son bought it for me last Diwali."

"Darling, we are not using your song book," Mona Auntie said. "Remember what happened last time?"

"Oh chup kar," Sonali Auntie snapped.

"Wait, what happened?" Benjamin asked.

Falguni Auntie didn't even look up from her menu when she responded, "Sonali Auntie wouldn't let anyone else sing and hogged the microphone all night. And she would only sing sad ghazals."

"Those ghazals are *classic*. Have some respect, Falguni."

Bobbi held up a hand to get everyone's attention again. "I am not talking about the Dholki, but I do think we should confirm the date and time for that." She looked up at Benjamin, then at each of the aunties. "We think someone is trying to sabotage Kareena and Prem's wedding."

The table went very quiet. The sound of conversation, laughter, and clinking dishes and glasses surrounded them. Benjamin held his breath. In that frozen moment, he felt like he was twelve again and he'd just told his mother or aunts that something very, very bad had happened.

"Bobbi, beta, what do you know?" Farah Auntie said in a deadly calm tone as she sipped her margarita.

Oh yeah, as still and silent as they all were, none of them were happy with this information and they were either about to explode or about to destroy someone's life.

Bobbi folded her arms on the table and nodded toward Benjamin. "We are supposed to work on the menu together, and someone left Benjamin a note saying that I picked the food for the venue. The selections were atrocious for a wedding. As if someone was intentionally trying to make it bad. I guess they assumed that Benjamin and I don't talk, and that Benjamin would call the venue and make trouble."

Benjamin then pointed the finger back at Bobbi. "Then she found out that someone called her specialty baker and canceled the wedding cake. Because the bakery is booked up a year in advance, they couldn't reschedule the order, so we had to find someone else to do the cake."

"Our Kareena's wedding cake?" Mona Auntie said evenly. She pushed her Marilyn Monroe glasses higher on her head, as if securing them there so she wouldn't lose them in case she had to fight someone.

Bobbi lifted her margarita. "We found an even better solution, so it worked out. But I don't think whoever is doing this will stop.

It's going to get worse, and I don't have time, nor do I know where to start in figuring out who is causing problems."

"I'll do pooja tomorrow for you," Sonali Auntie said, breaking the silence.

The other aunties immediately snapped.

"Sonali!"

"What the hell are you even saying?"

"Haan, and go ask bhagawan to give you two minutes of sense."

"Don't listen to her," Farah Auntie said, reaching across the table to pat Bobbi's hand. "Of course we'll help you try to find who is trying to make mischief."

Jake delivered heaping plates of papadum, aloo tikkis, and samosas with trays of chutney. His intuition must've kicked in. Benjamin smiled and gave him a nod before making a mental note to add a bonus to his tips.

"Why don't we eat something first, then order lunch?" he said. "While we're waiting, we can talk about—"

"We'll talk now," Falguni Auntie said.

Mona Auntie pulled her tote bag from under the table after Jake left and took out her tablet. "Here," she said and passed it to Farah Auntie.

"I forgot my ankhein," Farah Auntie said.

*She forgot her eyes?* Benjamin met Bobbi's gaze from across the table and she shrugged.

"I brought extra," Falguni Auntie said and removed a pair of bifocal glasses from her large tote bag. The glasses had a long, hot pink beaded chain attached to the end.

"Good," Farah Auntie said and slipped them on her nose. She looked down, then over the rim of the glasses and down again as she opened the iPad, removed the pencil that came with it, and began writing notes.

"Let's start with the first crime scene. The catering incident. When was the note delivered? What can you tell us about the handwriting, assuming you still don't have it? If you know what it said, that would be even more helpful."

Bobbi and Benjamin went back and forth, answering their questions as if they were being interrogated by the CIA. Only this was worse. They paused momentarily to put in their order for food, then resumed the questioning.

Benjamin was beginning to understand the aunties as individuals instead of as a collective as he most often did. He had to hand it to the beautiful woman who sat across from him at the opposite end of the table. She'd prepped him well for this meeting.

Sonali Auntie was indeed the most religious, even though she was on her third margarita. Her suggestions often included prayer and superstition.

Mona Auntie was very concerned with the aesthetics of the wedding and how the décor would turn out if they weren't able to get the best vendors.

Falguni Auntie was not afraid to fight dirty.

And Farah Auntie was the information specialist focusing on the perpetrator. It was questionable whether or not she consulted for the government at this point.

"I'm sorry, I wish I had more information for you," Bobbi said after running through all the details. "But that is the full list of people who know about the wedding, who know about me and Benjamin, and who may have access to information regarding wedding planning."

"You'll have to keep this a secret," Farah Auntie said, closing the tablet. "No one can know we are helping you. And no one can know what you're planning next for the wedding. That means Prem and Kareena will have to remain in the dark as well."

"Tell Mona to be quiet too," Falguni Auntie said. "She's the first one to open her mouth."

Mona Auntie gasped, her phone in hand. "I am not!" She discreetly put her phone away.

Bobbi cleared her throat, and everyone turned to her again. "You know Kareena. She's type A like me. She learned basic programming just so she could customize her own wedding website. There is no way she's not going to find out."

Sonali Auntie grinned. "She's so smart, isn't she? Our Kareena is the best."

All the aunties hummed in agreement, expressions of pride on their faces.

Benjamin had to smile. He knew that his father was always proud of him and his siblings. His mother expressed pride in her own way. But seeing the aunties and how they felt about Kareena now reminded him that no matter how nosy or aggravating they could be, they would always step in to find a shaadi saboteur.

"Bobbi, tell Kareena we are helping you with the planning, and that we want to keep some of it a surprise," Farah Auntie said.

"That might work, but none of you can *accidentally* share any of the planning details otherwise she'll get suspicious." Bobbi glared at each and every one of them, which was definitely an act of bravery. "If she finds out, Kareena will lose her mind. Then she'll tell Dadi, and Dadi will make it worse."

The aunties quieted at the thought of Kareena's grandmother finding out.

"If you're all on board," Bobbi said, "we'll keep wedding planning details to ourselves, and you'll help find the shaadi saboteur. Agreed?"

"Agreed," everyone at the table said in a mix of Hindi and English.

Benjamin watched as Bobbi's shoulders relaxed now that their impromptu meeting was over. Her entire face lit up with humor as she listened to Mona Auntie's story about her children. Then she looked at him, her brows furrowing as if she was asking *what's up?*

He shook his head, and she seemed to be satisfied with his response. Her pink painted nails ran over the spine of his menu before she flipped it open and started to read through the first page. Her phone, always within reach, was flipped upside down, as if signaling that she was present now and enjoying her time with everyone at the table.

He knew there was absolutely no reason he had to stay for the rest of lunch. But watching Bobbi in her element had become one of his favorite new pastimes.

He should probably stay away from her. It was the right thing to do. There was the likelihood that he'd be establishing a more permanent home base in California, which meant that he'd barely see her. Then there was their truce. They were still at the start of a delicate friendship, and he wasn't sure how long it was going to last after the wedding.

Would Bobbi resent him if their friendship became something more, and he chose to stay on the West Coast after Prem's wedding? Would his best friends resent him?

The very thought of leaving his found family, his restaurant, and New York City sat like rocks in his gut. One day at a time, he thought. Anything could happen before the wedding and the Naan King board meeting. In the meantime, he'd enjoy this moment where he had the opportunity to watch a beautiful woman command the table.

### *Indians Abroad News*
Relationship column

We're so thrilled to have our tech expert join us this week! He will be providing WhatsApp tips and tricks for online matchmaking. After all, WhatsApp is encrypted! Any secrets shared through the free messaging service cannot be hacked.

Mrs. W. S. Gupta
Avon, New Jersey

# CHAPTER 7

## Bobbi

*Note left in Bobbi's Phataka Grill to-go container:*

*Tactile sensory experiences are underrated. Return to eating with your hands, but during the dessert course, cakes and pastries should be served on banana leaves so guests can enjoy licking sugar off their fingertips.*

*GROUP CHAT: VERMANN WEDDING*

**BOBBI:** Thank you all for filling out the joint bachelor-bachelorette party Google survey. The bride and groom have selected Vegas for the location.

**DEEPAK:** Wait, seriously? We're ACTUALLY going to Vegas? No car shows, Taylor Swift concerts, conference trips, or remote medical abnormalities museum? Nice.

**PREM:** If you're going to be a smartass, we're leaving you at home.

**VEERA:** So exciting! I've never been to Vegas.

**KAREENA:** We know you all will have the most fun there, so you're welcome! But we reserve the right to go to bed early if we want.

**BENJAMIN:** Since we're going to Vegas, can we revisit the ban on strip clubs?

**PREM:** No.

**DEEPAK:** No!

**VEERA:** Wait, what kind of strip clubs?

**KAREENA:** I've always loved the Magic Mike movies. Did you know Chippendales was founded by an Indian dude? I think he was in the mob.

**BOBBI:** I can't promise Chippendales but I can book us a Magic Mike show.

**BENJAMIN:** . . . That's not quite how I thought this conversation would go.

Bobbi looked at the scrap piece of paper that she'd found tucked in her bag. It had Benjamin's now-recognizable handwriting scrawled across it in bold black ink. It included something about handheld desserts. She crumpled the paper and shoved it into a pocket on the side of her tote. She'd have to add it to her growing pile of notes. None of them made any sense to her, but it let her know that he was thinking of her, and that was . . . romantic.

"Bobbi?"

When her uncle called her name, she looked up, then scanned the expectant faces around the long dining table in her uncle's sprawling New Jersey home. All ten members of the planning team, including her aunt, uncle, and cousin, stared at her expectantly.

"Uh, sorry, Mamu. What was that again?"

His forehead creased and his bushy white brows lifted at the ends. "I was asking if you would like to start today's meeting."

"Oh, yes. Sure." She tapped the screen on her tablet in front of her. The team calendar popped up. It was meticulously color coded and labeled in the system that she had designed a few years ago. The precision sparked so much joy in Bobbi's heart. "All twelve of my events for the remainder of the summer are in motion. It is our busiest season, but fortunately, there are no problems on my end."

"What about your friend's wedding?" Bhua asked. She cradled a cup of chai in one hand, her layers of necklaces clicking together in musical harmony as she gestured with the other. "Do you need any help from us for Kareena's event at Messina Vineyards?"

There was a hush across the room. The other planners stared in wide-eyed wonder. Messina Vineyards. The coveted location that had so much potential but because of its exclusivity was out of reach.

Bobbi said a silent thank-you to Kareena for making that happen. Even though Bobbi was doing her best friend's wedding for free, having Messina Vineyards in her portfolio was a huge deal. If she could get in touch with them.

"I am still trying to connect with the events manager there to discuss logistics since this is most likely their first multiday Indian wedding," Bobbi said reluctantly. She glanced over at her uncle. "They have been hard to reach so far, but I'm confident I'll be able to connect with them soon."

"If you need support," her uncle said, "bring in Sukhi. She's wonderful with new vendors."

Bobbi's cousin sat up, bright-eyed, and nodded eagerly.

Bobbi loved her cousin, and was happy to bring her in, but Sukhi was the least experienced out of everyone in the room. She was also the only one who didn't manage her own events yet. The fact that her uncle thought Sukhi could do what Bobbi could not spoke to her uncle's lack of faith in Bobbi's ability.

And that burned her.

"I can make some calls if you want, Didi," Sukhi said, her stylus poised over her tablet. "Or I can drive out to—"

"Sukhi, thank you but I have it all under control," Bobbi said. Then winked at her cousin to soften the rebuke. "I love being your mentor, and if something comes up, I'll bring you in. Okay?"

She saw her uncle flinch at the word *mentor* out of the corner of her eye. Thankfully her cousin didn't mind and gave her a thumbs-up.

"That's it for me," Bobbi said, and motioned to the next planner to provide their update.

"We're having a good season," her uncle said, when the roundtable was complete. He motioned to the laptop in front of him, rattling off details with efficiency in his crisp American Desi accent. "We have a few big events next week, but the following will be twice as many so make sure you all pace yourselves. Now, the fall and winter season. I'm finalizing second installment payments for our October through December weddings. All your vendors should be confirmed, deposits paid, and RSVPs should be coming in. Any questions or concerns?"

Emily, one of their newest wedding planners who was responsible for award-winning design work in South Indian weddings, raised her hand. "Balakrishnan wedding. It's September. They didn't like their cake-tasting session. Instead, they asked for something quirky and original. I need a new bakery rec and, as expected, the suppliers I know are booked. Anyone have a backup that might be able to help? It's a small exclusive event. Fifty people."

Everyone around the table started scrolling through their list of contacts on their devices, rattling off recommendations. Unfortunately, Emily had called everyone.

"I have a suggestion," Bobbi said, raising the end of her tablet pencil. "But it's definitely quirky and original."

Emily nodded, adjusting her chic horn-rimmed glasses. "Those are the exact words my clients used."

"Would they be open to ice cream cake?"

Emily's brows furrowed. "For a wedding?"

"I met a new vendor a week ago," Bobbi said. "Her flavors are amazing. She's going to be doing the cake for my friend's wedding. It's unique, different—"

Her uncle held out a hand to stop her. "Is that really the best idea?" he said in Hind-ish. "Ice cream cake? I mean this isn't a child's birthday party we're talking about. It's a wedding."

Bobbi pressed her mouth into a thin line. She and her uncle were definitely going to have to have a conversation after this meeting. He was intentionally undermining her in front of everyone, and Bobbi was not putting up with that bullshit today. "Yes, I'm aware of that," she said coolly. "But because it's so different, it's a standout."

Her uncle shook his head. "It's too risky," he said. Then turned to Emily. "I'm sure we can put our heads together to find someone to deliver a classic cake for a replacement."

Emily's head volleyed between Bobbi and her uncle. "Actually, the more I think about it, the more I like the ice cream cake idea. Bobbi, can you send me the details? I'd love to give them a try. At least a taste testing."

"Sure," Bobbi said with a smile. She glanced over at her uncle and raised a brow.

Mamu still looked unsure, but he shrugged. "I guess it will have to be."

Bobbi couldn't spend the rest of the meeting trying to reassure him. There was too much to do, and too much information to go through. She looked back at her tablet and waited for her aunt and uncle to go through the rest of the agenda.

After everyone was dismissed, a few of the senior planners went down to the basement to gather supplies from company storage, while the rest headed out to start their event prep and to make on-site meetings with their teams.

Bhua flashed her a smile, then picked up the snack trays that she always filled to the brim. She disappeared into the kitchen without another word, with Sukhi following close behind.

Bobbi's uncle had slipped away into his office in the adjoining room. That wouldn't save him from a confrontation, Bobbi thought. She pushed up the sleeves of her suit coat, grabbed her tote bag, and charged across the hallway.

When she entered Mamu's office, he'd already settled behind the big mahogany desk covered in binders and books filled with color swatches. For as long as Bobbi remembered, her uncle would retreat to this massive cave and dream of inspiring celebrations for happily ever after. Along the wall were framed pictures from wedding magazines that featured some of his events over the past ten years. There was no doubt about it: he was incredible.

And she was incredibly pissed.

"Mamu!" she snapped. Then shut the door behind her.

Her uncle jumped in his seat. "Bobbi? Just the person I wanted to see." He slid his wire-rimmed glasses up the bridge of his nose, and quickly jotted a note on a notepad he'd retrieved from the edge of his desk. "There are so many things that could go wrong with an ice cream cake. The melting, the flavors, the number of people who are dairy intolerant."

Bobbi rolled her eyes. "If people are dairy intolerant, they most likely wouldn't have a regular wedding cake either."

He ripped off the top sheet of paper from the notepad and held it out. "I think you should call a friend of mine. Just ask them what their schedule is like—"

"Mamu, no." Bobbi braced her hands on the edge of the desk and leaned forward. "This is absolutely ridiculous. I am your oldest, most experienced wedding planner. I have been doing this a lot longer than most of the people in that meeting. Hell, when you started your business at the kitchen table, I would come home from school and help you assemble centerpieces! I've been in this with you from the beginning. But today you totally undermined my experience in there—"

"Undermined?" He looked startled as he leaned back in his chair. "Bobbi, you know I just want you to succeed. You're like my daughter, so of course I'll be the toughest on you."

"By *questioning* my skill and my authority? How do you think that makes me feel after all I've put into this company?"

Her uncle sighed. "Fine," he replied. "You have a point. If you think that this cake is going to be a good idea, then I'll support it. But consider a backup in case something happens the last minute. And remember, if there is a delay, and this cake is out in the open without a freezer, it's not going to look like a showstopping centerpiece."

The words came out of her mouth before she could hold them

back. Before she could stop herself from saying them out loud. "This is so much more than the cake, Mamu. It's everything! You're going to eventually have to trust me when you retire."

*Shit.*

"Retire?" he said, bewildered. "Whoever said anything about retiring?"

This was not the time or the place for her to have this conversation, but she was so fed up with the way he'd been questioning her ever since she'd lost one of their biggest clients almost a year ago. She'd overpromised a meeting with Benjamin's restaurant, and it had all gone to hell since. "Whenever you retire," Bobbi corrected. "I know you and Bhua want to start taking some time off. And that means you'll have to transition some responsibilities."

He took off his glasses and pinched the bridge of his nose. "Ahh, now I'm following," he said with a heavy sigh. "Beta . . . I'm not sure the company is ready for a leadership change. After you lost the biggest contract this business had ever seen, I think you're still making too many rash decisions."

*Bingo. I knew he was still holding that against me.*

Bobbi straightened on her stiletto heels. "We never *had* the Kaneria account so I couldn't have lost it. I at least got a meeting with them when most of the wedding planners in the city were rejected from the start! And I didn't see you or Bhua or any of the other wedding planners in there get nearly as close as I did."

"I think we would've secured the account if you hadn't set unrealistic expectations," her uncle argued. He was starting to turn red now, his weathered face changing with frustration. "Bobbi, I explained myself then, and I'll repeat myself now. That's not how this company operates. We only promise what we can deliver."

Bobbi's Punjabi was softened with her accent, but she knew her response came just as rapidly as his. "And I have always delivered except for that *one* moment in my past. But when else have I failed you? How many times have you told me that you think I'm made for this business? That I'm excellent at this job? I have been leading the biweekly team meetings for a few months now. I've implemented processes, connected with all of the best suppliers, sourced the best material from India, and I worked with the finance teams to make sure that we're constantly making profit and funneling it back into the business or to our teams. I am *ready*," she said.

Her uncle's eyebrows jerked, as if he was trying to think of something, anything to prove her wrong.

*Gotcha, old man.*

"I love you and value you more than anyone on the team," he said, switching to English, "because you are my family. But that doesn't mean I am going to give you the business without ensuring you have learned all the lessons you need. Your Bhua and I are not ready for retirement. Sukhi wants to come back and work in the business after graduate school. We'll stay until she's ready to take on her own clients as well. Then we'll determine when it's time to pass on the business. We hope that you both choose to run the business together since you are family and we know you love and support each other, but that will ultimately be your decision."

The idea of waiting for *years* had Bobbi's jaw dropping. "Sukhi hasn't even started grad school yet, Mamu."

He nodded. "And then after that, she's going to need an apprenticeship. We'll ask her to lead smaller events until she starts to develop her own relationships, vendor connections, and clientele list. Exactly the way we trained you from the beginning. I'm hoping in that time you'll learn a few things, too."

Bobbi felt a pang in her heart. Her uncle, the man who raised her since she was a baby, might never trust her to take care of a business he'd developed from the ground up after all. It was obvious that he was now making excuses, and there was nothing she could say that would change his mind. "We're going to have this conversation again, Mamu. Starting with Messina Vineyards."

His eyebrows jerked up. That immediately got his attention. "What about them?"

She was speaking before the idea had fully formed in her head. "I plan on doing such a successful wedding for Kareena that our company will be on their exclusive vendor list."

Okay, if she was being honest, she had no idea how she was going to do that when the events manager wouldn't even call her back, but being an exclusive vendor had to mean *something*, right? Her uncle chased exclusive vendor contracts for years because it was another avenue for receiving clients.

"If you can secure us an exclusive vendor for Messina Vineyards," her uncle said slowly, "then we can have this conversation again."

"Except without you being so bullheaded," Bobbi replied.

"You're just as stubborn as your mother used to be," her uncle said, his voice growing soft and wistful as it always did when he mentioned his sister.

Bobbi didn't have those feelings of nostalgia since she never met the woman, but it was always nice to hear that she had a wonderful ancestry. She walked around the big desk, then planted a kiss on top of his bald head.

"You're a pain," she said in English. "But sooner or later, you're going to be hiking Machu Picchu in your bucket hat and using your iPad as a camera, while I'm going to make sure that every wedding cake this company contracts with is an ice cream cake because you drove me nuts."

"That's it. I'm going to work until the day I die now."

Bobbi giggled, even though that pang still throbbed in her chest. "The horror!"

He grumbled something in response even as the corner of his mouth turned up in a smile.

When Bobbi was halfway out the door, her uncle called out to her. "Bobbi? I do trust you, even though you don't trust anyone else to help you. I hope one day you see that."

Since she had no idea what he was talking about, she gave him a backward wave, an absent "love you," and walked out of the office.

The car service was waiting for her when she got to the curb, ready to take her back to Jersey City. She had a day of client meetings at her apartment, and she could not be happier. Taking client meetings meant she could wear sweatpants if she wanted, and order takeout. Then, when it was all over and done with, she'd be able to take some time to process the argument that she'd just had with her uncle.

When she slipped into the back seat, she flashed a smile to the driver, then settled in to answer emails as the car pulled away from the curb.

She'd just started a reply to one of her January wedding clients when her phone buzzed with a new text.

**BENJAMIN:** Messina Vineyards' chef called me. Apparently, we have a mutual connection.

**BOBBI:** Vincent Marcon? What did he say?

**BENJAMIN:** Of course you would know Vinny. He is being an ass and wants me to come in and walk him through my ideas before Prem and Kareena do the taste testing.

**BOBBI:** That's extremely unusual.

**BENJAMIN:** He just wants a free Indian cooking course from one of the greats.

**BOBBI:** Gross, Bunty. Your ego is suffocating. Fine. Just tell me when. I'll squeeze it in.

**BENJAMIN:** We should probably go over some of the ideas again. Try them out for ourselves. Right now, they are just suggested notes. I'd like to be able to provide direction.

**BOBBI:** Is this all really necessary?

**BENJAMIN:** I can't believe you asked me that question.

Bobbi looked down at Benjamin's last text and sighed. She should be happy that he wanted to be involved, that he was taking this menu selection responsibility seriously. But she was . . . unnerved now whenever they were in the same room. She remembered the note he'd slipped her and removed the crumpled paper from her bag she'd set at her hip.

As she traced a fingertip over the bold, almost impatient scrawl of his handwriting, she thought about the promise she made to her uncle, and how Messina Vineyards would be an incredible partner. Maybe this was how she could secure a meeting with the events manager.

She quickly sent a text back.

**BOBBI:** Can you do the food testing? I don't know how to cook. I can pay for the ingredients as my contribution.

Seconds after she sent the last text message her phone vibrated again, but this time with an incoming call. Benjamin's name flashed across the screen. What in the world?

She hesitated for a moment before answering. "Yes?"

There was a roar of noise in the background. The sound of a honking car. "What do you mean you don't know how to cook?"

"Do I need to say it in Punjabi?" she replied.

"Everyone should know how to feed themselves. Didn't your mother—"

He stopped before he could finish that sentence.

"No," Bobbi said dryly. "Obviously not."

"Sorry," he said softly.

She couldn't be offended when he sounded so sincere. "It's fine. I'm used to it. She died when I was born, so it's not like it's really triggering for me or anything." It used to be, Bobbi thought, when she was in school, and everyone would talk about the bond they had with their mothers. But then her uncle would show up. He wore the matching princess gown for Halloween, volunteered for bake sales, and coached soccer the one season she wanted to play. Those memories only made the argument today even more difficult to swallow.

"I'm still sorry," Benjamin said on the other end of the line. His voice deep and warm. Familiar. "That was a shitty assumption to make. But my point stands. Everyone should know how to feed themselves. We'll make dinner. Don't worry about buying the food. I'm going to bring it with me. We'll have a cooking lesson together while we try something for the menu."

"What?" She sat up straight, practically falling off the car bench seat. She pressed the phone harder to her ear. "What do you mean 'we'll make dinner'?"

"I think *that's* self-explanatory, Bobbi. I have to fly out tomorrow. Unless you have an event? I guess we can push it back . . ."

"No, but—"

"Then it's done," he replied. His smug tone had her bristling. "You want to come to Deepak's apartment?"

"I didn't plan on leaving—"

"Okay, then text me your address. It's a date."

He hung up, leaving her reeling. Oh my god, *Bunty* was coming over.

# CHAPTER 8

## Benjamin

**CHOTTU:** Dad won't make it to retirement. I'm going to murder him.

**BENJAMIN:** What happened now?

**CHOTTU:** He's telling everyone that the gluten-free naan was his idea. That it was inclusive.

**BENJAMIN:** No one is going to believe that. Everyone knows it's you who conceived and launched the gluten-free line.

**CHOTTU:** Why does he highlight my mistakes, and then try to take credit for my accomplishments?

**BENJAMIN:** Because he's . . . Dad? I don't know. If you hate it, leave the company.

**CHOTTU:** No way. This is my legacy. I love this business. But I cannot wait until he retires.

**BENJAMIN:** Well, you won't have long to wait. October is around the corner.

**CHOTTU:** What do you mean?

**BENJAMIN:** Dad's retirement announcement. He's doing it in October, right?

**CHOTTU:** What the hell??? He's retiring in October???

**BENJAMIN:** Shit, I thought he told you.

**CHOTTU:** Obviously not. But he sure made a point to tell you. Does Didi know?

**BENJAMIN:** I assumed both you and she were aware.

**CHOTTU:** I'm calling Dad.

Benjamin read the last text from his brother and shook his head. "Dad, you need to do better for this kid. He's just like you."

Like all the times before when his brother and father miscommunicated, Benjamin was tempted to pick up the phone and call one of them to talk it out. But he couldn't think about family right now. If he got sucked in, then it would cost him his entire day.

He didn't know when he'd fallen into the role of family manager, but it had happened around the time his younger brother began talking.

Instead of following his instincts and old habits, he put his phone on mute and looked up at the three-story building close to Journal Square in Jersey City. A boutique occupied the bottom floor, and a small side door with an slim, grey intercom was situated to the left of the building. Kaur was listed on the third floor.

Benjamin pressed the button next to her name. It buzzed, and the intercom crackled.

"Yes?"

"Hey, it's Bunt— Ah, Benjamin. Let me up?"

The sound of her snort echoed through the intercom. He could almost hear the smugness in her voice. "Fine, Bunty Benjamin."

"Smart-ass," he mumbled and opened the door when it buzzed again. He walked up the three flights of stairs, taking in the wide hallways, the new hardwood floors, and the plants arranged on the landings. When he reached the top floor, there was only one apartment. He knocked, and Bobbi, with her shiny silk waves fluttering over her shoulders and her big brown eyes, opened the door.

It was the first time he'd seen her wearing a T-shirt and leggings.

God, he just wanted to squeeze her thighs now that he could see them on full display. Or better yet, be squeezed by her thighs—

Nope. No way, he thought, palms sweating. He was here on wedding business only. It was imperative that he behave himself. This was just a truce.

"Hey," he said after clearing his throat. He hoped he didn't have drool dripping from the corner of his mouth. He held up the large insulated cooler. "Ready to do some recipe testing?"

Her mouth pinched in a sultry pout. "Do we have to?"

"Yes," he said, and stepped past her into her apartment.

He didn't know what he was expecting, but the bright, colorful airy spacy wasn't it. The soft crooning of familiar Punjabi-Bollywood music played on a small speaker on the console table at the entrance. Late evening summer sunlight shimmered through tall windows against the far wall. A plethora of plants lined the windowsills and Benjamin knew then that the pots on the landings were from her.

The couch was a soft minty green, with pale pink throw pillows and an orange-and-yellow rug. A gold-framed TV was mounted on the wall, and shelves of books in a cobalt-blue stand sat beneath it. Bobbi's four-seater dining table separated the living space and the open kitchen with a small ledge and barstools. The table was decorated with a white vase in the center with a riot of colorful blooms.

Damn, he should've brought her flowers, he thought. Bobbi deserved beautiful, bright flowers.

She must've realized that he was staring at the bouquet. "I usually get a centerpiece straggler from an event," she said. "That one was from last night. Want some wine?"

He kicked off his loafers at the door and then walked straight into her kitchen. It was small, but clean and modern. "Yeah, that's fine. A red goes well with what I brought."

She paused, scrunching her nose. "I hate red. I only have a selection of white."

"Who only has—" He stopped, pinched the bridge of his nose, and let out a deep breath. He should've known that nothing was going to go smoothly with her. The idea of drinking white with the food he brought was appalling. But what else could he do? "Then white it is."

Bobbi walked over to the fridge, her pale pink toes drawing his attention against her white-tiled kitchen floor. After opening the stainless-steel door, she pulled out two cans.

Benjamin dropped his cooler with a thud.

"What the fuck is that?" he blurted out.

"Wine," she said. "In the last six months, I've stopped buying bottles. I was at a wedding in January where someone got hit in

the neck from a rogue champagne cork and had to be hospital-
ized. Couldn't speak for weeks. Permanently bruised vocal cords.
Since then, too much anxiety. Can or box only." She motioned to
him with one can. "I think this is called a Boss Babe sparkling
California white? I may have a fancier version. Some sort of Man-
eater Moscato and Ravishing Rosé."

He held up a hand to stop her. Then, removing his phone from
his pocket, he dialed his restaurant. The manager on staff picked up.

"Yes, Chef?"

"I'm going to text you an address. Can you deliver two bottles
of house wine? One red, one white. And one of our spare cork-
screws."

"Yes, Chef," she said.

He hung up and then copy and pasted the address into a new
message. Knowing his team, it would be at Bobbi's door within
the next half hour. When he looked up, Bobbi had popped open
the sparkling California white and had taken a big sip. "You
know," she said sweetly, "they can put wine in cans, but they can't
figure out how to lower carbon emissions. You'd think that would
be easier, right?"

"I don't think you realize how hard it is to maintain this truce
sometimes, Kaur."

She grinned, her smile sunny and warm. "It's been a long day.
I need to get my kicks somehow."

He unzipped the cooler and began removing containers. He'd
packed everything he needed, despite Bobbi's assurances that she
had *some* food in her kitchen. Onion, garlic, ginger, fresh mint
leaves, lamb chops, flour, and more.

He could feel Bobbi watching him as he set up a workstation
before she took another sip of her disgusting canned wine, then
retrieved a bottle of water from the fridge for him.

"Thanks," he said as he unwrapped the lamb chops to pat dry before seasoning. "Want to tell me about your day?"

"Not particularly."

"It's polite, Bobbi."

She huffed, then slid onto a barstool, leaning against the counter in a posture so unlike what he'd seen from her before. He was familiar with the business side of Bobbi, the troubleshooter, and the friend. Now he liked that he was able to see this relaxed version of her. It made her seem so much more approachable, with those delicious prickly layers peeling back to expose the softness. She was comfortable in front of him, and that made her look so much more attractive.

"Today was a biweekly planning meeting with my uncle's company," she started. "He basically told me that he doesn't trust me enough yet to lead his business. That I'm stuck as a senior planner, spinning my wheels for the next four years until my cousin becomes a senior planner, too. Then they'll pass off leadership duties to both of us after retirement."

There was something similar about her story. Something that was remarkably close to his. "Did you tell your uncle you were going to quit?"

"What?" Shock lit her face. "Absolutely not. This company means everything to me. I'm in it for the long haul. I love what I do and the people I work with. Besides. As much of a pain as my uncle can be, he's family. I just have to prove myself, I guess. Not like I haven't already done that over and over again, but maybe it'll finally click after Kareena's wedding—"

"Kareena's wedding?"

She looked up at him from her canned wine. "It's complicated. Never mind."

"Your uncle adopted you, right?" Benjamin began looking

through her cabinets, making a mental note of how little she owned when it came to cooking devices and utensils. It was as if he was in the kitchen of a college student who barely survived on Maggi noodles and takeout. At thirty, every household should own a regular-size blender, a food processer, a hand mixer, pots, pans, cast iron, and a few other things that Bobbi obviously didn't have. He rolled his eyes when he found a stack of bridal magazines where her spices should've been.

Benjamin was about to tell Bobbi exactly what she needed to do to fix her kitchen when she made a throaty and sexy humming sound as she sucked on her canned wine-juice. He whipped around just in time to watch. Her eyes sparkled as if she knew exactly what she was doing.

"My father was never in the picture," she said, with nonchalance. "After my mom died, Mamu stepped in. He was in his late twenties and working as a carpenter building mandaps for Indian weddings. He was an artist. Knew all the vendors, understood the process from end to end, and when his friends had daughters who were getting married, they asked him to help plan it. I watched him build his business through sheer determination. It was just the two of us until he met my aunt."

"And let me guess. Neither of you knew how to cook?"

Bobbi smiled, and Benjamin paused in his kitchen prep work because of how beautiful she looked when she was teasing him.

"My uncle paid this auntie next door to make these adorable veggie-and-fruit snack boxes for me," she mused. "When I remember how hard he tried to give me everything I wanted or needed, I feel so guilty fighting with him."

Benjamin stopped, grill pan in hand. He hated that the easygoing joy had slipped away. "Hey," he said, and put the grill pan on the counter. He leaned on his forearms, facing her from across the island. "It can't be as bad as my family argument. My brother has wanted to be the CEO of Naan King Emporium since he was a kid, and my father doesn't think he has it in him."

"Really?"

"Yeah," Benjamin said. He brushed a hand through his hair so he wasn't tempted to touch hers. "My parents have always been proud of all of us, even though they wished we all worked together for the family business. They're friends with the Singh family. The ones that own the tech empire? And the Singh brothers are heavily involved in their father's company, while Chottu is the only one who cares about naan."

"Well, as a chef, technically you do too," she said.

If only she knew how much he'd rather avoid naan for the rest of his life. "I'm not like Chottu. My younger brother started interning there at fourteen, working his way up through product development and marketing. Then he made one big, very costly mistake after college. My father, being the traditional Punjabi man he is, doesn't trust Chottu and his organic, gluten-free, market-fresh ideas anymore. And now that he's retiring, both Chottu and Dad are coming to blows."

Bobbi's jaw dropped. Her can hit the countertop with a thud. "Oh my god! We have something in common. I'm your brother, Bunty."

Benjamin picked up the grill pan again and flipped it with one quick flick of the wrist. "You are most definitely *not* my brother." He glanced down at her large breasts barely concealed from him under her thin T-shirt. Her wide hips and round ass he desperately wanted to slap. And then there was that small line that formed between her brows indicating that she was working out a complex problem.

Yeah, all of his thoughts so far were not family-like in the least.

"I so am," she said, getting to her feet. She pointed to her chest. "I'm a skilled professional with extensive experience looking to take over her uncle's—in your brother's case, father's—business. I also made one dumb mistake that my uncle is holding against me. And now my uncle wants my cousin to take over the business, too. The only difference is that your brother has a mediator. You!"

Okay, she didn't mean that she was literally like a brother to him. Just that they had similar patterns in their families. He could accept that.

The thought that Benjamin had something in common with Bobbi was . . . nice. They had been at odds for so long, and since they first met, he knew that he'd rather be friends with Bobbi than be enemies. But if he was being honest with himself, they were way too wise to enjoy each other peacefully.

"Do you want a mediator with your uncle?" he asked, pulling a way-too-small cutting board out from a bottom cabinet.

Bobbi shook her head. "I think that would hurt his feelings and I'd rather handle my own problems with him. I am not sure how I'm going to do that yet, but I'm working on it."

"And that is how you and my brother are different." He twisted open the bottle of water. "Well, technically you have more differences than your career aspirations. He's a California hippie who likes to surf before work, smokes hookah every night, and watches the TV show *Succession* on repeat. And I'm assuming he dates way more than you do."

"Hey!" she said. "I *date*. Just selectively. I have yet to find someone who is more interesting than my work."

"That long, huh?" Thank god.

She buffed her nails on her shoulder then looked at them. "My vibes do it better."

Vibes, plural? Benjamin couldn't hide his smile now. That

sounded like a lot of fun. "I can't fault you. Traveling every other week has been hell on my sex life, too." The last time he'd been with anyone in a meaningful way had to be, hell, a year ago. Before that day at Kareena's house.

He drank deeply from the bottle of water. Out of the corner of his eye, he noticed Bobbi watching him, her gaze directly on his throat, and his arm. He had to turn around to hide his smile.

"Come on," he said and motioned to her. "Let's get started. You're going to wash potatoes and boil them."

"Wash them with what?" she said, deadpan.

"I swear to god—"

"I'm kidding," she said. "I know you wash them with oil."

He didn't take the bait this time and waited while she got out a large pot. She filled it with way too much water and set it on the stove. Benjamin nudged her aside, then poured out half the water before replacing it on the burner.

She glared at him, then went to rinse the potatoes. His fingers encircled her wrist to stop her. Then he showed her how to scrub them underneath the cold-water stream. Her hands were soft, with short, rounded fingernails painted the same shade of pale pink as her toes.

When his palms brushed over hers, an electric current ricocheted through his body. He pulled away.

"You'll have to prick them a few times with a fork before you put them in the water. I'll tell you when."

"Yes, Chef," she said, her voice wavering. And then she moved to get comfortable in front of the sink. Her ass shimmied.

His mind went blank for a full five seconds, willing her ass to move again. When it didn't, he let out a deep sigh, flexing the hand that touched hers, and turned to wipe down the countertop.

Using a plastic bowl, he dumped in the flour and added a cup of filtered water.

Food. Benjamin would focus on the food, not on Bobbi.

He'd teach her some basics today and then he'd go home.

Even though he was confident that shimmy would remain in his memory forever.

Bobbi motioned to the pot. "What now?"

He flicked on the burner, then pulled her to his side. "Now we're going to make ajwain paranthas. This isn't for the wedding, but for practice. This was the first thing my mom taught me in the kitchen when I was barely tall enough to reach the countertop. She used to drag over a chair from the dining table and I'd stand on it and help her with dinner. It's super easy but you'll need to dig in there with your hands."

He positioned her in front of the clean countertop that he'd dusted with flour. He turned the shaggy dough mixture onto the counter and started the process. "Now you knead for five minutes," he said, motioning for her to take his place.

She looked at him with hesitation, then dug her hands into the sticky wet flour. Her fingers squeezed the dough like she was playing with wet sand.

"No, use your heel and push out in a V motion," he said. He stepped behind her and slid his hands over hers. Her skin was soft, and she smelled delicious. Gardenias. The same scent she'd used almost a year ago. But now it was laced with the rich wine she'd drunk. He leaned closer, careful not to bump his hips into her even as he closed his eyes to savor her. Benjamin guided her hands over the dough until she was able to create a soft, pliable mixture. His heart pounded, aware of how her hands moved under his.

They stood back to front, breath caught, rubbing and kneading the dough in long, smooth strokes. His hands guided hers as they worked together to build the elasticity.

"Done?" she said after a minute. Her voice sounded reedy, and she pulled her hands away from his.

"Yeah," he said. He couldn't look at her. Wouldn't. Not when they were still inches apart.

"You know, you're the son of the Naan King. Why can't we have . . . well, naan?"

He looked at the perfect dough, then back to her. Their incredible moment of connection was over. "Do you have an outdoor tandoor oven somewhere on your third-floor walk-up that I didn't see? I guess we can make naan on the tava but it's usually a bit denser, and—"

She crossed the small kitchen space to her fridge and freezer. Benjamin's stomach lurched when she pulled open the bottom drawer. Inside, stacked in neat rows, were every type of flavored naan his father's company produced. Waving at them like she was modeling a product, she said, "See? I've invested in some of the finest frozen naan your dad and brother make. I got my local grocery delivery to drop them off this afternoon."

He scrubbed his hands over his face. She was infuriating and delightful at the same time. How was that even possible? To be this smart, quick-witted, and beautiful while also pressing each one of his buttons. "You need to throw all of that out right now."

"What? No way." She began pulling out naan packets. "We got garlic naan and original. Then if we want some dairy, there is paneer naan. I was never a fan of paneer naan, but I'll try it with your lamb, especially if we're recipe testing for the wedding. There is onion naan. Also a good choice. Oh, I'm assuming this one is your brother's work." She held up a package that said "Diwali Naan."

"I don't even know what Diwali Naan is," she said pleasantly.

"But the packaging has these fun fireworks on the side. A little early for Diwali marketing, but I can get behind it."

"Do you know how much naan I've had to eat in my life, Bobbi?"

"But have you had enough Diwali Naan?" she said, shaking the package like she was trying to lure him closer with a treat. "When your mom taught you how to cook, I bet you were the only one at the table who ate rice."

He advanced, snatching the package out of her hand, then tossed it on the counter. She was giggling now, and the sound was like music. It hummed in his blood and had his heart pumping faster.

When Benjamin kicked the freezer drawer closed, Bobbi's giggles turned to cackling, as if she was thrilled that she'd made him lose his damn mind. He gripped her hands, then pressed her back against the fridge door.

Their chests collided, and even with her straining on her toes, he looked down at her upturned mouth, her teasing eyes, and remembered the delicious way she fit against him that first night they met. He hadn't been imagining the way she felt. No, she was just as perfect now as ever.

"We've been here before," he said, inching closer until he could feel her soft sigh against his lips. His dick hardened against her belly.

She whimpered, a breathy, needy sound, then said, "Are you going to fuck it up again by saying something stupid?"

"I'm not going to say anything at all," he said softly and let go of her wrists. Her hands rested on his shoulders as he wrapped his arms around her waist to pull her closer. Her head fell back against the stainless-steel door, her heart racing as fast as his.

Benjamin ran his hands down the curve of her ass and squeezed her hips until she strained against him. Then he brushed a soft, fleeting kiss against her lower lip just as the doorbell rang.

*WhatsApp Group: Operation Shaadi Saboteur*

**FARAH AUNTIE:** Darling, we haven't made much progress in finding out where there is an information leak with the wedding planning. I've done a few online searches but still nothing. Has anything else happened?

**BOBBI:** Not yet, but I'll let you know if something does! Thank you for your help. It is a huge relief for me to know you're all handling this.

**MONA AUNTIE:** Don't thank us yet! I'm turning my dinner party tonight into a working meeting. Hopefully we'll have some more information for you afterward.

**FALGUNI AUNTIE:** I'll talk to some of my old journalism contacts before then.

**SONALI AUNTIE:** There is a holy festival at mandir we should all go to.

**FARAH AUNTIE:** Shut up, Sonali.

**MONA AUNTIE:** Good god, shut up, Sonali!

**FALGUNI AUNTIE:** Oh just shut up, Sonali!

# CHAPTER 9

## Bobbi

*Note left on napkin in Bobbi's kitchen:*

*Thali with six different vegetable or meat options.*
*Puffed rotis or paranthas as main course. Play with*
*colors. Vibrant ombré?*

"When the wine showed up, he jumped away from me," Bobbi said. She pointed to the whiteboard she'd rolled in front of her living room couches. There was a diagram with stick figures that she'd sketched to illustrate her and Benjamin's sexy embrace.

"Then what happened?" Veera asked, hugging a pink pillow against her chest. Her eyes were as wide as saucers behind reading glasses. The air-conditioning hummed, and the soft strains of a Bollywood playlist echoed in the background. "Did he put the wine down and resume his position with you in front of the fridge?"

Bobbi pouted and looked over at her open kitchen. She wished. "He *apologized* as if the whole parantha thing never happened."

Kareena was sitting on the floor, Bellini in hand, even though it was a weekday. Her computer was propped up on the coffee table next to Bobbi's, with a Zoom screen open. They were about to chat with Prem's mother to get a wedding update. Auntie had used her status to convince Messina Vineyards to finally talk to

Bobbi on the phone. Since they had a few minutes to kill, Bobbi spilled all the details from her date night with Benjamin.

"He pulled a *Ghost* on you!" Kareena shouted. "Your situation is exactly like the pottery scene from that old movie we used to watch as kids. Except instead of pottery, it was dough. From standing behind you, to your hands working together with stroking fingers and palms. Making one parantha at a time. And then boom! Full-body contact against the fridge." She sighed, and fell back against the carpet, raising her glass in the air to avoid spillage. "Wow, I didn't know Benjamin had it in him to make passionate paranthas a thing."

Bobbi remembered the feel of his body, the low timbre of his gruff voice as he simultaneously lectured her on creating food at home to nourish herself, while correcting her technique. She shivered.

*No! No shivering allowed.*

"What am I supposed to do about Benjamin Padda?" she asked, capping the dry-erase marker. She rounded the coffee table to collapse on the couch again. "My body says 'let's go on an expedition!' while my brain is shouting 'evacuate mission!'"

"Expedition."

"Evacuate."

Her friends spoke simultaneously, and their heads snapped as they turned to each other.

"Okay, you first," Bobbi said, pointing to Veera. "You're usually the most positive out of the three of us. Why evacuate?"

Veera shifted until she was sitting up on her knees, cup in hand. "Easy. Forced proximity increases sexual tension. It's in every forced proximity romance novel that Kareena made us read in college."

"You bitches loved every minute of it," Kareena said, saluting them with her glass.

Veera shushed her. "Bobbi, what happens when he moves back to California? You'll get hurt, and then you'll say something rude because you always do—"

"Hey! I resent that."

"—and then you'll be alone. Your pride will kick in, and you'll overcompensate for your hurt feelings by diving deeper into your career until you convince yourself work is a part of your identity and the grinding cycle of creativity and burnout actually makes you happy."

Bobbi's jaw dropped. "Okay, Deepak Chopra. Tell me how you really feel."

Veera sniffled and hugged her pillow tighter against her chest. "Men are stupid. And this man is someone you'll have to see regularly if it doesn't work out. He's attached to Prem's hip like we are attached to Kareena. My vote stands. Evacuate mission."

Kareena pointed at her. "We're going to figure out what's happening in that brain of yours in a minute, but first, Bobbi." She turned around. "The last time you had a relationship was over five years ago. And that relationship lasted what, three months?"

"Six months," Bobbi corrected. Jesse was also her longest relationship. They'd been fine together, but when he started making comments about how his mother wouldn't like the way she *looked*, Bobbi ended that quickly. She'd been around enough Desi men at Rutgers to understand that some of them often blamed their mothers for things they believed themselves.

"I've dated other men after Jesse," Bobbi said. "I went out with Kuldeep a little over a year ago. I rocked his world so hard that he moved to Dubai two days later."

"Oh, that's right," Veera said. "That's the one we call the Sandman, right?"

"Yeah." That had been a confusing experience.

Kuldeep Krishan Kumar. After a few weeks of texting and then a few weeks of in-person dating, they spent a night having pretty good sex. The next morning she'd received a text message that had simply said, *It's been fun, but the desert is calling my name. I must go where the wind takes me.* She had no idea what it meant, and after sending it to Kareena and Veera, neither of them knew how to decipher it either.

"The Sandman doesn't count," Kareena continued. "Short-term hookups to blow off steam are not your thing, Bobbi."

"No, they aren't *your* thing. They work for me just fine. Well, it used to work for me." Had Kuldeep really been her last hookup? That had ended well before Kareena's birthday.

And then she'd met Benjamin. Damn.

She waved a hand in dismissal. "Just because it's been years since I've had a relationship doesn't mean that I need to jump into one."

"No, of course not," Kareena said, her voice coaxing and gentle. "But what it does mean is that if you're thinking about repeating your sexy, passionate parantha-making scene with Benjamin again, you have no excuses other than the ones you're about to make up to protect your feelings."

"That sounds like a good reason to me!"

"Agreed," Veera said. "Face it, Kareena. There are way more cons in this situation for her."

Kareena's eyes lit up. She jumped to her feet and handed Bobbi her glass. "Hold, please." She grabbed the pen and next to the erotic stick figures, drew two columns.

"We are not doing a pros and cons list about Bunty," Bobbi

said. Although the idea of making one with her friends had her heart beating with happiness. The tradition started when they were all living together in college.

"It's the only way!" Kareena picked up one of the black markers from the small metal tray and wrote the words PRO and CON next to the stick figures.

"I love a good pro and con list," Veera said with a sigh. "It's like crack for me."

"Then you can start," she said. "What was yours again?"

Veera cleared her throat and held up a finger. "Straight men are stupid."

Kareena carefully wrote "straight men are stupid" on the board. Then, in the pro column, she wrote "sexual attraction."

"Add 'California move' to the con section," Bobbi said. She'd spent enough time with Benjamin to know that he was serious about his family, and if they wanted him to be close, he'd do it for them. Meanwhile, Bobbi's entire life was on the East Coast. Their careers made sure that their schedules were not in sync.

Kareena did as Bobbi asked, then added "both in service industry" under the pro column. "I think I should also add that we're all part of the same friend group now."

"That should go in the con column too," Veera said. "If it works out, then it's great. If it doesn't, then all of us will be forced to pick sides."

Kareena wrote "same friend group" across both columns. She capped the pen and stood back. "What do you think? Do we need to do some more information gathering before you make an informed decision?"

"I also heard that he found you very attractive, Bobbi."

The auntie's voice had all three of them shrieking. Bobbi barely saved Kareena's Bellini she was still holding. Veera fell off the couch and dove behind the coffee table. Kareena tripped over the leg of the whiteboard and went sprawling.

"Hai, hai," the voice said again in a calm, almost distasteful tone. "Ladies, control yourselves, please."

The sound was coming from the computer. Bobbi motioned to the laptop that was still sitting on the coffee table. Kareena craned her neck to look at the screen and nodded.

Great, Bobbi thought. The first time she was going to talk business with Prem's mother, the woman got to hear about her love life. Not that love had anything to do with it, of course.

Kareena scrambled to her feet, grabbed the laptop, and squeezed between Veera and Bobbi on the couch so they all sat hip to hip.

"Hi, Auntie," they said in unison.

"Hello, my new bahu," Prem's mom said. She adjusted her bright red bifocals and looked down at the screen through the cat-eye shape. The glasses had a rhinestone chain that looped around her neck. "Hello, girls. I'm sorry I'm early for our meeting, but I wanted to make sure that we could discuss some points before Messina Vineyards joined. Because you were in the middle of your list, I didn't want to interrupt."

"Not a problem at all," Veera said. "It was our fault for not putting it on mute. We logged in early too so we wouldn't miss the start time. Ah, just out of curiosity, how much did you hear?"

Auntie raised a brow and gave her a bland look. "Veera, beti," she said in her crisp accent, softened with her years in California. "Do you *seriously* think I will tell you?"

"I guess not," Veera said.

"I'm glad you are all being so sensible and working on an honest assessment of your love life," Auntie said. She adjusted her tablet screen so that the camera was staring straight up at her chin and her nostrils. "I don't know if it helps, but I've heard from three different WhatsApp groups that that sweet boy Benjamin Padda may be interested in Bobbi Kaur."

Bobbi's heart thudded. "What—" Her voice squeaked. She cleared her throat. "WhatsApp groups?"

The woman nodded. "Ever since you were spotted sharing ice cream in Brooklyn."

*"Excuse me?"* How in the world did anyone know about that?

"Then two weeks ago, when you went out to lunch with Kareena's aunties, he looked at you over a dozen times in thirty-six minutes," Auntie continued. "Falguni counted. She likes having proof to back up her gossip."

"A dozen times?" Veera asked. She gaped at Bobbi.

"You went out with *my* aunties?" Kareena asked. "My mom's best friends? The ones who practically helped raise me? Why?"

"She was planning your bridal shower. Your Dholki," Auntie said smoothly. Then winked in Bobbi's direction.

Great. The smug smile was proof that Prem's mother knew someone was trying to sabotage Prem and Kareena's wedding. Hopefully she kept it quiet.

"The aunties wanted to go to Phataka Grill," Bobbi explained. "Benjamin was generous enough to offer his restaurant space for the planning meeting. The only time we looked at each other was when we were having a *conversation*."

"A dozen times is a lot, Bobbi," Auntie said smoothly. "Not to mention, he said something to Prem, who said something to his father, who said something to me."

"*What?*" Bobbi, Veera, and Kareena practically shouted.

"It's true," Auntie said. She picked up her phone, tapped the screen a few times with her well-manicured nails, and then held it up to the camera. Bobbi, Kareena, and Veera leaned forward, squinting to read the text screenshot between Prem and his father.

> **PREM:** Bunty said he's delaying his trip to SoCal until Tuesday night. You won't get my suit measurements before your appointment with the tailor. I'll send the measurements and the sherwani by mail.

> **ME:** Why is he delaying his trip? Shipping cost is expensive.

> **PREM:** He wanted to be available in case Bobbi needed him this weekend. They're working on the wedding together. He said he likes spending time with her.

> **ME:** Does he like her? Should I tell his father to arrange a family meeting?

> **PREM:** What are you talking about? No, that's Bunty's business. Stay out of it, Dad.

"Oh my god," Veera said softly. She turned to Bobbi, eyes wide. "He *does* like you. This goes way beyond passionate paranthas, Bobbi. He's talking to his friends about you."

"'He said he likes spending time with her,'" Kareena repeated. She was nodding like a bobblehead now. "Yeah, Benjamin likes you, Bobbi. That's as clear as it's going to get. I'll talk to Prem to confirm, but it's all right there."

Bobbi looked around the room, mouth slack. "What are you talking about? That's not clear at all!" Just because Bunty liked to spend time with her didn't mean that he was interested in her romantically. Or even sexually! He could've meant that they were no longer fighting, and he didn't mind her company. Yes, that had to be it. She remembered the feel of his large hands over hers.

Then the moment in the dressing room when his fingertips traced along the curve of her spine in that quick, almost careless brush. Or his quick wit when they were sparring in her kitchen and she was purposely needling him.

"Don't forget about the frequency with which he was looking in your direction," Veera said. "Trust the financial advisor. Numbers don't lie. With those two facts, and you two spending time together, the evidence leads to one conclusion."

Bobbi stood and walked to the other side of the coffee table. "That's enough," she said. "A few WhatsApp group chats and a side comment from Prem about his measurements aren't enough to convince me of anything other than the fact that we are in a friendly truce." A truce steaming with horniness.

Kareena and Veera stared at her, waiting for her to say more. Then Kareena slowly turned the laptop so Auntie could stare at her as well.

"*Fine*," she said. "We obviously have some sort of chemistry, but who's to say that's not because we've been at each other's throats?"

"But do you like him?" Veera asked. She was still clutching the pillow to her chest, her eyes wide with anticipation. Bobbi couldn't lie to her, or to Kareena.

"Okay fine," she said. "There is a small, tiny chance that I may like him too. I mean, he's single, smart, good-looking, and he's loyal to his friends. That is so impossible to find that it's like I'm conditioned to find that attractive—"

"And rich," Auntie interjected. "Very rich."

Bobbi shook her head. "That doesn't matter to me."

"Then you're an idiot," Auntie said blandly.

For the first time since they started talking about her love life, Bobbi smiled. "Auntie, are you always this sassy?"

The corner of the woman's mouth quirked up. "Always, beta.

Now, would you like for me to reach out to his mother to find out if he has said anything to her?"

"No, that's not necessary," she said quickly. She thought about the text messages again, and the aunties chattering in their WhatsApp groups.

Bobbi shook her head. No, she wasn't going to do this. She wasn't going to play the "does he like me?" game like some twelve-year-old at a sleepover.

Even though that's exactly what her living room looked like at that moment.

One mystery was enough for her to manage. She refused to sit around wondering about Bunty's feelings, too.

She walked over to the island in her kitchen and snatched up her cell phone. Her stomach knotted as she opened her texts and sent a quick message. Before she could second-guess herself, she turned off notifications and put her phone screen-down on the counter.

There, she thought. It was done. Whether she was prepared or not, Bobbi had thrown down the gauntlet. She'd learn if Benjamin was interested in her or if the scene in her kitchen was just a momentary distraction for him.

At that moment, a second woman popped up on the screen. She had coiffed brown hair and an almost uninterested expression on her face. When she saw Prem's mother on her iPad and Bobbi standing at a distance and the whiteboard featuring X-rated stick figures, her eyes widened.

"Hi, I'm Gwen. Am I catching you at a bad time?"

Kareena immediately twisted the laptop to face her, and Bobbi rushed to sit next to her. Damn the woman's timing. She was finally meeting the events coordinator at Messina Vineyards and she looked like a lunatic standing next to X-rated stick drawings.

"You're right on time," Auntie said smoothly. "Gwen? I'd like for you to meet our wedding coordinator, Bobbi Kaur. She'll be handling all of the details for us for Kareena's big day."

Gwen nodded. "Yes, Bobbi, so sorry I haven't been able to return your calls. You have to understand that we're making quite a few concessions for holding an event like this."

"Oh, I thought Messina was experienced in weddings," Bobbi said, eyebrows raised. She had been in the business long enough to know how to handle people who tried to other Desi culture. "Don't worry, I have done hundreds of them, and I can walk you through the whole process."

Gwen's eyelashes fluttered. "No, I mean—"

"In fact," Kareena interjected, "if this wedding goes without a hitch, Bobbi's very exclusive clientele might consider Messina for their events in the future. That is, if the venue can work with us for all of our needs."

"We hope that just because it is an Indian wedding," Veera added, "that a venue such as Messina Vineyards won't upcharge simply because of cultural differences. Because that would be unethical, wouldn't it?"

"No, of course not," Gwen started. "I didn't mean . . . uh, right."

Auntie's face was glowing. "See, Gwen?" she said. "I told you they were smart."

Bobbi had to bite the inside of her cheek to stop from smiling. Thoughts of Benjamin still lingered in the back of her mind, but she had to revisit her feelings about the situation later. Right now she was on her best friend's time, and she had a wedding to plan. And hopefully, Benjamin would respond to her text in a way that made it clear, once and for all, whether or not there was something more than just chemistry and bickering between them.

# CHAPTER 10

## Benjamin

"Then you just left?" Deepak asked. He sat across the small round table from Benjamin, an amber ale in front of him. "Not even a 'it's been fun'?"

Benjamin shook his head, twisting his IPA in his hand. He'd replayed the moment hundreds of times in his mind since he'd left Bobbi's apartment. She'd been so funny, and her laugh lifted the entire room.

But after they were interrupted, her sparkle quieted. She looked more shocked than anything. And because he wanted her to know exactly what she was doing when she was with him, he decided to give her some space. If she was interested, Bobbi would have to tell him herself.

But she hadn't texted.

Or called.

She hadn't even sent an S.O.S. via WhatsApp.

"It's probably for the best," Prem said. He clapped Benjamin on the shoulder. "I mean, you're moving back to California—"

"*Potentially*," he said. Even though that was more of a definite if his father had his way. Benjamin was thinking about his family obligation more seriously these days, and all roads led to California.

In fact, his flight was leaving soon, and he still had to go back to Deepak's house to pick up his bags.

"Bobbi is rooted here," Prem continued. "Her entire family is East Coast. And her best friends. I mean, they do everything together. From pretending to go to yoga classes, to a romance book club."

"Yeah, I know. It's pretty obvious, brother."

He had planned on keeping it light, flirty, and friendly while they spent some time together. But after dinner, he couldn't help but want more. It was as if they were planets circling that had gotten too close, and now they were sucked into each other's atmosphere, ready to crash.

Benjamin had even adjusted his flight so he could be available in case Bobbi needed him. It was inconvenient because that meant he was working remote longer than he wanted to be, but maybe it was good for his soul to do something out of the norm.

He looked around the crowded brewery packed with patrons wearing suits and skirts. The Financial District was the perfect central point for all of them to meet. Deepak was ready to head to Brooklyn after a long day at his family's company, while Prem was still on call at the hospital. For Benjamin, he was ready for the night shift.

Even with his flight change, and his distracted thoughts about Bobbi, his life was so predictable.

Every day followed the same pattern now. Work, friends, and family. Work, friends, and family. On repeat. To make matters worse, that pattern was very similar to what his parents had always wanted for him.

"When did life change for us?" he asked aloud.

Deepak and Prem looked puzzled.

"What do you mean?" Deepak asked.

How could he explain the disconnect he felt from where they wanted to go to where they were now as adults in their thirties? "I remember the days when we were talking about what we wanted to be, and where we were going. Now I feel like all we do is discuss Prem's wedding and business. We somehow fell into the South Asian immigrant culture trap." To make his point, he smacked his fist on the table, and the glasses jumped. "We're doing what they always wanted us to do, and what we truly desire is always just out of our reach. It's *disgusting*. We should be bucking the system!"

"As someone who prides himself on being his family's manager and putting their needs before his own, this should be good," Prem said. He motioned to the waitstaff for another round.

"No, I'm serious," Benjamin replied. "Prem, I remember the days when your only goal was to get through your residency and your fellowship program. You were determined to succeed and make a name for yourself."

"I have," Prem said blandly. He saluted Deepak and Benjamin with his soda. "I even did a fucking talk show."

Benjamin snorted. "You're missing the point. What happened to the dude with determination? The ace with the ambition!"

"Ace?"

"He's in love, brother," Deepak said, ruefully.

"And I never thought it would feel this good," Prem said as he gave them the finger.

"Pathetic," Benjamin replied. Judging by the grin on his friend's face, Prem didn't mind being a little pathetic. The truth was, he looked happy, and that was something that Benjamin was still having such a hard time understanding. Prem was doing exactly what his parents dreamed he'd do. He became a doctor, started his own practice, and was marrying a brown girl who was successful and kind.

There was nothing wrong with having the same ambitions that Prem's parents had for him. In fact, it made life easier when the community was supportive. But how did he know that he wasn't simply going along with a master plan designed for him out of convenience? How did he know that the years of parental pressure didn't brainwash him into thinking that his parents' version of happiness was his own? Maybe the truth was that Prem had a strong sense of identity separate from his family. But Benjamin's identity would always be tethered to the Naan King.

And if he went back into the business full-time, he was afraid that he'd never be able to do the things that he'd always dreamed he'd accomplish for himself. Or worse, he'd marry someone who fit his busy lifestyle, someone who wasn't like Bobbi with a schedule as packed as his, and he'd settle into a boring existence.

Benjamin stood and raised his glass. "Gentlemen, today I'm recommitting to my promise in front of both of you. Benjamin Bunty Padda will never fall at the feet of love. I will live until my last days as a bachelor. I'm going to do what brings me joy."

Prem's phone buzzed on the table, and he glanced at it. His eyes widened. "That's too bad," he said to Benjamin absently. "Because I'm guessing we're about to find out if Bobbi likes you, too."

Benjamin's breath caught. "What? What do you mean?"

"Hold on, my mom is calling," he said.

Benjamin almost strangled his best friend. How could he answer a phone call from his mother when they were in the middle of this incredibly important conversation about Benjamin's happiness? Was there no loyalty to friendship these days?

Prem, oblivious to Benjamin's suffering, pressed the phone to his ear and said, "Hello? Yeah, I'm with him and Deepak. Sure, one sec." Prem held out the phone, unexpectedly. "Here," he said to Benjamin. "It's for you. She has some information about Bobbi."

Benjamin almost fell over his chair, scrambling to snatch the phone from Prem's hand. If Prem's mother was the one who knew something about the way Bobbi felt, he'd talk to her for however long she wanted.

"Hello?" he said, pressing the phone to his ear.

"Hi, beta," Auntie replied on the other line. Her voice was clear and crisp, despite the overhead music and the loud chatter from other tables.

"Hi, Auntie, how are you? I hope you got my cranberry cardamom loaf I left with Uncle the last time I was in town."

Prem rolled his eyes at him, and Benjamin gave him the finger.

"It was so delicious, darling," Auntie said in his ear. "Thank you for thinking of Uncle and myself. You're such a sweet boy."

"That's only because you bring the best out of me," he said, smiling. Prem's mother reminded him of his own. The woman was doting, but she was also shrewd like a shark. They had to be to marry men who were practically strangers, move to a different country, and raise a family while building a community for their sons.

"Well, beta, as your reward, I have some interesting information for you. I had a lovely conversation today with Kareena, Veera, and Bobbi."

"Oh? Wedding planning?"

Deepak and Prem leaned in closer.

"Yes, of course," Auntie said. "And I just happened to join the Zoom meeting early. Enough to hear the girls talking about how Bobbi should handle her feelings for you."

Bobbi had feelings for him.

Bobbi. Had. *Feelings.*

His heart swelled in his chest as he jumped to his feet. Tapping the mic mute button on the screen, he shouted, "Bobbi has feelings for me!"

Prem and Deepak cheered with him, clinking their bottles together.

Benjamin cleared his throat, unmuted the line, and pressed the cell back to his ear. He could feel his heart pounding hard in his chest. "Wow, that's unexpected."

Auntie laughed on the line. "Duffer. Just like my son."

He grinned. "But a grateful one. Uh, I guess I'll reach out to her and ask her out."

"No!" Auntie shouted, jolting him in his seat. "No, no, you can't do that."

"I can't ask her out?"

"What?" Deepak said, hearing Benjamin's side of the conversation at the table. "What does she mean you can't ask her out?"

Benjamin shushed him then turned in his seat so he could listen more closely to Prem's mother. "Sorry, Auntie, what was that?"

"I told Bobbi I wouldn't mention anything. If you ask her out now, then she's going to know that I said something about the conversation. I need her to like me, Bunty. Because if she doesn't then she won't keep me informed about my son's wedding. You understand, no?"

Benjamin looked at the screen, then put it back to his ear. "Auntie, who else did you talk to before you called Prem?"

Auntie laughed again, the knowing chuckle full of secrets. "Beta, I tried to call you first. You didn't pick up."

"That's because I turned off all notifications," he said. It had been ringing nonstop or buzzing with texts from his assistant and restaurant managers since the morning. He needed a break to decompress with both of his friends.

He reached in his pocket for his phone and glanced at the screen, and his stomach dropped when he saw a missed text from Bobbi.

"Auntie?" he said. "I have to go. Thank you, ah, for the information."

"You're welcome, darling. Now can I speak to my son?"

"Sure," Benjamin said, and handed Prem back his phone.

He stared for a moment longer at his screen, debating whether he should open the text now or wait until he got home. Whatever it said was probably going to clarify if the chemistry between himself and Bobbi was something more than just part of his imagination.

What would happen if this one text message changed the nature of their entire relationship? Would they spend more time together, sleep together, and then move on? Did he want something more after he'd just committed to being a bachelor for the rest of his life?

Not that the commitment meant anything. People could change their minds, couldn't they? When he was a kid, he hated steak. Now? Loved it. The same principle applied here.

"What are you going to do?" Deepak asked.

Benjamin shook his head. "I'm about to find out." Before he could second-guess himself, he opened the message.

> **BOBBI:** Are you ever going to kiss me against a door or are you just not interested? Because I can always find someone else . . .

He grinned. Like hell she would find someone else. And wasn't that just like Bobbi to bait him? He sent back a quick text.

> **BENJAMIN:** Where are you?

When he didn't receive an answer after a beat, he sent a quick message to Kareena.

**KAREENA:** She had to help set up for an event at Riya's Banquet Hall over in JC. Just for a couple hours. Why? Is it wedding related? Is it the menu? You're not going to pick really gross food just to prank us, right?

He pocketed his phone, drained his beer, and stood in one easy motion. He was right. The text message had changed the nature of their relationship.

"Where are you going?" Deepak asked.

"Where do you think?"

Deepak nodded. He checked his watch. "Don't you have to be at the airport in a couple hours?"

Shit. His flight back to Cali. He couldn't delay it again because he needed to be on the West Coast for meetings first thing in the morning. He also had to spend some time with his family otherwise his parents would fly out to the East Coast themselves to see him. That was the last thing he wanted to deal with right now.

The aching need for Bobbi was too strong to ignore. They were officially on a collision course. It was consuming his thoughts and he'd never be able to last another week without giving her the kiss she wanted. The kiss she deserved. She'd thrown down the gauntlet, and it was his turn to respond. He'd go to her first, and then to the airport.

One kiss. That was all.

Benjamin opened his alarm app and quickly set a timer for the latest he needed to leave to get to the airport on time. Then, after pocketing his phone, he turned to his friends.

"I'll see you later. I have something important to take care of before I fly out."

# CHAPTER 11

## Bobbi

*Text message from Benjamin Padda:*

> **BENJAMIN:** Saffron rice cakes with pista ice cream. Pistachio and saffron together are a winner. Milk in the rice?

Bobbi rarely had to help with setup anymore, but this was an emergency. That was what she had to keep reminding herself as she stood at the base of the ladder while Neha climbed to the top to pin some of the drapery herself.

"They all called out on the same day?" Bobbi asked for the tenth time.

"Yeah," Neha yelled back from her perch at the top. "They went to Bollywood Blowout at that new place in midtown. The restaurant caters to the early twenties crowd that is more interested in the buzz than the taste of the booze. They got shut down twice for noise complaints. And now they're giving people food poisoning."

"That's awful," Bobbi called back. "It looks like you're almost done, though."

"I have to build the centerpieces, and I can take care of that by myself. There!" Neha pinched the drapes, fluffed them once, and watched as they flowed down to the floor in a glittery curtain.

"You are a magician at this," Bobbi said. She held the ladder steady as Neha climbed back to the ground.

Neha flicked her long, waist-length ponytail over her shoulder. Her skin was scrubbed clean, and she looked even younger than her twenty-five years. "Thanks! Sorry to interrupt your girls' night and your best friend's wedding planning. I know you get very few days off and you protect them fiercely."

"It's no problem," Bobbi said. "We were pretty much done, anyway. We had a long call with Gwen from Messina Vineyards, and I'm hopeful that everything will go smoothly there from here on out."

"Messina?" Neha let out a low whistle. "I can't believe they're still giving you trouble."

Bobbi nodded. "I'm trying to get my uncle to . . . ah, what I mean is, I'm trying to secure a relationship with Messina. I mentioned my plans to Kareena, and she's on board with letting me use her event as leverage."

"Thank god for best friends!"

"Exactly," Bobbi said. "So now I just have to show Gwen that I can make her money with Indian weddings."

"You will," Neha said. She grinned. "You're the best!"

Bobbi winked. "I like to think so. Hey, are you sure you don't want me to stick around and help with the centerpieces too?"

"Thank you so much, but I think I'm good," Neha said. She pressed a hand against her chest and let out a deep breath. "I know this is only our third event together now, but I felt like when I made that call, I was screwing it all up." Her eyes began to water, and her lashes sparkled with unshed tears.

"Neha," Bobbi said, rubbing her shoulder. She forgot sometimes how young her décor lead was. The woman's feistiness and professionalism hid all inexperience. "I would've been more pissed off if you hadn't called me and been stuck doing this by yourself and potentially getting injured. Now come on. I'll get this ladder in the back room, and you can start on the centerpieces. If you need me to stay, let me know."

"Thanks, Bobbi," she said.

The sound of the front door had both Bobbi and Neha turning in their spots. Benjamin walked in as if he owned the place. From his shining shoes to his fitted black Henley. His gold chain winked at the base of his neck under the bright overhead lights.

Neha sighed, soft and featherlight. "Oh my god. Who is *that*?"

Bobbi couldn't answer. Her first thought was that she was light-headed at the sight of him, and wasn't that an uncomfortable feeling? Her second was that Benjamin Padda was obviously here for her, and she couldn't remember the last time someone went out of their way to come to her, other than her best friends.

He ascended the stairs with quick, easy strides and headed straight toward them. When he was within earshot, she blurted out the first question that came to mind.

"What are you doing here?"

He paused midstride. "Didn't you get my text?"

"No?" She reached into the thigh pocket of her leggings and pulled out her cell phone. A new message popped up with Benjamin's name.

> **BENJAMIN:** Where are you?

> **BENJAMIN:** I checked with Kareena. Heading your way. Get ready.

He was responding to her taunt. She'd sent it to him hours ago, and with everything that had happened in the interim, she'd completely forgotten about it.

No, that wasn't true. She'd forced herself to forget about it otherwise Bobbi was going to be sitting at home by herself thinking about every moment she had with Benjamin "Bunty" Padda and whether she read too much into their interactions. They'd stopped pranking each other, stopped poking at each other in a way that had bite to it, and now every word had more meaning. She needed to know what that meaning was once and for all.

And now he was here. Did he want to—

"Hi," Neha blurted out, breaking the awkward silence. She extended a hand toward Benjamin. "Neha Wen. Nice to meet you. I'm Bobbi's decorator for the wedding events this week."

"Benjamin Padda," he said smoothly.

Neha squealed. She was practically vibrating out of her skin. "Oh my god! *The* Benjamin Padda? You own Phataka Grill! My family loves that place. Whenever my folks are in town, we always try to go."

Benjamin's shoulders relaxed. He gave Neha a disarming smile. "Thanks. Next time you're at the restaurant, let them know you're a friend of Bobbi's. Dessert is on the house. Hey, nice job decorating."

Neha was practically salivating now, Bobbi thought. She had pulsing hearts in her eyes. "Oh my god, thanks. All of this is because of Bobbi. I wouldn't be here without her."

Benjamin locked eyes with her. "She's incredible."

Bobbi's heart pounded hard at that declaration.

*This man can disassemble your armor with one look. Be careful or he might bruise you.*

They stood there staring at each other, Neha at Benjamin, Benjamin at Bobbi, Bobbi at the floor, for a solid thirty seconds before Bobbi motioned to the ladder.

"Hey, can you give us a hand?" she asked. "I have to take it to the back room for Neha. Then I should be getting home. Neha? Bun— Ah, Benjamin can help me. Don't forget, I'm a phone call away if you need anything this week."

"Yeah sure," she said, her ponytail bobbing with each nod. "I'll get back to work." She wiggled her fingers at Benjamin.

Benjamin moved forward, breaking their staredown, and quickly folded the ladder as if he'd done it a hundred times. Then, tucking it under one arm as if it weighed nothing more than a bag of feathers, he said, "Lead the way."

Bobbi nodded and followed the perimeter around the banquet hall so he would have the most room to maneuver the ladder. They passed a few lingering staff members who were unfolding chairs and laying out the tablecloths.

"You have a wedding event tomorrow?" Benjamin asked casually.

She glanced at him over her shoulder. "We have wedding *events* that start tomorrow. The first night is the welcome dinner for all the out-of-town guests. Then, in the library off this main hall, is a family pooja. On Thursday there is the mehndi, Friday is the sangeet, Saturday is the ceremony, and the reception is Saturday night."

Benjamin let out a low whistle. "That's a lot of wedding. Thank god Prem and Kareena's event will be a three-day thing versus a whole week."

Bobbi wasn't sure that was true. At least not yet. Prem's mother and Kareena's grandmother had just met, and their ideas were big.

Bobbi propped open the set of double doors that blended seamlessly into the pattern on the walls so Benjamin could walk through into the gray, industrial-like access hallway.

"It's through here," Bobbi said, motioning toward the end of the long corridor. They passed a mirror, and even though she only had a moment for a quick glance, it was enough to confirm that she looked like a mess. Her skin was shiny from the face mask she'd put on earlier, and her hair was piled up on top of her head. Her T-shirt was a slouchy number that she'd tied in a knot in front because it was so loose. She also wore neon purple sneakers because who wanted to decorate a room wearing fancy clothes?

"You didn't get my text," Benjamin said from behind her.

She paused midstride, then picked up the pace. "I wasn't expecting one. Especially since my first message was sent hours ago."

"I was out with Prem and Deepak for a quick visit and wasn't checking my phone."

She typed the code on the electric panel that was to the left of the last set of double doors and unlocked the storage closet. Once inside, she switched on the dim exposed bulb in the center of the room. "Right in here," she said.

Benjamin turned the ladder so it leaned up against the wall in the corner next to two smaller ones. "Wow," he said as he stepped back to take in the packed storage room. He scanned the stacked chairs, the neatly stored round tables in different sizes, and boxes filled with lights and fixtures. "This is a lot bigger than I expected it to be."

"It's a great place. Really well organized." She motioned to the far wall where the mandap was stored in pieces next to the throne chairs the bride and groom would use for their reception. Bobbi rarely did throne chairs anymore, and opted for a tasteful couch, but the mother of the groom selected them, and since she was paying for the reception, Bobbi relented in the design choice. As long as the bride and groom didn't mind.

Benjamin crossed to the two high-back red-velvet throne chairs and sat in the one on the left with a crown pendant embroidered at the top. His easy, relaxed pose, with an elbow leaning on one arm, didn't deceive her. The light flickered overhead and cast shadows on the hard planes of his face.

"Bunty, why are you here?" she asked from across the room.

"Why do you think?"

"I was just—"

"Don't be a coward now," Benjamin interrupted. He patted the seat next to him. "Bobbi Kaur, you have the name of a queen, and you deserve a throne," he said, referencing the twin chair next to his. It had a more delicate crown pendant embroidered in the same location as the first chair design.

Bobbi couldn't hide her smile and crossed the room to perch on the edge of the throne. "I could get used to being referred to as a queen," she replied in Punjabi.

Before she could get comfortable, Benjamin curled his fingers around the back of her neck, his grip firm and demanding, sparking electricity through her skin. He pulled her over the rolled arms, and with their eyes locked, he pressed his full mouth against hers.

Heat shot straight through Bobbi's body. She gasped, her lashes fluttering shut as he consumed her. There were fireworks in her head and her heart.

He kissed her like he couldn't get enough of her taste.

The firm pressure of his lips coasted over hers, coaxing hers open until his tongue slipped inside. His touch was demanding, seductive, systematically dismantling all her thoughts until her fingers were gripping the collar of his shirt and she was straining against him. Bobbi had never tasted a man like Benjamin, all spicy and sweet. His hand rough in her hair, while his other stroked the long line of her back.

When he pulled away, his mouth wet from hers, they were both breathing heavily, inches apart from one another.

"Does that answer your question?" he rasped, his voice deep and thick.

"Wh-what question?"

He nipped at her bottom lip. The quick sting had her straining forward, wanting more.

"Benjamin—"

His tongue laved over the bite mark. "Mhm, that's the first time I think I've ever heard you say my name."

"The moment calls for it," Bobbi replied. She was breathless, barely able to make complete sentences. And because she wanted more, she took it, cupping his face, smoothing her fingers over his beard, and pulling him closer.

He gripped her hips and yanked her forward until her breasts pressed against his chest.

When had she ever been kissed like this before? When had she ever felt this way? She wanted more—no, *needed* more. She'd been alone for so long, been touch deprived to the point where she thought she didn't care, didn't need it. Benjamin blew open a door she knew she'd never be able to close again.

"Do you need me, Bobbi?" Benjamin rasped, sliding a hand down the front of her shirt and squeezing her breast, running a thumb over the hard peak of her nipple. "Do you want me?"

"Y-yes," she said, aching now for some relief.

"Then sit back," he said, his voice taking on a desperate edge.

The lust-fog made it difficult to think clearly, to remember they were in a storage room at a wedding venue on the bride and groom thrones.

"Wh-what?"

She gasped when Benjamin fell to his knees and pressed a palm to her chest and pushed her against the high-back chair. "I want to hear what you sound like when you come for me."

Bobbi was wet for him, and she ached for his touch. When Benjamin ran a finger over the seam of her leggings, she gasped at the shock of pleasure, her thighs falling open, her eyes closing at the sensation.

"Lift your hips," he said. She did so automatically, responding to the thread of steel in his voice. He hooked his fingers in the waistband of her leggings and pulled them and her panties down to her ankles.

"B-Benjamin . . ."

"Any objections?" he asked, sliding his hands over her calves and thighs, exposed to the cool air.

She wanted this. She wanted this more than she cared to even admit. And in the dark, in her bedroom at home, she imagined this when she touched herself.

"No objections," she said, breathing heavily now.

In a move so quick and fast, he lifted her legs, bound at the ankles by her leggings, and looped them over his shoulders. She was trapped, tied at her feet resting behind his neck, with Benjamin squeezing her thick thighs like he couldn't get enough. He pushed them apart, and then without a moment's hesitation, pulled her to the edge of the seat, positioned her hips to tilt toward him so she was completely exposed, and buried his face against her wet heat.

Bobbi gasped, head falling back, fingers squeezing her nipples as Benjamin parted her smooth lips, licking her with the flat of his tongue, over the sensitive pebbled clit, like he was savoring an ice cream. Then he pressed a thick finger inside her slowly, pumping in and out as he teased her clit. He was thorough, working her over harder and faster with each demanding touch. His focus was that swollen nub that he sucked relentlessly.

She could feel the orgasm building, cresting like a wave that overwhelmed her.

"Don't stop," she gasped as she ran her fingers through his hair, lovingly, gently, coaxing him to press into her harder.

He pulled back and blew gently on her swollen lips. She jack-knifed forward, the sensation too much for her, robbing her of her breath.

"You're delicious, Bobbi. The best thing I've ever tasted. Now come for me like a good girl." He pushed a second finger inside her, curling it up, and then with his tongue, lapped at her clit and sucked hard.

She let out a silent scream, her fist pressed against her mouth as the orgasm took over. Her entire body tense as the pleasure wrecked her to her bones. She didn't know how long it lasted, how long she was overcome with the sensation, but Benjamin coaxed her the entire time, sending aftershocks up her legs until every muscle sang with pleasure and she was a trembling, gasping mess.

Countless minutes later, Bobbi lay limp in the chair as Benjamin unhooked her legs from around his neck, slowly slid her pants back up her thighs, and pulled her forward to rest against him as he lifted her and slid the waistband over her butt. She felt her cum, sticky between her thighs, as a reminder of the best oral sex she'd ever had in her life.

Her head rolled back, and Benjamin pressed a firm kiss against her mouth. She could taste herself on his lips.

"You okay?" he asked.

"Yeah," she said, stroking his wide shoulders. Petting him. "Yeah. Do you—"

Her words were cut off with the sound of a shrill alarm.

"Shit," he murmured.

"What is *that*?"

Benjamin took his phone out of his back pocket and stopped the alarm. "It's my cue that I'll be late for the airport if I don't go right now."

Her thoughts were beginning to knit together again after he'd fried her brain. "Airport? You're flying back to California?"

He pressed a kiss to her mouth again then stood. The thick bulge in his pants was evident. "I have to," he said. "Meetings with my West Coast restaurant staff and a family get-together. I hate to leave you like this."

He cupped her chin and tilted it up so she could look at him. His eyes were filled with concern. "Hey. You okay? I'll stay if you want."

"For the afterglow?" she said, amused. "No, I'm fine. Just . . . let me know when you're back East."

Benjamin leaned down and kissed her again with the intense focus that she knew she'd miss. The alarm went off a second time, and Bobbi pulled back.

"Go," she said. "Get out of here." She motioned to his crotch. "And try not to stop on your way out otherwise they're going to speculate about what we were doing in here."

Benjamin grinned, watching her as he backed away toward the exit. "Sapno ki rani, one look at you, and they'll know. Dream of us when I'm gone."

# CHAPTER 12

## Bobbi

*Wednesday morning*

> **BENJAMIN:** Even though I'm back Wesco, still thinking of you.

> **BOBBI:** You know, you really don't have to do that.

> **BENJAMIN:** Do what?

> **BOBBI:** Be charming.

> **BENJAMIN:** Ahh, you're on to me. That means I just have to get better at it.

> **BOBBI:** 😊 Did you read that line in a book?

> **BENJAMIN:** You know, for all those romance novels you devour, you're a bit cynical, aren't you?

> **BOBBI:** Guilty. When will you be back East?

> **BENJAMIN:** Don't know yet. I want more of you. I'm going to clear my schedule.

**BOBBI:** Okay.

**BENJAMIN:** OKAY? JUST OKAY?

**BOBBI:** Bunty, you don't owe me explanations, either. What happened last night was fun. I wouldn't mind if we had some fun again. What else do you want me to say?

**BENJAMIN:** I don't know, but something more enthusiastic than "okay."

**BOBBI:** If you want me to be enthusiastic, you'll have to come here and make me.

**BENJAMIN:** . . . That's more like it. I'm looking at flights now.

*Wednesday night*

**BENJAMIN:** ::IMAGE::

**BOBBI:** . . . Did you just send me a picture of food?

**BENJAMIN:** Yeah, I'm changing up the menu for the fall season in my LA restaurant. What do you think?

**BOBBI:** I mean, it looks beautiful. Passionfruit kachumber salad with goat curry is not something I thought I'd crave.

**BENJAMIN:** I'm craving something beautiful too.

**BOBBI:** Weak, Bunty. That was weak.

**BENJAMIN:** I don't see you doing any better.

**BOBBI:** ::IMAGE::

**BENJAMIN:** Wait, is that a spreadsheet of all the Indian restaurants in the tristate area? Holy shit, I never thought I'd be so turned on because of Excel.

**BOBBI:** Are you going to ask me to kick it up a notch and send a picture of my tits now?

**BENJAMIN:** I won't ask, but I wouldn't turn it down, either.

**BOBBI:** ::IMAGE::

**BENJAMIN:** Great. Now I have a half chub in the middle of my restaurant.

**BOBBI:** For the record, I have great tits. I don't mind showing them off.

**BENJAMIN:** The tits are great, but the face with it is even better.

*Thursday morning*

**BENJAMIN:** Hey, you up?

**BOBBI:** Yeah

**BENJAMIN:** What are you doing?

BOBBI: Are you trying to phone-sex me?

BENJAMIN: As much as I want to, no. I'm at the restaurant. I was just thinking of you.

BOBBI: You are full of surprises, Bunty.

BENJAMIN: Hopefully good ones?

BOBBI: Yes.

*Thursday night*

BOBBI: Hey, you okay?

BENJAMIN: Hey, sapno ki rani. Yeah, I'm fine. What's going on?

BOBBI: Nothing, it's just usually by now I'll get a few messages from you.

BENJAMIN: Ahh, looking forward to my text messages now, huh?

BOBBI: They keep me entertained.

BENJAMIN: Soooo am I the only man you text?

BOBBI: It's like you're in high school.

BENJAMIN: You didn't answer the question.

**BOBBI:** Fine. Yes. I'm assuming I'm the only woman who is sending you tit pics?

**BENJAMIN:** Yup. No one else is getting me hard with Excel spreadsheets, either.

**BOBBI:** Glad to hear that. I have a long night because the wedding festivities have begun.

**BENJAMIN:** Don't forget to eat something.

**BOBBI:** Sadly, food is furthest from my mind right now.

*2:00 A.M.*

**BOBBI:** ::IMAGE:: Did you have someone break into my apartment, stock my fridge, and leave food for an army?

**BENJAMIN:** If that someone is Kareena, then yes.

**BOBBI:** Kareena? Bunty, you know she's going to grill me with questions.

**BENJAMIN:** Let her.

**BOBBI:** Questions about us that I don't have the answers to.

**BENJAMIN:** Tell her we're figuring it out. In the meantime, eat something. I had my kitchen at Phataka make the passionfruit kachumber salad with goat curry.

**BOBBI:** OMG. Really??

**BOBBI:** ::IMAGE::

**BOBBI:** This is amazing. It's exactly what I needed after a long night. Thank you.

**BENJAMIN:** Take care of yourself, sapno ki rani.

*Friday*

**BENJAMIN:** It's wedding day two for you, right? Did you eat something?

**BOBBI:** I did. What are you up to today?

**BENJAMIN:** Mandatory board meeting at my father's company. This is my least favorite part about coming back home.

**BOBBI:** Why do you have to be there? I thought your brother was running things?

**BENJAMIN:** He wants to, but my father can't get over the fact that Chottu is finally at an age where he is mature enough to lead.

**BOBBI:** Want some advice?

**BENJAMIN:** Yeah, shoot.

**BOBBI:** Your interference will undermine your brother's authority. Let him fight his own battles.

**BENJAMIN:** It's hard because I've always been in the middle.

**BOBBI:** Bow out, Benjamin. You're the only person who'll get hurt in that situation. Take it from someone who knows family dynamics. I see them play out all the time.

**BENJAMIN:** I appreciate it. Tomorrow is family dinner, and I needed the reminder.

**BOBBI:** If it's anything like mine, then it's usually about work.

**BENJAMIN:** Haha, yeah. They usually are.

*Saturday*

**BENJAMIN:** Hey, sapno ki rani.

**BOBBI:** Every time you text me that, I think of those throne chairs. Which, by the way, are currently being used by the bride and groom at this reception, so I'm pretty much always thinking about the throne chairs.

**BENJAMIN:** Welcome to my world. Your taste is permanently embedded in my brain.

**BOBBI:** I'll take that as a compliment, Chef. What's up?

**BENJAMIN:** I had a thought.

**BOBBI:** Sounds dangerous.

**BENJAMIN:** Ha ha. I don't have a lot of time for myself. I'm usually working or thinking about work. But I use my flights to de-stress and binge-watch shows. I'm looking to switch up my flight entertainment. Prem mentioned you and Kareena and Veera have a book club. What are you guys reading?

**BOBBI:** A romance novel. That's usually our go-to. You want to read a romance novel? The same one we're reading?

**BENJAMIN:** Yeah, why not? What's the title?

**BOBBI:** Here's the link. But word of warning. If you make one misogynistic comment about it, I'm going to tell Kareena and let her read you the riot act about cis-het men and the patriarchy.

**BENJAMIN:** Noted. Downloading now.

*1:00 A.M.*

**BENJAMIN:** Oh, shit. Is this dude in the mafia?

**BOBBI:** 😏

*Sunday*

Bobbi needed her beauty rest, but she was still sitting up in bed with her laptop, waiting for Bunty's text. For the past few days, he would send a "good night, rani" message after he finished work and got in his car to drive home. She knew that she was being ridiculous and sacrificing her comfort in the hopes that she'd be awake to see it come in, but if he put the effort into messaging her before bed, it was the least she could do to respond.

In truth, she was starting to realize that Bunty was not the man she thought he was. Her first impression of him had been cocky, brash, and egotistical. He still pushed her buttons in a way that no one else had ever been able to do, but now she was beginning to like it. From thousands of miles away, he was trying to show her that he was an attentive and caring lover. He put a lot of effort into letting her know he was thinking about her while he was in a different time zone. In contrast, she'd been focusing on keeping things light and friendly.

But maybe it was time to accept that they'd moved past light and friendly and straight into something more serious.

She'd just finished reading the same page for the third time in a new vendor contract when her phone pinged.

> **BENJAMIN:** Good night, rani. Heading home from the restaurant now.

Bobbi looked at the text message for a moment and debated her options. Did she go with something glib like "your texts give me more heartburn than your food" or something classic like "sweet dreams"?

Glib was out of the question. Reading tone in a text message was too messy, and she wasn't interested in hurting his feelings anymore. Using a classic response was also a cop-out. That would read as "this text took little to no effort to send," which defeated the purpose of staying up late at night.

She started typing something, then quickly deleted it.

"Damn it, I wish I spent more time on practice dates," she murmured. She pulled off the eye masks that she'd plastered on her face and dropped them on her bedside table.

She began considering her options.

Thirty seconds later, she finished typing her sentence and hit send. "There! Perfect."

She was about to put her phone away when it buzzed in her hand. She jumped, fumbled it in the air, and managed to grab it while also saving her laptop from sliding to the floor.

"Hello, Bobbi speaking," she said.

" '*I stayed up to answer your text message*'? Seriously, that's the best you came up with?"

Benjamin's voice was laced with amusement. Bobbi couldn't help but smile in response. "I was going to go with 'sweet dreams,' but that was too easy."

He groaned. "You literally plan people's happily ever afters! You see romance every day of your life. How can you be so bad at sexy texting?"

He sounded like he was driving, his voice echoing in the enclave of what had to be a fancy car. Benjamin probably had a BMW SUV.

Or a fancy Toyota SUV.

"I feel like sexy texting is overrated," Bobbi said. She shifted in bed so that she could balance the phone on top of her ear without having to hold it. "As a wedding planner, I have learned to appreciate blunt honesty. I mean, what's sexier than that? Being completely transparent and straight with another person takes a kind of fearlessness, doesn't it?"

"Sexy texting and honesty aren't mutually exclusive, you know. That is, unless you don't find me sexy in the first place."

She reached out to poke the discarded eye masks that were drying on the table. She should really get up to throw the slimy gel blobs out. "Fishing for compliments, Chef Padda? I read your interview in *International Food* magazine this month. Looks like they kissed your ass enough to last a lifetime."

"Reading up on me? I guess that's a compliment on its own."

"It's kind of hard to miss. We both work in the service industry after all."

"That we do," he mused.

There was a pause, and Bobbi pressed her lips together, trying her best to hold back the question that circled her brain like a carousel. She lasted two seconds. "Ugh, I have to ask. How long are you staying out there?"

Benjamin sighed, and even though he had her on speakerphone, she could hear the frustration in his voice. "I don't know at this point. With my father's pending retirement, things are up in the air at the company. I feel like I haven't had a moment to breathe."

Bobbi sat up and shut down her laptop before she tossed it toward the end of the bed. She rolled onto her back and tucked the blanket around her. "Bunty, even if you had a choice, I doubt you would opt to do anything else besides work."

"Hey," he said, chuckling. "Pot, kettle, black."

"Guilty."

"Seriously, Bobbi, if you had a day off, what would you choose to do?"

She smiled and closed her eyes at the sound of his voice. "Is this the get-to-know-you portion of the relationship?"

"Humor me, Kaur. I have thirty more minutes of driving."

She switched off the bedside light and closed her eyes. "I don't know. I like working a lot, but I wouldn't turn down the opportunity to travel more. To explore different cities. Eat good food."

"Oh yeah? I love traveling. I wish I did it more, too. If you had a few free days, where would you go?"

She felt her muscles relax as she sank farther into her bed, lulled by the sound of Bunty's voice. "I want to visit India as an adult. The last time I went, I was really young. I think it would be interesting now that I'm thirty. But beyond the cliché, I'd love to see Paris. Rome. Munich. Singapore."

"Oh yeah? I bet you'd love Singapore."

He began to tell her about his trip that he'd taken for work a few years ago as she sank into the warm timbre of his voice. And when he finished, she sleepily told him about the absolute joy she felt doing nothing on a beach. Even as they shared parts of themselves in the quiet privacy of their late-night phone call, Bobbi knew in the back of her mind that if she wasn't careful, Benjamin could be the start of very dangerous feelings.

But maybe she was already too late.

# CHAPTER 13

## Benjamin

"What are you doing?"

Benjamin looked up from his phone. "What?"

His parents, Chottu, and his sister, Gudi, were all watching him expectantly from across the large rectangular patio table outside their Orange County home.

His sister, the nosiest of brats, leaned her elbow on the table and repeated, "I said, what are you doing, bhaiya?"

"Ah, texting Prem and Deepak." He tucked his phone away, even though he knew he'd be itching to take it out again in a minute.

"Do tell Prem that I am so excited to attend his wedding," Benjamin's mother replied. She pushed her large, round sunglasses on top of her head and leaned back in her seat. Her freshly dyed black hair fell in waves down her back as she tilted her face up to the last vestiges of evening summer sun. She didn't look a year over fifty, even though she was approaching her sixtieth birthday. Between tennis at the local country club, Kitty parties with the other Punjabi wives in town, and the copious amount of business dinners she hosted, his mother retained her youth through staying incredibly busy. He probably got his need for a chaotic lifestyle from her.

"I don't know why we all can't go," Gudi grumbled. "It's Prem Bhaiya. I never thought he'd get married." She slumped in her chair. Gudi may have inherited the same features as their mother, but she looked nothing like her with her bright pink curly hair frizzing around her face, her gold hoop nose ring, and her T-shirt that read *I'm not your model minority.*

"Gudi, not nice," Benjamin's father said. As the satisfied patriarch of the house, Gabbar Singh leaned back in his chair at the head of the table and folded his hands over his abdomen. "You know that the entire board of directors will be in town that week and my children have obligations to be available to them. Bunty is the only one who must leave after the meeting to go to the wedding."

"You need to start taking responsibility too, Gudi," Chottu replied. He was also glued to his phone, texting someone furiously.

"Hey, if I have to put my phone away, so does he," Benjamin said.

"Put the phone away, Chottu," his parents said in unison.

Chottu glared at Benjamin, then after tapping the screen a few more times, he tucked it in his pocket. "Fine. Why were we all summoned here? Gudi needs to return to her post in the seventh level of hell."

Gudi stuck her tongue out at him. "Hell looks a lot like my beautiful home in Oahu these days, dipshit, and I'm the reigning queen."

"Gudi!" her parents both yelled.

She snatched up Chottu's whiskey glass and tossed back the last shot, which only had Chottu cursing her out more.

"You are no longer children!" Benjamin's mother shouted. She clapped her hands together, her gold bangles jangling. "Enough! Your father has an announcement to make."

"What is it, Papa?" Chottu asked. He pulled out his phone again and began scrolling.

"I am retiring as the Naan King," he said, reaching out to grip his wife's hand. "I'll be announcing it to the board this October. Your mother and I are going to spend more time together."

"We know," Gudi said. "Chottu told me."

"And Bunty told me," Chottu said.

"And you told me, Pappa," Benjamin said to their father.

"You told the children already?" his mother snapped. She smacked her husband's arm with the back of her hand. "I told you I wanted to be in the room!" she yelled in Punjabi.

Gabbar Singh rubbed his biceps and glared at Chottu, then Gudi, and finally Benjamin. "You all couldn't lie for me this one time for your mother?"

"I didn't know we were supposed to," Gudi said. Benjamin and Chottu nodded.

When Benjamin felt his phone buzz again, he retrieved it to see a text from Bobbi. It was a picture of the red throne chairs Bobbi and Benjamin had occupied last week.

How could one moment with Bobbi shift all his thoughts and focus to her? His responsibilities should've been all-consuming. From his two restaurants to his expanding management team, to his family and his best friend's wedding. But he'd had a single taste of a woman who he'd just started to have feelings for, and it was as if everything before her was now a secondary consideration.

"Bunty, are you paying attention?" his father said.

He jolted upright. "What, no. I mean yes. What?"

His father shook his head. "Puttar, you are going to be at the board meeting, nah?"

Benjamin's brother was clenching his jaw. His hair was up in its trademark man bun and he was dressed exactly like their father. Button down. Slacks. Loafers. He was also hardheaded like Dad.

"I'll be there only if it'll help secure Chottu's role, Dad."

"And as an advisor?" he pressed. "Are you going to cut down your trips to the East Coast?"

This time his phone buzzed again, and he couldn't help but smile at the message.

> **BOBBI:** To honor our sexy escapade on those throne chairs, I've decided to use them in another wedding.

"Who's Bobbi?"

Benjamin pressed his phone to his chest, almost hitting his brother in the face. Chottu had leaned over his shoulder and apparently got a clear view of the name.

"She's Kareena's friend, and she's planning Prem and Kareena's wedding."

Gudi leaned forward, chin propped on her hand. "Bhaiya, do you like her?"

"Yes. No, wait—"

The word was out of his mouth before he could stop it. He knew it was too late to take back when his sister gasped. "You're kidding me! The 'I'm going to die a bachelor' Punjabi fuck-boi brother of mine is serious about a woman?"

"Gudi, don't be a brat."

Benjamin's mother waved at Gudi to settle down. "Don't say 'fuck,' Gudi. It's not appropriate."

"Why? You say bhen-ch—"

"Gudi!" her parents cried in unison.

Gudi rolled her eyes. "Whatever."

"Bunty, who is this woman?" his mother continued. "She's a wedding planner? Is she Punjabi?"

"Shit, Mom," Chottu said as he poured more liquor into his

glass. "Why don't you just show all your privilege, classism, and casteism and ask him what you really want?"

"Chottu, I'm speaking to your brother, not you," Benjamin's mom replied. "Beta . . ."

*Here it comes*, Benjamin thought. The inquisition. He preferred his single lifestyle, not only because of his career demands and how much time he spent supporting the family business, but because any information about his love life was like blood in the water.

And he was the prey.

"She's a great person," he said. "That's all you need to know."

His father leaned toward his mother. "With a name like Bobbi, she sounds Punjabi. Is it serious?"

"Beta, how well do you know this woman?" his mother asked, insistent now. "It's important to be with someone who has a good heart, and a good family."

"That's hypocritical, Mom," Gudi said. She pushed the wispy frizz off her forehead. "Your family sucks. Nani was a total bitch."

"We did not send you to the most expensive school in the country only for you to become a writer who has no common sense!" their mother yelled in Punjabi. "It's rude to call your dead grandmother a total bitch."

Chottu was back on his phone again, but this time he was grinning at his screen. "Bobbi Kaur," he said, delighted. "Just turned thirty. One of the best wedding planners in New Jersey based on these Knot.com reviews. She works with her family at her uncle's wedding planning business. He raised her as her parents are both gone."

Benjamin gripped Chottu's arm. "Where did you get that information? That can't be a basic Google or Knot search."

"I WhatsApp messaged Prem's mom," Chottu said.

Prem's mother. Damn it, he couldn't even fault her. She was the one who helped him out by telling him that Bobbi had feelings in the first place. But this was getting out of control now.

"Vah!" Benjamin's father said, slamming a fist on the table. "What a daughter! She works with her family, you say?"

He defaulted to the excuse that every Desi child used when they wanted to shake off their nosy parents. "Pappa, we're just friends." *Right now.*

"Do you think she'd move to California?"

Benjamin gaped at his father. "What part of 'we're just friends' makes you think she would move? But even if we were serious, the answer would be no. Her network is on the East Coast. She and her friends also think California smells like narcissism and avocados."

Even though Prem had warned him about Bobbi's roots, the more he spoke to her, the more the warning felt real.

The mischievous smile faded from Gabbar Singh's face. He grew solemn. "Then you must do away with any foolish ideas of getting serious with a Punjabi girl in New Jersey."

"Papa, my personal life isn't your business," Benjamin replied.

"It is if it means you'll be spending time again on the East Coast."

"I will spend time with whom I choose," Benjamin said, his voice escalating.

"Not if it affects the family business," his father shouted. He slammed his fists hard against the table. The plates and cups rattled.

"Now, boys," Benjamin's mother said, waving a hand between them like a referee. How many times had she done that before?

Benjamin watched as his father scanned the faces around the

table, then adjusted his collar. "Bunty, if you prioritize people on the East Coast, then it's going to divide your time. We talked about your active participation in the business."

The business that he didn't want anything to do with, Benjamin thought. But as the family referee, the manager, it was his responsibility. And even though he had always prided himself on supporting his loved ones, he was beginning to resent being told about his "responsibilities" when that's all he ever thought about.

"Papa, the business is yours and Chottu's concern. I'll help when I can, but my focus is my restaurants. And you should know that by thirty-five, I stopped following your orders."

Gabbar Singh's mouth pressed into a hard line. "If you have made up your mind, then so have I. I'm not going to endorse Chottu as the next CEO, Bunty, if you don't accept the role as an executive advisor, and an active member of our board of directors."

"*What?*" Chottu burst out.

"Dad, what the hell?"

"Oh boy," Gudi mumbled. She rested her chin on a fist.

"I wasn't going to give you an ultimatum," his father continued, "because I thought you would do the right thing. But now? With this woman in your life, I think it's important you know what the stakes are, and where your priorities should lie."

Chottu swiveled in his seat to face Benjamin. "Wait, he wanted you to be my, what . . . *babysitter*?"

"He mentioned it as a request, an option!" Benjamin replied.

"But now you're getting distracted, and we have to keep you focused," Gabbar Singh said from his seat at the head of the table. His resolve was clear in his expression. "Because you have a romance now, Bunty, and you can't let that get in the way."

This was probably part of the reason why he couldn't commit to long-term relationships. Because the family he loved always tried to tell him the choices they thought he should make. And those choices almost inevitably left him alone.

"Papa, remember the last time you threatened me?" Benjamin got to his feet.

"He went and opened Phataka Grill!" Benjamin's mother said. She grabbed her champagne flute and gulped before adding, "Beta, if this girl means so much to you that you are arguing with your father, then you should introduce us!"

"Mom, I think you need to pick up on the vibes here," Gudi muttered.

"I respect your career choices, puttar," Benjamin's father said. "But we all have to work together because we don't have anyone else here but ourselves. No one in America has our best interests at heart. They are expecting us, the immigrants, to fail. Even our own community sometimes sees us as competition. Chottu, if your brother supports you as an advisor, I know the both of you together can lead my empire into the future."

"I am more than capable of being the leader you refuse to see, but you'll never forgive me for making one mistake, will you?" Chottu said, hands planted on the table. "I screwed up one deal when I started at the company in my twenties, and to this day you're punishing me! Dad, I've more than made up for that loss."

"CEOs can't make mistakes," Gabbar Singh said. "Not if it costs millions of dollars and jobs."

*Some things never change*, Benjamin thought. Maybe it was Chottu's one snafu losing a big client. Or maybe it was his father's archaic belief that the oldest should inherit the business. Either way, he was wrong. Benjamin watched Chottu get to his feet and storm out of the backyard. He pointed at his father. "Old man, don't be alienating the kids that you want to love," he said. Then followed his brother.

With one last wave, he pushed through the backyard gate so he could walk around the house to retrieve his car that he'd parked in the driveway. If he stayed with his family for a moment longer, he was going to lose his mind.

He needed time to think. Time to understand Bobbi's role in his life before officially making his decision about where he was going to live. Benjamin was just having fun, right? That's all it should be.

Then why couldn't he just commit to supporting the Naan King Emporium like his father wanted?

He got behind the wheel of his car and pressed his forehead against the steering wheel. He needed to talk to Bobbi. In person. To figure out his feelings, and what he wanted to do before he just rolled over and accepted whatever life someone else designed for him.

Because if he said yes to joining the Naan King Emporium, he knew that he had so much more at stake to lose than just his restaurants.

# CHAPTER 14

## Bobbi

*Note left in take-out bag sent from Phataka Grill*

*For my next restaurant, I want an entire selection of salty desserts.*

*Monday*

**BOBBI:** How did your family meeting go?

**BENJAMIN:** Let's see. My brother and I walked out. And that was after alcohol, shouting, and my father issuing an ultimatum.

**BOBBI:** Sounds kind of nice. Our family dinners are usually quiet.

**BENJAMIN:** Yeah, I'm lucky even though they make me lose my patience.

**BOBBI:** Are you coming back East this weekend?

**BENJAMIN:** Can't wait to see me again, huh? 😊

**BOBBI:** This weekend is Kareena's Dholki celebration with the aunties.

**BENJAMIN:** I'll give it my best shot. For you.

*Tuesday*

**BOBBI:** The aunties haven't found anything yet, but I received a note from our shaadi saboteur.

**BENJAMIN:** What did it say?

**BOBBI:** ::IMAGE::

**BENJAMIN:** Wait, are those cutout letters from magazines?

**BOBBI:** Yes, and apparently that means whoever is doing this is over the age of forty because according to the aunties, anyone younger wouldn't waste their time.

**BENJAMIN:** That sounds . . . accurate. Okay. Well, if this person is threatening to have the venue cancel the event, are you going to talk to Gwen?

**BOBBI:** Yes, early next week. Wish me luck.

**BENJAMIN:** I will, but you won't need it.

*Wednesday*

**BOBBI:** ::IMAGE::

**BENJAMIN:** Are you in New York?? IS THAT CHICKEN AND RICE?

**BOBBI:** I ended up having lunch with Kareena's sister Bindu and her husband. I wanted to really make sure they weren't our shaadi saboteurs. They're too busy trying to diffuse Loken's toxic mother, apparently. And because Bindu was eating for two, she polished off my plate at the restaurant. I don't really mind, though. This is the best food cart food in the city. It's magic.

**BENJAMIN:** Sapno ki rani, please give a chef a heads-up before you send him food porn. Chicken and Rice is platinum plan porn. I need to grab extra kitchen towels for the drool.

**BOBBI:** I can top that.

**BOBBI:** ::IMAGE::

**BENJAMIN:** . . . is this what I think it is?

**BOBBI:** If you use the recipe for anything other than personal enjoyment, I've been told that both of us can be sued. It took me forty-five minutes to get this out of the Halal guys.

**BENJAMIN:** You're incredible.

*Thursday*

**BENJAMIN:** This book is fucking filthy.

**BOBBI:** You're still reading it, huh?

**BENJAMIN:** I'm about halfway through. I was going to wait until my next flight, but curiosity got the best of me.

**BOBBI:** I've said it before, and I'll say it again: you're full of surprises.

**BENJAMIN:** I can neither confirm nor deny that statement.

**BOBBI:** Why not?

**BENJAMIN:** It's a surprise.

**BOBBI:** That was such a pathetic line that I don't know if I can sleep with you again.

**BENJAMIN:** Fuck. Okay, give me a couple minutes. I'll come back with something better.

*Friday*

**BENJAMIN:** Hey, I'm so sorry but I can't make it this weekend for the Dholki. We're having a distributor problem at Namak.

**BOBBI:** Okay.

**BENJAMIN:** I wish I could be there.

**BOBBI:** Yeah, me too.

**BENJAMIN:** Make it up to you?

**BOBBI:** Okay.

*Saturday*

**BENJAMIN:** Hey, I haven't heard from you all day. You doing okay?

**BOBBI:** Yeah, sorry. I've been running around for Kareena's Dholki and for another wedding I'm trying to manage at the same time. It's insanity this weekend.

**BENJAMIN:** Do you have a team that can help?

**BOBBI:** Yes, but like you, I prefer to be onsite and handle things myself.

**BENJAMIN:** I can't tell if you're mad at me for not coming back sooner.

**BOBBI:** No, if I was mad, you'd know it. Am I disappointed? Sure. Sorry, Bunty. I have to go. We're setting up today.

**BENJAMIN:** Maybe we can talk on the phone tonight. We haven't done that in a while. Time zones have been our enemy.

*Sunday morning*

**BOBBI:** I'm not responding regularly because I'm swamped, not because I'm mad.

**BENJAMIN:** Any more sabotage?

**BOBBI:** Not since the note. I spoke with the aunties, and they said they may have a lead? Which sounds very . . . official. Between them, my work, and my uncle, I can't take much more.

**BENJAMIN:** Your uncle? Is he still in your business because of that wedding a year ago?

**BOBBI:** I think it's more than that, but I can't tell anymore. I've had full creative control for years, and all of a sudden he's decided he doesn't trust me.

**BENJAMIN:** One step at a time. I'll talk to you later?

**BOBBI:** Yeah. Here is what we did for the Dholki. Looks great, right? ::IMAGE::

**BENJAMIN:** It looks beautiful. I wish I was there. Send me a picture of yourself.

> **BOBBI:** Later. Promise.

> **BENJAMIN:** Looking forward to it.

*Sunday afternoon*

> **BENJAMIN:** ::IMAGE:: Chicken and rice tastes like I'm there with you in Midtown. I'll make these for our next date. We have to have another cooking lesson.

> **BENJAMIN:** Oh that's right, you're at the Dholki.

> **BENJAMIN:** I miss your face so fucking much, Bobbi Kaur.

Bobbi glanced down at her phone to read the last few text messages from Benjamin, her heart clenching at his words.

She had no idea how to stop herself from completely spiraling whenever she saw his name flash across her screen. She ached at night for him, and aching was a dangerous thing. Especially because she wasn't sure how he fit into her life.

The texting had been nonstop for two weeks. They had way more in common than she ever thought possible. From their ambition to their humor, to the people they loved and the things that irritated them.

Bobbi was sure that the conversation would deteriorate into nonstop sexting the minute Benjamin got back to the West Coast, but he'd kept everything relatively PG-13. And wasn't that confusing? She'd underestimated him.

The truth was, she couldn't stop thinking about him, and that meant she was spending less time thinking about work, when work fed her soul and gave her joy.

*But couldn't spending time with Bunty do the same?*

She tucked the phone back in her Patiala salwar pocket, even as a member of her team slid over to stand next to her.

"The appetizers are all a hit, Bobbi," Gina said. They canvased the room of fifty-some women wearing traditional Indian clothing from saris and salwars to lehengas and anarkalis. The small boutique venue in Red Bank had waterfront views and was tastefully designed with hardwood floors, a dome ceiling, and glittering chandeliers. The aunties insisted on paying her a fee to elevate the interior décor with bright jewel-tone chair drapes, lantern centerpieces, and a floor space for the folk singing.

Kareena sat at the end of one of the two long tables. She glowed as Veera placed a flower crown on her head.

She looked so beautifully happy.

"Boss?"

"Sorry, what?"

"I think most of the apps are gone," Gina said. "Right on time. We're finished with the speeches, too. Would you like to start the buffet?"

"How about we start the music first? Then ten minutes in, we'll open up the buffet line, and people can sing and eat, and go back to singing."

"Sounds good," Gina said. "Will you make the announcement?"

Bobbi caught Kareena's sister's eye, then in a moment of inspiration waved her over. "I think I'm going to have Bindu do the announcement."

"The cranky sister who told us we needed to raise the shades so she'd have better lighting to film her videos?"

"The same one." Bobbi winked at Gina. "If you give a family member with inflated self-importance a responsibility, then they're less of a pain in the ass in the long run. Makes them feel special."

"I don't think she needs any help in developing her self-importance," Gina whispered. She slipped away as Bindu floated over. She rested a hand on her perfectly round belly.

"What's up?" she said.

"Bindu, being an *influencer* and all, and having the ability to command a room, would you like to make the announcement that we're about to start the music?" Bobbi motioned to the padded cushions in jewel tones with yellow-gold thread embroidery. Low rolled-arm love seats were angled toward each other, and a Dholki sat in the center with two tambors and a set of spoons.

Bindu glowed. "Oh my god, I would *love* to. Should I do it right now?"

"If you think that's best," Bobbi said.

"I do, yes." She moved forward and clapped her hands to get everyone's attention. "Excuse me, ladies? It's time to make some music!"

There were cheers, and as Bobbi suspected, everyone wanted a chance to sing and celebrate the daughter of one of their old friends. Chairs scraped back as Kareena's aunties—Farah, Mona, Sonali, and Falguni Auntie—led the way to the center of the room. Kareena perched on one of the love seats, her dadi next to her, as another auntie lifted the Dholki drum into her lap. Her wrinkled hands smoothed over the canvas of the oval drum heads, and then with a few testing taps, began adjusting the strings.

Someone else grabbed the spoons and sat across from the Dholki, pinching them back-to-back between her fingers.

With a few testing beats, the drum began to play a quick, steady rhythm. There was chatter and laughter as Kareena's grandmother started singing first. Her voice lifted above the noise, and silence spread through the room as people began to listen. Her words were thick with emotion and age as she gripped her granddaughter's hand, rocking back and forth with each word of "Aaya Ladiye ni Tera."

Kareena's eyes brightened with tears, and she rested her head on her grandmother's shoulder. Mona Auntie, sitting cross-legged on the floor next to her seat, squeezed her hand, and Veera patted her other knee.

When Veera saw Bobbi standing across the room, she waved her over. Bobbi shook her head and motioned to the buffet. She then held up a hand.

*I'll be there in five.*

Veera nodded, then turned back to watch Kareena and Dadi singing.

The sound of the double doors creaking open had her turning to see the inn manager slipping through the crack. Sebastian smiled, then, adjusting the cuffs of his suit, crossed the room. He'd squeezed her in on a lucrative Sunday afternoon when most venues would've laughed in her face.

"How's it going? Do you need anything?" he whispered.

"No, we're good. Thank you so much for letting me know you had an opening. I really appreciate this," Bobbi whispered back.

He bumped her arm with his. "Hey, if it wasn't for you, I wouldn't even have a business. You gave the inn a chance when most people judged."

"And now look at you! One of the best in Red Bank. But you don't have to discount me every time I host an event with you."

"Take advantage of it while it lasts," Sebastian said with a grin. "When my brother-in-law takes over while I'm on paternity leave with Ying, he's not going to be so generous."

Bobbi chuckled behind her hand. Out of the corner of her eye, she thought someone was watching her, but when she turned back to the gathering in the center of the floor, all eyes were still on Nani.

"Let me know if there is anything else you need," Sebastian said, then turned to leave.

Bobbi got the thumbs-up from Gina that the buffet was ready when her phone began buzzing incessantly in her pocket. She retrieved it to see Benjamin's name on the screen. In their two weeks apart, they'd only spoken once on the phone because of their alternating work schedules. She tensed at the thought of something happening to him.

Glancing around, she answered, then quickly slipped out of the same double doors that Sebastian had entered through.

"Hello?" she said, after shutting the doors behind her.

"Bobbi?" Benjamin's voice sounded cool, and not at all in the friendly tone that his texts mimicked.

"Hi, is everything okay?"

"You tell me," he said. "Why did three different aunties send me pictures of a conventionally attractive man touching you?"

Bobbi stopped in her tracks. "What the hell are you talking about?"

"Who's the guy, Bobbi? Am I going to have to throw punches, or at the very least have a very serious conversation with someone?"

She quickly entered the small dressing room she had used for herself and her team off to the left of the lobby and locked the door behind her.

"Run that by me one more time."

Benjamin sighed. "Why am I getting pictures of some conventionally attractive tall man touching you? You look beautiful, by the way, but the man is the part I have an issue with. Because he's not me, in case that wasn't clear."

Bobbi pinched the bridge of her nose. "You're fucking kidding me. These aunties are ridiculous! Sebastian is the manager of the venue. He did us a favor and discounted this place for the Dholki. I was literally just talking to him thirty seconds ago. And our conversation was probably that long, too! Did they really think they were snitching?"

"*Sebastian?* Damn it, even his name is sexy." The tone of his voice shifted ever so slightly. He believed her. But then again, when hadn't he taken her word? The fact that he called her right away to ask her who the man she'd been standing next to had been instead of playing mind games with her via text was disturbingly sexy to her.

"You aren't seriously jealous, are you?" she said with a smile.

"I'm not there," Benjamin replied. "I'm not there and everyone knows it, which is so *frustrating*. The longer I'm away, the more I'm worried you'll lose interest in what we could be."

Because she had never been with a man who had been jealous of her time and handled it in a somewhat mature way, Bobbi decided that she'd humor Benjamin. She sat back on the faded gray couch, folding her legs under her hip. "I know it goes without saying, but I can do whatever the hell I want, when I want. But out of respect for you, I'll always explain myself if you ask."

"I know," Benjamin mumbled. "Do you know what irritates me the most? That it's been so long, and I can still remember how you taste, but because I had to go, our time together ended so soon."

His words twisted her gut in knots. "Benjamin Padda," she said softly. "Are you trying to phone-sex me as an apology for being a Neanderthal?"

"Is it working?" he said, his voice deep and dangerously protective.

"Maybe."

"Then I need you to hear me when I tell you that the next time I leave you in Jersey, I want you to close your eyes and remember exactly how my hands feel, how my tongue feels when I lick you, and the feel of my mouth on you. I want you to lose your mind at the thought of getting close to me, and I want the same from you. I can't wait to tie you up and feast on you, Bobbi."

Bobbi let out a ragged breath. He'd hinted at preferring bondage before, but the closer they became, the more she knew that she wanted for him to explore that kink with her. She squeezed her thighs together at his bluntness. "I want that too, Bunty."

"Are you alone?"

"Yes," she said. "Why?"

"Undo your salwar," he said quietly.

"Benjamin." Bobbi looked around the empty room. "We can't keep doing this in storage closets and dressing rooms."

"It'll have to work. Now, Bobbi." There was that thread of steel in his voice again that had her shoulders straightening, alert and eager. She was so wet for him already. She knew now that the text messages would never be enough when she could hear his voice like this.

"You too this time," she said, feeling her cheeks heat at the request.

"Yes," he replied. "Pull your salwar string undone."

With quick hands, she untied the string at her waistband. "Okay," she said, leaning back against the couch.

"Tell me what you feel," he said. "Lift your salwar out of the way and slide your hand under your waistband. Over your stomach and into your panties."

She closed her eyes, and gasped when her fingers coasted over her smooth mound and dipped into her wet folds. Her fingertips brushed her sensitive clitoris.

"I'm so wet for you," she whispered as she began to move her fingertips in soft circles.

"I want you to make yourself come," he demanded. Then she heard the sound of a belt buckle hitting a hard surface. "Touch yourself and think of me stroking my fingers over your clit, fingering your lips, and pushing inside you just like I've done before. I'm here in my office, so hard for you. I can't wait for you to stroke me, to suck me with that smart mouth of yours. Listen to me, Bobbi. You're going to do as I say, okay?"

"Yes," she said, chest straining off the couch. She closed her eyes and began rubbing her clit faster, in firm circles, as Benjamin whispered hot commands in her ear, demanding her to slow down, to slip her fingers inside, and pump. Bobbi's knees bent, her legs open, and she remembered the way he tasted her as if it were yesterday.

"I want you to come first," he said, their breathing in unison now. Bobbi gasped as the orgasm began to rise, steady and slow at first, until she heard the quick slap of Benjamin rubbing himself to the sound of her breath.

"Think of how good it's going to be," he said. "The way I'm going to fuck you slow until you'll feel nothing but me. You'll want my cock until it's an obsession, and I'll want nothing more than to make you come. To take all of you."

"I'm s-so close," she said, gasping as she fingered herself hard now, her hips rocking back and forth, chasing the orgasm. "Fuck, fuck me, Benjamin."

"Yeah, baby, come for me. Come."

The orgasm gripped her like a vise, robbing her of breath as Benjamin groaned in her ear. He called her name as he came. Bobbi fell back, limp against the couch. Her fingers still wet in her underwear, her salwar around her thighs.

"Are you okay?" Benjamin asked, his breath still fast and heavy.

Bobbi smiled, her face flush, her body lax. "One of these days, you'll have to stick around long enough so that you'll see for your-self that I'm fine."

"I don't know if I can wait anymore," he said, rasping. "Bobbi, I'm going to book my flight in a few days. Can you clear your calendar?"

She shook her head, trying to think clearly about what he was asking of her. She sat up and looked around the empty dressing room, removing her fingers from her pants and seeing the glisten of her own release. "Ah, what did you just say?"

"I asked if you could clear your calendar," he repeated. "For a long weekend."

"Yes, ah, well . . ."

"Well? *Bobbi*."

"No, no it's not like that," she said. "I am not leading any events next weekend, but I was asked to help on a few bigger contracts because it's so busy right now. I can juggle some of the work if I have to with our summer support. It's just that we need to go to Messina."

"Messina?" Benjamin asked. The sound of rustling followed. "Prem and Kareena's wedding venue?"

"Yeah," Bobbi said. "We have to see the chef, remember? He emailed yesterday asking if we can meet next weekend. What do you think?"

"Fine," he said. "I'll book the hotel room—"

"I'll book it," she said, cutting him off. The venue had a main hotel lodge and cabins at the back of the property. She wanted to be secluded with Benjamin. "One night?"

"Three," Benjamin corrected. "I want you for three nights. At least. Just you and me. And Bobbi? Pack your toys. We're about to have a lot of fun."

### Indians Abroad News
Relationship column

I am a woman of god, and I believe in the power of janampatris and romance written in the stars. But sometimes, it's up to parents, family, and friends to set the appropriate traps to usher love along.

Mrs. W. S. Gupta
Avon, New Jersey

# CHAPTER 15

## Benjamin

Note left in Benjamin's office

*This wedding will be a disaster. I'll make sure of it.*

Benjamin folded the note with magazine letter cutouts that was left at his restaurant earlier that week and tucked it into the outside pocket of his duffel bag. He'd have to talk to Bobbi about it later, considering it was the second note he'd received. The first had been about the fake food menu.

After waving off the driver, he swung the bag over his shoulder and looked up at the Italian villa boutique hotel. Behind the building was the vineyard that stretched for miles. Bright summer blooms grew on vines along trellises, and Juliette balconies were decorated with colorful window boxes.

Finally. Benjamin was in the same place and the same state as Bobbi.

His red-eye had run late, and because of the anticipation, he didn't sleep. Instead, he'd finished the mafia romance that Bobbi had recommended. That only made him want to get Bobbi naked faster, so the last leg of his flight had included a lot of shifting and fidgeting.

He approached the entrance of the villa with purpose. Bobbi

had texted him earlier that she was already in the lobby and she had checked in. All they had to do was go straight to their room.

He stepped through the glass doors into the blast of cold air-conditioning and saw her right away. She stood in the main foyer, a small lavender carry-on at her side. She had her cell in one hand, her eyebrows furrowed in concentration. She was talking to a woman with brown hair and a familiar older man wearing a white kitchen coat.

The man spotted Benjamin first. "Chef Padda!" he called out, then in three strides reached Benjamin, hand outstretched.

"Vinny," Benjamin said. He took the hand and endured the painfully uncoordinated greeting. How could this chef use a damn knife if he didn't know how to shake hands? "How's it going?"

"I'm so excited to see you," Vinny said. He had a whisper of an unfamiliar accent that had been more pronounced on the phone. "We have so much to do in the kitchen. The opportunity to learn from you for our first Indian wedding is huge—"

"Vinny, why don't you take a breath?" the woman with the brown hair said. She adjusted her dowdy slate-gray skirt suit and extended a hand as well. "Chef, my name is Gwen and I oversee events here at Messina. We're so glad you and Bobbi can stay with us for a few days and provide some clarity on this wedding in October." She tugged on the collar of her suit coat as if she were struggling to breathe.

"Gwen is a little nervous because she'll be the only event coordinator during the wedding and hasn't experienced a traditional Hindu ceremony and Indian reception before," Bobbi said as she joined them. When she reached Benjamin's side, he held out a hand, and as if they'd done it a hundred times, she linked her fingers with his.

Gwen and Vinny both saw the move, and their eyes widened.

"Ah," Gwen said, then cleared her throat. "Having your name attached to our vineyard, Chef Padda, is a big opportunity for us. We're more than happy to provide whatever you may need for the—"

"I'll defer to Bobbi on what I need," Benjamin said.

Gwen paused, her lips curling in a forced smile. "Of course. But we should probably address the biggest roadblock first. Bobbi, as we were discussing, we can't possibly block off all the rooms for the event—"

Bobbi's hand tightened on Benjamin's. "Gwen, you know the budget. What if I can promise you more bookings before the end of the year with similar or larger budgets? Would you be able to hire the staff we would need to pull off the wedding?"

Gwen linked her fingers together. "Of course, but—"

"If you have questions, maybe we can walk through them tomorrow at our meeting together," Bobbi said smoothly. "I know I've sent a lot of emails that have some of the information you're probably looking for."

"I would need additional reservation assurances prior to the event, Bobbi—"

"We can discuss tomorrow. If you don't mind, Benjamin and I would love to check out the grounds and the rooms?"

"Of course," Gwen said. She waved goodbye to Benjamin and after Vinny practically kissed Benjamin's knuckles, they were both gone. Benjamin was finally alone in the lobby with Bobbi, except for a few individuals standing behind the guest services desk.

Bobbi turned to look up at him. She smiled, a knowing expression filled with amusement. "Hi," she said. "I'm sorry about that. Gwen doesn't answer any of my messages even though we had a meeting a little while back. And Vinny only wants to use this as a learning opportunity. Hasn't studied the menu at all."

Benjamin nodded, but all he could think about was that it had been over two weeks.

Without another moment's hesitation, Benjamin cupped her face and pressed his lips against hers. They were soft under his, opening for him as she leaned in for more. The familiar smell of gardenias had him pressing closer, pulling her against him. When her fingers gripped at the fabric of his shirt, that was when he pulled back just a little, enough for their noses to still touch.

"Well, that was a nice hello," she said, her breath coasting over his lips.

"I have a lot more to make up for," he said as he nipped her lower lip. "It's good to see you, Bobbi."

"I have to say the same," she replied.

"So, you're promising Messina Vineyards future events, huh?"

She looked confused for a minute, then nodded. "Yeah. I know a ton of clients who would love having their weddings here. And I have a deal with my uncle that if I can become a trusted supplier here at Messina, then he'll consider me for a leadership role within the business. Kareena thinks it's a good idea."

"That's risky to promise, isn't it? Have you ever not been able to deliver a promise like that before?"

She winced. "Once. And that's why I am in this position trying to prove myself."

He stroked a hand over her shoulder. "I think you've mentioned a wedding plan-gone-bad before. What happened?"

Bobbi smiled up at him ruefully. "I promised a client that I'd get a meeting with one of the hottest Indian chefs in town for a conversation about catering, and I couldn't land the meeting. The client walked."

Benjamin's jaw dropped. "Oh shit," he said. "No wonder you hated me. I'm so sorry, Bobbi." He had no idea how she was even willing to give him another chance after setting back her career with her family.

Bobbi waved it off. "I didn't hate you for that, but it didn't help. And it's fine. I heard from a colleague that the bride's mother was an absolute nightmare, so I'm going to consider myself lucky to have escaped that drama. Come on. I checked in already. We can go straight to the room."

"Yes," he said. With their fingers still linked, palms pressed together, they crossed the lobby. Benjamin followed her as she led him through the back door of the main villa to a wide cobblestone path bracketed with flowers and pathway lights. The air was sticky and humid from the late summer sun, but a soft breeze perfumed the air with the scent of flowers from the beds.

"We have a cabin in the back of the resort," she said. "I'm hoping that they'll give us the cabins for the bridal party during the wedding weekend, but that depends on the very unreliable Gwen."

"If only Gwen had half of Vinny's enthusiasm, huh?"

"He's already set up a meeting tomorrow for you to be introduced to the kitchen staff." Bobbi paused, tugging on Benjamin's hand until he stopped, too. "This whole relationship you two have makes me nervous. I've never planned a wedding where the caterers had to actually learn how to cook the food."

"Vinny knows what he's doing. He can create what we want, too. He's just . . . overenthusiastic. But let's talk about work later, Bobbi."

"What? Why?"

"Because I can't think about anything else but being with you right now."

Her mouth formed a perfect O. "Maybe we should go to our cabin, then."

They didn't speak for the rest of the walk to one of the cottage cabins built at the end of a winding path. The single-story A-frame had its own porch with a swing and flower boxes on the porch railing. Through the small window, Benjamin could see a king-size bed, a seating area with a flat-screen, and a beverage center with a coffeepot, cups, and a fridge. There was a wine bottle chilling in the corner and robes hanging on the back of a door in the narrow hallway that probably led to the attached bath.

His pulse began to race, but he stood back, waited for Bobbi to use her key card to open the door and let them in. She rolled her suitcase to the side of the living room, kicked off her shoes near the entrance, and strode across the cabin, taking in the furnishings.

"Prem's mother and the aunties are going to love this place," Bobbi said, her voice slightly pitchy. "I think with thirty cabins, we can get all of the family and closest family friends first pick . . ."

Benjamin calmly toed off his shoes and socks. He closed the door behind them, then took his phone and wallet out of his pockets to leave on the side console table.

While Bobbi continued her nervous ramble, he unzipped his duffel and pulled out a coiled velvet corded rope, a flask, and condoms. He put the condoms and rope within reaching distance on the bedside table next to the door. He left his utility knife for emergency safety cuts in his bag for now until he understood Bobbi's comfort level.

His hope was that he could mentor Bobbi in exploring her kinks the same way he'd had the chance to explore when he found bondage. And because she was always working her high-stress job, he wanted to help her find a safe space to let go.

A vision of her sticky with sweat, breathless and naked, tied to each corner of the king-size bed flashed in his mind.

After setting up, Benjamin drew the shades. The room was cast in shadows. When he faced Bobbi, she stood on the opposite side of the bed, her arms across her chest. She'd finally quieted.

"Nervous?" he said.

"It's been over a year since I've gotten naked with anyone," she replied ruefully. She looked more serious than he'd ever seen her before. Beautiful and guarded.

"If you need more time—"

"No," she said. "I want you. I want this."

Then, after stripping back the comforter, he sat down at the edge of the bed. There was a part of him that desperately wanted to push her to the mattress, to take her the way they both needed, but this was their first time. And it should be something that she remembered with joy. It was important that the moments he gave her were moments that made her smile.

And as for him, his pleasure would be in watching her let go.

He circled her waist and tugged her closer until she was standing between his spread knees. He propped his chin against her stomach and looked up at her. She stroked a hand down his bearded cheek, then over his hair, almost as if she was soothing him as much as herself.

"Bobbi, are you ready?"

She nodded, her eyes softening as she looked down at him.

"Are you sure that the ropes are okay?"

There was that smile again, the one that said she was amused more by how he spoke to her than what he said. "I should've known you'd be a kinky bastard, Benjamin Padda."

He hadn't known he was one either until he went away for grad school. That was when he started to realize that all of the porn he watched included suspension or knots of some kind. He'd been weirdly ashamed of it at first, because he'd never known other South Asians who wanted the same thing. Hell, even his porn didn't include South Asians. But when he started working in the kitchen, in the chaos, his need for bondage in the bedroom became so strong that he began testing his limits. He was fortunate to have mentors, to have women who taught him what he needed to do to take care of their needs. He was content with sex minus kink, but this fulfilled him on a deeper level. And even though he'd never started a sexual relationship with ropes, he couldn't hold back with Bobbi.

As he sat in front of her, he knew that he wanted to build a scene, to push her to the edge of her limits and watch pleasure control her as she was consumed with erotic joy. He wanted to watch her as she lost her mind while she was the only thing on his. He wanted to test her.

But he wouldn't tell Bobbi that. He'd show her.

"I like the control," he said simply.

"Mhm," she said. She combed her fingers through his hair again. "I won't lie and say that I always wanted us to end up here, but I'm not mad about it. I've never used ropes, but I'll try with you. Is there a Bondage 101? An intro course you can walk me through?"

"Whatever you want. Whatever you're comfortable with. We can use the stoplight system. 'Red' to stop, 'yellow' if you're reaching your limit, and 'green' if it feels good, okay?"

She nodded again.

His hands slipped under her gauzy shirt and coasted along smooth skin. He traced her curves, the softness of her back until he hit her bra. Leaning forward, he pressed a kiss on top of the fabric, urging her to remove it. "First, I'm going to take all of these clothes off you so I can see every gorgeous inch of your body. Then I'm going to tie each of your wrists to the bed before tasting you, then feeding you my cock. I'll then fuck you deep and hard. That's our road map, okay?"

She let out a shuddering breath, and with a half-smile said, "Green." Bobbi tugged the shirt off and dropped it to the floor. Underneath were the most gorgeous breasts he'd ever seen. Round and supple, they were cupped in a lacy bralette with a corset tie in the front. The dusky tips of Bobbi's nipples were visible through the delicate fabric. He ran his thumbs over the quickly forming peaks and felt Bobbi's shudder straight to his groin. He hardened as she pushed her chest forward, begging him for more.

With a quick twist, he unhooked the bra and tugged it free, showing her beautiful nipples. He didn't hesitate in stroking his hands up her bare back and pulling her forward so he could take one in his mouth.

She was exquisite. Smooth and soft as he ran his tongue over the tip, and then nipped. She jerked in his arms, gasping.

"Benjamin," she said and tugged at the back of his shirt. He reached an arm over his shoulder and pulled it over his head, tossing it to the side even as he resumed his gentle, thorough care of her breasts.

Bobbi's arms went around his neck, her fingernails running over his shoulders, sending a trail of hot lightning across his skin.

He pulled back, examined his work on the first breast, and blew cool air across the areola to see it pucker even more. Then he switched his attention to the other, all while Bobbi's trembling fingers undid the hook on her slacks and pushed them down over her hips.

God, this was Bobbi. Thick and beautiful and perfect. He squeezed her ass then slapped one cheek, reveling in the sound.

Bobbi yelped, her knees going weak. Benjamin stood quickly and turned to position Bobbi on the edge of the mattress.

"Center of the bed," he said. "Now."

She pushed back on her heels while Benjamin unbuckled his belt and dropped his pants. He left his boxer briefs on when Bobbi's gaze dropped to his shorts. He needed her to listen. To pay attention. His nakedness would only distract her from his instructions.

Retrieving the rope, he made a basic knot around her wrists and tied them to each bedpost so that her arms were stretched open but with enough slack for her elbows to rest against the mattress. He checked her wrists for circulation before looking down at her cheeks darkened with desire, her eyes filled with curiosity and need.

"Does this feel okay?"

She nodded.

"I need you to tell me, Bobbi. Do these feel okay on your wrists? I can loosen them."

"They're good," she said with a testing tug. "My heart's beating faster. I didn't know . . . I didn't know how hot this would be, and how nervous and overwhelming it is at the same time."

"That's what makes it hot," Benjamin said. "Letting someone else lead." He straddled her hips, taking his time to appreciate her softness, the folds and divots in her body that he wanted to kiss and mark and make his. "That mafia book that you told me you read? It's hot, but it can't make you feel like this."

She smiled. "No, definitely not."

He pinched her nipple, reveling in her gasp. "I won't tie your feet. At least not the first time. But that's next. Then I want to hog-tie you. Suspend you. The possibilities are endless. Remember that stoplight system, okay?"

"I remember," she said, then closed her eyes as he stroked his palms down her arms and along the sides of her breasts.

"No," he said sharply. "Look at me. The last time we were together, I got to taste that pretty pussy of yours. Are you ready to taste me?"

Her eyes lit up. "Yes," she said.

Benjamin tested her restraints one more time for circulation before he got off the bed and pushed his boxers down. His erection sprang free, then lay thick and hard against his thigh. He'd shaved his balls and kept his cock neat just for her comfort. After he pumped a fist over it once, then twice, he climbed on top of Bobbi and straddled her abdomen. He inched forward until his knees were on either side of her head. Her eyes widened, but there was still desire in them, and a hint of nerves.

She nodded, and before he could feed her his dick, she'd taken it into her mouth. Benjamin groaned, his head falling back as her tongue swirled over the crown of his thick erection. She sucked in earnest, hollowing her cheeks as her lips moved over his shaft.

"I'm going to fuck your mouth now, rani," he said hoarsely. He linked one hand with hers. "I need you to squeeze if you want me to stop, okay?"

She squeezed his hand twice as she continued to suck him off.

He rolled his hips forward, pushing deeper until he hit the back of her throat. She gagged, but instead of squeezing his hand, telling him to stop, she continued to suck him like he was a delicious treat and she'd been craving him. Linking fingers, he began to fuck her mouth in slow, steady thrusts while Bobbi took all of him, urging him on with her tongue.

"You suck me so good, Bobbi," he hissed, bracing his other hand on the headboard, ensuring that he didn't rest his weight on her chest. He rolled his hips at the same pace as her firm strokes, shuddering when her tongue ran along the underside of his cock.

He was on the edge, the very precipice of his orgasm when he felt the gentle squeeze of her fingers. He immediately pulled out and shifted off her so he could lie on his back at her side. His erection was still thick and hard, begging for release.

They both gasped for air.

"Are you okay?" he asked, his voice breaking, his thoughts fragmented from need. He reached up to check her wrists, massaging them to ensure she wasn't in any pain.

Bobbi's voice was harsh and as desperate as he felt. "I need you inside me. I need you inside me, Benjamin."

"Not yet," he said. He sat up on his knees, gulping in air, desperate to slow his own pleasure for hers. Without finesse and with quick, uncoordinated jerks, he tore her underwear down her legs, revealing the smooth, fat pussy that he'd missed so much over the past few weeks. It was a perfect mound begging for him to taste.

He grabbed the flask from the bedside table, twisted the cap, then flicked it off. He took a swig and enjoyed the hot burn of whiskey down his throat. It was enough to get himself in control.

"Open wide, rani," he said, and waited for her to part her lips before pouring a shot straight into her mouth. Like a champ, she swallowed, then let out a gentle cough.

"Benjamin—" she croaked.

"I've been told that I look like I'm the kind of man to bring honey or whipped cream to bed," he said as he straddled her again, this time over her thighs. "But to me, that's just a waste of good food. Now, alcohol? That, I don't mind. I love my daru like any other Punjabi man would." Without another moment's hesitation, he poured a trail of whiskey between her breasts, down her curved belly. Rivulets dripped over her sides and into her belly button. She was already glowing with a soft sheen of sweat. The whiskey added a sticky shine that taunted him into tasting. He leaned down and laved at her skin. He licked the underside of her breast, the curve of her belly, and bit the flair of her hip. It was a generous spot that was quickly becoming his favorite.

She cried out, writhing underneath him when he reached the top of her thighs. Benjamin pressed a firm hand against her stomach. "No," he said firmly. "You move like that, and I'll stop."

She immediately froze, but to his delight, Bobbi's eyes flashed in mutiny.

"Don't you think you've made me wait long enough?" she said.

"Ah. I guess you're right."

Benjamin poured the barest hint of whiskey over her pussy, then, watching her as he bent between her spread knees, licked her hard and deep.

She orgasmed with one stroke. Tensing and quivering under him. She'd been tied tighter than a bowstring, and now that she'd come, he could make her insane all over again.

Checking her wrists, he poured more whiskey over her, well aware they'd need to change bedsheets with housekeeping, then tasted her neck, her shoulders, her clavicle.

He couldn't get enough as he worked his way down her breasts. This was his, he thought. This body, this soul was made for him. And when he caught Bobbi's eyes as she panted, called his name, and let out a high-pitched squeal when he stroked her in just the right way, he knew that he was not worthy of her star fire. He was so fucking lucky to have this moment with her, open and his.

When she was gasping, begging him to fuck her, to fill her up, he set the whiskey flask down and retrieved a condom. He tore it open with his teeth and rolled it on his cock. He'd never been so hard in his life, he was sure of it.

He pulled her wrists taut against the restraints and positioned himself on the bed between her thighs. His palms were slick over her skin, and he squeezed her softness to hold her in place, loving the way her feet arched and her toes pointed to the ceiling in response. Benjamin leaned forward, chest to chest, until their lips met, and he entered her in one hard thrust.

She cried out, muffled by his kiss, then opened for him, rolling her hips forward until his thick and hard cock was wrapped in her tight, hot core.

He pulled against the knots as he fucked his queen hard, the bed frame shifting with each move, the slap of skin against skin. Bobbi screamed with each thrust, and Benjamin's brain, hazy with lust, scrambled to memorize the sound of her pleasure and every feel, every touch in this moment as he fit inside her so perfectly. Then he was driving into her until neither of them could think, could speak, and their breaths and thoughts were robbed in the moment. Her thighs squeezed his hips, and the sound of their fucking wasn't nearly as loud as the roaring in his ears.

She screamed his name before she tightened around him, pulling him close. That was enough for his own orgasm to shoot straight up his spine, locking his body tight. His vision blurred and he buried his face in the crook of her neck as Bunty became Bobbi's.

# CHAPTER 16

## Bobbi

*Note slipped in carry-on bag:*

*Rasmalai cheesecake, gulab jamun tiramisu, or passionfruit kulfi? Cut sweetness with mint or South Indian bitter coffee concentrate.*

Bobbi woke at the gentle buzz of her phone on the bedside table. With her eyes still blurry from sleep, she reached for it and checked the screen.

When she saw Neha's name and the letters "S.O.S.," she jerked up into a sitting position. The bedsheets and blanket were a crumpled mess around her. Benjamin lay on his stomach next to her, his bare, muscled back on display. One hand was tucked under her pillow, which was frankly as much touching as she liked when she slept. But she learned that's how Benjamin operated. He respected her boundaries.

Damn, she wanted nothing more than to snuggle in, but an S.O.S. message was never a good thing.

She rubbed the grittiness from her vision, then slipped out of bed naked and tiptoed to her suitcase. She'd only opened it the night before for her toiletries, but now she retrieved the silk short set of pajamas. A quick trip to the bathroom had her mind racing with possibilities. What kind of S.O.S. was it this time? She hoped to god it wasn't the event that she'd off-loaded, otherwise her uncle would never let her take over the business. Not now, not when Sukhi graduated, *or* if Messina made them a preferred vendor.

It had been exactly three minutes since the text when she stepped outside onto the front porch, key card in hand, and sat on the swing to call Neha.

"Oh my god, Bobbi," Neha said when she answered. "I can't believe that I have two emergencies in the same month with you." Her voice wavered and cracked with tears. "You're my best client, and I really look up to you, and I can't believe this is happening to me, and I'm going to do whatever I can to fix it, I promise."

"Whoa, whoa, whoa," Bobbi said softly. Bobbi trusted Neha as her decorator because she was usually so calm and put together. This was scary. "Start at the beginning. What happened?"

"I ordered the special mandap design that you wanted for your best friend's wedding," she said with a hiccup. "The one with the beautiful gold filagree, the twisting metal vine work along the four posts? I even got the approval from your friend's mother-in-law and grandmother like you wanted. It came yesterday, and this morning I took a trip out to my storage units to see it. *The mandap is not the right design.*"

Bobbi dropped her feet to the ground to stop from swinging. "What did you say? Neha, what design is it if it's not the one we ordered?"

Neha was crying in earnest now, ugly wet sobs, like she was being tortured.

"Neha," Bobbi said with as much calm as she could muster. "Come on, pull it together. I'm not mad at you, I swear."

"It's not that," she wailed. "I mean, sort of, but here. I'm going to show you."

Her phone buzzed again, and Bobbi opened the picture Neha texted. Her jaw dropped. "Oh my god."

Even though it was in pieces, the mandap was easy to make out. It was a square platform in polka dot white and red, with a canopy in bright orange. But that wasn't the hideous part. In elaborate painted metal and plaster, two giant eyes protruded from the top of the canopy, two bulging white cheeks with red spots protruded on each side, and a honking red nose was positioned right in the top center.

The front of the mandap was a giant clown. A giant. Fucking. Clown. Worse, whoever was sitting on the mandap would look like they were inside the clown's mouth.

Who would've thought to even design a platform for a religious wedding ceremony in the shape of a clown mouth? She'd seen a lot in her years supporting her uncle and Bhua, and then on her own when she took over a roster of clients. But this was right up there with one of the most extreme situations. It fit between the groom who got caught in the bridal suite banging the bride's mom, and a dock collapsing in the middle of the wedding, tossing the pandit, the mandap, the bride, groom, and entire wedding party into a lake.

Hopefully, she would find this funny in the near future.

Now was not that time.

Neha began sobbing on the phone, and Bobbi rubbed her temples, counting to ten, before she spoke.

"Neha?" she said gently. "Babe, I'm going to need you to stop crying because we can't problem-solve this if we're hysterical."

"It's just so *scary!*" she wailed. "I'm all alone here with this thing!"

Good lord, Neha had a clown phobia. No wonder she went ballistic and sent an S.O.S.

"Why don't you go outside? Step outside your storage space and take a deep breath. Come on now."

There was shuffling, and the sound of more sniffling before Neha's voice came through again. "I really hate clowns, Bobbi. I'm so sorry about this screwup. I use a company that builds Broadway set designs to create these mandaps and they are always exactly to order. And more affordable than having pieces shipped from India! I'll cover this from my own expenses. I promise." She hiccupped.

Bobbi had a feeling there was more to the story than just a simple mix-up. This was a fucking *clown*. There was intention behind it, from the painted polka dot platform to the big plaster eyeballs. There was no way that a mandap in the shape of a clown face would ever show up unless someone was deliberately being an asshole and screwing with the wedding.

"Neha? Does anyone else have access to your supplier information?"

"I'm the only one who works with the designer," Neha said, sniffling. "But my team knows who they are, and the company has included me as one of their referred decorators for Indian weddings. People can figure out that we work together."

"Great," she mumbled. Bobbi looked out at the green lawn, dewy with late summer morning, the main villa of the hotel in the distance, and the fields of grapevines beyond that. She used her toes to push the cottage porch swing and began rocking gently back and forth as she thought through her options.

"Do you have any other mandaps that we can swap it out for?" Bobbi asked.

"Yeah, I have two others that won't be in use that weekend," Neha said, her voice miserable. "They aren't as big or as detailed as the one you had wanted for your friend's wedding, but I can create a unique filler design. I'll make this up to you. I promise."

"I know you didn't do this intentionally," Bobbi said gently. "Just do me a favor and send pictures of whatever you have in stock. I want to see the whole setup of each of the mandaps you can put up. Including the clown mandap."

There was a long pause. "I'm sorry, *what*?"

Bobbi leaned back against the seat, grateful for the calming sweet breeze as she rocked. "I need you to work your design magic and somehow manage to reconfigure that mandap into something spectacular. Because I'm a petty bitch, and I want whoever is trying to fuck with this wedding to hate the fact that we're thriving."

This time, Neha gasped. "Bobbi, do you have a shaadi saboteur? Is someone really trying to ruin your friend's wedding?"

"I do, and yes. I think you were targeted."

"That dickwad!" Neha snapped. "Oh my god, yes. I'm in. I'll see if I can get someone to do me a favor and repaint it so it may be in the shape of a clown, but it won't *look* like one. I'll send the other designs over, too. And thanks for understanding, Bobbi. If it was anyone else, I'm sure they would've just straight-up fired me."

"Brown girls have to stick together," Bobbi said. "And I know that this wasn't anything you could've stopped, Neha."

She heard the cottage door open and looked up to see a shirtless Benjamin, still yawning, step out onto the porch. His thick hair stood up in odd angles, and his beard was scruffy from a sleepless night. He stretched, and his hard chest, covered with just the right amount of hair, flexed. The gold pendant he always wore still hung around his neck, a religious symbol that she was very aware of pressing against her skin when they were chest to breast most of the night.

He was gorgeous, no doubt about it. Thankfully, the man had

put on a pair of athletic shorts, otherwise he would've had the neighboring cottages looking out their windows and seeing a fantastic view of his body.

When did he have time to work out to look like that?

"Hey, Bobbi, I'll do what I can to try to help find your saboteur, let me know," Neha said, interrupting her train of thought. "I'm going to figure out where there was a change in the order from my supplier and give you whatever details I can on that front. For the rest of your friend's wedding, I'll personally store and manage all the decorations."

Benjamin crossed the porch, dropped a kiss to the crown of Bobbi's head, then sat in the porch swing next to her. He slid his palms down her naked thighs and pulled her legs onto his lap before taking control of the porch swing's gentle back-and-forth movement. Bobbi shifted so she could lie flat on her back, the phone still pressed to her ear.

"I appreciate that," Bobbi said. "And if you could keep this between us . . ."

"Oh of course," Neha said. She let out a shuddering sigh, as if she'd come over the hump of her emotional outburst and was on the other side of it, ready to tackle what came next. "I'm going to close the storage unit for now. I can't look at this thing."

With one last goodbye, Bobbi hung up the phone. "Why me?" she said and closed her eyes.

"I take it that wasn't good news," Benjamin mused, as he began to massage her feet, from her toes down to her heels.

She opened Neha's text again and held it out for Benjamin to see. "This is supposed to be Kareena and Prem's mandap."

"Holy shit, is that a *clown face*?" Benjamin asked, taking the phone from her.

When Bobbi nodded, Benjamin, lacking all sense of self-control, burst out laughing.

"This is not exactly a funny situation, Bunty."

"Bobbi, it's a *clown face*. Of course it's funny! Clowns are hilarious."

*There are always two types of people when it comes to clowns.*

"I have to get this to the aunties. I hope they find something before the wedding because this is getting out of control. God knows what else this person will do."

"I got a note," Benjamin said.

Bobbi sat up. "Excuse me?"

He was still staring at the clown picture. "Yeah, I got it at the restaurant," Benjamin said. "I was in a rush to get down here to see you, and then *we* were in a rush, so I saved it for us to talk about later."

"What did the note say?" Bobbi asked.

"Something about how they're going to make sure that the wedding is a disaster. The letters are cut out from magazines and everything. Someone is playing a prank on us."

Bobbi lay back, covering her face with her hands. "This cannot be happening. How can there be this many gaps in my processes that one person is wreaking this much havoc? This is my best friend's wedding, and it should be the most amazing event I can possibly create! Instead, it's a disaster. And selfishly, if my uncle finds out about this, he'll bring it up every time I push him to change something."

"I'm sure we'll find a solution before that happens," Benjamin said, squeezing her calf.

She propped herself up on her elbows. "We?" she asked.

"We," he repeated. His voice had that hard, firm tone again. "We're in this together, right? Isn't that what you told me?"

She nodded, nerves fluttering in her belly. This was probably as good as any time to have the conversation since their brains weren't fogged with sex. "I guess I'm curious about what *we* means. Like as friends who are in a monogamous situationship? As people planning a wedding who have fun? Or as . . . more."

He grabbed her hand and pulled her up to plant a solid kiss on her mouth. "I mean me and you. *We* as in we aren't seeing other people because we're exclusive. And we're too old to get caught up in semantics and code words."

"How long is that 'we' until? Through the wedding?"

"Until the day I no longer make you happy," he said, his expression solemn.

Some of her nerves eased, but she wondered if *she* could make Benjamin happy in the long term. Where would his next restaurant be? Was he going to move back to California one day? And he was so close with his family. What if they didn't like her?

She could already hear the bicultural sides of her brain warring with each other. On one hand, she wanted to say, "Fuck them if they treat you like shit. They don't deserve you if they judge you." But then, the side that fully acknowledged the fact that her Desi identity was inherently community-driven instead of individualistic had to wonder how that would impact her relationship with Benjamin.

Benjamin kissed her again, his lips soft and sweet against hers. "You feel okay after last night, right?" His fingers fluttered over her wrists where he'd tied her. "We didn't get to talk about whether you liked it or want to do it again."

"Yes," she said, smiling for the first time that morning. "But thank you for checking. You gave me exactly what I needed and delivered way more than what I expected, Benjamin Padda." She'd never experienced bondage like that before. Once in college, the guy she was sleeping with bought fuzzy handcuffs from the sex shop in New Brunswick near campus, but they unlatched with one quick pull. No, those ropes were meant to keep her in. She'd wanted it since that first moment he'd tied her blouse at Cipriani's.

"You were perfect, Bobbi Kaur. Like fucking royalty."

This time, Bobbi kissed him, enjoying the feel of his thick beard against her cheeks. She stroked a hand over his shoulders. "Why don't we get dressed, get some coffee, and come back here to drink it in bed before we meet with the chef? I made reservations for dinner at the restaurant here on the premises, too, just to see how they do with food service."

"Since my flight is out of Philadelphia on Sunday morning, why don't we cancel reservations and order room service? In fact, we can get coffee later, and—"

Her phone buzzed and since it was still in Benjamin's hand, he was able to read the screen before she could grab it.

**VEERA:** Update please!

**KAREENA:** We want to know if your year of celibacy is over.

"Was it really a year of celibacy?" Benjamin said. His grin was so deliriously happy that Bobbi had to laugh.

"Sometimes, having sex with another person is way more trouble than it's worth," she said as she stood, phone clutched to her chest. "Work isn't nearly as complicated as a man."

"Until someone sends in the clowns?"

Bobbi rolled her eyes at the fact that it took Benjamin a solid minute before he could control his laughter. Clowns weren't even that funny, especially not when she had to deal with them for

Kareena and Prem's wedding mandap. Damn it, she really needed to talk to the aunties.

"Can you please go get dressed for coffee?" Bobbi asked after Benjamin's laughter subsided. "I need to make one last phone call before I come back inside."

Benjamin also stood, then wrapped Bobbi up in a hug, his palms stroking over the curve of her ass. She loved that he squeezed liberally.

"I like it when you're not being a dick," she said.

"I'll admit, I kind of like it when you are," he replied. Benjamin smacked her ass cheek with a firm quick tap that had her straining against him. She'd never felt this drawn to, this attracted to someone like Benjamin, and if he could have her melting with an ass slap, she was in big trouble.

"Dress, then coffee, then bed," she said and pulled away.

She waited until he opened the cabin door before she sat back on the swing to call Kareena and Veera.

"Sapno ki rani?"

"Mhm?" She looked up to see him stopped in the doorway.

He opened his mouth to say something, then paused, shaking his head. "Never mind."

"No, what is it?"

"It's nothing, really." He stroked a hand over his beard. "Hey, should I shave this off? It's getting a bit much."

She knew that he wasn't telling her the whole truth, but from experience, sometimes finding out the truth led to heartbreak. She wasn't ready to have her heart broken by Benjamin just yet. They'd just fit together, drawing closer with each conversation. How often had she felt like herself in front of a lover the way she felt with Benjamin? But their lives were chaotic, and the wedding was keeping them together. So the truth could wait for now.

"Keep the beard," she finally said. "I've always preferred a man with a beard."

He winked, then said in Punjabi, "Hurry up, Bobbi. I want us to have some coffee and sex before we must go to work, please!"

It wasn't until he closed the door behind him that Bobbi finally laughed.

# CHAPTER 17

## Benjamin

*Monday*

**BENJAMIN:** I'm still thinking of that spectacular weekend with you.

**BOBBI:** Me too. As great as phone sex was this morning, it's not the same as a weekend at a vineyard in a private cottage. But the #Vermann wedding party is getting fitted for clothes in two weeks. I guess you'll have to write me poetry or something until then.

**BENJAMIN:** Listen, I'm no poet, but I'll make it up to you in other ways. I promise.

*Tuesday*

**BOBBI:** Bunty. When you asked for me to share my location, I thought it was a little stalkerish, but I was curious to see what you would do with the information.

**BOBBI:** I didn't expect you to have someone deliver food every 4 hours.

**BENJAMIN:** You forget to eat when you work.

**BOBBI:** I'm not going to stop to finish a four-course meal every time!

**BENJAMIN:** My girlfriend should always have access to four-course meals.

**BOBBI:** . . .

**BOBBI:** You know, I think that's the first time we've prescribed the official label. And because of that, you're off the hook. For today.

*Wednesday*

**BENJAMIN:** I was going to fly east to get fitted for the tuxes, but now Prem's mom wants all the groomsmen and family to get fitted in OC. Apparently some uncle has a cousin-brother who can get a deal on suits. Both sherwanis and tuxes. We'll see how this goes.

**BOBBI:** She just told me, too. I guess our next rendezvous will be at the #Vermann Vegas trip the following week over Labor Day weekend.

**BENJAMIN:** I can try to move things around to come and visit sooner. Or maybe you can come out to California? I'll buy the ticket and come pick you up myself. I'll set you up in a hotel so you have space, and you don't have to stay with me at my parents' house.

**BOBBI:** Wait, how did I not know this? You live with your parents in Cali? And you live with Deepak here. Bunty, do you have your own space?

**BENJAMIN:** I have my own wing at my parents' place with a separate entrance, rani. The privileged Punjabi diaspora kid of the Naan King. Getting my own place never seemed necessary. So? Cali?

**BOBBI:** It's busy season for me. I can't leave for another weekend, especially not if I'm going to Vegas after that. I'm sorry.

**BENJAMIN:** I guess we'll just have to wait three weeks to see each other. But we'll talk every day. I promise.

**BOBBI:** Distance plus our work makes things difficult. We both know that. It's a lot harder than I expected and we've just started.

**BENJAMIN:** We'll talk tonight. I want you to feel like it's worth the effort, Bobbi. That I'm worth the effort.

**BOBBI:** I feel the same way. And thanks for lunch today. I was hungry and it showed up at exactly the right time.

*Thursday*

**BENJAMIN:** Hey, I didn't hear from you last night. Everything okay?

**BOBBI:** Long event. Super chaos. I tried calling this morning.

**BENJAMIN:** Afternoon meetings with the Naan King himself. I can try tonight?

**BOBBI:** More events. I can let you know when I'm on my way home?

**BENJAMIN:** I'll have my phone on me.

*Friday*

**BOBBI:** I tried to get you last night and this morning. I'm back-to-back today, but I should be able to step away for a quick phone call.

**BENJAMIN:** I'm looking at restaurant locations today, but I'll keep my phone with me.

**BOBBI:** Oh? For your new location?

**BENJAMIN:** Yes. My parents and family think it's a good idea for me to focus my attention on the West Coast. My father is still pushing for me to be the advisor to my brother for a year to help with the transition.

**BOBBI:** That makes sense if you think it's best for you, too.

**BENJAMIN:** I haven't made up my mind yet. We're weighing all the options, Bobbi. East Coast makes sense too.

> **BOBBI:** You really don't need to explain yourself. It's okay. Seriously. I understand that sometimes we have to make choices that move people apart from each other.

> **BENJAMIN:** But that is only a physical distance which can be rectified. I'll talk to you tonight. Heading out tomorrow for fittings.

*Saturday*

> **BENJAMIN:** Hey, I know our schedules have been insane. I miss you.

Benjamin stared at the last text he sent to Bobbi. She wasn't reaching out as frequently anymore, just like she'd disconnected before their trip to the vineyard. Except things were different now. They'd spent a weekend in Messina filled with quiet moments, sexy experiences, and hours of conversation. Now that they'd been together, that they'd spent so much more time with each other, the loss felt greater than before.

"Here," Prem said, and held out a whiskey glass. "If we have to deal with my mother for the next two hours, we should at least have alcohol. And if you want food, I put it over there." He motioned to a small folding table in the corner with a small cheese and crackers tray from the grocery store.

"Your mother isn't that bad," Benjamin said, taking the whiskey. He swirled the glass then sipped. It was perfect. "I thought this was just supposed to be us and your immediate family."

"This is my immediate family according to my parents," Prem said dryly as he motioned to the small, crowded shop. His entourage had taken over. There were two uncles standing on platforms in front of trifold mirrors getting fitted. Prem's father had just been fitted and was walking through the rows of tuxes, hands behind his back. He'd periodically lean down to squint at a price tag, then make a sour expression or bobble his head side to side.

Prem's second cousins from Vancouver had also come down to get fitted and were walking around in white undershirts, flexing in every reflective surface. Deepak was standing in the corner, his work phone in his hands, brow furrowed as he tried to coordinate his team in New York. Prem's mother, elegant in her matching linen pantsuit, was laughing with the store owner, a frail, older Desi man in a beige sweater and white kurtha underneath.

"I wish we could've done this back East," Benjamin murmured.

Prem nudged his arm, and when Benjamin glanced at him, his friend looked remorseful. "I'm sorry, dude. Really. My mom had her own plans and sort of made the decision before any of us could stop her. I know you wanted to see Bobbi. Especially since you just started dating her."

Benjamin shook his head. "That's not it. I feel like I've been in a relationship with her for so long. Maybe because she'd taken up residence in my head for months. Even when we were arguing, she *meant* something to me. Her words used to be as sharp as darts and each one hurt. And now that we're finally starting something together . . ."

"You don't know if she is with you because it's just passion," Prem said, finishing Benjamin's thought. "Or if it's something more."

"Exactly." He took another sip of the whiskey. Maybe he needed to stop overthinking everything and focus on just enjoying his time with her. They were both busy professionals who lived for work, had insane physical chemistry, and common beliefs and interests. Why should he spend valuable brain space thinking about whether or not she enjoyed their time together as much as he did, and if their relationship was worth going out of the way to coordinate schedules and responsibilities?

Even as he processed that thought, he knew it wasn't right. But the truth was still too uncomfortable to accept.

When his phone buzzed again, he unlocked it so fast to read the new message that he almost fumbled the whiskey.

> **BOBBI:** It looks like our shaadi saboteur is at it again. I just got this note delivered to our offices.

Underneath the text message was an image of a piece of paper that had cutout magazine letters in various sizes and shapes. The message read, *It's not over yet.*

"This is getting ridiculous," Benjamin mumbled.

"What is?" Prem asked.

He quickly pressed the phone to his chest, smiling sheepishly. Shit, Benjamin thought. He'd totally forgotten that the groom of the damn wedding was standing right next to him.

"It's nothing. Here, hold this." He handed Prem his whiskey glass and, taking a few steps to the left, typed a quick message back.

> **BENJAMIN:** Do you think we need to report this to the police? This person is starting to sound threatening, Bobbi. I don't like it.

> **BOBBI:** I'm going to ask the aunties what they think. I told them they had complete responsibility with this situation, and if they don't figure something out then I'm going to have to tell Kareena and Prem, which none of us want.

"What do you have to tell Prem and Kareena that you don't want them to know?"

Benjamin jumped and nearly crashed into a table of artfully arranged bow ties. He hit the corner, and a bolt of pain shot down his thigh upon impact. "Son of a bitch!" He rubbed at the spot even as he turned to face his best friend.

Deepak looked bored as he stood, hands tucked in his pockets. "Dude, I wasn't even trying to be sneaky."

Benjamin's heart was still beating like a drum. Where did this guy even come from? A second ago, he had been standing across the room on his phone, but now he was peering over Benjamin's shoulder.

"Hold up," Prem said. He put his and Benjamin's glasses on the nearest console table and made a T with his hands. "Who is texting you, Bunty, and what is it that you should be telling me and my fiancée?"

"It's nothing. We're just talking about the, ah, bachelor party."

"He's lying," Deepak said. "Bunty always gets twitchy when he's doing something he doesn't want us to know." He grabbed one of the glasses on the counter and took a sip. "Damn, that's good whiskey."

"Do you fucking mind?" Benjamin said to him.

Deepak shook his head. "Not at all."

Prem stepped closer, his voice lowering so that it reached just the three of them, inches apart. He looked like he was ready to cut Benjamin open, which he was completely capable of doing as a cardiologist. "Spill it."

Benjamin looked at both of his friends, and then weighed the pros and cons. If he told Prem and Deepak, then he could ask them for their help in finding the shaadi saboteur. Three heads were always better than one. But the cons were that this was Prem's wedding, and he hated for the day to be tarnished by the thought that someone was trying to ruin it for him. Not to mention, this was the one thing that Bobbi had asked of him.

To keep this a secret.

"You have three seconds otherwise I'm going to tell my mother that you're hiding something," Prem snapped. "And then let's see how quickly you cave."

Benjamin looked over at Prem's mother. She was now surrounded by the shop employees with stacks of shirts on the counter in front of her. Telling Auntie would be a terrible thing. The scales had tipped.

"Fine," he said. He looked around and noticed a small alcove sectioned off with a curtain at the far corner of the store. After making sure everyone in the wedding party looked like they were occupied, he motioned for his friends to follow him.

Benjamin knew realistically that they all looked fucking ridiculous as they piled into the fitting room space and closed the curtain. They were squeezed shoulder to shoulder, facing each other in the shape of a triangle.

"Prem, I hate to be the one who tells you this, but someone is trying to sabotage your wedding," Benjamin whispered.

"*What?* You're joking."

"You dragged us in here just to feed us some bullshit?" Deepak asked. He rolled his eyes. "Come on, man. I thought you were better than that. What's really going on?"

"That's it," Benjamin said quietly. "At first, someone tried to change the menu but that felt like a harmless prank. Then it got serious when the cake that Bobbi had ordered was canceled and she had to go to a different vendor. We started getting notes. Weird ones, with magazine cutout letters. And then last weekend, when Bobbi and I went to the venue, she got a call that said the mandap that came in was the wrong one and now Bobbi's problem-solving by finding something that's just as good if not better. Today she got another note."

Benjamin opened the image from Bobbi and held it out for both Prem and Deepak to see.

"This cannot be happening," Prem said as he scrubbed his hands over his face. "What the hell? Who would want to fuck with my wedding?"

Benjamin shook his head. "I don't know, man. But whoever it is really does not want this thing to go off without a hitch."

"I wonder if it's her sister," Deepak whispered. "Remember how she lost it on her family at her engagement party because everything wasn't perfect?"

"Bindu is focused on her baby," Prem said. "And her husband, Loken, is too busy trying to keep his mom happy. She's visiting from Italy right now, and apparently she's a tyrant."

"Bobbi already talked to both of them," Bunty said. "They've been ruled out."

"Then what are we going to do?" Prem asked. "Kareena wants this wedding now. It feels right to her. I want to give her this day that's just for her, about her, to celebrate. If anything happens to ruin it, I swear to god, I'm going to cause bodily injury, and I refuse to stop the bleeding. Fuck the Hippocratic Oath."

"Okay, Amitabh Bachchan," Deepak said, hands raised. "Slow

down. No need to seek vengeance just yet. Bunty, what have you done to try to figure out who it is?"

Benjamin winced. "We called Kareena's aunties."

Both Prem and Deepak let out a deep groan.

"Hey, Bobbi and I don't have the bandwidth to do any investigative work right now, but the aunties are determined to put a stop to it."

"The aunties are *chaos*, Bunty," Prem hissed. "God knows what they'll do!"

"Hey, you don't know that," Benjamin said.

"No, we all know that," Deepak said, crossing his arms over his chest. "They're loose cannons."

"You have not helped since the moment you showed up, you know that?" Benjamin said, his irritation growing.

Deepak shrugged. "I think that depends on your definition of help."

"*There is only one fucking definition, Deepak.*"

"Shh!" Prem said, closing one hand into a fist. "Did Bobbi come up with the idea to talk to the aunties?"

"Yeah, of course."

Prem seemed to calm then, settling back on his heels. "I mean, she has the most sense out of everyone in this situation, so if she thinks it's a good idea, then we'll just have to trust her."

Benjamin nodded. He hadn't been sure about telling the aunties either at first, but they seemed like they had it covered. Every other week, they texted both Benjamin and Bobbi whenever they found something, which frankly wasn't much.

"Why don't we give them some time before we make any decisions?" Benjamin said. "Until then, let's just keep this between us, okay? I don't think anyone else should find out. It'll become harder and harder for the aunties to find the shaadi saboteur if everyone knows about it."

Prem clasped both sides of Benjamin's neck and pulled him closer until they were nose to nose. "I love you like a brother, but I'm calling in a favor. The aunties aren't doing this by themselves. You're helping them."

Benjamin pulled back, racking his brain. "I don't owe you a favor!"

"Remember that video the South Asian Association posted on their website of you at Bollywood karaoke our second year? I got rid of it for you. I never called in the I.O.U."

Benjamin had erased that embarrassing moment from his memory. It came flooding back and pooled in his stomach as dread. He'd never live it down if his staff, his family, or, god forbid, Bobbi found it. "Fine," he said. "I'll get more involved than I already am and support the aunties in the search."

"Thank you," Prem said with a deep sigh. "Deepak, you also have to help."

Deepak's eyes bugged. "What? No way, man. This is out of my league."

"There is an unequal distribution of work in this wedding party," Benjamin said, nodding. He was already feeling the strain and pressure of all of it. "You have to carry your weight."

Deepak groaned, dropping his head back as if he were throwing a tantrum. "Fine. I have money. Can I use that to fix anything?"

"The Vegas trip," Prem and Benjamin said in unison.

"What? How is that fair? You know how expensive alcohol is in Vegas."

"It's that or you're added to the Auntie WhatsApp group with me and Bobbi," Benjamin said.

"Vegas it is," Deepak replied without missing a beat.

Prem nodded. "Thanks. I wouldn't be able to do this without both of you. Okay, we just have to get through the next six weeks and then this whole thing is over and I can settle into forever with the love of my life."

It was strange to hear Prem talk about love when he'd been so anti-love for years after his former fiancée's death, Benjamin thought. But it was good to see him healing and happy.

"We'll figure this out," Deepak said, clasping Prem's shoulder. "And your wedding is going to be great."

"Yes," Benjamin said, even though he wasn't sure any of them believed that. It was worth saying out loud in case manifestation was a thing.

"Okay, we're going to step outside," Prem said quietly, motioning to the curtain, "and pretend everything is cool. And after this, I need regular updates. I can then redirect information away from Kareena if need be. Got it?"

They all nodded, tapping their fists together as a trio, like the brothers they were.

When Benjamin opened the curtain, a look of calm collectiveness painted on his face, he was met with the entire wedding party standing around in a half circle staring at them.

All three friends froze.

"Busted," Prem mumbled.

"What are you three up to?" Prem's mother said, her eyebrow raised. She stood in the center of the semicircle, arms crossed over her chest.

"Prem wanted to get you and Uncle something for the wedding as a thank-you gift of appreciation, and he was just showing us pictures," Deepak said smoothly. "He didn't want you two to know, but oops! We got caught."

"Yes!" Benjamin said. Looping his arms around Prem's and Deepak's shoulders. "He's so grateful. We all are. This wedding is going to be better than anything your friends have ever seen. We're sure of it."

Prem's mother melted before their eyes. She sniffled, then shooed them away with one hand. "Bewakoof duffers."

The room seemed reassured that they were being sneaky for all the right reasons, and everyone scattered, returning to their corners and resuming what they were doing before the interruption.

When Benjamin's phone buzzed again, he was almost positive that it was going to be another catastrophe he'd have to handle, but Bobbi's name popped up on the screen.

**BOBBI:** I miss you too. Call me tonight. Let's have dinner together.

### *Indians Abroad News*
Relationship column

An Indian wedding is much more fun with chaos. It's best if children understand that and leave the wedding planning to their parents.

**Mrs. W. S. Gupta**
**Avon, New Jersey**

# CHAPTER 18

## Bobbi

*3:30 A.M. text message:*

**BENJAMIN:** Rich potato curry, hot and fresh, with baked parmesan shards.

*9:30 A.M. text message:*

**BENJAMIN:** I'll be waiting at the hotel for you.

*Auntie WhatsApp Chat 11:30 A.M.:*

**FARAH AUNTIE:** Bobbi, when you come back to New Jersey, we must talk. We have some developments that we think you should know.

**BOBBI:** Auntie, you have to tell me now. There is no way I'm going to relax with that kind of message.

**MONA AUNTIE:** Just tell her, Farah.

**FARAH AUNTIE:** Fine. We think it's someone within your wedding planning business that's actually trying to stop the wedding.

**BOBBI:** WHAT??? What makes you think that?

**FALGUNI AUNTIE:** Based on the timeline that Farah Auntie put in her spreadsheets, the only way this person knew about the mandap would be if they worked with you, beta.

**BOBBI:** Let's meet in person when I'm back. Thank you, aunties.

Bobbi looked at the text chain again before she put her phone in her oversize tote. She sat in the corner of the stretch limo, and for the past twenty minutes she'd listened to Veera talk to Deepak about Lisa Frank nostalgia from the seats next to her, and watched Prem and Kareena across the small aisle sit hip to hip, wrapped up in each other. The route from airport to hotel on the strip wasn't that long, but it made her feel so . . . alone.

Her partner—despite their frequent inability to coordinate their schedules while long distance, she was starting to think of Benjamin as a partner—was supposed to meet them in Vegas. She was buzzing with excitement to see him at the airport, but when her flight had taxied to the gate, he'd texted her that he'd meet her at the hotel.

That was disappointing enough, but then the aunties' WhatsApp chat came through.

Who could possibly be trying to sabotage her work? A small, bitter part of her thought of her cousin for one fraction of a second before guilt practically swallowed her whole. No, she'd grown up with Sukhi as if they were sisters. Sukhi was warm, loving, and always cheered Bobbi on. Any doubts of that were seeded from this fictitious competition she'd fabricated all on her own after her conversation with her uncle.

Everyone at the business worked as a team. Hell, they were *family*.

She was going to have to tell her uncle and aunt about this if it got any worse. That was the last thing she wanted to do.

Maybe Benjamin would have some insight into Farah Auntie's prediction. She rubbed at her temples, wishing she'd packed more aspirin than she did. And she'd packed a lot of aspirin, all in hopes of helping her switch between answering emails in the morning and going out at night.

She hated to admit it, but she overcommitted. She said yes to everything without thinking about whether or not she could actually handle the workload. Between her overflowing summer event list, the shaadi saboteur, and getting Gwen to email her back on the simplest shit for Kareena's wedding, Bobbi really needed this weekend to decompress before she jumped back into the work fray.

"You okay?" Kareena said, leaning forward in the limo seat. "You look stressed."

"I'm great," Bobbi said. She smiled, then reached out to squeeze Kareena's hand. "This weekend is going to be great. Hey, Deepak, thanks for the limo."

He leaned around Veera and winked at her, then held up his champagne flute. "I want to make sure I do my part so that Kareena and Prem have a wedding that no one will forget."

"Idiot," Prem mumbled.

Bobbi had no idea what that was about, but when it came to the guys, she'd learned in her brief interaction with all of them together that it was best to leave it alone. "We have a pretty loose itinerary," she continued, "but since we're all here, maybe it's a good time to give you all your uniforms."

Kareena pushed her glasses up her nose. "Say what now?"

This was the one thing Bobbi didn't regret spending her time and money on. She unzipped her tote bag and pulled out the tiara she'd stored away earlier that morning.

"I knew you'd do this," Kareena said, smiling. She gently placed it on top of her head and fixed it as firmly as possible. "What do you think?" she said, turning to Prem.

"Perfect," he said. "At least I don't have to—"

"Yes, you do!" Bobbi retrieved the T-shirts that she had made. They were rolled up and tied with different colored ribbons so she could easily identify them. She gave Prem his first, and watched as he unfolded it and held it up against his chest. His, like the rest of the shirts, had a faded image of an album cover similar to the vintage music T-shirts in the early nineties.

"You and Kareena are *Folklore* and *Evermore*," Bobbi said. "I, of course, am *Midnights*, and Benjamin is *Reputation*. Deepak and Veera? You're *Lover* and *Fearless*."

Kareena's eyes widened as she shook out her T-shirt to see for herself. "Oh my god, this is brilliant! Bobbi, you're the best!"

"How can we have a wedding party weekend in Vegas without Taylor Swift album cover shirts to match?" Bobbi mused.

Veera held the T-shirt over her chest to look at the faded pink *Fearless* image. "I would've preferred *Red*."

"I bought a backup in case you were feeling more *Red* than *Fearless*."

Veera brightened. "Kareena said it already, but you *are* the best."

"I think we're all going to look weird as a group of brown people with the picture of the same blond woman on our chests," Deepak grumbled. He shoved his shirt into the leather backpack he'd tucked between his ankles then picked up his champagne flute again. "When are we supposed to wear this? To that Magic Mike show, or to Bunty's fine spirits and burrito food crawl?"

"We'll figure it out," Bobbi said smoothly.

The limo slowed and turned into the wide U-shaped drive in front of their hotel. It was a newer one. Trendier than the classic statement hotels on the strip. The rooms were reportedly bigger, and suite balconies were curved outward to allow for lounge chairs. Although Bobbi hadn't booked the place, Deepak proved to be as meticulous as she was and provided an itinerary with links and calendar-synced notifications. He'd also been nonchalant about the fact that there were only four bedrooms in the massive suite they'd secured, and Bobbi was assigned to the same room as Benjamin.

Bobbi felt someone kick her shin and she looked over at Kareena, her eyes bright behind her clear plastic frames. The new floral maxi dress fluttered around her knees as she shifted closer until they were practically cheek to cheek. "Do you remember how freshman year we signed up for the astronomy club because we thought it would be cool to do some space things together as roommates?"

Bobbi snorted. The memory was so easy to recall and felt as fresh as yesterday. "You mean the astronomy club that was really a cover for a bunch of people going to the middle of a field and smoking weed? We were so naïve that when they told us it was called the Sky High Club, we thought that was a clever way to refer to the stars. We were probably the only nerds there interested in astronomy."

Kareena giggled, then her voice softened to a whisper. "Did you ever think that those nerds would be the kind of people who went to Vegas with a bunch of hot men in a limo?"

"Absolutely," Bobbi said. She turned and gave Kareena's cheek a smacking kiss. "Because even then, we were always the type of nerds to go after whatever the fuck we wanted."

The limo came to a stop, and Bobbi's nerves returned with full force as she realized that she was finally in the same space as Benjamin. Her heart began to pound as she scanned the entrance of the hotel through the tinted window.

Good god, what was she doing? She was acting ridiculous. She'd been with Benjamin a few times . . . okay, a lot of times over the course of one weekend. But before that, it had been . . . well, it had always been *something* with Benjamin.

The door opened, and Prem and Kareena exited first. Then Deepak. Veera stopped before she scooted out and turned to face Bobbi.

"Hey, you seem a bit off. Is everything okay?"

Bobbi nodded, hating that her best friends could easily pick up on the edginess she felt from wanting to see Benjamin. "I feel like an idiot, but I'm really excited, Veera."

Veera had the softest heart out of all their friends. Her expression softened and she wrapped her arms around Bobbi, squeezing her in a hug. "If you want, I can pretend there's some sort of emergency for the next few hours so you and Benjamin can have some alone time."

"I'm not even going to lie to you, I'm very tempted to take you up on that offer."

Veera nodded, her mouth set in a line of determination, then scooted out of the limo. Bobbi followed close behind. She stepped out into the heat, the burning hot, dry air enveloping her. After getting their bags, they strolled in through the thick glass sliding doors and into an air-conditioned, opulent lobby filled with glass and chrome. There, in the center of the lobby, Benjamin stood in a button-down shirt, cargo shorts, and flip-flops. He looked absolutely wonderful with his thick hair groomed back, his beard trimmed, and that ever-present gold chain hanging against his collarbone, glinting in the light.

All he had to do was open his mouth to puncture her ballooning joy. ·

"The Vermann have arrived!" he said, arms outstretched. Like absolute fools, Prem and Deepak made a run for him and the three tackled each other in a group hug.

"I bet that fantasy about three hot men in Vegas isn't so hot anymore, is it?" Bobbi said to Kareena.

"They all can't be perfect."

She laughed, and this time when she turned to face Benjamin, he was looking right back at her. His piercing gaze reignited all those feelings that surged within her whenever they were together. She was in so much trouble. She had to be careful, so very careful, if she wanted to come out of this with her heart intact.

He crossed the lobby and without a second's hesitation, wrapped her up in a hug that she didn't know she needed. Then, pressing a sweet kiss against the corner of her mouth, he said, "I missed you the most."

Aware that their friends were watching them, Bobbi pulled back, the only connection between them was the soft touch of knuckles brushing against each other. "We should check in."

"Already done," Benjamin said. "I dropped off my bag too. Deepak, you outdid yourself. The suite is incredible."

A hotel luggage concierge appeared at that moment with a cart and began loading their luggage. "This will be waiting for you in the room when you're ready," they said before rolling the cart away.

"Since it's lunchtime," Deepak said, "I was thinking that we could probably just order room service and eat out on the balcony. Then maybe head to the pool or something—"

"Actually," Veera started, "I'd love if we can go check out this pizza place that I heard about. The last time I was in Vegas I was here for work, and I didn't get a chance to really explore. But everyone who was at the conference with me said that the pizza place was the best thing on earth. Deepak, do you mind if we do that?"

He looked startled but shook his head. "Are you sure? I mean, we can order it in and just hang out in the—"

"I want to see it," Veera said.

"I mean, we still have to go upstairs to put these things in the room—"

"Bobbi can do that," Veera said. She motioned to Bobbi and Benjamin. "I *hate* that you have to work, Bobbi, but why don't you finish up now so we can have some fun tonight together?"

"I think that's a great idea," Benjamin said. He gripped Bobbi's hand in his. "You know what? I'll show you the room, and guys, I'll meet up with you in a bit. Why don't you head out now?"

"Does everyone think that we were born yesterday?" Prem asked Kareena.

"No, which is why they assumed you were smart enough to keep your mouth shut," Kareena replied.

"I don't know what the fuck is going on," Deepak said, hands up in surrender.

Prem shook his head. "It's fine, dude. Play along because it's a little weird seeing those two together and not wanting to kill each other. Veera, did you say pizza?"

"Good idea, right?" Veera responded, nodding like a bobble-head. "Bobbi, Bunty, we'll see you guys soon." Then she winked at Bobbi before ushering everyone through the glass doors again.

"Are we really alone?" Benjamin asked after a minute.

Bobbi looked around the crowded lobby, swarming with

groups ready to begin their long-weekend celebration. Strangers. They didn't count because what happened in Vegas was supposed to stay in Vegas.

"It seems that way."

Benjamin slipped Bobbi's tote off her shoulder and onto his. His fingers intertwined with hers as gracefully and easily as if it had been second nature to him. Their palms pressed together warm and sure as he tugged her toward the elevator bank against the far wall of the lobby.

They didn't say anything as they made the journey up to the thirty-sixth floor. There were a few passengers with them, so they waited patiently as people got off at various stops.

Bobbi thought her heart would be pounding nonstop at this point, but Benjamin's presence made her feel more at ease than she had in weeks. What did that say about their relationship? What did that say about the risk that she was taking when there was a very good chance that he would stay on the West Coast?

When they reached the thirty-sixth floor, there was only one room at the end of a very short hallway. Benjamin pressed a thumb against a biometrics reader. "I think we all have to get our fingerprints scanned if we want to have individual access," Benjamin said. "Have you ever been in an executive suite?"

"For weddings, yes."

"I have as well, but this still blew my mind." He pushed open the door, and Bobbi's jaw dropped. This was no run-of-the-mill executive suite. This was the type of space that people toured on HGTV.

The foyer was a study in marble. There was a grand piano against two-story windows in one corner, an open kitchen, and a long, deep sectional in a sunken living room to the right. A wide spiral staircase led to a second floor. In the corner, lined up in a single row, were their suitcases already delivered from the lobby.

"Oh my god," Bobbi whispered. "How the hell did we get this lucky?"

"Deepak said that his father is colleagues with the guy who owns this place. Apparently the people who had booked the room canceled for the long weekend."

She toed off her shoes at the entrance out of habit and walked across the cool marble tiles into the living space. There were sheer curtains on the outer walls of the living room, but she could see the massive balcony with the deck chairs just begging for her to lie down for a nap. And the kitchen! It was a dream, even though she knew next to nothing about cooking and had been relying on Benjamin's delivery service for almost three weeks now.

Three weeks. She spun to face the man who had tied her up in knots for so long. "Hey," she said. "Where are we staying?"

He pointed up to the second level.

Bobbi didn't say another word. She bolted for the stairs and heard Benjamin's deep, rich laugh right behind her as he followed.

There was only one door that was cracked open, and she assumed that was theirs. She was two steps into the room awash with light when she heard her tote hit the floor, and Benjamin's arms grabbed her from around the waist.

In a move that delighted her so much that she would have given him whatever he wanted in the moment, he picked her up from behind, spun her around, and toppled her onto the king-size bed. She was breathless from the impact, from the scent and feel of him, the softness of down blankets under her.

Benjamin rolled her onto her back and didn't waste any time in kissing her again.

It felt like coming home, and the twin feelings of fear and something beautiful wrapped together inside her chest she worried she'd forget with time and distance.

She kissed him hard, turning their sweet embrace into something more desperate, as she released all the stress and anxiety that had been tightly packed away over the three weeks they'd been apart. As he took over the kiss, holding her head in place as his mouth tasted hers, Bobbi told herself it was stupid, it was utterly ridiculous, to miss someone with such ferocity.

But the more she tried to dismiss her feelings, the harder it became to control them. So she tucked her legs around his waist as they rolled until she was on top, straining against Benjamin with lips and tongues and hands desperate for more.

When they pulled apart for air, Bobbi felt more centered than she had in weeks.

"It has been too long, sapno ki rani," he said, his voice ragged with need as he pushed back her silky blown-out hair that fell in a curtain around their faces. "It's been too long and I *missed* you."

"Me too," she whispered back.

There were no more words as they got undressed, pulled at each other's clothes until they were skin to skin, hands coasting over nakedness, legs intertwining. Benjamin pulled off the sheer lacy underwear she'd purchased just for this trip, and when she was exposed to him, he spread her knees then slapped her pussy with one hard tap. The sound, and reverberating sting, had her hips lifting off the bed, straining for more. She was already so wet for him, writhing against the bed now, begging for more.

"Not yet," he said hoarsely. "Not yet."

He slid off the end of the bed and reached for his bag. Bobbi was desperate for release, so she trailed her fingers over the curve of her belly to touch herself when his sharp retort stopped her.

"Don't you dare finger yourself. That's for me to do."

"I need you."

The bed dipped as he returned to her side, this time with the familiar rope in his hand. "I brought more," he said. "But I want you in this first."

"Yes," she said. Knowing that she now wanted this as much as he did. It thrilled her in a way she'd never experienced before when Benjamin took responsibility for her pleasure so she could find her release.

When she stretched her hands toward the headboard, Benjamin shook his head. "On your stomach."

A thrill rushed through her, and she squirmed in anticipation of what was about to happen. She complied, turning over to reveal her naked back, hands at her sides. Benjamin looped the rope around her so that it created a cross between her breasts. Then he pulled her wrists back and quickly, efficiently, put one on top of the other then tied them together. Unlike handcuffs, this tie had a long tail that fell between the cracks of her cheeks.

"Beautiful," Benjamin said hoarsely.

She pulled, her heart racing at the feeling of being helpless and in his control. Where did he even get the tie from? Did he have it ready for her in his pocket? The idea that he'd been waiting for this exact opportunity had her breathless.

Benjamin tested her pulse, his thumb brushing over her wrist. "Do you want to choose your own safe word this time?"

"Red," she said.

"Okay, rani. We'll keep it light and easy, but I want you to trust me to take care of you. Know that I'm going to make you come, okay? Let go of your control and try to relax your muscles."

She nodded and forced the tension in her shoulders and arms to release.

"Perfect," he said, checking the restraints again. "Are you ready?"

"Yes," she said. "I want you so much." The need was gnawing at her now.

"Me too, rani," he said. He gently helped her to her knees, and then adjusted her legs so that she was facing the sliding closet doors. They were mirrors, and in the well-lit room, she could see everything.

Bobbi was a study in lust. She looked like an image from ancient Indian artwork with voluptuous women showing off their bellies and hips, consumed with pleasure. Her arms tied behind her back, knees spread, breasts and body on full display. Her head tilted back as Benjamin, naked and ready for her, his cock at full attention, began stroking his hands over every exposed inch of skin until he cupped her pussy.

He kissed the shell of her ear and said, "Watch."

She had to stop her eyes from rolling back when his fingers dipped inside her pussy and began teasing her clit in slow, steady circles. Bobbi tried to roll her hips forward, desperate for more, but he had a firm hold on her with the ropes.

"What do you see?" he said in her ear, as his other hand squeezed and fondled her breast. "What do you see, Bobbi?"

"I see you playing with me," she said softly. "I see you t-teasing me."

"Do you want more?"

"Yes. Benjamin, I need you."

Instead of sliding his fingers inside her, instead of rubbing her clit until she came, Benjamin pulled back and returned to his bag at the foot of the bed. She opened her mouth to protest, when he produced a round lavender vibrator, no bigger than a mango, flat on one side with an opening that looked like petals with a round nub in between.

"You like toys, right, Bobbi?" Benjamin said casually. "You have some yourself."

"Wh-what?"

He returned to his position behind her, then pushed between her shoulder blades until her chest was pressed against the bed. Positioning her knees wide, Bobbi heard the soft whir of the motor of the vibrator. Then the cool silicone slide against her pussy and the vibrator moved in a rotating motion, teasing her clit in quick, steady strokes.

Bobbi gasped, a cascade of pleasure wracking through her body, and she shrieked at the onslaught. When her hips lifted off the mattress, the vibrator fell away.

"No you don't," Benjamin said with a soft chuckle. "You move, you'll lose the vibrator. If you want pleasure, baby, you have to stay still, okay?"

"Benjamin," she cried. This time when he put the vibrator in place, her body was coiled tight, her wrists straining at the small of her back, and she rolled forward, pressing into the quick rotating nub that massaged her clit and had her on the verge in seconds.

"Benjamin," she whined. "Take care of me. Please."

"I'm going to fuck you now," Benjamin said. There was the vague sound of a wrapper tearing, and then Benjamin used the long tail of the rope that was tied to her wrists and torso to pull her up. Bobbi gasped when he held her with his strength, suspended over the bed.

"Are you ready for me?"

"Yes!" she shouted. "Green, green, green!" she panted.

The thick head of his cock pressed against her opening, and because she was already so wet, so eager for him, he slid inside her, stretching her until she felt so full, she was choking, gasping for air.

"You're so tight, Bobbi," he said hoarsely. "You're squeezing my cock; did you know that? Your hot little pussy is gripping me like a vise."

She couldn't think, couldn't focus on anything other than the image in front of her in the mirror. A rope wrapped around Benjamin's forearm and fist as he held her up with one hand, his other teasing her clit mercilessly, stroking in and out of her with smooth, coordinated thrusts.

The orgasm came hard and fast. She screamed with it, begging Benjamin for more. Then before she could catch her breath, Benjamin pressed the vibrator against her clit one more time, pushed her chest into the mattress, and held her hips in his wide hands as he fucked her with fast, deep strokes. Their skin slapped together, a sheen of sweat coating her back and her thighs. Then he reached forward, wrapped her hair around his knuckles, and pulled so that she had no choice but to watch in the mirror, tied, spread, and fucked so hard her ass vibrated with each thrust.

She closed her eyes, reveling in the feeling of his passion, of his need for her, and welcomed the rise of another orgasm, this one stronger, fiercer than anything she'd ever experienced before, and as it rolled over her, Bobbi knew that Benjamin had claimed a part of her for the rest of her life.

# CHAPTER 19

## Bobbi

*Note left on the hotel bathroom mirror, traced in steam from a shared shower:*

*There isn't a single dish that I could create that would taste as good as the both of us together.*

Bobbi woke up sore, aching, and completely sated. She'd heard their friends enter the suite a little over an hour ago, but Benjamin had been sleeping, and she'd been too tired to get up herself. Now the itch to check her messages had interrupted her blissful peace.

Turning over, she pressed a kiss against Benjamin's exposed cheek, right about at the razor-sharp cut of his beard. She touched the gold chain at his neck, then his bare shoulder before she slipped off the bed. Benjamin slept peacefully, his hand still tucked under the pillow she was using. Her heart warmed at the sight.

She hated how she felt knowing that he wasn't close enough to see regularly, but what they had was so new and that meant she had to keep her feelings to herself. For now.

After quickly using the bathroom, she put on a pair of her favorite Patiala salwar pants that ballooned at the thigh. She'd ordered them from a South Asian American designer who made them out of the softest yoga pants material for plus-size women.

With that, she added her *Midnights* T-shirt and cinched it under her breasts as a crop top.

"I'm too old to look like this," she whispered to herself. She grabbed her phone, cringing at the number of messages on the screen, before she exited the room.

The suite was quiet, except for the hum of the TV that someone had left on in the living space. Outside the glass wall, Vegas was brightly lit with orange and pink skies as a backdrop. It was already sunset. How was that possible?

She slipped through the door and walked over to the chaise lounges facing the skyline. When she saw Deepak sprawled in one of the chairs, she let out a small yelp.

"Holy shit," she said, pressing a hand to her chest.

Deepak's lips curved in a half smile as he focused on his phone. "Yeah, Bunty is a little jumpy, too."

Bobbi paused at Deepak's comment. She'd yet to see him that way, but then again, they hadn't been together too long. That would be a fun fact to discover on her own, though. Bobbi sat in the empty chaise.

"Working?"

"Yeah," he said absently.

When he went to put his phone away, Bobbi waved a hand at him. "Oh no, keep doing what you need to," she said. "I have to check my messages, too."

"Thank god," Deepak muttered.

They sat in companionable silence for quite a bit of time, answering messages on their phones. Bobbi had almost forgotten that he was there as she emailed distraught brides who weren't sure about color combinations, moms with obscure requests, and vendors struggling with supply chain constraints.

When the soft glow of the balcony lights turned on and the sky began to twinkle with the Vegas skyline, Deepak got up from his seat. "I'm going to go make some coffee. Want some?"

"God yes, I could use a decent cup of caffeine. Is ch—"

"Chai? Yeah, the instant kind, I think. I can bring you a cup," he said. He straightened his shirt, Taylor Swift's face splashed across the front of it, and walked back into the suite.

Bobbi sent a quick message to Benjamin to let him know where she was in case he woke up while she was still outside. Then she dealt with a bridal fitting conflict and two other messages before her phone buzzed in her hand. Gwen's name flashed across the screen. The events manager from Messina Vineyards had rarely picked up the phone, let alone called Bobbi first.

Taking a deep breath, she prepared herself for the worst. "Hi, Gwen, how are you?"

"Bobbi," Gwen said, her tone already bored and dismissive through the receiver.

God, Bobbi hated this woman, and she barely knew her. How was she supposed to work with her long term if this one wedding had such poor communication? Bobbi stood up and paced to the railing. "How can I help you?"

"I finally got through all of the emails you've sent me in preparation for this wedding."

Bobbi wanted to tell her that there were only three emails, and the rest were follow-ups, but that probably wouldn't help her position. "Yes, I wanted to confirm the menu that Chef Benjamin reviewed with Chef Vinny. I provided you a list of all our vendors, and I updated you with information pertaining to our hotel block."

"Yes, that's the one that I have the issue with," Gwen said. She said "issue" like "iss-sue," even though she wasn't British. "Because we weren't sure that there would be enough people to fill the block, we opened the rooms to outside guests, so we actually do not have enough space for your guest requirements at this time."

This was not Bobbi's first rodeo, and she'd been in this same exact position before. She took a moment to censor herself, and said, "We already spoke about this when we were on-site at Messina. We even gave you additional assurances, so you should've been prepared. Based on the agreement we signed with you, we were promised a number of rooms. I'm sorry, you'll have to advise those other parties who've booked that their reservations will be canceled."

Gwen paused on the phone, as if she was processing what Bobbi had just told her.

*That's right, bitch. I just told you that it's a you-problem.*

"That's not in the best interest of Messina," Gwen said, her voice crisp, as if she was trying to reprimand a child for suggesting something so ridiculous.

"It's not in the best interest of Messina to deliver on your contracts? To host weddings with a six-figure budget? To ensure client satisfaction?"

Bobbi turned at the sound of the sliding door opening again. Deepak managed to step outside, chai in both hands. He used a foot to push the door closed behind him as much as possible. When he saw her by the railing on the phone, he made a beeline for the chaise chairs and put the chai on the small round table between them.

When Gwen stuttered, Bobbi turned her back to Deepak to focus on the conversation.

*I can't believe you thought that I would just roll over and be okay with this.*

"Gwen, I promised you that I'd secure more events at Messina Vineyards. I can't do that if you can't deliver on one event. We've already had a poor service experience. Now I can tell Dr. Dil's mother, and their entire network of families, that Messina isn't interested in hosting their wedding based on this conversation—"

"No, no, no," Gwen said in a rush. "Ah, you're absolutely right. With the potential for us to do more business together, I'll work on getting this sorted. But we'd like some assurances that you're looking to be a long-term wedding planner of ours to justify adding staff, canceling rooms, purchasing equipment that you'll need for your *cultural* event . . ."

Bobbi closed her eyes and counted to ten before she said, "It's a cultural event to you, maybe. To us, it's just a wedding. And if Messina Vineyards doesn't want to service South Asian families, then—"

"Of course not," Gwen replied. "No, we believe in diversity, equity, and inclusion. We appreciate the opportunity to learn and provide services to . . . ah, your community."

*Sounds like your human resources department had to do some training, Gwen.*

"Great, then I trust you have it covered. As for assurances, we aren't bending over backward anymore than we already have. I'm so sorry but I'm currently on the West Coast and I'm unable to talk about this any further. Isn't it like, ten over there, Gwen? You should consider starting fresh in the morning, too. Why don't you let me know how the room situation is sorted out, and then we can talk about future opportunities?"

"Of course, I—"

"Have a good night," Bobbi said, then with a little more force than she should've used, she pressed the end button on the call.

"Wow, she sounds awful," Deepak said.

Bobbi turned to face him. "I'm glad that Prem and Kareena secured one of the most exclusive properties in New Jersey, but why does it have to have one of the worst event coordinators I've worked with in recent years?"

Deepak sat in his vacated chair, stretched his legs out, and then picked up one of the mugs. "Prem also told me that the event coordinator is a pain. I think it's something more than just incompetency."

Bobbi crossed the patio. She knew exactly what Deepak was talking about. Even living in New Jersey where there was a huge Desi population, there were a lot of pushbacks, too. Stories of real estate agents drawing lines around counties for their non-Indian clients to avoid because of the large immigrant population were commonplace. "It doesn't matter if Gwen has sour feelings about Indian weddings. I still have to work with her."

"Well, after this wedding is over, you'll never have to see her again."

Bobbi winced.

"Wait, you *do* have to see her again?" Deepak asked, eyes wide. "Why?"

"I have an agreement with my uncle that if I could convince Messina Vineyards to use us as an exclusive planning business, that he'd consider my role at our company more seriously for an executive position. I want more creative control. I need it. I feel . . . stale. I spoke with Kareena about it, and she's supportive and willing to help, but I know that I have to figure out this relationship with Messina on my own."

Bobbi picked up the second cup and took a sip of silky smooth, hot and spicy sweet tea. It was perfect.

Deepak patted the chaise next to him that she'd occupied earlier. "Can you tell me, from one businessperson to another, why the hell you think you have to do this on your own?"

Bobbi took a moment to sit since he had gone to the trouble of making her chai. "Because I've always had to do anything that I've wanted by myself. And I know if I have complete control, then it'll be done the right way."

"Which is why you're trying to handle Gwen on your own," Deepak said. He drank more of his tea. "That makes sense."

Bobbi stared out at the skyline. "I really thought that since Kareena and Prem's mom introduced me to Gwen, that she'd be all onboard with working with me. I guess I just have to try harder."

Deepak chuckled. "Have you talked to Bunty yet about your situation? It sounds like you're in a similar role as his brother."

"Oh yeah," Bobbi said with a grin. She cupped her mug in both hands, enjoying the warmth when a breeze glided over her exposed arms. "He did not like that comparison."

"He has a lot of experience helping Chottu. You can always ask him for advice—"

"No," Bobbi said. That was the last thing she wanted to do. She didn't need a fixer, and she didn't need a man to step in and try to manage the work that she was doing. She'd been on her own for years, and even when it was just her and her uncle, she'd been the one who brought ideas to the table. What meals to cook, when she had to register for extracurricular activities, what to bring for the PTA bake sale. "I can not only figure this out on my own, but I am going to make sure this doesn't impact Kareena and Prem's happiness."

"Asking for help isn't a bad thing, Bobbi."

She turned to look at him. "It can be if you're a woman, Deepak."

He nodded. "Or is that what they want you to believe?"

They sat in silence, until finally Deepak's phone pinging interrupted the peace. "Speaking of Bunty," Deepak said. "His sister just texted. Apparently he might only be able to come for the ceremony and the reception before he has to go back."

"*What?*" The wedding was supposed to be Friday through Sunday. And she had hoped that she had that much time to celebrate with Benjamin alone before he went back to California. "That's so soon. I thought—"

Deepak continued to scroll on his phone with one hand while drinking from his mug with the other. "I was hoping we'd see more of him, but with his move back to California to support his brother inheriting the company—"

"Wait, Bunty is moving back to California? That's a sure thing?" No, it was too soon. They were going to be over before they had a chance to begin.

"You didn't know," Deepak said softly when he finally looked up from his phone. "I'm so sorry, I didn't realize that—"

"It's fine," Bobbi said. "Really." She felt like her rib cage was cracking open. When had this happened? When had they gotten so close that now, the thought of losing someone she never had hurt more than any of the losses she'd faced in her life before?

No, she couldn't allow it. She wouldn't. She had so much going on, so much to live for that Benjamin's presence in her life was only a small speed bump. It had to be. There was an expiration date from the beginning.

"Bobbi," Deepak said. He reached out and brushed her arm. "Are you going to be okay?"

"Of course," she said, and put on her brightest smile for him. "Bunty and I knew it was going to be hard. We are both too dedicated to our work. And I always said that I'd die a bachelor."

Deepak smiled. "Bunty used to say the same thing, you know. His mom would get so upset with him over it."

Even though breathing hurt, she tried to inhale deep. "My uncle would also get upset with me for the same reasons. I'd tell him that the day I died, God was going to shake their head and say, 'Go back to New Jersey, Bobbi Kaur! There are so many bachelors in Edison that you should be able to find someone in your next life!'"

Deepak laughed. "I bet when you were born and your star chart was created for you by the pandit, your family said that you were the raunak, right? When you walk into the room, you brighten all the dark spaces."

"Aww," Bobbi said, touched at how sweet he was being. Deepak reminded her so much of Veera. He had a heightened awareness, a sensitivity to those around him. "Unfortunately, my mother cried on the day of my birth. And then she left me. But that's okay. Because I have family here."

"You do," Deepak said. This time he put his phone down on the table and gripped Bobbi's hand.

She squeezed. "I'm going to be okay," she whispered, her voice shaking. "I mean, we haven't even spent the night at either of our homes yet. It's so new. It's fine. I'll be fine."

Deepak let go, then after a minute, he said, "You know Bunty doesn't even have a place of his own, let alone a bed, right?"

Bobbi laughed, and some of the ache eased.

# CHAPTER 20

## Benjamin

Benjamin woke alone in the big hotel room bed. It was dark outside and the lights from the Vegas strip were shining through the curtains. He reached out to the other side of the bed, and when it felt cool to the touch he sat up. The sheet pooled at his waist.

"Bobbi?"

There was no answer from the adjoining bath. He climbed out of bed, and when he saw the rope on the floor, he grinned at the memory of her tied and suspended. He picked it up, coiled it quickly, and tucked it back in his bag. Retrieving his phone from his previously discarded pants, he saw that it was already 8:00 P.M.

He scrolled through his most recent texts, the ones from his attorney and his restaurant manager congratulating him for finding the perfect location for their next business investment, to his employees letting him know that the opening shift went off without a hitch. He saw Bobbi's name and opened the message.

> **BOBBI:** Downstairs balcony. Having chai with Deepak. ♥

He tapped a fist against the center of his chest, the place that ached when he thought of her. And then read the message again.

"Ugh, god knows what that idiot is going to tell her." He made quick use of the bathroom, then dressed. When he stepped out onto the landing and listened for the sound of his friends, nothing but silence greeted him. It wasn't until he made his way down-stairs to the living space that he heard Bobbi's voice. Moving closer to the slightly ajar balcony doors, he saw his girlfriend and best friend were sitting on lounge chairs under the glow of the overhead lights.

"Do you think that Bunty is ever going to buy his own house?"

Benjamin had gripped the door handle and was ready to walk out when Bobbi asked her question. He froze, brows furrowing.

"I don't think he's ever had a need for his own place," Deepak mused. "When he's ready to settle down, maybe?"

"That's what I was thinking," she replied. The regret in her tone had Benjamin rocking back on his heels. "Maybe when he moves back to California, he'll take the time to figure out what he wants."

"You don't think he's ready to settle down now?"

Benjamin could hear Bobbi's sigh through the screen. "It's more that I don't know how that affects us if his obligations to family are out here on the West Coast."

Benjamin's gut twisted. He didn't know what it meant ei-ther. Because the truth was, right before he left for Vegas, he'd found the perfect location for his third restaurant. It was in Or-ange County, a respectable distance from home, and far enough from Namak that he wouldn't be competing for his other client base. He had some time before he could make an offer on the location, and he planned on taking advantage of every moment. This commitment meant that the majority of his time would be in California, and he would be able to work closely with Chottu as an advisor, which was in the best interests of the people he loved the most.

"I'm not the greatest when it comes to relationship advice," Deepak said, his voice carrying into the house. "But I will tell you this. Bunty will be dedicated to making it work between you two. When he told us about you, Prem and I weren't surprised. Because it felt like you were already an important part of his life."

"I feel the same way about him," Bobbi mused. "But if he's going to be in California more often, then maybe that bachelor lifestyle is the best for both of us after all."

He wanted to barge through the door, to tell her no. How could she believe that now? Benjamin clenched his hands at his sides, forcing himself to think about it from her perspective. Okay, if he was being honest, he hadn't given her a reason to believe anything else.

"Well, if Bunty is out of the picture, I am more than willing to marry you in a heartbeat."

Bobbi laughed, the sound loud and sultry. "Honey, not even if I swore to be on my best behavior for the rest of my life would you and your softness be a good fit for someone like me. I like them a little sarcastic and sometimes grumpy."

Benjamin backed away from the sliding doors, tiptoeing so that the two outside wouldn't hear him. His heart was pounding, and a trickle of sweat itched at the base of his neck.

Deepak's casual reference to marriage unlatched a gate he'd erected a long time ago when he prioritized work and family over everyone and everything else.

"Hey."

He jumped, hand clasped over his mouth to hold back a scream. He faced an innocent-appearing Veera, who looked like she wouldn't scare a bug with her Taylor Swift *Red* shirt, leggings, and high ponytail tied in a pink scrunchy.

"Holy shit, you scared me."

Veera shrugged, then motioned to the doors. "Sorry. Are you eavesdropping?"

"That wasn't my plan but then I heard Deepak propose to my girlfriend and it definitely had me stopping in my tracks," he said, gasping for air.

Her eyes went wide. "Wait, Deepak proposed to Bobbi?"

Once Benjamin caught his breath, he was able to recognize the surprise and shock on Veera's face. "I'm pretty sure it's a joke. I'm not going to throw punches."

She tried to smile, but it looked more like a trembling lower lip instead. "Yeah, of course. I mean, obviously. She *is* his type. I guess that's why I wouldn't be surprised if he was serious."

It was Benjamin's turn to do a double take. "What do you mean she's his type?" The idea that anyone other than him was Bobbi's type immediately had his hackles rising.

"Nothing," Veera said, crossing her arms over her chest. "But hey, while we're on the topic. I'm not going to tell you that if you hurt Bobbi, I will ruin you to the point where you'll have to get a whole ass other career if you ever want to make money again. Because you should already know that."

Veera was the nicest out of Bobbi's friends, and the fact that she was able to threaten him with a straight face had Benjamin pulling at the collar of his shirt. "Scary, but fair."

"And here is my other unsolicited piece of advice," Veera said, her voice softening. She glanced at the sliding doors, at the sound of Bobbi and Deepak still in conversation, and said, "Bobbi always does what she can to make other people happy. She's made a career out of it. She needs someone who is going to understand that about her. Someone who knows that she can take care of everything by herself but is ready to step in and help her when she asks for it. Because if Bobbi asks for help, it's a big deal for her. You understand that, right?"

"I do," Benjamin said. "I know that she wants to take care of everyone." He'd seen her answer phone calls first thing in the morning, only to reassure the person on the other end that they were being completely reasonable and not overstepping boundaries. He knew she skipped meals because she was so busy making someone's wedding the most perfect day of their entire life. She never pushed the work on someone else if she could handle it all by herself. And if he was being honest, Benjamin had also witnessed how much grace and patience Bobbi had with him and his travel schedule.

Veera stepped closer, leaning in so that Benjamin had no choice but to hear every word of what she had to say next. "Do you love her?"

Love. It was one of the scariest fucking words in the English language. It meant there was so much room for getting hurt and hurting others. And love came with strings that he didn't know if he was ready for yet.

"We're getting to know each other—"

"You've had the last year to get to know each other," Veera said. "Don't lie to me, Bunty. It hurts my feelings. Do you love her?"

"Yes," he said. Because that was the truth.

*Yes, but I don't know if we will last if we're always on different work schedules.*

*Yes, but I don't know if I can make her happy if I'm not what she needs.*

*Yes, but I'm still prioritizing my family over her, and I don't know what to do about it.*

*Yes, but does she love me enough so that I should stay?*

"You should tell her," Veera said.

"I don't know—"

She stepped forward and sandwiched his face between her

palms, forcing his mouth into fish lips. "Tell her, because that will let her know that you're worth it."

"Mhmk," he managed to say. He'd also have to admit that he was planning on officially opening up his new restaurant in California. And that meant he would see less of Bobbi. And because she was always as busy as he was, the proof of which he could see from the gaps in their texting timeline, he wasn't sure she'd want him once the wedding was over.

Veera, unknowing of his thoughts, wrapped her arms around his waist in a crushing hug. The top of her head barely reached his collar bone.

Benjamin sighed and patted her on the back. He appreciated her need to comfort him, but it wasn't necessary.

When the screen door opened, Deepak entered the living room first. His jaw dropped.

"Dude, what did you do to her?"

Benjamin pointed to Veera's back as she was still barnacled to him. "I have no idea, but do you know how to turn it off?"

Bobbi walked through the screen door after Deepak and closed it behind her. Her eyes widened when she saw Veera hugging Benjamin.

"What happened? Veera?"

She pulled away, and Benjamin was certain that he'd see tears in her eyes, but they were dry, bright with happiness. "Bunty promised me that we're going for great food, and I'm so hungry!"

"Oh yeah? I'm hungry too," Bobbi said.

Shit, she hadn't even had lunch because they'd gone straight to their room. He had only thought about his need to be with her, and that was so damn selfish on his part. "Come on," he said, extending a hand for her. "Let's hit the strip."

"What about Prem and Kareena?" Deepak asked. "I think they're still napping."

"Let's text them where we'll be," Veera said. "If they're up for it, they can join us, or we'll bring something back for them."

"Sounds like a plan," Benjamin said. And when Bobbi took his hand, he knew the feeling that filled him up was the love he had for her. He lifted it to his mouth to kiss her knuckles and smiled at her when she shot him a confused look.

He was the son of the Naan King. The spoiled rich kid of a frozen food empire who everyone in the culinary world underestimated. A true nepo kid who forced others to judge him for his skill, not his connections. If he fought for what he wanted his entire life, why couldn't that include loving Bobbi? He'd make it work. Living in California and dating Bobbi on the East Coast was possible. It had to be. Because she was worth fighting for long after the wedding was over.

God, that sounded so cheesy, Benjamin thought. But what the hell? He was already discovering that love tasted better with a little cheese.

# CHAPTER 21

## Bobbi

*Note on food delivered to Bobbi's event:*

*Energy wrap, handheld sweet and salty? With protein or cheese? For the businesswoman in my life.*

**BOBBI:** Thank you for the kathi rolls. How did you know I needed comfort food?

**BENJAMIN:** You're meeting the aunties first thing in the morning. It seemed like an appropriate breakfast delivery item.

**BOBBI:** Everything going okay over there?

**BENJAMIN:** Yeah, it's been busy. Miss you.

**BOBBI:** Miss you, too. Heading over to Kareena's house. Her clothes are in and we're going to measure for any last-minute tailoring before the aunties and I talk wedding security.

Three weeks. Her best friend was getting married in three weeks, and Bobbi had finally cleared most of her other events so that she could focus on Kareena. Things were going great with Gwen after their conversation. She hadn't gotten another note or heard a peep from the wedding saboteur. Life was finally as it should be.

If life meant that she and Benjamin hadn't seen each other in weeks.

She sat curled up in the living room space in Kareena's home, scrolling through her tablet filled with notes. She purposely avoided the file where she'd begun documenting all of Benjamin's food scribbles that he'd sent her. Seeing those incomprehensible notes, the ones that she now knew were because he was thinking about her, made the longing a little bit worse.

"Bobbi, let me make you something to eat," Kareena's dadi said from the kitchen. The older woman held a spatula in one hand, waving from her spot in front of the brand-new kitchen island. She yelled, as if the wall that had separated the two rooms was still there.

"No thanks, Dadi. But I appreciate you for asking. How are you liking Florida, by the way? It's a lot warmer in the summer, right?"

Dadi's smile was infectious. "It's perfect for my old, tired bones. I miss the girls, but there is a group of grandmothers my age who play cards and go for walks in the neighborhood."

"That sounds wonderful," Bobbi said warmly.

The mudroom door opened and, as usual, the aunties made their grand entrance filled with loud conversation, hugs, and cheers. Bobbi got up from her position on the couch and crossed the room so she could also be a part of the hellos.

Farah Auntie was the first to reach her, and when she hugged

Bobbi around the shoulders, her grip turned ironclad. She whispered in Bobbi's ear, "Are we talking after the bridal fitting?"

She hadn't forgotten. How could she? "Yes, we'll meet down on Oak Tree Road."

"What is all this ghusar-pusar?" Sonali Auntie said as she came closer in the guise of hugging Bobbi hello. "Is this about the—"

"Sonali, go help with the chai," Mona Auntie said. "You're being a pest again to the girl. Hi, beta." She gave Bobbi a quick air-kiss. "Sorry we're late. All that morning rush hour traffic."

It was already 10:00 A.M. and most of them lived within a seven-minute driving radius, but Bobbi wasn't going to bring that up. "It's okay, Auntie. You're here, and it's going to be a special moment."

"Yes, where is Kareena?" Falguni Auntie asked. She dropped her tote bag sporting the *Indians Abroad News* logo on the new dining table that acted as a separation between living room and kitchen. The natural wood top and black metal detail was different from the small round table with a plastic tablecloth that had been there before.

"She's upstairs trying on her clothes," Dadi said. "She wanted all of us to stay down here so she can show us at the same time. Why don't you all take a seat?"

"She should have just gone to India to get her clothes," Mona Auntie said. "It would have been so much easier to pick everything out at the designer studios there."

"Probably cheaper, too," Falguni Auntie said.

The archaic belief that wedding attire could only be purchased in India was no longer true. Bobbi would never be able to throw the extravagant events that she'd been able to manage if she couldn't get affordable design material shipped. But then again, some people preferred to believe what they wanted about India.

"Auntie, she used one of my new vendors. I really like them, and they've done good work for some of my other brides."

"I hope so," Dadi said. "She wouldn't even let me see what she purchased. I'm putting a lot of faith in you, Bobbi, for making my granddaughter look gorgeous on her day."

"She already looks gorgeous, but she'll be dressed beautifully, too."

"Hey, Bobbi?" The voice came from the stairwell.

Bobbi clapped, anticipation running in her veins. "Coming! Aunties, this is it. I'll go bring the bride."

Bobbi knew that Kareena would've wanted her mom to see her in her dress for the first time, but the aunties had helped raise her, and Bobbi was going to try to make this moment as special as possible regardless. Even though they were at home, and even though Kareena had to go back to the office after they were finished, it was still going to be a good memory.

She left her tablet on the table and quickly made her way down the hall to the staircase at the front of the house. When she looked up, her mouth dropped. "Oh no."

"Yeah, that's what I said when I opened the box just now," Kareena replied ruefully.

"What is it?" one of the aunties called from the kitchen.

"Is there a problem?"

"Wait, we're coming."

The sound of chairs scraping across the new hardwood had Bobby jumping into action. She jogged up the stairs and then ushered a half-dressed Kareena into her childhood bedroom, which was converted into a temporary wedding dressing room space.

Bobbi shut the door and leaned back against it. In the light, the bridal lehenga looked even more hideous than it had from the base of the stairs.

"Oh my god, Kareena."

Kareena pushed her glasses up the bridge of her nose. "Damn, this is ugly."

Her mind raced through all of the ways this could've happened. "I can't believe it! I've never had a problem with this vendor before." Based on the pictures that Kareena had showed Bobbi, the long flowing skirt was supposed to be a deep vibrant red with the subtle hint of gold peacocks embroidered up the sides and embellished with green fabric and sparkling rhinestones. The blouse they had ordered was in a matching red, but simpler with embroidery on the hem of the cap sleeves. The chunni was the star of the show, a long, shimmering fabric that would be expertly pinned against one shoulder and draped over Kareena's head.

But what Kareena got was the exact opposite of what she wanted. The fabric looked like the shiny material on a Halloween costume a third grader would wear for a class parade. The colors were bubblegum pink and emerald green with orange embroidery.

The sound of thudding echoed through the house, and the aunties' chatter grew louder.

"Should I show them?" Kareena asked, motioning to her lehenga.

Bobbi shook her head. This was one of those rare occasions when she didn't know what to do. She felt like she let her best friend down. The beautiful outfit that Kareena had wanted with her whole heart was not the one she received, and because they were so close to the wedding, it would be next to impossible to find the exact replacement.

What was worse, she didn't know if she was to blame or if someone was still trying to ruin Kareena's big day.

"I know that face," Kareena said, moving forward. She gripped Bobbi's arms. "This is not your fault. Don't even think for a second that it is. You had no idea that they were going to send knockoff Indian bridal Barbie clothes to me. I've seen some of the other outfits that your clients have worn from this place and I was the one who told you I wanted to go with them."

"Let's problem-solve this," Bobbi said. "I'll pay for a new outfit. We can either go into New York and visit one of the new designers that are coming from India who have set up shop in the village in hopes that they have something that's ready-made or can easily be stitched. Or we can go to Edison and try a store down there. There is a little bit of an upcharge, but like I said, I can pay for it."

"Bobbi," Kareena said again, this time her tone gentler. "You've done this a hundred times and you know that some things are out of your control."

But this time, according to the aunties, someone in her uncle's business was intentionally trying to stop Kareena's wedding. That meant it was her fault.

She was the reason why Kareena's wedding had had one hiccup after another.

"Open this door," Dadi said with a loud knock. "I want to see my granddaughter."

"Let us see!"

"It can't be that bad."

"My mother-in-law picked out my wedding outfit and it was so hideous, too."

"Give us the number to call them so we can give them a piece of our mind."

Bobbi pressed her fingertips to her eyeballs. If she was destined to have problems, why did it have to be at her best friend's wedding?

There were sounds of whispering, and then Dadi's voice cut clear through the door.

"*What shaadi sabotage?*"

Kareena's brow lifted, and her gaze went razor sharp. "Excuse me?"

Bobbi lunged for the door and pulled it open. All five women practically fell through the opening. When they saw Kareena, they gasped and not in a good way.

"It's definitely not Sabyasachi," Sonali Auntie said.

"*Shut up, Sonali,*" they all said in unison.

"Hey, what were you talking about earlier outside?" Kareena asked. "A shaadi, what was it? Sabotage?"

"Nothing," Farah Auntie said smoothly. "We were just wondering if someone would do this intentionally because it is such a hideous outfit."

Kareena's shoulders relaxed. "Well, gee, don't sugarcoat it."

"I'm going to fix this," Bobbi said to the aunties.

"No, you're going home," Kareena replied.

Bobbi spun to face her best friend. "Why? Is it already time for you to go to work?"

"No," Kareena said. "But this is above and beyond. I can handle this."

"I'm closer to Edison here. I'll just drive you over and we can look for a replacement while I call the vendor in India and make sure that you get your money back."

Kareena shook her head. "You've done so much for me. We had the most incredible time in Vegas and I know that you had a lot to do with that. You've pretty much taken all the stress off my shoulders and acted as a buffer between everybody. This is one thing I know that I can handle. I already have the contact information for the boutique in India. I'll call them myself and tell them what happened and that this is not the outfit I ordered. And while the aunties are here, we'll all go together to look for a backup outfit."

"But I can—"

Kareena shook her head. "I love you and this is supposed to be fun for you too. I'm getting married! You're my best friend. I don't want you to have to work through every single second of pre-wedding events. I can do this one small thing. Just do me a favor and go home, go read, watch movies, whatever. Relax! It's been a long summer for you, and I think you need a day off."

The room had gone quiet, and she saw that all the aunties were standing, waiting to see what she would do and say next.

She wanted to push back, but there was only one rule that she refused to break as a wedding planner. The bride always got what she wanted, even if Bobbi didn't agree.

"Okay. But please call me if you want me to fix it."

Kareena wrapped her in a warm hug and squeezed. "Thank you for everything that you've done. Really. But we're so close to the wedding day that I think it's time for all of us to start sharing the workload so you can spend more time with me. Okay?"

"Okay."

"Great. I'll change and drive you to—"

"No. No, it's okay. I'll call a car. I can make some calls on my way home. Then I'll relax. That's my compromise."

Bobbi squeezed Kareena's hand, then looked at Farah Auntie, who nodded. They'd have to have their conversation about the shaadi saboteur later.

With as much pride as she could collect, she made her way down the staircase, grabbed her bag and her tablet, and called a car service to take her to the train station.

It wasn't until she was halfway to Metropark that her phone buzzed. She pushed in her earbuds to answer.

"Did Kareena call you?"

Benjamin chuckled, the sound soft, intimate and low. "No, the aunties texted. They said you looked stressed and that I should check in on you. Is everything okay?"

She felt tears burn in her throat and wasn't sure why she had the urge to cry. She was usually so put together but maybe it was because she was missing Benjamin and her nerves were fried at the thought that someone close to her could be trying to hurt her.

Bobbi took a deep breath and said, "Kareena's wedding outfit is a disaster. I'm trying to figure out solutions to make it up to her. But she kicked me out."

"What? She kicked you out? Did she think you were the reason why her outfit was ugly?"

"No, she kicked me out because she said that she wants me to start enjoying her wedding. She wants to handle the mix-up with the vendor herself."

"I mean, that seems reasonable to me. But why does that make you sad, sapno ki rani?"

*Because I want to be a part of what makes this event special.*

*Because that's how I show how much I love her and that she's important to me.*

But Bobbi couldn't say any of those things. They just wouldn't come out of her mouth. Instead, she opted for the facts. "This beautiful moment that I wanted to create for Kareena showing her grandmother her outfit for the first time, showing her mother's friends her outfit, just didn't happen, and I really wanted to create that for her."

There was the sound of a siren, and then honking cars. In the back of Bobbi's mind, she didn't think the OC was so noisy, but what did she know about California?

"Bobbi, I always want you to have whatever you want for

yourself, but it's okay if your understanding of an ideal moment didn't happen. I mean, when Kareena looks back on it, she'll have something to laugh about, and that could be even more special to her."

"Kareena won't be laughing ever if she is forced to wear that outfit for her ceremony," Bobbi said.

"Okay, then we'll be the ones laughing."

Bobbi couldn't help but smile. The pang in her chest intensified. "Is it too soon to say I miss you?"

Benjamin sighed. "No, not at all. I miss you, too. But the wedding is in a few weeks, and we'll be at the venue for the long weekend, celebrating Prem and Kareena together."

Then they'd have to figure out how to make things work after that, she thought.

"Can I say something that is going to sound desperately needy and a little pathetic?"

Benjamin laughed. "Since I've never heard you sound desperate, needy, or pathetic before, yes, please do."

She let out a deep breath. "I hate not knowing who is trying to ruin my best friend's wedding. I hate not being able to get my uncle to understand that I am ready to lead the wedding planning business and then have this happen to make me doubt my own skills. And I hate that I can't even complain and fall asleep next to you at night. How's that for needy?"

There was a long stretch of silence before Benjamin said, "It's not needy at all. Bobbi . . . I feel the same way."

Bobbi closed her eyes and dropped her head back against the headrest. Why was having a little bit of Benjamin so much worse than being alone? It was as if all or nothing were the only two ways she could protect her heart.

"Maybe we can FaceTime tonight," Bobbi said.

There was a long pause. "Rani, I hate to do this, but I have to get going. I'll talk to you when I can, okay?"

"Yeah, okay."

Bobbi hung up, then waited in silence until the cab came to a complete stop in front of the train station before she got out. She had to get used to this, she thought. Because sooner or later, Benjamin wasn't going to be calling or texting her at all, and she'd be by herself again.

BOBBI HAD GONE to bed early when she didn't hear from Benjamin for the rest of the night. But, out of a newly developed habit thanks to Benjamin's hours at the restaurant, she slept with her phone under her pillow in case he called. When it began to vibrate at midnight, she jerked up in bed and pressed it to her ear before she was even able to read the screen to find out who had disrupted her sleep.

"Mhm, hello?"

"Hey."

"Bunty? Is everything okay?" She checked the clock on her bedside table. "Did you just get out of work?"

"No, I left early. Can you let me in?"

She was wide awake now. "Let you in where? *Here?* Are you in New Jersey?"

"Yeah, I'm outside your door. I think your neighbor recognized me from the last time I was here and let me in. I don't know how I feel about your safety after that."

Bobbi didn't care that she was wearing her oldest pair of pajama sleep shorts and tank. She didn't care that she still had zit cream on her cheek or that her hair was piled high on her head and probably sticking out in ten different directions. She bolted through the dark apartment to the front door. She paused, then looked through the peephole, and there, in the dimly lit hallway, was her Benjamin. Her Bunty.

She flung the door open and launched herself at him.

He chuckled, then buried his face in her neck. Gripping her thighs, he hoisted her up, carrying her into the apartment.

Then, when the door was shut firmly behind him, he flipped on her kitchen light. The glow highlighted the shadowed planes on his face, the haggard exhaustion.

"I can't believe you're here," she said, cupping his face.

He kissed her, a quick, hard peck. "Well, you sounded like you wanted to be with me, so I came." He dropped the backpack he carried and toed off his sneakers. "Sorry I cut you off on our phone call earlier today. Getting a last-minute flight was a bit of a mess."

She could feel tears pooling in her eyes, but she wasn't horrified at the thought of crying in front of him. She was filled with so much love for this man. How did it happen so quickly? How did her love for him consume her whole heart in the space of a single sigh?

"Bunty, this makes me feel so much better. This is hands down the sweetest thing anyone has ever done for me."

He picked up his bag and gripped her hand in his. "Come on," he said. "Let's get some sleep."

Bobbi dug in her heels. "Wait, that's it? You came all this way to sleep?"

"To sleep next to you," he said. He tugged again and she followed him this time, only because she was so thunderstruck by what was happening. This sweet, sweet man flew across the country, probably paying an exorbitant amount of money for a last-minute flight, waiting on standby for whatever he could get, just so he could *sleep* next to her? Her throat burned with more unshed tears. No one had ever waited in an airport standby line for her like that.

In the dark bedroom, he pulled back the comforter and nudged her into bed. "Stay here," he said softly. "And give me your phone."

"What? Why?"

"No screentime, otherwise you'll be lying awake. I think we could both use the rest."

She couldn't argue with him about that, so she handed over her phone. He put it on the bedside table next to his cell and wallet.

"I'll be right back," he said and walked into the bathroom with his bag. She closed her eyes, letting the tears fall, sliding down the side of her face. Bunty was here. He was here and everything was fine.

Benjamin exited the bathroom a moment later, dressed in a pair of sleep shorts. He then left the room again to shut off the kitchen light.

When he came back, he slipped under the covers next to her, pulling her close so that her cheek pressed against his curling chest hair, her fingers brushed at the chain he always wore, and his arms held her close, with one hand smoothing over the curve of her butt. She felt the cool steel of his kada on his wrist kiss her skin.

"This," he whispered against the shell of her ear, "was worth every moment of that flight. Hey, can I tell you something that's really strange?"

"Mhm."

"I love you more than anything else in this world, Bobbi Kaur."

Bobbi's heart burst when she heard the words, and she turned in his embrace, a little sluggish from sleep. She stroked a hand over his scruffy beard until he looked down at her.

"I love you more than anything else in this world too," she whispered back.

He ran a hand down her hip and thigh, easing some of the tension that still tightened her muscles. "We'll figure out the rest, okay?"

She closed her eyes and snuggled closer. "Okay," she said, knowing that even in the deepest part of her heart, there was no way they'd be able to make it work. But feeling loved, being loved in this moment would be worth all the pain that was to come.

**Indians Abroad News**
Relationship column

As Bollywood has taught us, do not try to be a
hero in an argument with your children. This
new generation has no qualms about treating us
as if we are already dead should there be a fight
regarding marriage.

Mrs. W. S. Gupta
Avon, New Jersey

# CHAPTER 22

## Bobbi

SUKHI: Hey Bobbi, can we talk? I have really been trying to take initiative, just like mom and dad told me you used to do when you got into wedding planning, and I could really use some help. I joined some of the wedding planning message boards, but I don't think I'm using them the right way. Anyway, it's been a long time since we had a cousin-sister date. Maybe when you're done with the season?

Benjamin and Bobbi made love in the morning. It was soft and sweet, with sighs as warm as the light filtering through the curtains. This time, Bobbi climbed on top of Benjamin, and when he slipped inside her to the hilt, she was breathlessly full. She rolled her hips, lifting up and down with the help of his strong thighs guiding her, his hands cupping her breasts then fitting them in his mouth. He sucked hard on her nipples until they were red, and squeezed her ass as if he couldn't get enough. Then, with their hands linked, she came, shuddering and crying out with the intensity of it. Benjamin thrust once, twice, and claimed his own release inside her.

"This is the first time that we've slept together in a bed that one of us owns," Bobbi said to him quietly as he held her, stroking a hand down her arm. She could hear the steady beat of his heart underneath her ear. It was so soothing and felt so right.

She was in love, and even though their futures held vastly different things for them, she would cherish it while she had it.

"How about I make you breakfast?" he said softly. "We can get ready together and then maybe you eat something while I eat you—"

She giggled, and the sound was so foreign to her own ears even as she rolled onto her back. "God, Bunty, that was so cheesy."

"Love is always better with cheese," he said as he leaned down to press a kiss between her breasts. Then he rolled her over once more toward the edge of the bed, slapped her ass, and ran his thumbs under the curve of her butt, sending delicious shock waves to her lower belly. "Come on, sapno ki rani. I have a plane to catch."

The reality of him leaving so soon dimmed some of her light, but that was okay. She had work to keep her occupied. She would check in with Kareena about the wedding outfit and speak with Gwen about securing all the rooms at Messina.

But for right now, she'd enjoy the moments she had with this man, she thought as she got up to start her day.

After showering, Benjamin insisted on teaching her how to make breakfast, which meant they had to have groceries delivered first. They talked about everything from their childhoods, to the music they listened to when they were trying to clear their heads, to their dislike for capers. They already knew so much about each other that it felt like the most natural thing to start planning future events together.

"When we go to India, I'll take you to one of my favorite street food markets," he said as he slid some eggs onto a plate.

"When *we* go to India? Aren't you supposed to ask me first?"

He rolled his eyes. "Don't be a brat, Kaur."

"Don't be so damn pushy."

He scooped some eggs off her plate and held it to her mouth to taste. She took a bite and closed her eyes at the delicious spicy, salty tastes and texture. "God, that's good."

"You know what else is good? Street food in India."

"Ahh, I see how it is. You're on a mission to wear me down."

She'd never known how thrilling it was to be with a man with whom she could act as her whole self. There were no filters, no second guesses.

And when Bobbi was sure that her world would be okay, that everything was right, her cell phone rang.

"I thought you only had to focus on Kareena and Prem's wedding from now until their event," Benjamin said. He stood across from her at the kitchen island drinking a cup of black coffee. His hair was freshly washed and his beard groomed. "Who is calling this early on a Thursday?"

"It's Messina," Bobbi said, checking her screen. It was normal to get a call from the venue a few weeks before a big event but something in the back of Bobbi's mind told her that there was an issue.

"Hello, Bobbi speaking," she said when she answered.

"Hi, Ms. Kaur," Gwen responded. Her voice was colder than it had been since the first time they spoke one-on-one. "We have a problem with the Prem Verma–Kareena Mann event."

"Oh?" Bobbi said. She set her coffee cup down. "What's going on?"

"We'll have to cancel your event."

"*Excuse* me? Why is that?"

Bobbi saw Benjamin's inquisitive expression and quickly turned on speakerphone.

"Because"—Gwen's voice came out dull and irritated—"half of the guest rooms that we have reserved for you have canceled in the last few hours."

"No, that's a mistake," Bobbi said. She mentally reviewed the status of the hotel block. "We've fully booked your venue as promised. There should be no cancellations."

"That is what you had informed me, but I personally spoke with a guest early this morning who said that the wedding has been called off."

"*What?*" This time Bobbi couldn't stop her voice from cracking. "It absolutely is not!" She looked up at Benjamin, who had the same shocked expression on his face.

"Well, forty families seem to think so as that is the number of rooms empty in my Vineyard. Unless you can rectify this within the next business day, we will have to void the agreement, or the Verma–Mann families will have to pay for the rooms."

Bobbi was already running through mental gymnastics trying to figure out what the hell was happening. "Gwen, you know that is absolutely unreasonable. I'll need at least the rest of the weekend. How about Monday morning we'll set up some time to talk?"

Gwen let out a long, heartfelt sigh. "Fine. Monday. But it'll have to be early because we are currently looking for a new chef and I'll need to be conducting interviews."

This had just gone from bad to worse.

"Is she talking about Vinny?" Benjamin whispered as he motioned to the phone.

Bobbi repeated the question even though she wasn't sure she wanted to know the answer.

"Yes," Gwen said. "He was offered a teaching position at a prestigious school in Florence, Italy, with a fully paid relocation package and a bonus. If you are able to rebook the rooms, we will also have to make accommodations to your custom food menu because we do not have anyone on staff who will be able to deliver on recipes outside the scope of our standard catering menu."

"Gwen," Bobbi said. She rubbed at her temple, feeling the start of a headache. "I can't serve a four-hundred-person wedding, where the guest list is ninety-eight percent Indian, a buffet with Italian food. Even if the food is the most incredible thing they've ever eaten, they have certain expectations."

"*If* there will be a wedding."

She ignored Gwen's snark and judgment. "Can we bring in a caterer?"

There was a long pause, and Gwen cleared her throat. "*I've been told*," she said with exaggerated emphasis, "we have to follow certain state restrictions when it comes to food services. No outside food services can be vetted in this short amount of time."

Benjamin was out of his chair and slipped the phone from her fingers. "Hi, Gwen? This is Benjamin. I have a restaurant in Jersey, and I know there isn't a law that prohibits outside food services as long as they are licensed and certified."

Gwen remained silent for a moment, the sound of papers shuffling. "I'm afraid it's just not possible."

Bobbi knew this conversation was going nowhere. She had to regroup, come up with a solid plan, then call Gwen and ask for a face-to-face virtual meeting to instruct them exactly how this was going to go down. She took the phone back and spoke directly into the receiver.

"Gwen? We are going to have this conversation on Monday about how to address some of the guest misconceptions. And you are going to look at making an exception to our outside food services rule."

"I don't think—"

"That's right, you don't think," Bobbi snapped. Her voice rose an octave. "There are very few circumstances in this country where people from my community can get together and feel like they are welcome because they are able to enjoy their music, their food, and wear their clothes that they feel comfortable in. The guests look forward to a wedding not only because it's a celebration for someone that they know or they love, but because it's also an opportunity for them to be unapologetically Desi. They can celebrate the way that they would have if they had access to all the resources available to them in India, a country many of them left behind. Now, I know you have absolutely zero respect for Indian weddings, but we have no choice but to work together. Are we clear?"

There was a long pause, and then Gwen sighed, as if this was the biggest waste of time.

*I feel the same damn way, lady.*

"I will be expecting your call first thing Monday morning."

Bobbi pressed the end button as hard as she could then tossed her phone clear across the counter until it fell to the floor in a loud crash.

"Fuck me," she said with a groan. This could not be happening right now. Her best friend needed her, and everything was royally screwed. She whirled to face Benjamin. "How could this be happening? It has to be the person who is trying to stop Prem and Kareena's wedding. I have absolutely had it with this bullshit! I've handled some of the worst situations that you could possibly imagine, but this is ridiculous."

"Oh, honey," Benjamin said. He crossed the room and wrapped Bobbi up in his arms. A hand stroked over her back in soft, gentle circles. She felt as tense as a wooden board and couldn't relax no matter how hard he tried to squeeze her.

"I hate to see you so stressed and upset like this. Tell me what I can do to help you?"

She pulled back, hands on his chest. "I want this fucking shaadi saboteur *ended*."

Benjamin's eyes widened. "Okay. Uh, well, I don't know if you think I should challenge this person to a duel or something, but murder is illegal, rani."

Of course he would say it like she was being unreasonable. Bobbi began pacing her living room. "We have to tell Kareena and Prem and that is absolutely the last thing I want to do. Maybe if we start with the aunties? God damn it, I have to loop in my uncle too."

"Wait, why do you have to tell your uncle anything?"

"Because he owns the business, and when there is a code-red situation like this, our policy is to loop him in to help with trouble-shooting. He'll go the conservative route, which will not work in this situation. My hands are tied because he doesn't trust me, and now there is absolutely no way he's going to ever consider me for a promotion."

Benjamin nodded, hands shoved in his pockets. "Ah."

"'Ah'? That's all you can say? 'Ah'? If I owned this company, I would sniff out this roach and squash her until her guts squeezed through my fingers!"

"Maybe I should get you some water. Then we can sit and eat."

There was a loud buzzing sound on the kitchen floor against the tile. It had to be Kareena, Bobbi thought. She dove over her coffee table and scrambled for it. She pressed the cell to her ear on the third ring. "Hello?"

"Bobbi?" Kareena said. The pitchy panic in her voice had Bobbi freezing in place.

*Oh no. She found out.*

"I just got a call from one of our family friends. They said that the wedding was canceled? Is there a problem with the venue?"

"Oh honey, it was just a misunderstanding," Bobbi said. Her phone buzzed again with another incoming call, and this time it was her uncle. She had to pick it up. There was no way that he was calling and didn't know what was going on. "Kareena? Hang tight. I'm going to find out what happened, and I'll call you right back. It's going to be okay."

Kareena sniffled then said her goodbye before Bobbi switched lines.

"Mamu?"

"Bobbi, what is going on?" her uncle burst out. His tone was as high-pitched as Kareena's had been a moment before.

"What do you know?" she said. This was just getting worse and worse. She closed her eyes, hoping that he was calling about something, anything, other than Kareena's wedding.

"One of our family friends who is a guest at the Kareena Mann–Prem Verma wedding said that the event was canceled? And the hotel might charge a cancellation fee?"

"There was a miscommunication," she said. Her voice was so frosty it could form icicles. "I am working on it."

"No, you are not," her uncle said.

"What? Of course I am. This is my event."

"And this is still my business," her uncle retorted. "I am taking over damage control. Send me all your vendors, the client file, and information about the event. *Now.* Hopefully I can straighten this out."

"Mamu, no, I said I can fix this. You have no right—"

"I have every right!" he shouted over her. "You were supposed to secure more opportunities with Messina Vineyards, not lose the only one you had. And that for your best friend, too. I told you that you take too many risks and take on too much work!"

"Mamu, don't you dare turn this on me when you are just looking for excuses to prove that I am not as qualified as you are!"

"What did you just say?" he said, his voice going deadly quiet.

"You heard me," she shot back.

"Bobbi, your misstep can affect everyone on the team. It can affect our ability to get more clients! It already looks bad that we aren't ahead of communication yet."

Tears clouded her vision and scraped her voice raw. She began to pace the kitchen. "If you so much as make a single call interfering in my event, you'll not only lose an event planner, the best one you have, but you'll lose me as your niece. I told you I can fix this. And I *will*."

She hung up before she said anything else she regretted.

When she turned back to Bunty, he was glancing at his Rolex, then at the door before he turned back to Bobbi.

"Wait, you're not leaving, are you?" she said. She was about to cry, and she wanted so much to lean against him, to sob at how stressed and fucked up everything was until she was done, then pick herself up and put together the pieces.

He looked guilty as he checked his watch again. "I can try to change my flight. There might be a red-eye. I'm so sorry that I'm leaving in the middle of the chaos, but there is a lot to do to prep for the big board meeting . . ."

Benjamin had said that he loved her. That meant she should be honest with him.

On a deep breath, she said, "Bunty, I know I said that I can figure things out on my own, but I could really use your help. Please. Will you stay? For a few days."

He looked gutted, like the request was something he didn't expect, nor wanted to hear. "Bobbi, I'm cutting it down to the wire. My family needs me. And then after that, I have to meet my attorney. I'm signing the new lease for my next restaurant."

"The one in California."

He gaped. "How did you . . . Deepak told you."

This time, Bobbi felt like the hope that was slipping away was so much greater than she could brace herself for. "You're going to work for your family's company."

"It's temporary," he said softly. "While my next place is being renovated. It's not my first choice for location, but it's a good one. I think it'll be enough to set me for a Michelin star. I can help my brother."

"It's just that I thought—"

"My family needs me, Bobbi."

"No," she said, her voice hardening. If there was one thing she wouldn't tolerate, it was a lie. She crossed her arms over her chest, holding herself together. "That's not true. They don't need you. They want you, but they don't need you to be there. Your father is no better than my uncle. He's making excuses about your brother, but his goal is to get *you* under his control."

Benjamin blanched. "You don't know my family."

"I don't have to know your family to know of them," she said, squaring off with him now. "Bunty, your worth is not determined by how helpful you are to your family."

"I think you're just projecting," he shot back. "Whenever someone needs you, you always put their needs in front of your own. It's as if you're constantly trying to be helpful to someone else."

The verbal blow had her rocking back on her heels. "It's my job! And for this wedding? I'm helping my best friend because why wouldn't I use my skills to make sure that she has the best day of her life?"

"But it's more than that," Benjamin said. "Sometimes I feel like I can't see you because you're hiding behind your work."

"You work just as much as I do!" Her voice rose an octave, wavering. "Maybe I just say the unspoken truth out loud. Whether you love me or not, this relationship ends after Prem and Kareena's wedding, right? Because I will never be as much of a priority to you as the Naan King, that company, and your California family."

"What, so now you want me to choose you over my family?"

"No, no, you don't!" she shouted. "Don't you ever put this on me. Bunty, I deserve to be with someone who loves me enough to think of me first. I deserve to be a priority, too! And I want that to be a *choice*."

He shoved his fingers through his hair. "Damn it, Bobbi. This is my brother. If I miss this flight, if I don't help with this board meeting, then my brother could lose everything he's ever wanted. Why wouldn't I try to be there for that?"

"Did your brother even ask for help, or was it just your father issuing an ultimatum?"

He didn't answer at first. He simply walked over to his coffee cup on the counter and placed it in the sink.

"I get that you're mad that I can't cater a wedding for you—"

God save her from men who miss the point by a mile, she thought. "I asked you for help, not for food. This isn't about the wedding now. This is about us. In three weeks, when the reception is over, you are moving back to California for good where you will have to be for extended periods of time with your new restaurant. Where does that leave me?"

He took a step toward her. "People have long-distance relationships—"

"If they try to make them work, then yes! But how often do we get to talk when we're bicoastal? And if your work takes up the rest of your time . . ."

He motioned to her apartment. "I'm here, aren't I? I literally put your needs before everyone else's in my life."

"I want you to be here because you think this is important. Not because you'd rather be with your family and this is just to make me happy, but it makes you miserable."

He didn't say anything, and that seemed to hurt more than his words. Because his silence was confirmation that one day he'd resent these flights he'd have to take to come and see her. Bobbi dropped to the edge of her couch, wrapping her arms around her knees.

"Please just go. It's harder the longer you wait."

"Bobbi, I love you," Benjamin said, his voice fierce and firm. She could see the guilt, the desperation on his face. "I love you more than anything."

"You may love me," she said, looking up at him from across the room, "but that's not enough when I don't fit into your life. Right now, I can't count on you when I need you."

The longer Benjamin remained silent, the worse her heart broke. "Please go," she whispered again.

"Bobbi, I—"

"Bye, Bunty," she said, cutting him off. "It was fun while it lasted."

She didn't watch him as he went back to her bedroom to retrieve his bag. Then she listened as he slipped on his shoes and exited the front door, closing it quietly behind him.

When she was alone in her apartment, the way she'd been for so long before Benjamin came into her life, she let the tears fall. She curled up into her couch pillows and sobbed.

# CHAPTER 23

## Benjamin

Benjamin knew the universe was telling him something when his flight was canceled. He screwed up, and now he had no idea how to fix it.

Bobbi had asked him for help, something that he knew took a lot of courage to do, and he'd looked her in the face and said no.

What made it worse was that he didn't want to say no. He was determined to be there for her because she really was a priority in his life. But it was as if all of his training, his past commitments made to his family, the motto of "family first," came bubbling up and took over. So now he needed to clear his head, to figure out what to do next. Which was why in the back of a car service, in the middle of a Thursday morning traffic jam, he texted his lifeline.

**BENJAMIN:** Heading to Deepak's. S.O.S.

**DEEPAK:** It'll take me a minute to cancel my meetings. Be there in an hour.

**PREM:** If you haven't heard, the wedding is a disaster right now. I also need an hour.

**BENJAMIN:** Bring whiskey.

It was more like two hours before they were all able to get together. Benjamin had arrived first, using his time in the car to secure another flight, communicate to his restaurant, his attorney, and his father that he was going to be late. Then, while he waited, he sat in the living room watching reruns of *The Golden Girls* until Prem and Deepak arrived.

His friends showed up quietly, without complaint, and soon after, they sat side by side at the kitchen island, three tumblers of whiskey in front of them along with heaping servings of Cocoa Puffs. Benjamin gave them the highlights of what had happened since the night before. When he finished, they were mostly done with their cereal and the gallon of milk was still left uncapped on the counter in front of them. Thoughts of Bobbi and his heavy broken heart circled his brain. He took another bite from the lingering puffs now soggy at the bottom of his bowl.

"This tastes like chocolate-covered cardboard. I can't believe we used to do this every Sunday."

"Your mind isn't in the right place," Deepak said, hunched over his bowl like a troll under a bridge with treasure. "If you weren't so heartbroken after Bobbi dumped you, you'd realize it tastes just as good as it always has."

"Bobbi didn't dump me," he said, leaning forward so he could glare at Deepak, who sat on the other side of Prem. "We just had an argument. We can recover from this. I just have to figure out a way to apologize."

"I don't know," Prem said. "It sounds like she broke up with you to me."

"No way," he said. Panic churned in his gut, souring the milk that he'd just slurped. "We've barely gotten started."

"You chose your family over her. What did you expect to happen?" Deepak said.

"I didn't choose anybody over her." Even as the words came out of his mouth, he knew that wasn't true. He looked her right in the face and when he heard her asking for help, he ignored it because he was so determined to get back to California for the board meeting prep. "My family needs me."

"I think the question you need to start asking is what do you need?"

Benjamin pushed his bowl aside and leaned on his forearms. He rubbed the heels of his hands against his tired eyes. "That doesn't really matter. There are people depending on me—"

"If you're talking about your brother and father, those people are all adults who can figure things out themselves," Prem said. "Deepak and I have been telling you for so long that all you're doing is making their life easier and your life more difficult. Pretend that their wants and needs are out of the equation. What does Benjamin Bunty Padda want in his life?"

Bobbi's face was the first thing that came to mind. Their weekend together at Messina Vineyards. Their long text chains discussing work. The copious notes he'd taken for his new restaurant filled with recipe and design ideas inspired by her. Cooking lessons. Their deeply erotic and personal sexual chemistry that kept him company during the nights he had to spend apart from her. It wasn't enough. It wasn't nearly enough. He wasted months being at odds with her, and he had so much to make up for in that lost time.

"We've barely gotten started," he repeated quietly.

Prem picked up his whiskey tumbler and swirled it in his hand. "When Kareena and I were dating—"

Benjamin and Deepak snorted. Benjamin wasn't in the mood for humor, but it was marginally funny that Prem rewrote history and called the four months with Kareena dating. No, they had one memorable night of conversation, a very public argument on Prem's show, and they slowly slid into something more because they were destined for each other.

Unlike Benjamin and Bobbi.

*Two planets orbiting each other until they got too close and were drawn together with impossible force.*

His muscles ached as he shifted on the counter stool, staring into his empty bowl. It was so strange to him that admitting love for someone made losing that love so much more painful. He felt Prem's hand clasp over his shoulder.

"Whatever Kareena and I were," he said softly, "I knew that I loved her when my entire world shifted and I couldn't picture any future goals, ambitions, or plans without her right next to me. I'm assuming that's how it is with you and Bobbi."

"I told her I loved her," Benjamin said slowly.

"What did she say?"

"That she loved me, too."

"Then you're lucky that she sees your flaws and still thinks you're perfect for her," Deepak said.

Benjamin gave Deepak the finger. "By the way, thanks a lot, asshole, for telling her about my decision for California."

"You're welcome," Deepak said. "Are you still going through with that dumbass plan?"

Benjamin looked at the expectant faces of his two friends. He was in the city he'd learned to love in college and grad school. And Bobbi was here. He could make California work, but he wouldn't thrive. And his restaurant probably wouldn't thrive either. Because he needed heart and soul to make award-winning food, and his heart and soul would be in New York and New Jersey.

"Look, man," Deepak said, looping an arm around Prem's shoulder. "We will support whatever you want to do, but there is no one who understands family obligations more than I do. There has to be a moment when you stop living for other people and start living for yourself. You're thirty-five fucking years old. When are you going to finally make the jump?"

Prem nodded. "The way you put your family first is one of your greatest qualities, but it's also your greatest weakness."

"You don't even have your own place," Deepak said. "Your restaurants are your passion, but they've always come second. Don't put Bobbi second, too. You can't hire people to manage her while you run and answer your father's calls in California."

The idea of anyone managing Bobbi had him smiling. "Yeah, she would cut me."

"With a knife as sharp as her cat eyeliner," Prem said with a nod. "What?"

Prem's eyes widened and looked back and forth between Benjamin and Deepak. "What? Nothing. Anyway. What we're trying to say is, put your grown-up pants on and tell your father and your brother they are on their own. If your father loves Naan King Emporium as much as he tells you he does, he's not going to give his company to anyone else."

It was like a light bulb flickering on. He'd never thought about what his father would do if he said no. Which was probably what dear old dad was expecting.

That bastard.

"I really fucked up," he said.

He didn't want to be another oven in the Naan empire. He never had. He hated coming home to play mediator and family manager. His heart was in his restaurants.

And his heart was with Bobbi. He loved her and he wanted to be East Coast with her and his friends.

And he wanted his restaurant here, too.

Benjamin got to his feet and picked up his bowl. "I don't know if she'll forgive me."

"Trust me when I say this," Prem replied. "Grovel."

Grovel Benjamin could do. And because Bobbi was as ruthless as she was generous and softhearted, he knew he'd be doing a lot of it. "I'm going to have to fucking cater your wedding, aren't I?" he said.

Prem nodded. "Yeah, probably."

"Okay, well, if my father doesn't kill me when I tell him my plans later tonight, you'll have earned that catering service."

# CHAPTER 24

## Bobbi

*Text message from Benjamin Padda*

> **BENJAMIN:** The Grovel: a sour dessert with a soft center.

Bobbi gave herself exactly twenty-five minutes to cry it out before she got up, went to her bathroom to wash her face, and put on a gel under-eye mask. She cleaned up every corner of her apartment that Benjamin had touched, including the dishes in her sink and her bedsheets, before she propped open her laptop and got to work. After deleting the messages from her uncle, she sent Prem and Kareena a quick text to let them know that she had everything under control. She promised them perfection and that's what she'd deliver.

She spent the first hour and a half confirming with all of the vendors that the wedding was still happening. Thankfully none of them had received cancellation notices. Next up was the communication for the guests. It was the distraction she needed.

Why did she ask Benjamin to help her anyway? She had this. Never trust a Punjabi munda to do a Punjabi kudi's job.

When the doorbell rang, she jumped, and her heart pounded with the secret hope that it was Benjamin coming back to see her. She rushed to the door, and when she pulled it open, she was greeted with two familiar faces. Kareena stood in her signature sweater-vest work attire with Veera by her side, a paper bag in hand.

"What are you doing—"

"Not only is Benjamin a complete idiot, but some bastard is also trying to fuck up my wedding and you think you're just going to try to handle it all *yourself*?" Kareena burst out.

She pushed past Bobbi into the apartment, and after kicking off her stilettos at the door, she dropped her tote bag on the counter.

"Who told you about the shaadi saboteur?"

"Is that what we're calling this person officially? If so, I want this shaadi saboteur *ended*!"

Okay, now she felt marginally justified. "That's what I said!"

"*Kareena*," Veera hissed, and made a quick cut-it gesture across her neck before giving Bobbi a more sympathetic smile. "We got a call from Deepak and Prem."

Bobbi shook her head. "No," she said. "No, no, no. You two did not leave work in the middle of the day because you thought I needed your sympathy."

"Well, that's exactly what we did," Veera said as she put down the bag that smelled suspiciously like Shun Lee Palace.

Kareena held open her arms. "Let's address one idiot at a time. Honey, I'm sorry about Bunty."

Bobbi started to sniffle again. She did not have time for any more tears.

"I'm fine. Really. But, Kareena, if you're here, I can tell you everything I plan on doing to make sure your wedding is the best day ever."

When Kareena and Veera glanced at each other and back at Bobbi, she felt her eyes water. "Damn it, when the doorbell rang, I thought he'd returned," she admitted, rubbing her nose with the back of her hand. "It's totally fine. We knew whatever we had was only during this wedding. He made his choice, and he's going to be spending a lot more time in California, so it's for the best."

She was surrounded by her friends before the last words left her mouth. Their familiar scents of fresh powder and sweet floral perfumes. And as the arms tightened around her, and her head rested against Veera's shoulder and Kareena's arm as they squeezed together, she let out another sniffle.

Falling in love was incredibly inconvenient. Damn Benjamin for putting her through this. Then Veera rubbed her arm, and she began to cry in earnest. Everything inside her hurt, and she didn't know if she'd ever feel better again. Closing her eyes, she gave in to the sobs, in to the broken heart.

She lost track of time after that point. Kareena pulled out a four-pack of Boss Babe white wine from her bag, while Veera took off Bobbi's gel eye masks and replaced it with a new set. Bobbi was nudged to the couch where Veera handed her a container of chicken in spicy garlic sauce with dan dan noodles. *The Golden Girls* was playing on low volume from the television because there was nothing else worth watching in the middle of the day on a Thursday.

She ate between hiccups and sniffles as she told her friends everything. From what she felt to the way she was quickly dismissed. She complained about her uncle, the shaadi saboteur, and how she should've been able to take care of everything by herself, but nothing was going the way that it was supposed to.

Kareena put down her plate, her chopsticks propped at the edge. She took Bobbi's hand and squeezed. "Bobbi Kaur, I love you so much but it's not because you're a wedding planner."

"I know that, but—"

"No buts!" Kareena said. "I love you because you're funny and generous and loyal and the best friend a girl could ask for."

"Amen!" Veera said from the other end of the couch.

"But you constantly think you have to do things by yourself! You should've told me what was going on. At the very least, you should've told Veera! We could've been here for you to help. We're family. You never have to be alone when things get hard."

"It's literally my job to be able to plan your wedding," Bobbi said, shifting in her seat. "I feel like such a failure because I should be able to handle it—"

"This is not a normal wedding situation, and you know it," Kareena said. "You have to deal with that racist bitch Gwen, and Uncle, who is being an absolute butthead. It's the way you're feeling right now. You love Benjamin and he's planning on staying in California."

"Yes," she said with a shaky voice. She looked at Veera, then back to Kareena. "Pretty stupid of me to fall in love, right? I feel like I should know better by now."

Veera nudged Bobbi's shoulder. "No. You two had so much chemistry, how could you not? We all saw it from the beginning. But are you sure Benjamin has officially chosen California?"

"He hesitated, Veera. He looked right at me, with that guilty frown, and hesitated when I brought it up." Bobbi took the tissue Veera handed her and blew her nose. "I hate how much it hurts when I knew this was coming. Over the last few weeks. I was bracing for it, thinking that we'd just drift away or something like some couples do. And then when he told me he loved me, I had this weird moment where I wondered, what if I moved to California? What if I did national-scale weddings? But that would never work. I'm rooted here. My client base is here. And our drifting apart was more like a deep wound."

Veera and Kareena leaned in against her side, wrapping her up in their arms.

"I'm sorry," Kareena said quietly. "I really haven't been here as much as I should've been. But I'm here now."

"And so am I," Veera said. "I have totally neglected my co-maid of honor duties. That stops immediately. Whatever you need, Bobbi. Just tell us you'll be okay."

No, she thought. She wasn't okay right that moment, but she wasn't going to let heartache get in the way of being a total badass like she was. This time together that was so special for the three of them because Kareena was going to be the first. "I will be once this saboteur is caught."

Kareena tucked her feet under her hip and leaned back against the cushions. "If focusing on this wedding is what is going to make you feel better, then fine. But in love and life, you have us. You're still not going to do this alone. Tell us what needs to be done and split the load. We'll call the aunties, too, since they've been in this from the beginning."

Bobbi's phone buzzed, and she saw from her position on the couch that it was her uncle calling. Veera and Kareena also saw the name.

"Ignore him," Kareena said. "We'll handle him, too! Family or not, he needs to realize how shitty he's been treating you."

"No, I'll deal with Mamu personally," Bobbi said. She took a deep breath, and for the first time since Benjamin left, she could feel her entire lungs fill with air without crushing pressure. These two were right. She had family. The *best* family. Even her uncle was incredible when they weren't working together.

She moved her food container from her lap to the coffee table. "I love you guys so much, do you know that?"

"We know," they said in unison.

Kareena picked up Bobbi's phone and handed it to her. "Now,

let's get the aunties on the line. The fastest way to get the communication out is through WhatsApp."

"Of course it is," Bobbi said. "I was working on the communication plan before you showed up. I don't know why I didn't think of it, but the easiest and quickest way to do damage control is to start a phone tree."

"We'll get those rooms rebooked in no time!" Veera said. "The shaadi saboteur made a big mistake underestimating pissed-off women."

"Pissed-off women and one livid wedding planner," Bobbi said calmly. "Kareena? I promised you a wedding you'd never forget. You're about to get it."


It took Bobbi the entire weekend with the aunties to ensure that all of the rooms were re-booked. Then, at 7:00 A.M. on Monday, she got a text from Prem and Kareena that said they were able to solve the caterer problem and would work directly with Gwen on it. Bobbi had to actively hold herself back from asking questions, but she'd promised that once she assigned a task to someone, she wasn't going to backtrack to try to do it herself again. She had to trust the people she loved to help. She didn't have a team because she had been so sure that she could do all the prep on her own before the event. Thankfully, her friends were there to make sure nothing was left undone.

She'd be lying to herself if she didn't admit that she still felt a teensy bit like a failure. But Bobbi had been in the industry long enough to realize that sometimes there were weddings that were destined to be chaos. Her uncle taught her that.

After her call with Gwen, she caught a car service to Mamu's house. She used the front door code and strolled right in. After waving to her aunt, who was in the kitchen drinking chai, she headed toward the office. Her cousin, Sukhi, was coming down the staircase just as she approached the door.

"Bobbi!" She faltered on the last step, laptop tucked under her arm.

"Sukhi, I'm just here to talk to Mamu."

Sukhi nodded. She hugged the laptop to her chest now. "I was actually going to come and try to talk to you today. Maybe when you're done with Dad?"

"Sure. I'll come and get you." She knocked twice on the office entrance.

"Come in," a voice called back.

Her uncle was just where she'd predicted. Behind the big wooden desk, wire-frame glasses perched low on his nose, and a file in hand. He looked up, eyes widening when he saw her. Then cooling.

"I know you're mad at me," Bobbi said as she shut the office door at her back. "But you've treated me like absolute shit for *months*. You used to trust me, and now it's like you're trying to get me to quit! I just wanted to let you know that I resolved all of the problems that popped up with Messina Vineyards and with the Mann-Verma wedding."

Her uncle continued to stare at her as he took off his glasses. He looked so much older than his years in that moment. The deep grooves of his wrinkles were pronounced as he frowned, and the age spots on his hands and his cheeks weren't there in Bobbi's childhood memories.

"This is my fault," he said.

*Wait, what?* "What's your fault?"

"The fact that you don't trust me anymore. That you never talk to me anymore. You only treat me like your boss and not your family."

"Maybe that's because if I tell you what's wrong, you just use it as another excuse for why I'm not ready to take over the business."

"That's not true, Bobbi—"

"Don't gaslight me," Bobbi said sharply. She'd had enough of his bullshit, and this had gone on for far too long.

"Gas . . . do you need Tums?" He opened a drawer and pulled out one of the largest bottles of antacids that Bobbi had seen outside of a Costco.

Bobbi shook her head. "Gaslighting doesn't mean gas. Mamu, stop trying to convince me to believe something that we both know isn't true. You know that any mistake I make you immediately use as an excuse for why you think I'm not ready. But everyone makes an error every once in a while, and my record has always been pristine. Yet I'm the one who gets berated the most for it. Is it because you really don't want me to take over? You promised me that I would one day have this legacy, but is it because Sukhi is your daughter by birth—"

"Don't!" He stood, vibrating with fury. "Don't even think that for one minute. From the moment you came into my life, you were always mine and you will always be mine. Your Bhua has only ever treated you as one of hers as well. Your presence in my life is what gave me courage to start this business so why wouldn't it belong to you?"

Bobbi brushed a tear off her cheek. "Then why?" she said, her voice hoarse.

Her uncle sat down, his shoulders sagging as if in defeat. "Maybe it's because if I am here, you will always need me, little girl. But sometimes I feel like regardless of my presence, you have already moved on."

This time, it was Bobbi who got up. She rounded the desk and wrapped her arms around her uncle. He was undoubtedly the only man who never ruined anything in her life. Quite the opposite. He had been with her for all her memories, encouraging her, cheering her on, and even putting his own uncomfortableness aside so that she would always have a safe space to go to if she needed anything.

"You will always be one of the most important people in my life, Mamu. Count your blessings because you will never be able to get rid of me."

He sniffed, then hugged her waist. "Is that a promise?"

"Yes. But this doesn't mean you get to keep hurting my feelings. If you're worried I'm just going to usher you out, and that is the only thing holding you back—"

"Now, Bobbi—"

"Don't you 'now, Bobbi' me," she replied. She pulled away, fists on her hips. "Let me put it to you this way. If you don't promote me to, at a minimum, yours and Bhua's partner within the next year, then I'm going to open up my own business. I want more responsibility and I want to grow this business, but I can't do that if I'm stuck in the same role for another ten years."

"Fine," he said. He let out a deep sigh filled with the sound of frustration. "I'll talk about it with Bhua, if you *insist*."

"I do," Bobbi said. She pressed a kiss to his bald head. "You didn't raise no pushover."

He looked up at her, pride shining in his eyes. "No," he said, his voice wavering with so much happiness that it hurt her heart. "No, I definitely did not. I'm sorry I yelled at you, beta."

"Same, same," she said, mimicking his accent.

*Same, same.*

He would say that to her when she was a child and they apologized to each other.

"Now, is there anything that I can do to help with Kareena's wedding?" He held his hands up as if surrendering. "I don't want to take it over. I am just offering whatever resources I have."

She thought about it for a moment and realized that she had the perfect task for him. "When was the last time you worked on building a mandap?"

His eyes widened. "Not since the early days in the planning business. But I did it for years before I switched over to this desk job." He motioned to the mess in front of him. "I could do it in my sleep. Why, doesn't Kareena have a mandap?"

"It's more like the mandap needs to be completely redesigned."

He perked up with interest. "Well, well. I know exactly how to help with that."

There was a knock at the door followed by the sound of Sukhi's voice. "Papa? Bobbi? Can I talk to you?"

Mamu cleared his throat just as Bobbi dabbed at her eyes before sitting in the chair across from the desk.

"Come in, beta," he finally called out.

The door creaked open, and Sukhi burst into tears three steps into the room.

This was apparently the day for crying, Bobbi thought. She got to her feet and motioned Sukhi forward to comfort her. "Hey, what's wrong? Is everything okay?"

Sukhi shook her head. "Papa, I heard what you were telling Mom last night. That Bobbi's guests for the wedding had canceled. Bobbi, it's all my fault! I'm the one who shared the guest list."

"*What?*" This was definitely not something on Bobbi's bingo card. She was looking for a stranger, a person who may have a personal vendetta against her. Definitely not her cousin.

"Sukhi," Bobbi's uncle said. "I think you better sit down and start from the beginning."

She practically collapsed in the chair next to Bobbi, and pulled a tissue from the box that Bobbi handed to her. "This woman approached me online on this New Jersey wedding planning board. She said that she's heard of the company that was in my signature block and that she has attended some of Bobbi's weddings."

Bobbi continued to rub her cousin's back. "Can you tell me what happened?"

Sukhi nodded. "This woman promised to bring us her business if I could get her information about the Kareena Mann wedding. She made it seem like she was competing with the wedding, and she wanted to make sure that her stuff was better. I thought this was some Indian community drama about throwing the better party. I swear I didn't know that she was going to try to mess up the event when I started talking to her. I'm so sorry! I can't believe I put you in such a terrible position without knowing it."

Sukhi started sobbing again in earnest. Bobbi met her uncle's gaze over Sukhi's head. He shook his head, disappointment in his eyes. Unfortunately, there was nothing anyone could do at this point. The damage had already been done.

"Can you do me a favor?" Bobbi asked. "Please don't share any of our personal information with anyone outside of this company without getting the approval of myself or your parents, okay? That's a huge breach of privacy and I'm going to have to tell Kareena what happened. Why were you trying to get clients on a message board, anyway?"

Sukhi leaned into her side, sniffling hard. "I'm so sorry! I didn't mean to hurt you, but I really wanted to bring in clients of my own. I wanted to contribute. To take initiative just like Dad said you used to do." She then listed everything she had shared, including her cake vendor, her decorator, her florist, and everyone in between. She'd pulled the information from Bobbi's files on the company shared drive before Bobbi had locked down the information.

"It's okay," Bobbi said, rubbing. "I know you didn't do this on purpose." This time when she met her uncle's eyes over Sukhi's head, he looked very, very tired. "Sukhi, do you have any idea who this woman was?"

Sukhi shook her head. "She didn't seem like she was American though. I promise, Bobbi. I thought that I was helping by securing more business."

This meant that their shaadi saboteur was still at large and had the capacity to do a lot more damage before Prem and Kareena made it to the mandap. Bobbi grabbed her bag and got up to leave. "I have to go talk to the aunties," she said. "Mamu? I love you and I expect to see that business partnership agreement soon. Sukhi, I love you, too, but no more online boards. I promise you we'll do that cousin-sister date soon. Maybe a girls' weekend during your next break from grad school, okay?"

She didn't even wait for her cousin's nod before she left the house. She called Farah Auntie as she slipped into the back seat of the ride share.

"Hello?" a voice answered on the second ring.

Bobbi felt lighter than she had in months. "Hi, Auntie. I found the leak in my company. We're getting closer, but we're also running out of time. Whoever this person is might not stop at trying to cancel the wedding."

"What do you and Bunty think we should do?"

"I don't know about Benjamin, Auntie. But I know now I can't do this on my own. We're all in this together."

### Indians Abroad News
Relationship column

It's best to put bygones aside for weddings. Families who have not connected for years will come together for a time of celebrating. Holding grudges will only draw the attention away from the happy couple.

Mrs. W. S. Gupta
Avon, New Jersey

# CHAPTER 25

## Benjamin

**BENJAMIN:** I know we haven't spoken since I left, but is there any way we can talk when I get to Messina?

**BOBBI:** I'll be really busy. Listen, it's okay. We knew that our truce was temporary. Don't worry about it.

**BENJAMIN:** Yeah, that's not happening. I'll see you in Messina.

*Family WhatsApp Chat: FAMILY FIRST*

**DAD:** The board meeting is today. Bunty, you should be here instead of flying back East. This is absolutely neglectful.

**BUNTY:** Chottu has it handled. Like I said last week, this is between you two. No more ultimatums or threats, otherwise Chottu is going to do Christmas Naan or something just to piss you off.

**CHOTTU:** Thanks, bhai. Dad, stop bothering Bunty. He already has Gudi submitting his proxy vote.

**DAD:** This is a family business.

**BUNTY:** And you are surrounded by your family. We already talked about this. I will not be manipulated just because it makes you happy. You lived your life. Let me live mine.

**DAD:** I don't know what kind of white nonsense you've learned from these American schools you went to.

**GUDI:** Hey, if you wanted us to think the way you and Mom do, then you should've thought about that before raising kids in a different country than your experience. We adapted. So you have to as well, Papa. Hey, Benjamin, I want to come out and visit you soon. Bobbi sounds awesome.

**MOM:** I am ordering mithai and jewelry for your sagai, beta.

**BUNTY:** MOM, we are not engaged!

**CHOTTU:** MOM! He doesn't even know if she's going to forgive him!

**GUDI:** Typical.

*iMessage Chat: Benjamin Padda, Deepak Dutta, Prem Verma*

**BENJAMIN:** Are you ready to get married, buddy?

**PREM:** I've been ready since the moment I met this woman.

**DEEPAK:** We'll allow the sap since it's your wedding week.

**PREM:** Hey, guys? Thanks. Because you're allowing the sap, I just want to tell you both that I love you, and I'm glad that you'll be here with me.

**BENJAMIN:** Don't thank us yet. We have a wedding to save first.

Deepak rented a car so douchey that it should've had a sticker in the back that said: "We're assholes and we know it." But since he was paying for it, Benjamin couldn't exactly complain. At five in the morning on Wednesday, exactly twelve hours after Benjamin had landed in New York City, they piled into the douche-mobile, a red tank of a vehicle with white leather interior and fuzzy dice hanging from the rearview mirror, and drove out to Jersey City to pick up Prem.

The ride was predominantly silent, with the windows closed and the radio off. When they pulled up in front of Prem's apartment building at five forty-five, he stepped outside in the early dawn with the barest hint of sunlight on the horizon. He carried a bulging garment bag and two massive suitcases that could each fit a body.

Benjamin and Deepak rolled down the windows, put on neon

orange sunglasses that read "Dulha Party" across the top, and turned on the stereo to blast the song "Dezi Boys."

Prem stopped in his tracks, staring at the car for a few seconds, then with a shrug walked toward the trunk, bags in tow. Deepak and Benjamin got out to help him, and the first thing Prem had to say to either of them was "The glasses are a nice touch, but what's with the douchey car?"

"I told you," Benjamin said to Deepak.

"Shut up," Deepak mumbled, and after adjusting the bags, they all got in and headed toward the wedding venue.

Benjamin didn't know if it was because they were all feeling nostalgic at this very permanent shift in their lives, but they chose not to talk about the wedding the entire drive down to the vineyards. Instead, they relived their college days, the shitty apartment that they shared their last year, and all the memories that followed. There was that time in Boca when they all thought they could play golf, but they just wanted to drive around in the cart. There was also the night that Prem and Gori had gotten engaged the first time, and Benjamin and Deepak had fallen asleep in the fountain in front of the country club after the party. Years of sheet pan nachos, sneaking into movie theaters, whiskey tasting, and adventures together.

When they reached Messina, Benjamin was ready to celebrate the start of another adventure. He knew that Prem would always be in his life, regardless of how many changes he was going to experience moving forward. And when it was Benjamin's turn, he knew that Prem would still be in his life cheering just the same.

AFTER THEY CHECKED in and settled into their cabins, Benjamin left Deepak and Prem to explore the property while he went straight to the kitchens.

He had a slight bounce in his step as he made his way through the empty restaurant that was prepping for lunch service and to the double doors in the back. He loved being in the food service industry. It energized him, the rush, the sounds, the smells around him. Because he'd been so caught up in the development phase of his restaurants, he hadn't spent as much time as he wanted in the back, but he was going to change that. Now that he had a regional partner managing Namak back in California, he would only have to travel to the West Coast once a month. And as he built his new location in New York, he was planning on a lot of recipe testing in a kitchen of his own.

When he pushed through the double doors, the prep team froze, their starched white coats perfectly pressed exactly as they should be.

A petite older woman approached him first. "Chef Padda?" She wiped her palms on her jacket.

"Yes," he said. "Are you Chef Catherine?"

"Yes. I am interim chef de cuisine until Messina can get a replacement. Then I'll resume my responsibilities as sous chef. It's an honor to meet you. I've eaten at Phataka Grill and it is hands down my favorite Indian restaurant."

"Thank you, Chef," Benjamin said. "And thanks for letting me invade your domain for the next few days. I have never catered before, but I've worked in kitchens for most of my life. I understand the food has arrived and has already been inspected for quality?"

"Yes, Chef. I checked the shipment myself and sorted by event. They are currently stored in our catering fridges," she said, motioning to the alcove off the opposite end of the massive prep space.

Benjamin smiled. God, he loved efficiency. Bobbi wouldn't have anything to worry about if this person was in charge. "Wonderful.

I understand we have meetings tomorrow. My team arrives later today, but as we discussed, your team will take the lead."

"Absolutely. We understand where the expertise is here, and frankly, we're excited to support catering something different."

"Great," Benjamin said. He glanced at the curious faces, then back at Catherine. They were all going to have to make this work together if they were going to pull off three days of food for four hundred people. "Would it be too much trouble if I help with lunch rush to get a feel for how you work? If it's too much of an intrusion—"

She gaped at him, shaking her head until her hat almost slipped off her head. "Not at all, Chef. It would be our honor. Most of us will be working the event as well, so your timing is perfect." She turned to the kitchen staff, and there were unanimous nods. "We have some extra coats and aprons in the back. If you'd like to take over—"

He shook his head. "I can just work as relief. I don't have my knives with me, but I can fit in anywhere else."

"Yes, Chef," she said, her shoulders straightening.

Benjamin grabbed the largest chef coat they had, which fit just a bit snug, but it worked. After washing his hands, he followed his orders. Then, when the lunch flow started, he moved on to grilling, followed by the sauces.

The kitchen worked in a mix of silence and companionable conversation. He began to understand its rhythm and its flow. He learned everyone's names, the way that they functioned together, and what they excelled at.

He wanted this again, he thought. He wanted to have this experience and then go home to Bobbi and talk to her about everything that happened during his shift. Then he wanted to make her dinner and hear about her day, too.

Two hours later, the double doors swung open. The events manager, Gwen, with her permanent scowl, was followed by the love of his life. He froze at the sight of her.

He'd missed Bobbi so much that his bones ached from it. She scanned the kitchen, her eyes widening when she saw him.

*There you are.*

Out of the periphery of his vision, a member of the waitstaff picked up his order from the metal racks that divided the back end of the kitchen from foot traffic.

"What are you doing here?" she said in Punjabi, over the sound of sizzling pots and pans. The metal counter separated them so he walked around to her side so he could be close to her. He wondered if they were in her apartment, or in the privacy of his cottage behind the hotel, he'd be able to smell the gardenias on her skin.

"I'm catering Prem's wedding," Benjamin replied in the same language.

"But you hate catering! You said you refuse to feed the masses—"

"You asked me for help."

Her eyes widened. "But—"

"We should really keep it moving," Gwen said. "Is everything okay in here, Chef?"

"It's great, Gwen. Catherine has been fantastic." He motioned to the woman in charge, who beamed at the praise.

"I'm . . . grateful that you're doing this for Prem and Kareena," Bobbi said, reverting to English. "But this is not what I thought they'd do when they said they'd take care of the food. I wish you had told me—"

"Bobbi, I have it under control. I'm using the same menu that Vinny was supposed to coordinate. Catherine is familiar with it, too, along with both of our teams. This made the most sense as a solution to the problem." He knew that having her insight and input would've been invaluable, and since she was the wedding planner, it was also part of her job to be involved, but he wanted this to be a surprise for her too. He was here, and he wasn't going anywhere.

Except she didn't look surprised.

She looked pissed.

Had he screwed up so much that she wasn't even willing to see that this was his attempt at a grovel? He couldn't possibly do the same song and dance routine that she read about in her romance novels. Most of the time, the mafia heroes were committing a crime. The best he could do was tie her up and feed her freshly made samosas.

Or cater a wedding.

"I guess I should've realized that Prem is your family, too, and you'd prioritize him as well," she said. Her demeanor remained cool and collected. Professional. Guarded.

*Damn stubborn idiot woman doesn't even realize this is all for her.*

"Chef Catherine?" he called out, even as he pinched his nose in an attempt to stall the tension headache.

"Yes, Chef?"

"Can you please fix a plate for our wedding planner here?"

Bobbi shook her head. "What? No, I—"

His glare cut off her excuses. "You need to eat something before you start running around in those heels." Chef Catherine discreetly passed him a gorgeously plated serving of gnocchi in a creamy blush sauce through the pass-through, and he thrust it into Bobbi's hands.

"Gwen, don't take her anywhere or show her anything until she finishes at least half of this plate."

"I'd prefer not to get in the middle, thank you. I feel like I'm already too involved."

"Benjamin," Bobbi said. This time she sounded absolutely exasperated. "What the hell?"

He wanted to point out that she made him feel the same exact way.

"We'll talk later. About my family, California, and everything else."

Bobbi glanced at the kitchen staff over his shoulder, at the line cooks pretending to look busy when they were most definitely paying attention to the scene. "Chef Padda, we will most definitely be talking about this later." She tilted her chin up as she snatched the fork out of his hand and strode through the kitchen double doors with Gwen following closely behind.

Chef Catherine issued a directive to speed it up, and everyone got back to work.

"Is that your partner, Chef?" the pastry chef asked from the corner station where she was dipping ladyfingers into a coffee syrup.

"She is," Benjamin said with a rueful smile. "And whether or not she wants to admit it, she's so much more."

# CHAPTER 26

## Bobbi

*Preliminary logo sketch texted to Bobbi:*

RANI
A Punjabi Fine Dining Experience

Every second of her first day at Messina Vineyards had been consumed with last-minute details for Prem and Kareena's wedding. First there was the run-of-show meeting with Gwen. Then Neha arrived with the décor. After that, the florists needed additional accommodations because the Messina fridges were too small. Prem's cousin brought the welcome bags, but he was late so Bobbi had to coordinate with Messina's on-site staff to drop them off in guest rooms.

That didn't stop her from thinking of all of the reasons why Benjamin was here instead of at his family business board meeting or planning his new California restaurant. He wasn't supposed to arrive until Thursday night, which meant *something* had changed.

Was he trying to hold on to her and expecting her to compromise her wants and needs? Because that would be shitty.

When she brought it up to Kareena and Prem, neither of them was willing to say anything other than "ask him yourself." Then they were off to greet their families, who had just arrived from the airport.

Six hours later, Bobbi realized that it was next to impossible to have the closure she desperately needed. Benjamin was running on a completely different schedule from hers, and she hadn't seen him all day. She didn't want to text him because this conversation had to be done in person.

After she'd given up finding peace for herself that night, she turned all of her attention back on the person who deserved it the most. Her best friend.

It was seven by the time she changed into a pair of linen capris and a tank top. Her little cabin cottage seemed so empty compared to last time she and Benjamin had come for the food testing. But that was fine. She could be alone again. It would hurt at first, but she'd be okay.

She grabbed a large cooler and her bag of snacks she'd packed from home, and stepped outside into the crisp, early fall weather. Kareena was getting her bridal mehndi tonight, and this was Bobbi's favorite part in a wedding celebration. The quiet moments with just the bride and her friends.

Bobbi walked down the narrow walkway lit with twinkle lights to the bridal suite and pushed open the door that had been left ajar. Kareena was already in the room, dressed in shorts and a tank, leaving her arms and legs bare. Hanging from the top of the doorframe of the coat closet off the living room was the brilliant red bridal gown that Kareena had ordered from India.

Bobbi dropped the bags on the floor and rushed forward. "Oh my god, it *came*."

Kareena grinned at her. "It did. And it's because of you, and all those strings you managed to pull. I'm so glad, Bobbi. I know I told you I'd manage it myself, but I can't thank you enough for fixing my dress fiasco. I really wanted to wear something that reminded me of my mother's lehnga." She walked over to the gown and ran her fingertips over the delicate paisley designs along the hem. "I never thought I'd want this fairy-tale wedding, but I'm so *glad*."

Bobbi wrapped her arms around Kareena's waist, while Kareena leaned her head on top of Bobbi's. They looked at the dress together in silence.

"I'm so sorry," Bobbi finally said. "That I've been caught up in the details of this, and I haven't been around to enjoy the moments with you as much as I should have. I just wanted it to be perfect for you."

"You could've literally done nothing, and this weekend would've still been amazing because I have you here with me," Kareena said, brushing Bobbi's hair back over her shoulder. "I know I've already said this, but Bobbi Kaur, I don't want you in my life because you planned a party for me. I want you in my life because you and Veera are my best friends."

Bobbi sniffled, and she dabbed at the corner of her eye with a knuckle. "I know that. I love you."

"Love you too." They hugged, and Bobbi truly felt like this was finally a celebration that she was a part of, not standing in the background helping others to build memories.

"Hey," Bobbi said, once they wiped away their tears. "I brought snacks!"

"Yay! I hope some of it is chocolate because I want to spend every moment until I go home gorging myself. Now that I know the food is going to be excellent."

Bobbi paused, halfway across the living room, her arms filled with chip bags. "Yeah, about that. Why didn't you tell me that Benjamin was going to cater your wedding?"

Kareena smiled. "Did you talk to him yet?"

"I just ran into him in the kitchens earlier today. He's been so busy with Prem and Prem's family that we're on completely different schedules."

She smiled. "I'm sure he'll find you tomorrow."

Bobbi wanted to ask Kareena again if she knew anything about Benjamin's plans for California. Except she was right. Benjamin was the one who should be answering those questions, not Kareena. She'd just have to wait.

Bobbi unzipped the cooler she'd dropped at her feet. "I'm going to set up the food, and then your mehndi chair and station. Do you know when everyone else is coming? Your sister and grandmother?"

Kareena's smile faded. "They aren't coming tonight."

"*What?*" Bobbi shouted. This was one of the most personal and private moments for a bride and the women in her family. "It's your bridal mehndi! They're supposed to get their mehndi done tonight, too. Why can't they make it?"

Kareena shrugged. "They said they are going to get their mehndi done at the party tomorrow night. It's too late for them to stay up, even though it's only seven thirty. We all know that they just didn't want to sit here for me."

Bobbi felt a pang in her heart. Kareena always tried so hard to have a relationship with those two women. Sometimes they were incredibly supportive, but only if it suited their interests first. Bobbi was determined to make up for the gap they caused in Kareena's life if it was the last thing she had to do.

"Hey," she said, and ran her hands down Kareena's arms. "We're going to be here and we're going to have a blast, okay?"

Kareena gave her a sad smile. "Yes, absolutely."

Bobbi retrieved a tumbler that said "Dulhan" on it from the tote she brought with her. "I think it's time we toast. What's your poison tonight? Watermelon wine cooler? We'll start drinking before your mehndi ladies get here. I'm celebrating now with you, so I'll get as intoxicated as you do, I promise."

"Considering the last time you got as intoxicated as me was maybe six years ago, that's quite a promise," Kareena said.

The front door opened, and Veera's head popped through the opening. "Hey! Is this where the party's at?"

"It is!" Kareena said. "Come on in. We're just getting the snacks set up."

"Good," she said, then pushed the door open. "Look who I brought with me?"

One by one, Falguni Auntie, Mona Auntie, and Sonali Auntie walked in, chatting away.

"What are you all doing here?" Kareena blurted out.

"It's our baby's mehndi," Falguni Auntie said. She walked over to Kareena and cupped her face. "We're missing her tonight, too, darling, but we're going to represent her every step of the way, okay?"

Kareena's eyes dampened, and Bobbi couldn't help but feel her own tearing up.

"Is Farah Auntie coming too?"

The aunties looked at each other, then back at Kareena.

"She is doing some last-minute digging for our shaadi saboteur," Mona Auntie said. "But she'll show up before the night is over."

"I'm so glad you're here," Kareena whispered, her hands pressed against her chest. "It feels like Mom is here, too."

There was another knock on the door. Before anyone could open it, Prem's mother stepped inside the doorway, arms outstretched as if she were making a Broadway entrance.

"I'm here! Sorry I'm late." She retrieved a bulk-buy-size container of petroleum jelly and a bottle of lemon juice from her purse. "I brought the supplies. With these two things, your mehndi will come out such a beautiful dark red, beta."

"Auntie?" Kareena said. "Uh, hi?"

Bobbi was also surprised. Since the Vermas had the most guests on the list, she had assumed that Prem's mother would be focusing on her family friends.

The woman reached for Kareena and said, "I think it's time you started calling me Mom. Just please don't use that irritated tone my son tends to use." With a soft kiss against Kareena's temple, she said, "There is nowhere I'd rather be tonight than with my daughter."

Kareena wrapped her up in a hug, her sniffles loud enough to trigger everyone else in the room. Bobbi did not anticipate these many wonderful opportunities for tears to celebrate.

"Okay, enough," Prem's mother said briskly, pulling away. She dabbed at her lashes with a manicured fingertip. "Have you seen the second season of *Fabulous Lives of Bollywood Wives*?"

Everyone shook their head.

"Oh my goodness, darlings. You must! Let's put that on the television in the background. We'll have some entertainment."

Episode one had already begun by the time Gwen arrived escorting the three mehndi artists from the main house down to the bridal suite. There was cheering, laughter, and pani puri shots, along with gulab jamuns and bags of Flamin' Hot Cheetos. Kareena sat in the low chair, held out her arms and stretched out her legs so that her artists could begin their work.

There were two additional women who set up stations on either side of the room for the aunties, Veera, and Bobbi to get their mehndi done as well. And as the garden lights outside the suite windows twinkled, Bobbi couldn't stop smiling. Her best friend was getting married, and she was going to enjoy every moment of it.

# CHAPTER 27

## Benjamin

Benjamin adjusted the headlamp that he wore so that the beam of light shone straight down on the large building plans rolled out on the scarred wooden table. The smell of cedar and wine surrounded him and the other members of their elite task force in the rare-wine cellar of Messina Vineyards. Gwen waited by the door, her fingers wringing together as she stood watch by the staircase.

"What do you think?" Deepak said, adjusting his headlamp.

Prem pointed to the long corridor, and then the section marked as a side panel exit. "I think if one of you takes my shoes through there, you can then hide them in the service closet off the left side of the hallway. There is no way that Bobbi and Veera are going to know to look in there for the duration of the ceremony."

"I think that's too close to the wedding hall," Benjamin said. "If we're going to hide your shoes so no one steals them, we need to run them back to one of the cabins. It's not that far if we jog, and it's even faster if we ask to borrow one of the golf carts."

"You know, this tradition of the bride's sisters stealing the groom's shoes is supposed to be a celebratory and fun process," Prem's father said from one end of the table. "It's not a serious enough event to pay someone three hundred dollars at the county courthouse for the hotel floor plans, boys."

"I think an entire generation has been impacted by that movie *Hum Aapke Hai Kaun*," Kareena's father said from the other side of the table. "Why don't you just give the girls the money like they want, and let them take your shoes?"

"Uncle," Deepak said, turning off his headlamp. "This is about honor. And Veera is a hedge fund financial executive. Do you think she and Bobbi would settle for anything less than a grand each? Prem doesn't have that kind of money right now. He's building a community health center. He's saving for a honeymoon and offsetting the cost of the wedding."

"He's not paying enough for the wedding, if you ask me," Prem's father mumbled.

"Dad," Prem said with a sigh. "You insisted on coming here tonight. At least be supportive."

"I came to help you find out who is trying to stop this bloody wedding," he grumbled. "Which is not going to happen on my watch. The alcohol was too expensive for even a moment of this weekend to go wrong."

"I told you," Kareena's father said. "We should've just let the children elope."

"You've met my wife. Do you think that is even an option for me?"

The door at the top of the stairs opened, and Gwen jumped. She hadn't said a word since they descended into the basement, but the peep she let out now was enough to remind everyone why they were hiding out in the first place. Deepak quickly rolled up the floor plans and tucked them under the table they'd been standing around.

"It's just me," Farah Auntie said as she trudged down the stairs. First her shoes appeared, then her matching tracksuit, then her face. She adjusted the tablet she carried under one arm and waved to everyone. "This is the task force?"

"It is," Prem said. "Come on down, Auntie."

She nodded and then approached the table. "Very nice," she said, scanning the racks of wine. "Very, very nice. Pity we don't drink wine in our home."

"I said the same thing," Prem's father said. "Now, if this was whiskey—"

"We have to get to work," Deepak said, interrupting the chit-chat. "Our time is running short and god knows what this person is going to do on the day of the wedding. Farah Auntie, do you have anything else to go off of other than what you've already shared?"

Benjamin watched as Farah Auntie pushed her glasses up her nose, then set up her tablet. She tapped the screen a few times before saying, "The saboteur received information from Bobbi's wedding planning business. Bobbi's cousin shared the details, in hopes of securing this stranger online as a new client. Bobbi's cousin assumed that this stranger wanted a bigger and better wedding, which is the only reason why she was asking for specifics."

"Are you sure this wedding planning business is legitimate?" Prem's father asked. "This sounds like it's—"

"It's not only legitimate, but also the best in the country," Benjamin said. "Uncle, this had nothing to do with Bobbi. If anything, she's the only one who was able to save the event after this random person tried to ruin everything—"

"Calm down, Devdas. No one is blaming Bobbi," Prem said. "Dad? Benjamin is a bit protective about his girlfriend right now, so if you could stop needling him?"

"Ah. Sorry, puttar. Didn't realize that you were sensitive about her."

Benjamin gritted his teeth. He wasn't *sensitive* if what he was saying was the truth, but arguing with Prem's father was like arguing with a brick wall. The man was the reason why Prem was a stubborn idiot sometimes.

"As I was saying," Farah Auntie said from across the table, "this person managed to leave a note about the catering at Benjamin's restaurant, which seemed harmless. Then left another, more sinister threatening note with Benjamin and Bobbi over the last few months. There was the canceled cake, and the mixed-up mandap."

"What happened to the mandap?" Kareena's father asked.

"Someone called the supplier and changed the design, so it looked like whoever was on the platform was inside a clown's mouth. There was a red nose and everything."

"Oh my god, *that's* what it looks like!" Prem's father said, snapping his fingers. "I saw the frame of the mandap in the hall where the wedding will occur, and I swear it looked familiar. It's a giant clown! That is *terrifying*."

"Don't worry, Dad," Prem said. "Bobbi's uncle used to design mandaps before he planned weddings. He built these extension pieces so when the decorator sets it up, you'd never be able to picture the clown."

"That's not even the worst prank," Farah Auntie said. "The most criminal act was sending the guest list a cancellation letter and sending the current chef on an all-expense-paid trip to Florence, Italy, for a teaching position."

"Did you say Florence, Italy?" Kareena's father asked. He rested his knuckles on the table and leaned forward. "*The* Florence, Italy?"

Everyone nodded.

His eyebrows pinched together, and he stroked a hand over his chin. "I don't think it could be him . . . but then again, I didn't think anyone would want to ruin my daughter's wedding either."

"Could be *who*?" Prem pressed.

"One minute." He pulled out his phone, and after everyone stood around and painstakingly watched him send a text message, he put the phone down. "I called my son-in-law over. He should be here any minute. His family is from Italy. I don't know if that is the connection, but it's the only lead we have so far."

*Lead?* Benjamin had to shake his head. It was as if every single person around this table thought themselves equipped to solve a crime when they had probably watched only a few marathons of *Law & Order* as their experience.

"If you're talking about Loken," he said, "Bobbi has already checked with him and your daughter Bindu."

"Did you check with Loken's mother?" Kareena's father asked, his bushy salt-and-pepper brows arching with the question. "She's a nightmare."

"Uh, no. Would she have a reason to act like a criminal and destroy a wedding?"

"Maybe?" Kareena's father said. "She's beyond upset at Bindu and the rest of our family for canceling the wedding. She thinks it's our fault that Bindu and Loken eloped. She has an over-inflated sense of importance and thinks the entire Italian Indian community is mocking her because her son ran away with my daughter. Even though they'd been together for quite some time before the wedding."

"When they eloped," Prem's father said, stroking a hand over his face, "how much did that cost you?"

"Dad, quit it," Prem snapped.

Less than ten minutes later, an unfamiliar voice called out from the top of the stairs.

"Hello? Bindu's Papa?"

*Bindu's Papa?* Deepak mouthed to Benjamin.

Benjamin shrugged.

"I'm here, Loken," Uncle called back.

Kareena's brother-in-law appeared a moment later. He nodded a hello to Gwen and moved into the light. Benjamin remembered seeing him almost a year ago at his engagement party that Benjamin and Deepak had attended as Prem's support. That party did not go well, especially since Kareena's father punched Prem in the face.

They had obviously made up since then.

"What is happening here?" Loken asked as he approached the table. He looked Gujarati but sounded very much Italian. Which shouldn't have surprised Benjamin since there were second-generation desis all over the world, but it felt a little rarer to hear the Italian accent. He was average height, with black hair combed straight back. He was slender, and tucked his white shirt into fitted jeans that rode high on his hips. When he approached the table, Benjamin noticed that his hands trembled.

"Loken, beta," Uncle started. "Do you know the name of the cooking school in Florence?"

Farah Auntie rattled it off.

Loken shrugged. "Yes, of course. Everyone knows of the school."

"Do you or your family have any connection to the school personally?"

Loken cocked his head, his mouth pursing. "Why? What is this about?"

Benjamin shared a look with Prem and Deepak, then with Farah Auntie. Farah Auntie was the one who spoke first. "The chef who was supposed to be here for the wedding decided to study at the school. We just didn't know if there is a way we can reach out to him about his . . . uh, butter chicken recipe."

Loken seemed to relax at that excuse. "I can ask my mother. When she and my father first moved to Italy, that's where she worked as an assistant. She still has a lot of friends there."

*Bingo.*

Kareena's father shook his head. "This is about to get ugly," he muttered.

"Is your mother here?" Farah Auntie asked. "At the wedding?"

"Yes," Loken said. "She's been living with us for the last few months and will stay until the baby is born. I was just with her. She and my father are at the end of the left row of cabins. Bindu and I are next door. I can call her—"

"I don't think so," Prem's father said. He charged around the table. "Beta, lead the way. We'd all love to talk to her face-to-face." He hooked an arm around Loken's, dragging him along.

"Shit," Prem said and raced after his father. Kareena's father followed close behind, then Deepak with his building plans in one hand and headlamp in the other. Farah Auntie, who already had a cell phone pressed to her ear, trailed behind Deepak. Benjamin was the last to go. He paused in front of Gwen.

"Thank you for letting us use this room, Gwen."

She shook her head. "This is all very different from the weddings I'm used to."

"Please don't hold this against any other South Asians who want to have their wedding here," he said, pausing on the first step. "Especially since there is about to be a lot more . . . ah, entertainment."

Benjamin raced after the group and met them on the path toward the last cabin at the end of the left row. He could hear Prem trying to talk his father out of losing his shit on Kareena's sister's mother-in-law, but the way that the older man was man-handling Loken and dragging him along didn't look like that was going to happen. Most of the cabins they passed were brightly lit and already occupied by family friends, which meant that everyone was about to hear the confrontation with the shaadi saboteur.

It didn't help that Kareena's father was listing his grievances against Loken's family loud enough to wake the dead.

It was dark outside now, with only the pathway lights brightening their way. When they reached the last cabin, most of the aunties had spilled out of the bridal suite in the distance and were coming toward them.

"And somehow it's gotten worse," Benjamin mumbled.

"Maybe we shouldn't have invited the dads," Deepak said.

"You'd think they'd have more of a control on their tempers," Benjamin said. "But no. They're the reason why Punjabis have the stereotype that we're all hotheaded."

"We heard you found the saboteur!" Mona Auntie said. She had a giant margarita glass in her hand with what smelled like—

"Hey, is that pani puri water?" Benjamin asked.

Mona Auntie nodded, then handed him the glass. "Farah, who is the culprit?"

"We actually don't know for sure yet," Prem called out, even as he stepped onto the front porch of Loken's parents' cabin. His father was already pounding on the door, and Loken stood between them, with an expression of a deer caught in the headlights.

Benjamin turned, glass in hand, to see the love of his life cross the lawn with Veera. She had mehndi on one hand and carried her phone in the other. "What's happening?" she called out.

*I love you*, he thought. *I love you, and I can't wait to start my life with you, you absolutely infuriating, sexy queen of my heart.*

Instead, all that came out was "Prem's dad is about to have a throwdown with Loken's mom. They're getting ready to rumble."

"*What?*"

"For fuck's sake, Bunty," Prem snapped.

The door of the cabin opened, and a woman who looked like she spent her entire life sucking on lemons stepped outside. Her hair was perfectly coifed, and she stood defiant, her arms crossed over her crisp white button-down shirt.

"What is all this commotion?" she said.

"Did you try to ruin my son's wedding?" Prem's father boomed. "With your stupid pranks and parlor tricks?"

She gaped at him, a hand pressed to her chest. "*Excuse* me?"

"Lily," Kareena's father said. "Please tell us the truth." He put palm to palm as if in prayer. "We're just looking for answers. Your son told us about—"

"My son deserves more than to be married into your family!" she shouted. It was as if she was waiting for someone to confront her so she could explode.

The crowd that had gathered outside of the cabin hushed. Benjamin did a slow circle and saw that some of the other neighboring cabins were beginning to step outside to watch what was going on.

"What did you say?" Kareena's father said softly.

"My son." The woman vibrated with anger. She pounded a fist to her chest, her eyes bulging like golf balls. "This wedding should've been his! But instead your eldest daughter ruined everything for them! I saw the way she and her boyfriend interrupted their engagement. Kareena and that Dr. Phil—"

"Dr. Dil!" the crowd echoed back.

"Whatever!" She was practically foaming at the mouth, spittle flying between words. "They are the reason why my son was forced to break my heart and elope. He would never make that decision on his own. Do you know that I had to go back to Italy, to face all of my friends and family and tell them that this big expensive celebration was no longer going to happen? That my son snuck away instead of celebrating with family!"

"Loken?" Bindu's voice cut through the darkness as Kareena's sister stepped out onto the porch. Her jaw dropped at the sight of the entire wedding party and a fraction of the guests standing in front of her mother-in-law's cabin on the grassy lawn. "What's going on?"

"Your mother-in-law tried to ruin your sister's wedding," Deepak called out. "Because you and Loken eloped. She's got it twisted that it was Kareena's fault and not because you're a selfish b—"

"Oh my god!" Bindu pressed a hand to her large pregnant belly and hobbled off her porch. "Muma, you're the shaadi saboteur?"

"Way to go," Benjamin murmured to Deepak. He looked down at the glass, then passed it back to Mona Auntie, who was busy recording the entire event with her phone.

"You two should be getting married," Loken's mother said. "Not them!" She pointed a finger at Prem, and then at Kareena, who stood at a distance with her arms stretched out at her sides, already covered in mehndi. "Then I wouldn't have to be stuck here, hiding from my friends in shame."

"Did you really have to try to sabotage the wedding out of revenge?" Kareena's father said. "Couldn't you have talked to us like civilized people? This accomplishes nothing, Lily."

The woman stepped into the porch light as if she were walking into a spotlight onstage. Her hands fisted and her voice trembled. "If my son cannot get the wedding he deserved, then none of you will. It's bad enough he has chosen a—"

"Hey!" Kareena shouted. Her voice carried like a sharp blade over the lawn as she moved closer, waddling as she walked so she wouldn't smudge her mehndi. "You will not speak about my sister in any way other than with respect, do you hear me?"

The woman shrieked, then pointed at Kareena's father, her finger crooked with a long coffin-shaped nail at the end. "Do you hear that? Do you hear how shameful—"

"You will be checking out of this hotel tomorrow morning," Kareena's father said. The crowd went whisper silent.

"Oh shit," Benjamin whispered.

"Here." Mona Auntie shoved her margarita glass at him, and he took another sip before handing it back.

From the stories he'd heard, Kareena's father was more of a "hands-off" parent. He'd never said anything to protect his daughters, so the fact that he was speaking up now felt like a big deal.

"Lily, you will be leaving the premises," Uncle continued. His voice remained neutral, but it carried across the lawn. "You are no longer allowed at my daughter's wedding, do you hear me?"

"Fine, then I'm taking my son with me!"

"Okay, that's enough," Bobbi called out. She pushed through the growing crowd until she was also on the porch, a siren commanding attention.

No, Benjamin thought. A queen.

"You!" She snapped, motioning to Loken's mother. "Get inside right now. We're about to have a long-overdue conversation about how you've made my life very difficult. I don't take kindly to bullies. Loken and Bindu? Inside now." It took her less than thirty seconds to get the entire family into the cabin before she turned in the doorway.

"Veera!" Bobbi shouted over the murmur of conversation. "Get Kareena back in the bridal suite. She has mehndi to finish."

"On it!"

Bobbi pointed to the people on the porches of neighboring cabins. "Everyone who is not related to the Mann or Verma family, please go back to your rooms, otherwise I will escort you off the property as well."

With one last glance in Benjamin's direction, she entered the cabin and shut the door behind her.

No one moved.

Benjamin heard Kareena call out in the distance, "Veera, I'm not going anywhere, so stop trying to shove me back."

"Well, I shall pray for their family," Sonali Auntie said loud enough for everyone to hear.

"*Shut up, Sonali!*" the aunties echoed in unison.

"Dude, all I can hear from here is Bindu crying," Deepak said.

He was right. Kareena's younger sister was wailing now, and the sound poured through the cabin windows like a cry for help. It was cut off abruptly a moment later.

"I apologize for my daughter and her in-laws," Kareena's father said. He held out a hand to Prem's father to shake. "I hope you can forgive us."

"Nothing to forgive," Prem's father replied, and shook the hand. "You didn't do anything. Maybe we should go get a whiskey—"

"You're not going anywhere yet," Prem's mother called out from her spot in the back of the crowd. She looked like she was trying to keep Kareena at a safe distance while also listening to what was happening in the cabin. In the soft glow of the garden lights, Benjamin could tell that she was holding a margarita glass, too, but the contents were clear.

From what he knew about her, he was pretty sure she was drinking straight vodka.

"I have never met a more selfish group of people in my entire life!"

Bobbi's hollering was louder than Bindu's crying could've ever been and carried clear across the hotel property. "Do you know how much time, money, and effort you cost everyone? You should be ashamed of yourself! And you'll be lucky if Kareena, *who is a lawyer*, doesn't press charges against you . . . I don't give a shit if you're Italian! Your son is here. Do you want Kareena to sue him instead? . . . No, I don't care about your Italian Indian community either. And neither will you once the news gets out that you acted like a damn fool . . . Oh yes, I plan on calling up that gossip columnist Mrs. W. S. Gupta in *Indians Abroad News* right now so she can do an entire exposé on your family. What do you think of that? The aunties are right outside, and probably recording this whole thing to post on WhatsApp. You're going to fix this right now!"

"Bobbi's great, isn't she?" Benjamin said out loud. She was so . . . efficient. He loved hearing her like this in her element.

"Shh," Falguni Auntie hissed. "I can't hear. Mona, you're still recording, right?"

Mona Auntie saluted her with her glass.

Thirty seconds later, Bobbi stepped out of the cabin, with Loken and a sniffling Bindu following behind. The couple didn't look up or make eye contact with anyone. They quietly walked hand in hand to their cabin, slipped inside, and shut the door behind them.

She looked fierce, a woman in charge, Benjamin thought. Her thick glossy black hair billowed around her face, and that deliciously full mouth set in a straight line. She handled a situation getting out of control quicker than anyone possibly could.

Benjamin knew without a doubt that he wanted a second chance with her, not only because of love, but because he was so proud of her incredible talent. He wanted a million more moments to watch her do this again.

"Are you going to have a problem?" she asked the fathers, who were both still standing on the front porch.

"No," Kareena's father said.

Prem's father shook his head. "Bobbi, are there cigars at the main house?"

Bobbi sighed. "There is whiskey, but no cigars tonight. You're health professionals, for god's sake. Have some decency."

They grumbled but didn't argue as they descended the short stairs of the cabin porch.

"Now," Bobbi said to all of the wedding guests and family friends standing around. She was the person in the spotlight. "Loken's parents are packing up and they will be leaving the premises tonight. Their pranks will not be a topic of conversation for the rest of the wedding. We are going to focus on Prem and Kareena. Do I make myself clear?"

There were a few nods and yeses.

"I said, *do I make myself clear?*"

"Yes!"

"Absolutely."

"To Prem and Kareena!"

Bobbi tilted her chin up, satisfaction on her face. She propped her hands on her waist. "Does anyone else have anything disruptive to say, because after this, I'm focusing on my best friend, and I don't have time to deal with—"

"I have something to say," Benjamin said, his hand shooting straight in the air.

The crowd turned en masse to stare at him.

"What the fuck are you doing, brother?" Deepak hissed at his side.

Benjamin had no idea. His heart began pounding thick and

heavy in his chest. He didn't want to wait until after the wedding was over before they spoke. He wanted to talk to her now. In front of everyone. So they all knew that he was in love, and he was giving up his bachelor lifestyle for a lifetime with this woman.

He cut through the aunties and the dads, then ascended the porch until he stood in front of Bobbi, looking down at her confused expression.

"Bunty?" she whispered. Her face was void of makeup, and her skin glowed in the overhead lighting.

"My family is always going to be important to me, Bobbi. But you're my family now, too. I love you."

There was an echo of awws around him, but he didn't stop. He couldn't, otherwise he'd never get this out. "I want to relocate to New Jersey and New York," he said, loud enough for everyone to hear. "I want to be with you and my friends. I want my life on the East Coast. This decision is for me and for us."

Her brows furrowed and her voice trembled for the first time since she stormed out of Kareena's bridal suite. "But the board meeting—"

"I told my father and brother that they have to figure it out between themselves. I am not rejoining the company in any capacity. I'll have my hands full over the next few weeks so I can spend some time finding the right location and starting on my next restaurant. I've already gotten the name and most of the menu, so I'm hoping things will move quickly once I sign the lease."

"The name?" she said softly. She leaned closer to him, and he felt his heart bursting. She was going to believe him. Thank god, he thought. He didn't deserve her forgiveness, the way that she loved him so readily, but he'd take it and cherish her.

He linked his hands with hers so that they stood facing each other. "Rani. After my queen."

There were more awws from their audience, but he could hear Bobbi's words as clear as if they were alone and surrounded by silence.

"You are the most infuriating person, Benjamin Padda. God knows why I love you too."

He looped his arms around her waist and pulled her close. "That's because you and I are way too smart to love without a little bit of fighting, Bobbi Kaur."

"Thank *god*."

Benjamin and the rest of the crowd turned around to face the event coordinator, who was standing in the back, barely visible in the darkness. She jumped, as if she'd just realized she'd spoken out lout.

"What was that, Gwen?" Bobbi said, her voice dripping with a false sweetness that had Benjamin wincing. "Why don't you come into the light and say it again."

"I'm sorry," Gwen said. She brushed a hand over the front of her beige suit coat, then spoke loud enough for not only Bobbi and Benjamin to hear, but also the cabins across the lawn. "It was so exhausting holding on to the Prem Verma–Kareena Mann secret this entire time."

"What secret?" Bobbi asked.

"About how we don't accept outside caterers. We do, actually. And we have a popular Indian restaurant we work with in town. But the bride and groom made some pretty scary threats, uh, I mean requests that we keep that information from you two. I think it's safe to say it doesn't matter anymore if you know."

"*What?*" Bobbi's shriek sounded suspiciously like Bindu's now.

Benjamin scanned the crowd until he spotted Prem toward the back trying to slip away into the darkness. That son of a bitch. "Prem, you asshole!"

Prem stopped, then gave Benjamin and Bobbi a sheepish smile. "We just wanted you to be happy," he shouted back, his shoulders hunched. "It was exhausting watching the both of you circle each other every time we were together."

"Kareena!" Bobbi shouted, but the bride was already waddling back to the bridal suite as if she hadn't heard anyone call her name.

"I think you'll have to chase her, rani," Benjamin said.

Bobbi whirled to face Benjamin. "Did our friends seriously get a wedding venue and a few people to lie to us just so we'd spend time together?"

Benjamin motioned to the crowd that was skulking away. Every single one of them retreated like they were guilty as hell. "I have a feeling it was more than just a few people. And I've never been so grateful to a nosy community." He pulled Bobbi close again and pressed a kiss to her mouth.

It felt like coming home, and all he wanted to do was sink into the delicious feel of the moment.

Except Veera's voice cut through his dreamy happily ever after.

"I feel so much secondhand embarrassment, and I hate that for myself," she said loudly.

Benjamin pulled back to see her storming up the steps. "Okay, lovebirds. This has been great, but we need to break it up. We're currently standing in front of the door of a woman who single-handedly tried to destroy a wedding. Bobbi? We still have mehndi to do."

"Oh my god! Yes, okay." She followed Veera down the steps, then looked over her shoulder at Benjamin. "We'll talk tonight?"

He nodded. He knew there were so many missing details to his confession, but that's all they were. Details. Fortunately, both he and Bobbi were pros when it came to details.

And he had to kick Prem's ass for tricking them in the first place.

"Tonight, love."

Hand in hand, she and her best friend skipped down the stone path toward the bridal suite. He could hear Veera call out, "I told you so."

Benjamin motioned to guests on the opposite side of the lawn, the few brave enough to stay back and watch the end of the show. "Welcome to the Vermann Wedding! Now the party can begin!"

As they cheered, he watched Bobbi's retreating back into the darkness. She turned at the last minute before she reached the bridal suite, and in the soft glow of the porch light, he could see the shadow of a smile, and he grinned.

Yup, he thought. He was going to wife her up soon. He was in love, and his happily ever after had just begun.

# CHAPTER 28

## Bobbi

*Text from Bobbi to Benjamin:*

**BOBBI:** ::file transfer::

**BENJAMIN:** What is this?

**BOBBI:** It's all the notes you've been sharing about recipes over the last few months. I put them in a database, sorted by keyword.

**BENJAMIN:** Just another reason why I love you.

Bobbi gasped as she pressed her hands against the mirrored wall. The only thought that kept running through her mind was that Benjamin Padda had singlehandedly changed her mind about heterosexual Punjabi men.

Her lehenga blouse with its row of eyelet hooks along the front was completely undone and her heavy, round breasts bounced with every thrust. Her skirt was bunched around her waist as she bent over, legs spread. Benjamin's hands gripped her hips as he guided her in quick and hard thrusts from behind.

"Benjamin," she gasped, meeting his eyes in the mirror. He had a ferocity, a look of sheer determination on his face, as he fucked her thoroughly in her reception outfit. The sound of her bangles clinked hard against the glass as she desperately searched for purchase.

With his eyes still on her, he licked two fingers, then reached under her skirt from the front to tease her clit.

Bobbi's eyes nearly rolled to the back of her head. Her legs were shaking so hard now that she was afraid she was going to collapse any minute.

"Come for me, Bobbi. Come for me now like the filthy queen you are."

She tossed her head back, shuddered, and let the orgasm take her as she rode Benjamin's hand, his hard cock still driving in and out of her. Then she heard him shout, his thighs tensing behind hers as he came as well.

Bobbi would've fallen to the floor if Benjamin hadn't pulled her back to lean against his chest. They were both breathing heavy and hard. Her breasts still bared to the cool air-conditioning.

"We were supposed to grab Prem's reception shoes and take them downstairs for him," she said with a gasp. "Especially since Deepak and Veera lost his wedding shoes."

"I have a lot of time to make up for," he said gruffly. He kissed the curve between her shoulder and neck. "I have to take advantage of whatever opportunity I have." His hands came up to massage her breasts, and his fingers were still wet with her come. "And god, you look so sexy like this, I couldn't help myself."

She felt sexy, Bobbi thought. She felt loved. But she was also acutely aware of four hundred people in the venue at the main building who would most likely wonder about her and Bunty, especially after the scene Wednesday night.

The wedding had gone on without a hitch. From the mehndi to the sangeet to the ceremony and reception. Kareena and Prem beamed with joy, but their parents were even more thrilled to be celebrating their children with their friends.

And Bobbi was just happy that the wedding saboteur case was finally resolved and she could move on with her life. She hadn't felt this relieved at a wedding . . . well, ever.

"Come on," she said quietly. She stood on her tiptoes to kiss his bearded chin. "We have to get back."

They cleaned up quickly, adjusting their clothes to pre-sex status, then Benjamin helped Bobbi back into the golf cart they'd used to drive up to the main house.

"I have to check on the kitchen after we drop the shoes off," he said.

"I'm sure it's under control."

He raised a brow. "Okay, Ms. Wedding Planner. Are you telling me that you wouldn't do the same thing?"

She thought about it and shook her head. "Let's check on the kitchen together. Once the reception is in full swing and all of the speeches are over, I usually eat with the staff, anyway."

"So do I," Bunty said. He maneuvered the golf cart into its designated parking zone. "Maybe we can snag a few plates and go sit in the back together."

"That's perfect," she said. The idea of sharing a meal with Benjamin, just the two of them, warmed her heart. They had barely gotten any solo time even though he had moved into her cabin. They'd dressed together before every event, but there was always a time limit.

"When are you going back to California?" she asked as they walked hand in hand up the steps to the double doors.

"I don't have to go back to wrap up some meetings for another week," he said. "The place I liked in DUMBO is still available, but I want to check out a few more spots before committing."

A week of Benjamin. That sounded amazing. They could actually go on a date and spend time together in person instead of all of those hours on the phone or via text. When she went to open the door, Benjamin pulled her to a stop.

"Hey," he said. "I spoke with Prem, and he said that if I was interested, he'd sell me his apartment in Jersey City."

Bobbi's jaw dropped. She thought about the exposed brick, the state-of-the-art kitchen, and the floor-to-ceiling windows. "The beautiful loft apartment? You'll be close to me!"

"Yes," he said. "He's officially moved into the house in Edison with Kareena, and now that space is empty. I love you, and I want us to think about the long term, but since we haven't been in the same state for long periods of time, what do you think about me moving in there for right now?"

He wanted to give her time and space, and he couldn't have offered a more romantic gesture than that.

"I think it's amazing. Thank you." She stood on her tiptoes again, this time in her sparkling juttis, and waited for him to lean down so she could kiss him properly. When some of her lipstick transferred to his mouth, she brushed it off with her thumb.

"I never thought that we'd have this bizarre and incredible love story, Benjamin Bunty Padda. But I'm so glad we do."

"Same, sapno ki rani. But this is only the beginning."

# EPILOGUE

## Veera

Veera knew it wasn't fair to think that just because her friends were paired off that now Deepak would think of her in a romantic sort of way, too. They'd spent so much time together; they shared their deepest, darkest feelings about their futures, their hopes and dreams. And Veera had thought that maybe, just maybe, Deepak might feel something for her as more than a friend after all of that.

She was so horribly wrong. Instead, she watched as he flirted with other women during the sangeet and mehndi. Then he danced with everyone but her at the reception. He practically ignored her the entire night. So she'd done what she did best and she slipped away to the bathroom where she could hide in one of the stalls to cry in peace.

She was so happy for Kareena and Prem, and for Bobbi and Benjamin, obviously, but for just a minute, she needed to be sad for herself.

Veera had closed the lid to the toilet, sat, and tried her best to catch her tears before they ruined her makeup. The doors, thank the lord, went floor to ceiling, so no one had to know she was in here, crying for a man who didn't even know she had fallen in love with him.

The sound of people entering had Veera's breath caught in her throat. She prayed that no one would know it was her in the last stall.

"It's so beautiful."

*No, no, no,* she thought. Her mother could *not* be in this bathroom while she was being all emotional. Mom would only want to try to fix things for her, and she'd just make it worse.

"Bobbi really outdid herself."

This time, the voice belonged to Deepak's mother. *What? Why was her mom with Deepak's mom having a private conversation in the bathroom?*

"I hope you're looking forward to your son's marriage," Veera's mother said. "I'm sure you have wonderful plans for that happy occasion."

Veera pressed a fist to her mouth to stop the startled gasp from coming out.

"I do! But of course, he doesn't want us to announce anything quite yet."

Veera could feel her heart breaking in her chest.

"Well, it will have to come out soon," Veera's mother said. "Especially when our husbands announce the company merger."

*No.*

*Oh my god, no.*

"It'll be good to grow our partnership. My children have meetings with their father next month to discuss. When will your girls be told about the deal?"

"I'm sure my husband will tell them soon. Veera will be so happy that she and her best friend will be coworkers now."

"They're so adorable together."

There were sounds of stall doors opening, more conversation through the walls, then the sinks running. Finally, the footsteps faded until Veera was alone again.

She couldn't hold back the sob this time. She dug her phone out of the discreet pocket in her lehenga skirt, and before she could call the first number in her favorites, it rang in her hand. She immediately pressed it to her ear.

"Sana?"

"Twin-tuition," Sana said with a yawn. "Is everything okay?"

Veera shook her head, then croaked out a "No."

"Veera? What's wrong?" Sana asked, her voice going hard. Even from a distance, she sounded alert and ready to fight Veera's battles for her.

"Do you think you can come home now? I really need you."

The sound of a bed shifting, and then a chair scraping back. "I'm booking the flight now."

# ACKNOWLEDGMENTS

*Much Ado About Nothing* is my absolute favorite Shakespeare play, which is probably why there are more overt nods to the source material than there are references to *The Taming of the Shrew* in the first book in the trilogy, *Dating Dr. Dil*.

My intention with this book was to focus on the way we associate worth with work. Specifically, how children of immigrant families become the "family manager" and conflate their value to the degree of help they provide. This is in part because I absolutely love the idea of exploring my personal toxic behaviors as a child of immigrant parents, but also because of the relationship Beatrice and Benedick had to their cousin/friend respectively in *Much Ado About Nothing*.

And, of course, I wanted to write a love story.

This was my first novel with my new Avon editor, Carrie Feron. Carrie, I'm so glad that we have the opportunity to work together now. To Asanté Simons, Jes Lyons, DJ DeSmyter, and the entire Avon team who helped get this book and *Dating Dr. Dil* off the ground.

To my ride or die, Joy Tutela. Joy, I'm on this journey because of you and the team at David Black Literary. Thank you from the bottom of my heart.

To Lauren Clarke, Sanjana Basker for the incredible story guidance, and to my entire team of supporters helping with social media, marketing, website design, and publicity.

To Namrata Patel, who was with me on this writing journey at 7:00 A.M. (sometimes 7:30 or 7:45 A.M.) finishing this book. I'm so glad that our friendship has bloomed into this incredible gift.

To my Desi romance writer friends, including Farah Heron, Falguni Kothari, Mona Shroff, Alisha Rai, Sonali Dev, and so many more new ones who have come into my life this past year. Writing is a solitary endeavor best done with the support of community, and I'm grateful to have you as part of my community.

To my author friends who have lent me their ears (not to get all Shakespearean) when I needed to talk through plot or strategy. Thank you so much, Sarah MacLean, Andie Christopher, Dee Earnst, and Katee Robert. Thank you to Sierra Simone for being the smartest freaking woman I know and for always blowing my mind wide open whenever I call whining about Shakespeare themes or taxes (thankfully never at the same time).

Thank you to my real-life friend, former college roommate, and neighbor, Jordan, and her husband, Tim, for the endless support, guidance, and levelheaded advice.

To my life partner who is my real-life hero, my support system, and my sounding board. I'm forever grateful to my Alaskan husband who prefers anonymity.

To Smita Kurrumchand, my adopted sister, who is always so open and willing to support me and read whatever garbage I write just to tell me that it's her favorite and I should keep going. To my sister by blood, Shikha Sharma, my parents, and my in-laws for all of your support, love, and guidance.

And last but not least, to my aunties. I love that you always ask, "Is it like *Fifty Shades of Grey*? Because then I'll read it." Thank you for being there for me during my lowest lows and highest highs. You are the community I wish upon all of my readers.